Into the World

Stephanie Parkyn has always wanted to write, growing up in a book-loving home in Christchurch, New Zealand. A fascination with science, research and the environment led her to a PhD and a career as a freshwater ecologist. In 2010, she moved to Hobart in Tasmania with her husband and embarked on her other passions of art and fiction. Here she learned of the remarkable voyage of Marie-Louise Girardin. The story had all the elements that inspire her: mystery, adventure, natural history and injustice. Stephanie loves travel, learning and sharing stories. She enjoys the challenge of illuminating historical figures who dared to question social rules and conventions. She now lives in Launceston, Tasmania.

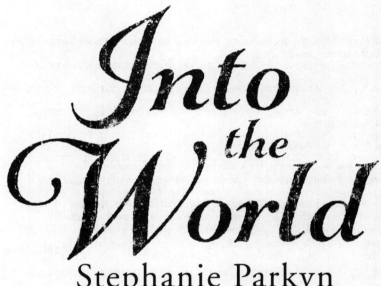

Into the World

Stephanie Parkyn

ALLEN&UNWIN
SYDNEY·MELBOURNE·AUCKLAND·LONDON

This is a work of fiction. Names, characters, places and incidents are used fictitiously or are products of the author's imagination.

First published in 2017

Copyright © Stephanie Parkyn 2017

All rights reserved. No part of this book may be reproduced or transmitted in any form or by any means, electronic or mechanical, including photocopying, recording or by any information storage and retrieval system, without prior permission in writing from the publisher. The Australian *Copyright Act 1968* (the Act) allows a maximum of one chapter or 10 per cent of this book, whichever is the greater, to be photocopied by any educational institution for its educational purposes provided that the educational institution (or body that administers it) has given a remuneration notice to the Copyright Agency (Australia) under the Act.

Allen & Unwin
83 Alexander Street
Crows Nest NSW 2065
Australia
Phone: (61 2) 8425 0100
Email: info@allenandunwin.com
Web: www.allenandunwin.com

Cataloguing-in-Publication details are available
from the National Library of Australia
www.trove.nla.gov.au

ISBN 978 1 76029 651 3

Set in 12.6/17.9 pt Garamond Premier Pro by Bookhouse, Sydney
Printed and bound in Australia by Griffin Press

10 9 8 7 6 5 4 3 2 1

The paper in this book is FSC® certified. FSC® promotes environmentally responsible, socially beneficial and economically viable management of the world's forests.

For Marie-Louise Victoire Girardin

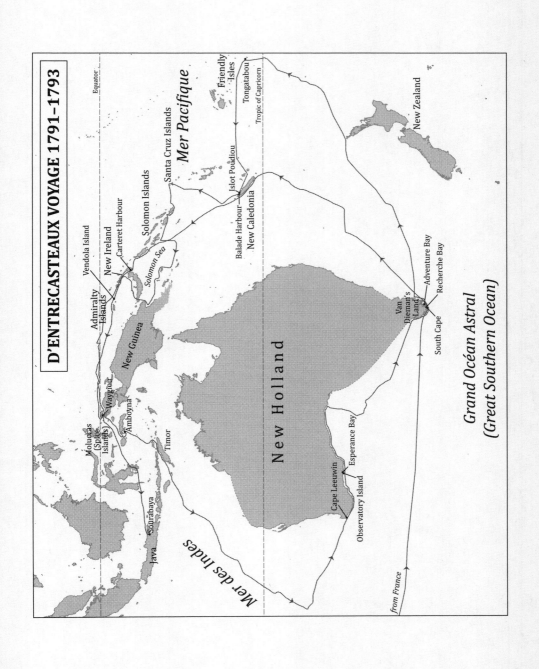

List of characters

Armand   Old sailor aboard the *Recherche*
Aubry de Gouges, Pierre   Son of Olympe de Gouges
Beautemps-Beaupré, Charles-François   Cartographer and hydrographer, one of the observatory trio
Besnard, Thomas   Cook of the *Recherche*
Bruni d'Entrecasteaux, Antoine-Raymond-Joseph (The General)   Commander of the expedition, aboard the *Recherche*
D'Auribeau, Alexandre d'Hesmivy   Captain of the *Recherche*
De Gouges, Olympe   Playwright and political activist during the revolution
De Saint-Méry, Mérite   Midshipman of the *Recherche*
Girardin, Jean   Father of Marie-Louise Girardin
Girardin, Marie-Louise (Louis)   Steward of the *Recherche*
Hébert, Jacques René   Journalist and founder of radical republican newspaper *Le Père Duchesne*
Huon de Kermadec, Jean-Michel   Captain of the *Espérance*, sister ship of the d'Entrecasteaux expedition
Joannet, Denis   Surgeon of the *Espérance* and chief surgeon for the expedition

Labillardière, Jacques-Julien   Naturalist aboard the *Recherche*, specialising in botany
Lahaie, Félix   Gardener of the *Recherche* and assistant naturalist
Le Fournier d'Yauville, Madame   Sister of Jean-Michel Huon de Kermadec
Piron   Artist on the *Recherche*
Raoul, Ange   Pilot of the *Recherche*
Renard, Pierre   Surgeon of the *Recherche*
Riche, Claude-Antoine-Gaspard   Naturalist aboard the *Espérance*, specialising in zoology
Rossel, Elisabeth-Paul-Édouard   Lieutenant of the *Recherche*, one of the observatory trio
Saint-Aignan, Alexandre-François   Lieutenant of the *Recherche*, musician, one of the observatory trio
Sirot, Michel   Servant of Claude Riche
Trobriand, Jean-François-Silvestre   Lieutenant of the *Espérance*
Ventenat, Louis   Chaplain of the *Recherche*

Part One

Fuire: to flee

Chapter 1

IN A COACH-HOUSE ROOM ON THE EDGE OF PARIS, MARIE-LOUISE Girardin stood beside a dying fire in clothes that were not her own, holding a baby she could not keep. She wore a royal-blue coat with epaulettes that sloped off her shoulders and white breeches that bagged above her boots. Beneath this loose and ill-fitting costume her breasts were bound with linen bandages, stretched taut and knotted so tight each breath was cut short. She could feel her milk leak into the bandages, feel the brutal waste of it, as she pressed her son to her chest.

'I have no choice,' she whispered to him, throat closing. Tears dripped from her chin. One splashed on her baby's cheek and she watched it roll into the whorl of his ear. He did not wake. Milk-drunk, he lay fast asleep in her arms. The hair on his head was pale, like hers, and already it grew in wild directions. She marvelled at his perfect skin, not a freckle or blemish or crimson stain. She stroked his plump pink arm, so full of health and hope. Bending forwards, she kissed his nose, his forehead, and then inhaled, committing him to memory.

Olympe de Gouges paced in front of the fire, her gown tracing lines in the dust of the floor. With her straight back and her snowy wig of hair piled high on her head, there was something of the proud swan about her. Marie-Louise needed her friend's spirit now. Olympe's son, Pierre, an ensign in the French navy, knelt to prod and scatter the embers. It was his cast-off uniform that Marie-Louise wore. The remains of her dress, her old life, burned in the grate.

'Will you name the father?' Olympe asked her. 'Shame him. He has responsibilities.'

Marie-Louise shook her head sharply. 'It will do no good. I cannot name him.'

Olympe released a heavy breath. 'Bastard children have no rights. As well I know it.' Her voice was bitter. 'Nor their mothers.'

But Marie-Louise could not admit his name, not even to her one true friend—especially not to her. Shame reddened her face. She had been a fool. Her lover had discarded her, flicked her away as carelessly as if she were a blowfly that might lay a maggot in his plate of pie. She would not entrust her son to his mercy.

'Then there is no other way,' Olympe said, and the two women shared a look of bald despair. Find a man, Marie-Louise thought, or take this desperate course. Find a man—or become one. She swayed, on the brink of a stagger. The room was warm and the air fusty with mildew and smoke. She had the sudden urge to cut her bindings, run to the window and fill her lungs. This disguise was insanity. How was she to become a man?

'I could take my chances on the streets.'

'You will likely die disfigured and diseased! What sort of life would that be for your son?' Olympe paced across the floor, her hands in fists. 'They deny us even the chance to work to feed our babies. They would rather see us die as syphilitic whores than grant an unwed mother the means to feed her own child. Such is our civilised society. It sickens me.' Olympe was rigid with anger.

Olympe spoke the truth. It was the way of things. And women who were cast out from their families did not last long on the streets, if they could bear the life at all. Marie-Louise imagined seeing herself on the Pont Neuf, watching herself fall as though looking up from the bank of the Seine at a stranger plummeting from the bridge with the air snatching at her skirt.

'I will fight for you,' Olympe said, coming to her side. 'There is still hope we will change this world.' Marie-Louise felt her friend lay her chin on her shoulder and fold her arms around her waist. Their heads rested against one another. Her son stirred in his swaddling.

Marie-Louise was grateful for Olympe's strength, but she no longer believed the revolution would change anything for women. It was 1791, almost two years since the Palace of Versailles had fallen to the people. The revolution was surely over. The National Assembly governed France now and Louis XVI was held prisoner in the Tuileries Palace. The monarchy was no more. She had helped to deliver France to the people and free them from tyranny. Once these thoughts would have fired her blood, but now she felt no such warmth. Only the thudding of a small, quick heart against her own.

Olympe was still strong, still earnest. Olympe de Gouges would not stop at the rights of all men to be treated equal, she would stand on street corners and preach that women should be treated as citizens, not property. But Marie-Louise felt her own revolutionary flame stutter and smoulder. She doubted whether women would ever truly be free.

Pierre stood suddenly, dropping the poker to the hearth, startling her from her thoughts. 'The last coach will leave soon.'

She turned her face to him, distraught. 'Already?'

His voice softened. 'I'm sorry, but I must return to my ship. I have delayed too long. It must be tonight.'

Marie-Louise pulled away from Olympe and rocked forwards, cradling her baby. She gazed at her son's face, memorising the curve of his chin, the splay of his eyelashes. A few days was all she'd had with him, and yet this bond that joined her to him was already as complete as a grafted vine.

'You have the letter?' Olympe asked her.

The letter of introduction to Olympe's friend in the port town of Brest was in the pocket of her coat, flattened against her chest. She nodded.

'Keep it safe.'

Marie-Louise met her friend's eyes. The moment had come. Olympe held out her arms. 'He will be cared for. The nuns...' Olympe's voice trailed away.

The lie was no comfort. Marie-Louise backed into the corner, the dark panelled walls closing in, her heart hammering at her bound chest. Could her baby feel it beating? she wondered. Could he feel her dread and know that she did not want to do this?

She pictured the stone wall behind the chapel, the *tour d'abandon* at the corner of the street. How many nights had she spent in the shadows, arms cradling her belly, staring at that wooden door? Some nights she crept closer, laying her hand on the wrought-iron latch, wondering what it would feel like to draw it open. Or, worse, to push it closed. Would it sound as heavy as the door of a crypt? She had listened for the echoes of abandoned voices, torturing herself, convinced she heard the wail of an infant marooned. Once she almost opened the portal, wanting to know what darkness lay inside, but instead she turned and kicked the lurking, scrap-fed dogs away. 'There is nothing for you here.' Tonight, the wooden doors would be drawn back and her son would be laid down inside and left behind.

'This is the only way you will be free,' Olympe said, stepping forwards, arms outstretched.

Olympe would do it for her. Olympe would take her baby to the church while she, the coward, would seize her chance and run.

'Wait!' She felt a surge of panic. 'I haven't named him!' Nothing had fitted, nothing had felt right. She had to give him a name; it was all she had to give.

'Rémi,' she said. The oarsman. She pictured her son grown into a strong young man, expertly navigating his boat in the current of the Seine, staying safe and dry while others might be swept away. 'His name is Rémi.' She lifted him and pressed her lips to his forehead for the last time.

As soon as the weight of her son was lifted from her arms, Marie-Louise wanted him back. She almost snatched him from Olympe. Instead, she gripped the gilt buttons of her coat, crossing her arms over the loss of him. She heard herself release a deep, guttural moan.

Pierre plucked a heated coin from the embers of the fire.

'I will do it,' she said to him, her voice choking. He passed her the coin, but her gloves were too large and her fingers unwilling. The coin slipped. She saw the silver écu fall and Louis XVI's head spin upon the floorboards.

She bent to retrieve it and felt the white heat of it through her leather glove. *God forgive me.* Her son was asleep in Olympe's arms. Marie-Louise lifted his hand and pressed the coin beneath his forearm until it seared his newborn skin.

Rémi woke, screaming, and she was lanced by guilt. Quickly, she pulled back her sleeve and let the heat of the coin bite into her own skin. She pressed the coin harder, holding it, letting it singe, listening to her baby's anguish. She bared her wrist for him, showing him the brand, flaming bright red like a beacon.

In return, the red weal on Rémi's skin swelled in ugly accusation. 'It will heal,' she sobbed to him. He punched his outraged arms and would not let her blow upon the burn. She offered her finger for him to squeeze and felt his hand grip it hard. She prayed he would one day understand what his scar meant—that he would see the round, red mark on his flawless skin and know she would return for him.

Chapter 2

AT THE GATES OF PARIS, A GUARD STOPPED THEIR COACH AND inspected the paperwork Pierre had forged for her. Marie-Louise flicked a glance at Pierre. Olympe's son risked everything to help her and her heart swelled with gratitude. Both their lives would be ruined if they were caught. He was tight-lipped and she saw the youth of him in his thin and carefully groomed moustache. He would not look at her. She held her breath as the guard peered into the carriage window. She kept her collar turned up high. For months, noble men and women had been escaping Paris in disguise. Was that what the guard would think if she was discovered? That here was some pampered aristocrat fleeing the new regime? After what she had done for the revolution, the thought was laughable.

With a bored flick of his wrist, the guard sent them onwards. As the coach jolted forwards, Marie-Louise stared back at the lamplights of Paris casting their burnt sienna glow up into the dark sky. By now her son would be lying alone and afraid on a slab of cold stone inside the *tour d'abandon*. The burn on her arm throbbed as the carriage lurched and rocked, carrying her away.

The route from Paris to Brest took her through Chartres, Le Mans and Rennes. She had never been so far from home. She had never seen so much black-hearted forest, never heard the howl of wolves after dark. When they finally reached the coastal town of Saint-Brieuc, in Brittany, Marie-Louise caught her first glimpse of the sea. It frightened her. A grey blanket stretched out from the cliffs to a grey sky as the sea mists rolled in, concealing the horizon. Pierre assured her that land lay to the north, but all she saw was emptiness.

Limping along the cobbled streets of Brest, she felt drained by weariness. The coach had slammed her spine with each stone and rut of the rough road and the wounds from the birth of her son had barely had time to heal. At night she had lain awake staring at the ceiling of each wayside inn, trying to recall the shape of her son's nose, the feel of his skin. It had been nine days since she abandoned him.

The marketplace was crowded with the stench of mackerel and oysters. Gulls screeched and swooped overhead. Here children brawled among the fish heads and oyster shells, she saw babies carried in slings around their mothers' chests, and with each wail of hunger her breasts leaked into the bandages beneath her costume. Two boys pushed past Marie-Louise as they chased turds down the swollen gutters towards the sea.

Pierre forged ahead into the crowd and women pulled their children out of his way. Marie-Louise followed into the fug of wet armpits. To her relief, men's eyes slid over her without interest. Her fingers crept into her pocket, checking for the reassuring feel of parchment. Without this letter of introduction, all her hopes were lost.

A sharp tug of her elbow made her turn. A smile of yellowed teeth and carmine lips leered close. The woman's face was caked in white lead and daubed with rouge to disguise the pox marks on her cheeks.

'We like the officers, don't we, girls?' she said, turning to address three more garish faces staring with predatory appraisal from the step of a tavern.

The whore was skin and bone. She slipped her bodice down and jiggled a pair of flaccid breasts, like chestnuts swinging in pale pink stockings.

Marie-Louise stared at the dangling nipples and then back up to the flint eyes of the prostitute. She could be my age, Marie-Louise thought. She could be me.

These women were caricatures, she realised, pantomime women. Living outside society and despised for their freedom, for the power they held over men. Yet proud, unashamed. Could she wear this mask, she wondered, if her life depended on it?

'Oh, he likes what he sees!' the woman simpered, slipping her breasts back within the bodice. 'If you want any more than that you'll have to pay for it.'

Pierre gripped her arm. 'Louis, come with me!'

'Don't forget me, Louis!' the whore called out, laughing. Marie-Louise glimpsed plugs of cork in her mouth instead of molars before Pierre yanked her away.

Marie-Louise followed Pierre, dodging a splash of grey water as a barmaid sluiced vomit from the tavern wall. She pressed her hand to the parchment in her pocket, feeling the rapid pounding of her heart.

The letter she carried was for Madame Le Fournier d'Yauville, a friend of Olympe de Gouges, and the sister of a naval captain. Their plan was simple: to gain her a position on board a ship. Olympe had been excited. 'I have heard of women who have disguised themselves before. Think of Jeanne Baré.' It had all seemed possible in the weeks before her son was born. It was not forever, she had told herself. She would return for her baby. She had not imagined this wrenching loss would feel the same as the death of a child, like a hole that opened her inside out.

A young boy with a wad of papers in his arms cried out from a street corner, 'Père Duchesne is fucking angry today!'

Marie-Louise froze.

'Our father is damn angry!' the boy called.

The Paris papers, even here, Marie-Louise thought with a tremor of disgust. Père Duchesne was an invention, a caricature father of the nation, styled by a man who could not be trusted. Looking around her, she wondered if these people knew that their crass-mouthed, straight-talking hero of the revolution was a figment of the imagination. That the writer of these words, Jacques Hébert, was a man who still wore silk culottes and rode about in a carriage like an aristocrat. She felt the tide of people turn towards the boy.

'The King flees! The King flees!'

Elbows jostled against her. The mob snatched for the papers. The great mound of sheets tilted. The boy vanished from her view as he was pushed into the muck of the street.

Around her the voices grumbled.

'He means to abandon France.'

'Flees to Austria to raise an army against the people!'

'Disguised themselves like common servants. Even dressed the Dauphin as a girl!'

Marie-Louise held her breath. She pictured the King trapped in his study at the Tuileries Palace, gazing at the paintings of ships with their white sails puffed like pregnant bellies. He had always wanted to sail around the world.

'At least they caught the traitor!'

A gob of phlegm splattered against her boot. She looked up, eyes wide. A grey-whiskered man breathed stale garlic and tooth-rot into her face. 'You're not welcome here.'

Marie-Louise held her cloak tight around her, aware her naval uniform marked her out as a supporter of the King. Pierre shouldered the man aside, dragging her towards an alleyway.

Marie-Louise pulled back. 'Wait,' she cried out to him, reaching for one of the papers trodden into the manured cobbles. 'I must know.' She stuffed the paper in her pocket.

Pitiful light filtered between the tall buildings. The shadowy doorways stank of urine and most were filled with dark shapes, the round humps of bodies sheltering beneath rags. Her breath was short. Surely the air here was too thin to support life.

A woman in a long skirt and tattered shawl brushed past Pierre. Even in the low light, Marie-Louise saw her hand flicker and snatch the handkerchief from Pierre's pocket. Their eyes met. The woman showed no fear, no alarm; her eyes were hollow. Who was she to deny this woman a square of fabric? What might those simple threads buy for her or her children? Pierre turned back, aware that Marie-Louise had stopped behind him. He looked impatient, nervous. The woman had deftly balled the handkerchief into her fist. I will keep your secret, Marie-Louise said with her silence, and hurried past her.

The stinking alleyways opened out to the stately homes of the Recouverance. Before long they found the house of Madame d'Yauville on Rue Saint-Malo. It was an imposing structure. The grey block walls were stained black where water dripped from the slate roof. Stone steps led up from the street to a thick oak door flanked on either side by iron-barred windows. From the dormer windows on the top floor, Marie-Louise saw a woman's face peer down at her. She shivered.

Pierre had already climbed the steps and rapped on the door. He was eager to be relieved of his charge, she realised.

Suddenly, she remembered the pickpocket from the alley. Fumbling beneath her cloak, she felt for the letter, pulling the pamphlet from her pocket instead. She glimpsed the cartoon of Père Duchesne, an old man clutching his groin and leering at her. A footman opened the door. Pierre was looking at her now. She pushed her fingers deeper in her pocket. Her fate lay with the reception of this letter. Her fingers grazed the raised edge of a wax seal. Retrieving the neatly folded parchment, she placed it into the upturned palm of the footman.

Chapter 3

Marie-Louise chewed the corner of her thumbnail, her pale brows drawn together. Her hair was damp on her forehead. They had been shown into a salon to wait. Tapestries and portraits cluttered the pastel yellow walls. Here, the ancestors of Le Fournier d'Yauville were displayed for all to see and she ducked her eyes from the condemnation in their oily gazes.

Marie-Louise flattened the pamphlet she had taken from the marketplace against her thigh. The King and all his family made it as far as Varennes before being recognised and seized. His escape had failed. She folded the paper into ever-decreasing squares and clasped it in the palm of her hand.

The doors of the salon swept open and Marie-Louise leaped to her feet.

It was only the servants, delivering coffee. She returned to her perch on the edge of her chair.

Pierre attempted a lopsided smile. 'All will be well,' he said, but his expression was unsure. She smiled back, grateful for his concern, and tried to relax her shoulders and loosen the stiffness of her spine, for his sake. Whatever the outcome of this meeting, she could not be a burden on this boy.

When Madame d'Yauville eventually appeared, she was not what Marie-Louise was expecting. Madame wore a black gown of mourning. Her thin lips were pinched and her forehead deeply lined. Marie-Louise felt her hopes plummet. Mourning women had no sympathy to spare for others, as she well knew. Widows treated the world as fiercely as they themselves were treated. Marie-Louise stood with her hands gripping one another.

Madame's black skirts inflated and deflated like a breath as she sat on the edge of her chaise. Her face was severe. 'Please, sit.' On the wall behind Madame, the portrait of her dead husband glowered down.

Marie-Louise sank back into the hard chair.

Madame dismissed her servants, waiting for the sound of retreating footsteps before she spoke. 'What makes you think I will help you?'

She won't help, Marie-Louise thought. Why would she? 'I need to support myself.'

Madame retrieved Olympe's letter from her black skirts. 'For the child?'

Marie-Louise dropped her head. She slipped her thumb beneath the sleeve of her shirt and rubbed the blistered welt, still sore to the touch.

'But surely this plan, this scheme, is ludicrous? The danger! And if you were to be discovered—' Madame leaned closer '—I cannot bear to think of the consequences.'

Marie-Louise took a deep breath, feeling her bandages cut into her ribs. 'I am prepared.'

'Have you no family to turn to?'

She thought of the night she had returned to her father's doorstep. She saw her stepmother's sour-sucked face and her father in his brocaded waistcoat, stroking his belly in front of the fire. Her stepmother's condemnation was shrill. A bastard child! What curse did she wish upon this house? At thirty-six years of age had she not learned the meaning of shame? The top of her foot ached where her father had leaned upon his cane to pin her to the floorboards.

She shook her head.

'Is there no other way? A position as a maid?'

'I have no references.'

'But that is easily fixed! I can provide you with one.'

Marie-Louise paused. Could she go back to that life? Could she empty chamber pots and scrub linen for the rest of her days?

'But how will I reclaim my son?' she asked. 'What household would employ an unmarried mother and let a bastard child under their roof?'

Madame d'Yauville could not answer her. Marie-Louise saw her flick her eyes towards the door, suspecting the servants might be listening. Indecision played across her face.

'It is my only hope,' Marie-Louise pleaded.

'There is another way.' Madame raised her chin. 'A wealthy patron?'

Marie-Louise shook her head, just once. 'I am no beauty,' she said, surprised Madame could not see that for herself. Had she not been told that so many times in her life, by her father, her stepmother, her lover? 'And I no longer have youth on my side.' Besides, Marie-Louise promised herself, I will not be another man's whore.

Madame sighed, then nodded. 'I will petition my brother, Jean-Michel, for you.'

Marie-Louise rushed to kneel before her. 'Thank you, Madame, thank you.' She felt a kindling of hope, like the first smoulders catching in a handful of twigs.

'Do not thank me! I fear the future I could be sending you to. Jean-Michel is to leave soon for a long and treacherous journey. He will think this scheme is madness, of course. There is no guarantee that he will help you.'

He must help me, Marie-Louise thought, with a glance towards Pierre. Olympe's son had risked enough. He was returning to his ship and she could ask no more of him. Soon she would be alone in this port. Her new-found confidence wavered and she saw the lead-white faces of the marketplace whores, like beckoning ghosts.

Madame d'Yauville gave her a room on the top floor and Marie-Louise endeavoured to keep away from the prying eyes of her household. For a week she waited for news. Eventually, Madame brought word from her brother, and an assortment of worn sailor's clothes.

'He cannot take you on his ship. There is no position for you.' Madame d'Yauville helped Marie-Louise remove her shirt, stripping it over her head. 'Thank the Lord. Imagine it—a long sea journey to the ends of the earth? I could not forgive myself if he suggested it.'

Marie-Louise sat pale and shrunken, slumped forwards, naked above the waist except for her bandages. Her arms were crossed over the loose skin of her belly. She turned her face away from Madame d'Yauville to hide her distress.

'But I have found you something more suitable instead,' Madame d'Yauville continued. 'A baker's assistant on the gun ship *Deux Frères* while it restocks in Brest. It is only for a few months. Promise me—'

she shook Marie-Louise's arms '—that you will disappear before it sails. Promise me I will not be sending you off to war.'

Marie-Louise said nothing, her emotions in turmoil. Was she relieved? It was what she wanted, wasn't it? A navy post. The navy would feed her, house her, pay her. But in truth, she could not see her future. Before Rémi was born it had seemed so simple. All she had thought about was running away.

She clasped her elbows, shivering despite the warmth of the room. Madame had been so kind, hiding her these past days, keeping her secret safe. In Paris, Marie-Louise had constantly feared her father would come for her. His boiled face when he saw that she had returned to his house, pregnant and forsaken, still haunted her. She had been weak and he despised weakness. What she had done, the scandal, could ruin him. He would never forgive her. Even here, at the out-flung fingertip of France, she did not feel safe.

Scissors scraped on bone. Behind her, Madame cut through a whalebone corset to bind her breasts made heavy by the needless milk. Gently, Madame wrapped it around Marie-Louise and then wrenched it tight. Marie-Louise gasped. Surely her heart and lungs had collapsed. The bones pinched her flesh. She began to pant. Madame tugged the laces one final time and knotted them in front of her chest. 'You must tighten by another notch each day.'

Marie-Louise touched her flattened chest. Obsolete.

How many reincarnations could one life hold?

The uniform Pierre had given her lay crumpled on the floor like a shed skin. She thought of the dress she had burned in the coach-house—once a chambermaid's uniform and yet another of her disguises. Who she was, who she might become, was as clear to her as that first sight of the sea, a horizon smudged by fog.

'Did Olympe suggest this ridiculous scheme?' Madame asked. 'She was always one for pranks and disobedience.' She snorted. 'We knew each other at school.' She drew out the word, as though considering the definition. Marie-Louise turned to face her. 'The convent that we were sent to,' she explained, 'with all the inconvenient wives and the daughters who had babies by the wrong men.'

Marie-Louise's heart knocked against her caged chest. So that was how Olympe had come to know Madame d'Yauville. They both had bastard children.

'We have that in common,' Madame said, reaching out to cup Marie-Louise's jaw in her palm, her eyes full of understanding. 'Our families took our babies away from us.' Her hand fell away from Marie-Louise's face. As she turned to the wall, Marie-Louise blinked away hot, welling tears. She wiped them quickly, not wanting Madame to see.

'Now,' Madame said, gathering herself. 'Put this on.'

She held out a rough tunic. It fell loose and square over Marie-Louise's shoulders.

Marie-Louise pulled on wide, striped trousers beneath the tunic.

'Let me see.' Madame stood back, appraising. 'Good,' she said, knotting a tricolor scarf around Marie-Louise's neck. Taking up a comb and a pair of scissors, Madame tugged the tines through her grease-thickened strands. Marie-Louise's head jerked. Clippings littered the floor and she saw her hair, once shining honey, was now the colour of stale straw. Madame took some ash from the grate and smudged it above Marie-Louise's top lip. 'There. They might take you for a boy. What about your voice?'

'Like this?' Marie-Louise choked the words from the back of her throat.

Madame screwed up her nose. 'Tell me to go fuck my grandmother.'

Marie-Louise recoiled.

'Go on.'

Marie-Louise grunted the insult, feeling ashamed to utter such words to this kind woman.

'Deeper.'

She tried again.

Madame shook her head. 'Growl. Be menacing. From your gut. Think of someone you hate.'

The image of her lover's face came to her in an instant, his pocked skin and eyes too close together. She remembered his sweetened, sickening, truthless whispers.

'Go fuck your grandmother!' She hurled the words. The hairs rose on the back of her neck.

Madame d'Yauville smiled. 'Perfect.'

Chapter 4

MARIE-LOUISE MADE HER WAY ALONE THROUGH THE DANK ALLEYways to the port. She hovered in the shadows of the warehouses, the brim of her hat pulled low, watching a queue of men waiting to board the *Deux Frères*. A rat lurked at her feet, thrusting its nose and whiskers out into the light, poised as if to run. Ahead, the harbour was a forest of masts, bare of leaves, stark like winter in the pale morning light.

She waited. Her scarf was too tight and she tried to loosen it, feeling it pull like a noose around her neck. Perhaps it was not too late to change her mind, to abandon this disguise. A door clanged open behind her. Men carrying barrels on their shoulders filed out, cursing at her to move, and suddenly she was pushed and jostled into line.

The smell of men, their sweat and grime, overwhelmed her. Yet she moved along with them, one small discordant thread in a braid of rope, pulled along the dock. Muscled shoulders and backs banged against her. Thick, hairy forearms were exposed beneath their sleeves and, terrified, she clasped her own fine wrists behind her. She wanted to run, but knew she could not. The cord of men came to a halt and she saw the rat sprint between the legs of the men ahead. Each man was counted into a small boat by a *garde marine*. She pressed close to the sweat-stained back of the man in front of her, willing herself invisible.

The boat swayed as she stepped into it and her stomach lurched at the unfamiliar sensation. Suddenly, her neck was tugged back by her scarf.

'You there!' The *garde marine* was glaring at her. 'What do you think you are doing?'

She could not speak. How could she ever have imagined she could look like one of these men?

He tugged again at her tricolour scarf. 'You are in the service of the King now. Take it off!'

She hastily undid the knot and tossed the fabric into the water. The soldier pushed her down into a seat as the rowers took up the oars.

Trembling openly now and not daring to look up, she felt a clap on her shoulder. As the boat drew away from the *garde marine* in his bright uniform, she heard sniggering. 'Good on you, lad.' 'Stick it to 'em.'

On the *Deux Frères*, she was led below deck. Here, she was to bake bread for the crew who worked to repair the ship and ready her for sail. It was dark in the galley, the gloom broken only by yellow lantern light. The baker regarded her, unimpressed. She shrank beneath his appraisal. His arms were thick and he stood with fists on his hips. He sniffed and shrugged then tossed her an apron.

Marie-Louise steadied her hands against her thighs, hardly daring to believe her disguise had carried her this far. In the mess hall, the baker showed her the chest for her belongings and the hammock she was to sleep in. The canvas coffin hung from the roof along with dozens of others, fourteen inches of space for each man. She began to pant, feeling her chest swell against the whalebone. *How can I sleep among all these men? How will I relieve myself? What do I do when I have the bleeds?* The bundle of cut rags she had tucked into her waistband seemed a feeble defence. *What if they see a stain? What if they smell me out?*

'The crew are housed ashore until we sail,' the baker said.

Marie-Louise let her breath escape. She forced herself to be calm as she returned to the galley. Right now she had a barrel of flour to transform into loaves of bread.

Years ago her husband, Etienne, had taught her to bake. She thought of him as she worked the dough, imagining herself back in his café kitchen. She closed her eyes, remembering his arms wrapped around her, his big hands covering hers, and his soft lips touching her ear as he taught her to knead. He was dead now. Buried more than ten years ago. Beneath the heel of her hand she felt the dough stretch. *You can do this. You have to do this.*

Her first batch earned her a clout about her ear. 'Do you want them buggers brawling over the size of a bun?' the baker demanded of her. 'They're like children that lot, just with bigger fists. Don't give them an excuse.'

She quickly learned the knack of rolling out a log of dough and slicing each bun precisely. The baker—she had not yet been told his name and he did not seem inclined to learn hers—tossed them in his floured palms and grunted approval. Her muscles ached. No sooner was one batch left to prove than another was started. All day she worked and the pressure in her bladder grew. She glanced around the empty mess hall, her eyes resting on the dark stairway to the hold below. She crossed her legs.

Heavy feet pounded on the floorboards above her head. The baker shut the oven door and stood, listening. Marie-Louise looked up to the vibrating boards. Her hands were glued with wet dough. She heard a shout.

The baker peered up the steps. 'Stay here,' he said as he began to climb. 'Mind the oven.'

She held her breath. The shouting grew louder. She dunked her hands into a bucket of water and scratched her hands clean. Crouching, she listened to the cries of the men. Angry? Hostile? What was happening?

The baker did not return. Torn between the desire to hide and the desire to run, she did neither. Her bladder threatened her. She found a pot and searched for privacy, a cupboard or an unused room; there had to be a place. Smoke drifted through the galley and she remembered the loaves. Swearing, she opened the oven door just as an explosion rocked the ship. She was thrown across the galley with hot loaves sliding from the oven. A barrel of flour smashed against the wall. The matter of her bladder was decided for her.

Squinting through the cloud of dust, she scrambled for the stairs.

'Fire!' The call rang out as Marie-Louise emerged on deck. She turned to see black smoke billowing against an orange sky. Men rushed past her, but she could not move.

'Come on, lad,' a voice rumbled in her ear. A rough hand grasped her wrist. 'There's mutiny and the fools have set the ship alight!'

The grey-haired sailor dragged her towards the side of the ship where rickety scaffolding had been erected against the hull. Men tumbled down the stairs, pushing and screaming as they fell into the waves. Longboats were rowed out from the dock to rescue them.

'Jump!' a man from a longboat called to Marie-Louise.

'I can't swim!'

A monkey scampered along the deck and launched itself, arms and legs suspended like it was swinging between trees, and bounced onto the backs of the men in the boat.

'Go, lad!' The sailor who had pulled her from the burning deck grew impatient. He shoved her over the side of the ship. She screamed and landed hard upon the edge of the longboat, arms and legs splayed like a spider. Winded, she hauled herself over and rolled into the wet swill in the bottom of the boat as, one after the other, more men elbowed and kicked and scrambled on top of her.

As the rowers pulled the boat away she heard the terrified shouts of men left behind and the splash of bodies hitting the water. She imagined their hands striking the hull of the boat, fingers searching for purchase against the copper bolts.

At the dockside someone slipped an arm beneath her armpits and heaved her onto the flagstone quay like a sack of grain. Marie-Louise rolled onto her hands and knees, feeling bruises in her ribs and back as though she had received a beating from her father's cane.

'We're not safe yet, lad.'

Carriages clattered towards them as the municipal guards chased the mutineers. The old sailor pulled her up and she stumbled after him for no other reason than she didn't know what else to do. The sailor ran with a bandy-legged gait. He ducked between the tall warehouses that lined the docks.

'Where are we going?' Marie-Louise demanded, suddenly fearful in the maze of alleys.

He didn't pause or reply. She swore and hurried after him. Eventually he stopped, swinging out his arm to push her back into the shadows. Pressed close beside him, he smelled of pipe smoke. She noticed a pointed tooth punctured his earlobe. His face was weathered and lined and his forearms were like tanned leather and heavily tattooed in blue ink.

The sailor checked the alley was clear of the guards before crossing to a large doorway. He gave four sharp knocks.

As the door opened she saw a tall man silhouetted against the golden light. Marie-Louise watched him drop coins into the hand of her rescuer.

'Thank you, Armand,' the man said as the sailor pocketed his coins.

She frowned. What was happening? Was she being delivered? Before she had time to run, the man stepped out into the pool of light on his doorstep. 'You had better come in.'

Chapter 5

MARIE-LOUISE BEGAN TO SHAKE AS SOON AS SHE SAT IN FRONT of the fire. They were in a study, that much she could tell, but she kept her head bowed and said nothing.

The man took a seat in a stiff-backed chair and stretched out his long legs towards the fire. She sat hunched like a fist. From the corner of her eye she saw him watching her, taking in her wretched state: wet, ragged clothes, her hair hacked short, her face made ghostly from the blast of flour.

'What am I to do with you?'

She glanced at him, measuring his intentions. The coins in her purse would not last more than a week.

'Allow me to introduce myself: I am Jean-Michel Huon de Kermadec.'

She looked up quickly. So this was the brother of Madame d'Yauville. Had he been keeping a watch on her? She thought of the coins he'd paid the sailor at his door. He was younger than she had expected, perhaps forty, and his face was like creamed butter, not leathered by salt and sun like the sailors of the *Deux Frères*. He wore an ivory-coloured wig in the modern style of Louis XVI, two curls above each ear and tied at the nape of his neck with a long black ribbon. He gave her a reassuring smile.

She flicked her gaze away. He knew she was desparate. She could not trust him.

'My sister asked me to look out for you.'

The fire crackled and spat. The tang of warmed urine rose from her clothing. When she closed her eyes she saw the flames of the burning ship, saw herself teetering above the waves. Her eyes snapped open.

From floor to ceiling, the walls of the room were almost entirely lined with books. Among the leather bindings she saw books on mathematics, geography and the voyages of great navigators. She recognised the comedies of Molière and philosophy of Rousseau. She had been in rooms like this before. It reminded her of the Paris salons and her intellectual friends. It reminded her of revolution.

'The difficulty is knowing what to take and what to leave,' he said, following her gaze.

In the corner of his library stood crates half filled with books. Some of the volumes were flipped open on the floor as though he had been rediscovering each one as an old friend, unable to choose between them. Propped up against the crates were oil paintings in ornate gilded frames and perched on top was a silver flute, glinting in the firelight.

'What will you do now?' Huon de Kermadec asked.

Marie-Louise stared into the flames. She could not answer. What options did she have? Stay here with the dockyard whores and live a short, ruined life. Or remain in a man's skin and seek a placement on a naval ship, perhaps even go to war. Above the mantelpiece, two frigates with full sails crested the bow of a turquoise wave.

'That's the *Resolution*,' Huon de Kermadec said, pointing to the oil painting. 'I sailed in her under Commander Bruni d'Entrecasteaux from the East Indies through to China. The voyage was exceptional; they still talk about it today. Instead of waiting a whole year to avoid the typhoon season, d'Entrecasteaux proposed we sail an untried route virtually without charts! And we had to navigate in darkness through the Makassar Strait when the wind blew only at night. A brilliant man. There is no safer commander in all the French navy.'

She admired his conviction, but he was talking nonsense. Safety. There was no such thing. Safety could be stripped from you in an instant.

'I am to captain the *Espérance* on a rescue mission. Perhaps you have heard of this?'

She nodded curtly. Was he boasting? Of course she had heard of the famous navigator who sailed from Brest six years ago and never returned. 'La Pérouse,' she murmured. In fact, she had been at the Tuileries Palace when Fleurieu, the Minister of Marine, came to collect the King's signature for the rescue mission. Old, fat Fleurieu—she knew of him from the servants' gossip. Everyone talked about his fresh bud of a fiancée, and the fact that he had been intimate with both her mother and her grandmother before engaging himself to her. Marie-Louise had dropped into a curtsey with all the other servants as he strode past, flanked by two naval officers in shining uniforms. Fleurieu carried a scroll of parchment in his hand. Everyone knew this was all for show, that the National Assembly ran the country now, and seeking the King's signature was a matter of etiquette only. But she could never speak of this.

She caught the earnest look in Huon de Kermadec's eye. Not to this man.

'Exactly. The King sends us on a mission in search of La Pérouse and his two ships, the *Astrolabe* and the *Boussole*.' Huon de Kermadec crossed the room to his desk and began to unroll a massive sheet of yellowed parchment.

She craned her neck.

'Would you like to see?'

She rose cautiously. Huon de Kermadec weighted down the corners of the large map, smoothing its surface with his palms. The whole of the known world stretched out before them.

'This is where we shall sail.' Tapping the map at Brest, he traced a line from France past Spain and down along the coast of Africa. At the pointed tip of the continent his finger tracked across a great expanse of ocean, the Mer des Indes, until it hit the half-formed outline of another large landmass, the uncertain shape of a continent. 'New Holland. Great lengths of its southern coastline remain unknown.' The black line along its southern coast stopped abruptly and his finger ran into nothingness.

Marie-Louise clasped her arms around her. The world was a large and terrifying place. 'How will you find La Pérouse?'

'He was heading for the Friendly Isles—' Huon de Kermadec pointed to a group of islands north-east of New Holland '—so we will follow him there.'

She read the name written across the blank paper: *Mer Pacifique*. The islands were barely dots of ink upon the paper. It was a fool's errand. Like searching for raindrops in the ocean.

'We shall return as heroes!' His cheeks were flushed and his eyes shone.

She snorted. 'You have the blind faith of a child,' she said aloud without thinking. She stepped back beyond his reach, horrified. She had let her thoughts run away with her tongue.

But Kermadec laughed. 'Oh, you wound me,' he said, clasping a hand to his chest in mock pain. 'I am the boy who ran away to sea and never grew up. You sound like my father. He thinks a man of my age should return home to the country and provide our family with heirs.'

She dropped her eyes to the patterned rug at her feet. Duty to your father above all else.

Kermadec poured himself a brandy and offered a glass to Marie-Louise. She took it.

'You puzzle me,' he said.

She looked away, made uncomfortable by his searching gaze.

'I see your eyes linger on these volumes; I see you scan their spines. You can read.'

She did not deny the accusation. She thought of Olympe and her friends. If she had never joined their circle she would know nothing of Rousseau or Voltaire.

'Can you write?'

She nodded.

'Who are you? How have you ended up here, and in this state?'

Who am I? she thought. Daughter, widow, mother or whore? Which one would she pick?

'My father held a post at the Palace of Versailles when I was young,' she said. It was true, but he hadn't worked in the palace. Kermadec did not need to know that she had been a gardener's daughter. Perhaps if he believed her to be the daughter of a courtier rather than a gardener he would treat her with more respect.

'Will you return to your family?' he asked.

The question cut her to the quick. None of them would help her. Not her brothers nor her sisters. Her father would see to that. She was dead to them. 'My family have disowned me,' she murmured.

Huon de Kermadec frowned. 'The father of your child? Where is he?'

Her eyes flashed wide. So he knew about her son. About her disgrace. She regarded him from beneath her brows. His question was bold, but he would not meet her gaze. She shook her head.

'An honourable man would know his responsibilities,' Kermadec said. 'He would accept the consequences of his actions.' He emptied his glass in one gulp.

She turned her head from him, staring down at the map of the known world, letting her eyes trace the meridian line through the centre of Paris. She sipped the brandy in her glass, feeling it burn above her heart.

He tapped the map with his finger. 'You should join us.'

She cocked her ear towards him, unsure if she had heard him correctly. He was staring at her intently. 'Our expedition has two ships, and the *Recherche*, our sister ship, is in desperate need of a steward.'

Think of the adventure, Olympe said in her ear. *All the wonders of the world you will see.*

Think of the danger, Marie-Louise thought, looking towards the door.

He saw her indecision. 'You were prepared to risk this subterfuge on the *Deux Frères*.' He gestured to her clothing. 'What is the difference?'

'How long will you be gone?'

'Two years at most.'

Two years was too long. How would she ever find her son again? She saw the heated coin pressed onto her baby's skin, heard him cry out. Her hands shook and she set her glass down onto a lacquered side table with a rattle.

'I cannot turn you out on the street.'

She narrowed her eyes. Why did he care?

He rocked slightly from his heel to his toe. His eyebrows flicked upwards in challenge, like a boy enticing her to mischief. 'I made a promise to my sister to watch out for you,' he said.

How could she trust him, this man she barely knew?

He spread his hands lovingly across the map as though it were the skin of a beautiful woman. She saw the tiny dots of the islands, the looping letters of the *Grand Océan Austral* marking the vast southern seas, and the faint, hair's-breadth lines of unfinished coasts, drawn with all the surety of a suggestion. She recalled her first sight of the sea and the white haze obscuring the horizon, blocking all sight of the way ahead.

And yet. She felt a strange sensation; a throb of possibility. For the first time in her life she felt opportunity opening before her. She could do this. She could be this woman that would sail across the world and back again. Until a familiar mocking voice spoke in her ear: *You are not brave enough, you silly slut. This is not for the likes of you.*

She turned for the door. She would leave. Crossing the worm-eaten floorboards, her heel caught on a hole in the floor. Looking down, she was suddenly reminded of the fairy she once found trapped in the floor. All her brothers and sisters had crowded around the creature, staring in wonder at its squashed and hairy face wedged in the crumbled floorboards. The more it struggled and flapped, the more it tore its wings. She had knelt and tried to prise it free. Her father's cane had cracked over her knuckles. 'It's a bat,' he told them. And stomped his heel to its head.

She swung around to face Kermadec. 'How much does it pay?'

Huon de Kermadec raised his eyebrows. She saw at once that he had never had to feed a family with soup made from onion skins. 'Thirty-three livres per month.'

Thirty-three livres! That was three times more than she could earn as a domestic servant. Her heart beat faster. That would be enough to claim back her son. She could start again.

'Two years?' she asked.

'More or less,' he answered.

Chapter 6

'You should not have deceived me in this way!' Bruni d'Entrecasteaux growled at Huon de Kermadec, who stood with head bent beside Marie-Louise in the commander's cabin. 'We sail on the tide!'

'But, sir, we have need of a steward. Where are we to find another at this late hour?'

'This ship is no place for a woman, Huon. I expected better of you.'

Marie-Louise saw herself reflected in the commander's expression—a mangy, shipyard rat; for all he knew, a whore who had come aboard to ply her trade.

The commander turned to her. 'Tell me why I should not have you put off this frigate along with the other stowaways we cannot afford to feed?'

Huon de Kermadec looked shocked. 'Sir, she would have no chaperone, no protector!'

'If she is prepared to sail around the world, surely she is resourceful enough to find her way home from a European port.'

'I can cook,' Marie-Louise blurted.

'You will need to do more than that! The steward is responsible for our stores. You must decide how we can feed one hundred and ten men over many months. When there is no fresh food, you must ration the rice and beans and salted meat. Calculate how much flour we have left for bread. Do you understand how important this role is?'

Marie-Louise nodded, glancing at Huon de Kermadec for reassurance. His face remained grim.

The commander was right. She could not do this job. Look what had happened to her beloved Etienne's café after he died. It sank faster than a scuttled ship. If she had been capable of saving it, she would not be standing here now.

Commander d'Entrecasteaux took a deep breath, his powdered cheeks flushed. He turned away from her. In profile, she saw the sharpness of his hooked nose, the angles of his forehead. His thin lips were drawn tight.

'Leave us now, Huon,' the commander said.

Huon de Kermadec hesitated. She glanced at him, suddenly afraid to be left alone with the stern commander.

'You must have many details to attend to aboard your own vessel,' Commander d'Entrecasteaux said firmly to the younger man.

Huon de Kermadec bowed to him in acknowledgement and winked at Marie-Louise before he closed the door behind him. It did not reassure her. Alone with the commander, she tried to calm her pounding heart. He gestured for her to draw up a chair beside him.

Sitting so close, she noticed the spot marks of age beside his eyes, barely concealed by powder, and the loose flap of skin beneath his chin that the white ruff of his cravat did not hide. His wig was traditional in style, a short crop of tight grey curls tied crisply at his nape.

'Tell me,' he said, 'what of your father? Can he not provide for you?'

She shook her head. 'I cannot go back to him.'

'What manner of man is he?'

How could she explain? Her father had been a gardener once, that was true, but now he was a different type of man altogether. A wine merchant. A wealthy man. A burgher of Versailles. 'I have dishonoured him,' she said. 'It is not safe for me to return.'

Commander d'Entrecasteaux stared at her, one eyebrow raised. 'There was a child.'

Tears blurred her eyes as she hung her head. The commander was a nobleman, a military man—he would understand her father's position. Peerages could be lost, generations ruined by the scandal. She heard her stepmother's shrill voice: 'Did anyone see you on the step?' No, she could not go back to Versailles.

The commander leaned back in his chair. For a long while he was silent. 'I was duty-bound to resign my post on the staff of the Minister of Marine because of the scandal caused by the actions of my nephew. I was sent far from France.'

Marie-Louise screwed her eyes tight shut. It was as she'd feared. He understood family dishonour and he had been burned by it. She would be set ashore. Her thoughts whirled. How would she survive?

'Fortunately,' the commander continued, 'it meant I could return to the sea.'

She looked up to see a smile of unexpected kindness. His stern face had softened.

'Have you heard of the corsairs of the Barbary Coast?' he asked.

She nodded, confused. Of course she knew of the pirates who raided the Mediterranean towns for Christian slaves. Parents relied on these chilling tales. *Behave, or the corsairs will come for you.*

'As a young man I served on frigates protecting French trading in the Aegean Sea. There I heard a story that has remained with me all these years.' He leaned forwards in his chair. 'A feudal lord had stolen away the daughter of a rich Italian merchant. Enraged, the merchant hired seven corsair ships to sail to the palace of the lord. The pirates raided at night, in a surprise attack, and the merchant gained entrance to the palace.' He drew back. 'But the merchant did not seek out the feudal lord for revenge. Instead, he found his innocent daughter and strangled her with his own bare hands.'

The commander held out his hands as though contemplating the weight of wrath that might be contained in them. He shook his head.

Marie-Louise held her breath. Did he understand? Did he see why she could not return to her father? A memory of her father's rage forced itself into her mind. Her father was drunk. She saw her mother's bone-white hand gripping the edge of the table. Saw her mother on her knees, her belly hanging low, broken shards of the brandy bottle still rocking on the floorboards. She had dropped his last bottle. Marie-Louise dragged her brothers out from beneath the kitchen table. In the last look that passed from mother to daughter Marie-Louise thought she saw gratitude, but at ten years old, would she know? Her mother's teeth bit into her bottom lip to keep from crying out, to deny him that one last satisfaction. Marie-Louise had watched her father raise his cane and strike her mother's back. Anger pulsed through her at the memory. *I need your courage now, Maman,* she thought.

'All women know how to budget for their families,' she spoke up, feigning a confidence she did not feel. 'All women know how to make the soup stretch when meat is in short supply.'

'But not on this scale.'

'A matter of multiplication.'

She thought she saw the commander struggling to hide a smile.

'I cannot guarantee your safety,' he said. 'You would be at grave risk.'

She nodded.

'I expect you to perform your duties like any other member of our crew and I will treat you no differently from the men.'

Hope began to swell inside her.

'I need to depend on you.' He leaned forwards, holding her gaze.

'You can rely on me,' she said, hoping that was true.

'And you must never reveal your gender. On board the *Recherche* only I will know; not even the ship's captain will be told. I cannot risk the jealousies—the divisions—that might arise should you make yourself known to the men.'

'Of course.'

'What is your name?'

'Girardin,' she said without pause. 'Louis Girardin.'

Part Two

Cacher: to hide

Chapter 7

Port of Brest, 28 September 1791

LOUIS GIRARDIN HELD UP THE LANTERN AND SLOWLY TWISTED about. Her cabin was narrow and crammed with wooden crates. It had no windows. She looked down into a stinking pail that had not been emptied for some days and the sight of it nearly made her weep with relief. She leaned her forehead against the door and turned its heavy key, hearing it lock with a reassuring solidity. She pulled the key out and held it tight in her fist.

A tall man would have to stoop, but being just shy of five foot, she could straighten her backbone and walk freely. Girardin paced the length and counted to four. With crates of ship's biscuit lining one wall, the width was not much more than her fingers could reach when she stretched out her arms, but the size of her room was not important. She stroked the sound planks that enclosed her space and obscured her from view.

On the other side of her door the crew were sleeping. It worried her that the crewmen slept so close to her cabin. By day the area was a mess hall, but each night the tables were replaced by dozens of hammocks swinging from the rafters. Above her head was the gun deck with the galley in the bow and officers' cabins in the stern. Beneath her feet was the hold, filled with barrels of fresh water, food and trinkets for exchange. She was yet to be shown the full extent of the ship. For now, she was thankful to be left alone in a place all her own.

The solid shaft of the foremast ran down through one end of her cabin. She rested her back against it, feeling its strength like the trunk of a tree. Even without the sails raised she could feel it vibrate against her shoulderblades as somewhere high above the wind pushed against the yards. Tomorrow she would feel it creak and strain and shudder as the wind leaned into the sails, pushing them away.

Her hammock was slung up high against one wall with a chest beneath to store her spare clothing. There was a desk with its chair pulled out, as though the previous steward had just stood up to greet her. She took off her aged jacket with its dull brass buttons and laid it over the back of the chair. It looked at home there. Opening the chest, she found the belongings of another man: a used cake of soap, a nub of tallow candle, a sewing kit, a Bible. She stared at them, feeling a vague sense of indecency to see them still there. It passed quickly. From the sewing kit, she cut a length of cord and tied the key around her neck. She had a locked door. She had privacy. Here, she could wash herself and her bloodied rags without being seen. In this dark cocoon, she dared to hope she would be safe.

Lifting up the greatcoat that lined the bottom of the chest, she recoiled from the reek of empty brandy bottles stashed beneath. The smell brought with it a vivid memory of her childhood. She saw the brandy bottle fall from her mother's hand, the liquor splash across the kitchen floor, the scattered shards of broken glass rocking on the boards.

Her father's beating had brought on her mother's labour that night. Still drunk, her father had banished all the children from the house. They sheltered in a toolshed. Her older sister sat cross-legged with the toddler upon her lap. Together they listened to their mother's screams. Marie-Louise imagined her mother sweating and twisting in her sheets. 'We have to do something,' she hissed to her sister.

But what? Clemence mouthed in response.

As Marie-Louise crept from the shed, her toe clipped a spade leaning against the garden wall and she froze, listening as the metal scraped in a slow arc against the stone. She ran. Turning her back to the palace walls, she weaved through the tight streets, past the cathedral of Saint-Louis, searching for the house with flowers painted on the door. At night the streets of Versailles were owned by rats and dogs, the homeless and the drunks, but she ignored their shadows. She had no time to be afraid.

At last she found the door with geraniums and yarrow painted on its wood and roused the midwife from her sleep. The old woman gathered her implements in a canvas bag. She plucked some bunches of dried herbs from her ceiling and suffered herself to be dragged from her home.

All through their slow progress in the dark streets, Marie-Louise feared they would be too late. Nearing the wall of the palace garden, she listened hard for the sound of her mother's birthing cries. She tugged the old woman along, almost slipping in her haste. When they reached her home, the house was black and silent. Marie-Louise was afraid to go inside, but the midwife pushed the kitchen door open.

Her father had passed out, slumped sideways in his chair. The smell of brandy stained the air. The candle had burned down to a nub and Marie-Louise stared from the doorway at the glistening pool of wax beneath a glutting flame.

'Stay here,' the midwife commanded, and began to climb the stairs.

Marie-Louise turned to the yard and saw the haunted faces of her brothers and sisters peering out from the shed. She slid down to the threshold and hooked her skinny arms around her bruised shins. All was silent.

Sometime later, Marie-Louise heard the midwife creak back down each step. She remembered the bone-hard squeeze of the old woman's hand on her shoulder and the hopelessness in the shake of her head.

Louis Girardin kicked the chest away from her and the brandy bottles shifted, clinking and chiming like bells in the wind. Tomorrow she would pitch them over the side of the ship. This was not the time to dwell on her past. She kicked the chest again and the lid slammed shut.

Chapter 8

Port of Brest, 29 September 1791

THE CREW OF THE *RECHERCHE* CROWDED THE DECK TO WAVE farewell to France. Louis Girardin joined them, taking her place on the forecastle deck in the bow. On shore, there was fanfare and celebration to launch the rescue mission. Girardin heard drums and trumpets and saw muscians marching along the quay. She saw tricolour banners and flags of red, white and blue proudly displayed alongside the King's white Bourbon flag. Naval regiments came out to salute them. Cannons boomed. All of Brest must have come to wish them well. The expedition had raised the spirits of the town, and she wondered if the families of La Pérouse's men were among this crowd, watching them cast off. She felt the hopes of the wives and mothers, who had thought never to see their husbands and sons again. We will bring them home, she promised them silently.

The ropes binding ship to shore were quickly looped undone and thrown back to the ship. Girardin gripped the rail and felt the liquid sensation of the earth sliding beneath her. A gap appeared between the wharf and the ship as men in rowboats towed the frigates out from the docks. The murky water stretched out between her and the shore, the gap becoming further than she could leap. The crowd roared louder. Women waved handkerchiefs. Children skipped like rats along the quay, running after the ships. Her heart lurched. *Wait*, she wanted to cry out to them, *I am not ready! I am not ready to leave.*

A mass of ropes writhed across the deck and Girardin was afraid to move lest they snag her feet. Her knees trembled. The bosun called commands and the crew responded in a singsong way, with words she barely recognised as her own language. Sailors tugged on the ropes to hoist the sails.

'Make fast!' came the command as the canvas rolled down with a solid *thwap*, the sound of wet washing slapped by the wind. The ship surged with the choppy waves. Girardin bent her knees as the deck shifted beneath her and her stomach rolled uneasily.

Captain Kermadec's ship, the *Espérance*, was already out in the middle of the bay, surrounded by an entourage of smaller boats sailing alongside to farewell her. Marie-Louise wished that she had seen him before they had sailed. His reassuring smile might have settled her nerves. This first leg of their journey was to be a short one. First stop Tenerife in the Canary Islands, off the coast of Africa. Perhaps he would seek her out there. But for now, she had to find her own courage.

To think, when she was seventeen she had begged her father to let her travel with him to the vineyards of the Mediterranean. By then Jean Girardin was a successful wine merchant, and had long since left the gardens of Versailles behind. After her mother's death, her father had married the widow of a wine merchant and the family moved into a larger home in a better neighbourhood. She remembered being presented to her new stepmother along with her brothers and sisters, all lined up in decreasing order of size. Then, she had been just tall enough to see out a window overlooking a courtyard filled with barrels. Looking down into that walled courtyard for the first time, she had felt certain there would be no escape.

'Send me with your journeyman,' she had begged her father. 'You know the travel aggravates your gout.'

'No daughter of mine will be seen in a common coach!' Jean tossed the last of his cases at the carriage driver. 'I didn't work myself out of the compost heaps of the royal gardens to have my daughter bring down our family name. The only women who travel are prostitutes and actresses! Do you want people to talk of you like that?'

'No, Papa,' she had whispered.

The town of Brest faded into haze. The entourage of boats had returned to shore, leaving only the two frigates under full sail, heading out to the horizon. I am travelling now, Papa, she thought. I am travelling as far away from you as I can.

But as the land retreated behind them, her doubts rose. She rubbed the raised welt underneath her forearm. The route back to her son had been broken by this stretch of water. If she stepped off this ship, she would plummet to the sea floor. They were no longer linked by the same piece of solid earth. They were cast adrift from one another and she was the one floating away.

The sails snapped as they filled with the freshening wind and the ship gained pace, rising and falling on the waves. As the coast fell further and further behind, she began to panic, convinced she had no hope of returning for her son. Mocking voices filled her head. *What kind of mother would run away like that? Doesn't deserve to be one. Worthless bitch.* The voices knew her darkest thoughts. Even the tiniest blackbird will launch itself against the circling hawk, not flee and leave its young to be torn to pieces.

Oh God, she thought, I am going to be sick. Leaning out over the side of the ship, a stream of vomit poured from her. She coughed and spat, her throat burning. The ship rocked again and another gush of vomit rushed from her. Whether the pitch of the waves or her guilt had overturned her stomach, she could not say.

She wiped her mouth on the back of her sleeve. Oh Lord, help me, she prayed even though she knew He would not listen to her. What have I done?

Girardin clutched a wooden pail to her chest as she reported to the galley. Two men watched her sidle past the coal-black beast of an oven in the centre of the space. She steadied herself against the benches built into the bow of the ship that served as their kitchen. At her feet, water sloshed in a pail as the bow surged and fell with the waves. Girardin held her bucket tighter. What a sight I must look to these men, she thought. How could Louis Girardin be disguise enough to fool them at such close quarters? A look of incredulity passed between the head chef, Thomas Besnard, and his assistant, a leek-limbed youth named Luc.

'Not been at sea much, then?' Besnard nodded at the pail.

She shook her head, not daring to trust her voice.

'Where did they find you?' he asked. 'Never seen a ship's steward look so feeble.' His sly gaze slid all over her.

She felt the queasiness of her stomach return, the anxious rolling of her gut.

'Hope you're better than the last one.' Besnard looked at her directly, his eyes made small and piggish by the fullness of his face. 'Steward was a drunk. Fell off the ship at port and drowned.' He laughed, a hog-like snort.

She swallowed the urge to vomit and carefully set down her pail, drawing her spine up straight. If he meant to intimidate her by his disregard for the steward's life, she would not give him the satisfaction. Yet Captain Kermadec had not mentioned that the sudden death of the steward had allowed her this berth. It was not an auspicious start.

It fell to Besnard to show her the ship and its storerooms. She followed him, keeping her eyes trained on the long braid hanging down his back. He was a big man with a lopsided walk that made his braid swing like a pendulum. She found its motion ominous.

Beyond the galley were gangways on either side of the ship that joined the forecastle deck to the quarterdeck, leaving the centre of the ship open to the sky. Animal pens had been constructed beneath the gangways of the gun deck, and she saw cows wedged between cannons. She breathed the manure and greased-wool scent of the sheep. The animals pressed back into the dark as she passed, their eyes wary. A kid goat bleated beneath its mother's legs and Girardin turned her face away.

The longboats were stored in the centre of this space. At its widest point the ship must only be thirty feet in breadth, she estimated. Looking up to the masts, the sky was crisscrossed by taut ropes that felt like a net trapping her within.

At the stern of the ship were the officers' cabins, and in the common space outside the officers' doors, hammocks were hung in the roof space. 'For the midshipmen,' Besnard said, waving his hand at them. He pointed out the great cabin at the far end of the ship.

'The officers' dining room,' he said. 'Twelve officers to feed and half-a-dozen civilians.' He sniffed. 'They'll be expecting fine dining, no doubt. Our grub won't be good enough for the likes of them.'

The thought of civilians on board surprised her. So far she had only seen sailors in rough clothes like hers, and officers and soldiers in their naval uniforms. She wanted to ask what the civilians were doing on board but did not yet trust her voice.

Besnard nodded up the stairs towards the quarterdeck. 'You'll be cooking for the commander. And serving him his breakfast, lunch and dinner.'

She counted the eight steps up to the quarterdeck and estimated the short number of paces to his cabin door, wondering if she would ever have to seek sanctuary behind it.

They climbed down through the hatch to the orlop deck. Besnard sidled past barrels of salted meat in the passageways and the makeshift storerooms erected in every spare nook and cranny of the ship. He explained the frigate had been transformed from a naval supply vessel to an expedition ship, and this whole deck had been conjured to create more room for the extra crew and stores. He pushed open a door. She was shocked to see the supplies jammed haphazardly inside with barely room to squeeze between them. Behind her, she heard the chef clear his nostrils onto the floor.

In the middle of the ship was the mess hall for the crew. Men sat on wooden chests at tables made from planks of wood suspended on ropes. They chewed slowly. She felt the men's eyes follow her and she prayed their curiosity was piqued out of boredom and not by the shape of her figure or the style of her walk. At the end of the mess hall she saw her own cabin with the title of *Steward* painted on the door. Her hand crept to the key hanging around her neck.

'The sailors eat and sleep here,' Besnard said. 'Three watches. We feed them at the end of each watch.'

Besnard led her past the separate area where the *garde marines* slept. This small core of soldiers would protect them if force was necessary. 'Against the savages,' Besnard said, with a knowing nod.

They climbed down a rope ladder into the hold. The floor was wet. Besnard swore as the flint he struck refused to spark. Girardin stretched out her arms in the darkness and touched a clammy wall. On the other side of her fingers, through planks of wood, studded nails and copper straps, the ocean pressed against them. Water was now above her head and beneath her feet. How insignificant she felt. How tiny. Like Jonah in the belly of the whale. Sweat beaded her brow. She tried not to breathe, made nauseous by the stinking bilge water swilling around their feet. Below decks, in the dark and foul-smelling air, her seasickness felt worse. She blocked her nose, choking back the urge to heave.

Finally the tinder flared and Besnard lit the lantern.

The stores in the hold were a jumbled mess. Sacks of grain spilled on the floor. Ammunition was piled among barrels of water. Boxes with bolts of cloth, beads and mirrors had been opened. As they shuffled forwards, she found room after room filled with unmarked crates of food. She saw Besnard looking at her.

She threw up her hands, finally incensed enough to speak. 'How are we supposed to find anything?'

He shrugged. 'Not my problem.'

She clenched her jaw.

'That's what they pay you "learned" men for.' The chef did not trouble to disguise the sneer in his voice.

The ship climbed a wave and the bilge water rushed out like a tide beneath the planks she stood on. Outside, she knew, the waves were growing taller, giving the ship a greater distance to fall.

'High water,' Besnard said. 'We'll have lost sight of land by now.'

The flicker of candlelight cast grotesque shadows across his face. It was as if the chef knew all her fears and was determined to magnify them. Bile surged into her throat. She had to leave the hold; she could no longer stay in this tight and gasping space. She fumbled for the rope ladder, climbing quickly.

'Take this,' Besnard called up to her when she reached the deck above. He passed her the lantern as he took his turn on the ladder.

The air on the orlop deck was stale. The ship was lurching, pulling her stomach with it. Besnard grunted as he followed her through the hatch. Nausea rising, she ran for the stairs and climbed to the deck above. She barely had time to fill her lungs before she was knocked and sent sprawling to the floor.

'I'm so sorry! Excuse me!'

A concerned face with a head of loosely curling brown hair loomed in front of her. A young man, mid-twenties, in a full-sleeved shirt and waistcoat. She ignored his proffered hand and pushed herself to her feet. Behind him, a taller man wearing a well-cut civilian coat and top hat ran past.

'The lantern, you fools!' Besnard growled. His disembodied head appeared at the top of the stairs.

Girardin gasped. She had dropped the lantern when she fell. It now rested on its side, the candle still alight, but as the ship nosed downward, it began to roll.

The man with the curling hair dashed after it. He had almost corralled it when the ship listed to one side, sending the lantern skidding back towards her. She lunged for it, missed, and watched it plummet past Besnard down the stairs. The glass smashed on the deck below.

Besnard's eyes popped wide. 'Imbecile!' He leaped with surprising fleetness to the lower deck.

Girardin sank down to a crouch. She listened as Besnard stomped out the flame. She remembered the burning ship *Deux Frères*, the sailors screaming to be saved, left with no choice but to leap into the waves to escape the flames. Who would save them here, in the middle of the ocean? She had almost drowned them all.

'Lahaie, come quick, we will miss our chance,' the tall civilian called back to his companion.

Girardin turned her head and was startled to see a pistol in the man's hand.

'Idiot!' Besnard rose out of the hatch and bore down on her. 'You could have killed us all.' He raised his hand, about to cuff her, and she shrank away, feeling suddenly like a child again, grovelling at her father's feet.

'It was my fault.' Lahaie stepped between her and the cook.

Besnard stalled his blow, his face red and round as a boil about to burst. 'Useless, the lot of you,' he hissed, spitting at her feet. 'Noses in books, heads with the fairies.' He pushed the waistcoated man out of his way.

Girardin sat upright, shaking.

'Félix Lahaie.' The man stuck out his hand to her with a bashful grin. 'Call me Félix.'

This time she clasped his rough hand in thanks.

Chapter 9

Latitude 29°6′ N of the equator, longitude 18°8′ W of Paris, 10 October 1791

AFTER TWO WEEKS AT SEA, GIRARDIN FELT HER STOMACH BEGIN to settle and grow used to the motion of the ship. At first she survived on diluting liquors, lukewarm water sweetened with sugar, but now she could manage some plain bread and the occasional bowl of soup. In those early days on board, she observed much and said little. In the galley, she feigned a strength she did not feel. She rose early to weigh out the flour and knead the dough for the officers' loaves, enjoying that quiet time before dawn when the ship was not yet fully awake.

No one questioned her lack of whiskers. Each morning when she went to serve the commander's breakfast, she passed the crew shaving each other's chins and braiding one another's hair. She ducked her eyes, focusing on the tray in her hands and wishing herself as small and unremarkable as a flea in dog's fur. No one challenged her. As a week passed, and then two, she grew a little more confident, a little more hopeful that her disguise would hold.

Today was fine and calm and Girardin ventured up onto the gangway. Here she could watch everyone. The sailors, officers and civilians had all come out to enjoy the air. She wished she had learned the knack of smoking so that she might stand against the rail with a clay pipe in her hands and be like any one of them. She kept her back to the open sea, still unsettled by the immensity of blue.

No man should be idle, the commander had declared, and today the off-duty sailors were fishing. She marvelled at the weird and wondrous creatures dangling on their lines; fish with snouts and spines and sails. An enormous fish with bright yellow belly and blue sail along its back was pulled onto the forecastle deck. Its colour astonished her, its beauty as well as its size drawing a crowd.

A group of civilians had gathered on the forecastle deck, conspicuous by their gentleman's attire and by the way they clung to one another, moving as a cohesive shoal between each fisherman to inspect his catch. These men were savants, she had been told, engaged to make scientific discoveries in the lands the expedition visited. Among them were naturalists, an astronomer, and an artist. Even the chaplain, Louis Ventenat, appeared to be an enthusiast of the natural world. Dressed in a black cassock with a silver cross hanging from his neck, he was wrestling a curiously shaped fish into a jar of spirit. The two men she had met on her first day were now dissecting the stomach contents of a large tunny. She had learned the tall man in his tailored coat was the botanist Labillardière and his companion, Félix Lahaie, was a gardener.

The gardener was not considered equal to the other savants, so he was not permitted his own quarters. 'Head pupil at the Jardin du Roi,' Félix had grumbled to her when she chanced upon him one day in the great cabin. 'Recommended by André Thouin himself, and reduced to slinging a hammock with the crew.' She had said nothing, terrified he would ask to share her own sliver of space. As a form of protest, Félix had commandeered one end of the dining table in the great cabin, his packets of seeds spread about him. 'They need constant care,' he said, laying each seed on a linen bandage to dry and painstakingly turning them one by one. 'To protect against decay.'

The commander strolled among the crew. Girardin saw the men sit up straighter and stand taller in his presence. They beamed when he touched a hand to their shoulder or took an interest in their fishing prowess. She watched him compliment a drawing made by a young ship's boy. On the journey, he had encouraged feats of strength and sprint races along the gangways that spooked the animals into bleating terror at the pounding above their heads. The men now called him 'the General' after his promotion to rear-admiral in the King's sealed orders. He did not appear to mind the title, taking the greeting in the spirit intended, as a mark of affection.

As promised, the General treated her no differently from the other men. He expected her to provide the same standard of duty as any male steward. But when she delivered his breakfast and he asked her to drink coffee with him, she could not be sure if this was a pleasure that had been extended to the previous steward. The General asked no questions about her past; he preferred to tell her stories, and Girardin was more than content to sit and listen.

Gradually, she began to relax in his presence. From his maps, she saw their two ships had already sailed past Spain and were now off the coast of the great continent of Africa. To Girardin, the General's careful plotting of their course seemed miraculous. Outside, the flat blue ocean stretched to the horizon in all directions, interrupted only by the distant shape of the *Espérance* trailing behind. How did the General know, with his instruments and tables, where in the world they were?

The General had shared with her his high hopes for the expedition. 'We shall open up the waters for generations of mariners to follow in our wake.' He meant to survey the unknown southern coast of New Holland and explore the archipelago of islands that were scattered through the Pacific. She had looked at the map pinned to his cabin wall, thinking of La Pérouse and his two ships lost somewhere in that expanse of emptiness.

While the General was well respected by the crew, the same could not be said of their ship's captain, Alexandre d'Auribeau. She saw men scowl as he walked past, his tricorn hat pushed low on his brow. Once she saw his face bewitched by strange tics and spasms, and his voice when giving orders was feeble and prone to being taken by the wind. He spent little time among the crew, preferring to cloister himself inside his cabin, but today he strutted along the gangway opposite her. There was a coldness in his gaze and Girardin found herself wishing that Captain Kermadec had been assigned to the *Recherche* instead of the *Espérance*. Even from their brief acquaintance, she sensed how much safer she would feel if he were on this ship.

She was thinking of Huon de Kermadec when she noticed a wizened sailor sitting amid a coil of rope splicing two lengths into one. She recognised the tooth through his earlobe and the tattoos on his arms. A demon-faced monkey perched on his shoulders. He was the sailor who had dragged her from the burning *Deux Frères*, the one who had delivered her to Kermadec's house. Her breath quickened. What had Kermadec told him? Did he know her sex?

The sailor did not look up. Both man and monkey were intent on their work, fingers quick and deft, the monkey parting the roots of the sailor's hair and nibbling at the roving lice. It made her head itch to watch. As Captain d'Auribeau passed by them, she saw the old sailor make a sign to ward off evil. Even the monkey bared its teeth at the captain. It seemed she was not the only one to consider him a poor choice of man in whom to entrust all the souls on this ship.

To Girardin, the second-in-command, Lieutenant Rossel, would have made a more robust choice of captain. With his ruddy cheeks, port barrel stomach and sturdy stance, he gave the impression of a man prepared to meet all weathers. On the quarterdeck, opposite to the savants and fishermen, the officers had gathered for lessons in navigation. Their white breeches, shined boots and gold buttons flashed in the sunlight. Lieutenant Rossel held an instrument they called the Borda Circle. From a distance, it looked like a brass wheel with a small telescope attached. When the General joined his navigators, he took the instrument in his hands with great care and put the telescope to his eye. How did this Borda Circle tell them where they were? she wondered. Perhaps one day she would be brave enough to ask.

The General passed the instrument to Beautemps-Beaupré. 'The boy is a brilliant cartographer,' the General had told her proudly. 'Been in the map business since the age of ten. Draws exquisite charts.'

Girardin looked doubtfully at the narrow-shouldered young man, the only civilian standing with the officers. Of a slight build and not much taller than herself, he looked insubstantial next to the stout Lieutenant Rossel. He maintained a meticulous care about his dress. Instead of a wig, his dark hair was curled about his temples and lacquered down so that even in a brisk breeze not one hair stirred out of place. He had the mannerisms of a sparrow, she thought, watching the precise movements of his small head. His nose was hooked and narrow and when he turned in profile she had the distinct impression of a beak.

To complete the trio of navigators was the lanky Lieutenant Saint-Aignan. In the evenings, this officer liked to practise his violin, his angular form silhouetted against the colours of the sunset, knee raised, elbows pointed, chasing the sailors from the deck with his endless scales. Now without his violin, she noticed his hands fidgeted. He shifted from foot to foot waiting for his chance to hold the navigation instrument. Beautemps-Beaupré seemed reluctant to relinquish control.

Girardin lingered on the gangway, in no hurry to return to the galley, even though she knew she must. Soon there would be fish to prepare for the sailors' dinner and she would need to warn the cook. The duties of a steward were diverse, she had discovered. Not only was she required to take charge of the stores, plan the meals, bake bread for the officers and serve the General, but she had come to realise that the chef and all the commis staff reported to her. She was to be the leader of these men. The prospect terrified her.

These past two weeks had confirmed her suspicions: Thomas Besnard was a pig of a man. She had watched him sniggering and whispering to his sous chef, Luc, only to fall silent when she walked into the galley. He left vegetable peelings and spilt sauce on the floor and benches. She was forced to trail in his wake, sweeping and mopping up his mess. His bulk seemed to take up the space of two men in their narrow enclave around the oven. His bowels rumbled and filled the air with the reek of rotting cabbages. And after each trumpeting release, Besnard would lean back, rub his rotund stomach and sigh with contentment. Girardin despised him. With heavy heart, she pushed herself out of the sunlight and down to the galley.

'Fuck me, this stings worse than my cock after a week in port! Fuck it.' Besnard sucked his finger. Girardin raised an eyebrow at the cook as she entered the galley. He held up his finger to display a splinter. The coarseness of the language had shocked her at first, but she had learned to regard the constant swearing as mere punctuation of the men's speech. No simple statement should start or end without reference to fornication.

Worst of all, she thought, observing the slovenly cook, he made her think of Etienne. The contrast was extreme. Her husband had been careful, deliberate, and had created beautiful food. People would travel from far and wide to visit the Café Lesserteur and taste Etienne's famous leek-and-salmon pies. Girardin remembered the scent of sautéed leeks and herbs and the hot puff of buttery air when the oven door was opened. In the mornings, the sun would stroke their café with warm lemon light. She heard Etienne singing from the kitchen, while her son, Jojo, crawled across the black-and-white tiles towards her.

Her father hadn't wanted her to marry Etienne. Marie-Louise would've gladly left home at age fourteen like her sisters, but she had been repulsed by the men he chose for her—all of them lecherous, bulbous-nosed, claret-cheeked members of the guild. She watched as each of her sisters was sacrificed, while the colour and quality of her father's wine grew richer.

'Wilful, disobedient, wicked girl!' her stepmother spat when she declined another elderly, lip-licking suitor. 'Twenty-two years old—who will want you now?'

Marie-Louise shrugged. Her stepmother slapped her face with a glove. 'Marriage is about duty to your family, not love!'

Marie-Louise had no reason to expect love or affection; she had no concept of it. She had hopes for a tolerable companionship, that was all. Until she met Etienne.

He was four years older than her but looked like a gangly youth. All arms and legs and wide, bony shoulders. She had first noticed him among the wine barrels in the courtyard of her home. A new customer, she had presumed, peering down from the floor above. He rolled up his sleeves and she watched him lift the barrels onto his cart. He flicked his hair back and caught sight of her at the window. His smile was the largest she had ever seen.

Over the weeks and months that followed she contrived to meet him in the courtyard. Stolen moments in dark corners. She loved to touch his large baker's hands, rub her fingers over the powerful knuckles, and curl her own small hand snugly into his palm. She loved it when he talked of his café and heard the joy in his voice when he described his delicious food. He had great plans for his future—the humble pie could be taken anywhere, he said: meat, vegetables and sauce all bound up in a golden crust. He would cup his hands together as he spoke, like a nest. Food that can be eaten anywhere, at any time ... now that was the future! All he had need of now, he said, was a wife.

'The piemaker?' her father said with a measure of disgust when she told him of Etienne's proposal. 'I will not allow it.'

'Too late,' she said, spreading her hands across her belly.

He lashed out with the back of his fist. It struck the side of her head and her ear fired in pain. She tumbled, losing her balance, striking the hard tiled floor.

'Slut! You disgrace us all.'

So began the happiest years of her life. Free of her father, living with a man she loved and a child growing inside her. They lived in a tiny back room, not much larger than their bed, but it was all she needed. She worked with Etienne, serving customers until she grew too big, and then she sat in the corner of the kitchen with her feet up on a stool and a little plate of pies cooked especially for her. Etienne liked to surprise her. Each parcel of pastry kept its flavour hidden so she never knew what she would get. He laughed at the burst of pastry flakes across her breasts and kissed the bump of her belly.

Her son was born with a smile ready from the start, or so it always seemed to her. He had his father's smile. When it slowly stretched across his entire face, it melted her insides like warmed raclette cheese. He was growing fast and long; he would be tall, just like Etienne, who had to stoop to kiss the top of her head. They had named him Jean to appease her father, but at home they called him Jojo. Everyone said Jojo had his mother's clear blue eyes. When those eyes danced at the sight of her, she was happier than she ever imagined she would be.

But then she lost it all.

First her son. An illness, the doctor said; not uncommon. She had sat by his side, sponging the sweat from his pale skin. Barely one year of life on this earth. Gone. She felt fractured after that, like mended pottery that leaked because some small piece had been lost. Her love for her husband was still strong, but now subdued. She rarely saw Etienne's golden smile in the three years she had left with him. Often it seemed to falter before it could bring pleasure to either of them and she would reach out and stroke his lovely hand.

Etienne was killed by a runaway horse. He had stepped out of their café carrying a tray of freshly baked pies when the beast threw its rider. Terrible timing, the undertaker said, so tragic. Marie-Louise did not see the impact, but she heard it. The pies smacked against the window, splitting open and streaking the glass pane with their flesh and juices.

Without Etienne, she was bereft, unable to rise from her bed. Without Etienne, the bakers lost their way. No one opened the doors each morning with a long-limbed stretch and a smile. Whenever she thought of the café she felt sick and rolled over in her bed to face the wall. She didn't want to live. No one remembered to shop for fresh fish or place the orders for beef. The customers drifted away. The café was ailing and she could not pay the rent or the staff. By the time she forced herself to dress and open the door of the kitchen, she found it empty. Even the flour bins had been cleaned out. Next the debt collectors took their turn. They picked over the remains of the café like vultures at a carcass, tugging at the innards, pecking out the eyes. They pulled the chairs and tables out onto the street and took the hand-painted sign from above the door. Her beautiful café was stripped bare. She stood shivering on the street, her arms clasped around herself. All Etienne's dreams were gone. She had failed him. The bailiff locked the door with a heavy padlock. She had nothing left of her beloved family but memories.

And no option other than to return to her father's house.

That night, Girardin rocked gently in her hammock, listening to the creaks and moans of the ship. She felt the uncertain ocean slipping beneath her. This time, she couldn't afford to fail. Rémi needed her.

She had to keep herself and these men alive so she could return to him. She held the vision of the sunlit café tight behind her closed eyes as though it could seep out between her eyelashes and fall to the ocean floor.

Chapter 10

Latitude 29° N, longitude 18°19′ W, 12 October 1791

Gentle kisses landed on her eyelids, brushed her cheek and fluttered in her ear. Girardin murmured in her sleep. Feathery touches tickled the downy hairs at the corner of her mouth, nudging with increasing insistence at her lips, urging her to part them. Is that you, Etienne? she wondered in her drowsy state, but another man was conjured to her vision. His kisses smothered her and she brushed them from her mouth. Doubling their intensity, they slapped against her nostrils, stealing her breath. Girardin opened her mouth and gasped.

Moths whirled into her mouth and she gagged on their powdery wings. She coughed and spat, tasting bitterness. She beat her hands about her head. Her hammock rocked and tossed her to the floor, where she landed on her hands and knees and felt more winged bodies squish beneath her palms.

She lit her lantern. The moths had erupted from the cases of biscuit through the night. They swirled and flickered against the golden light. She sat on the floor of her cabin and stared up at them. The traces of her dream still lingered with her like a guilty conscience. It was not Etienne but a more recent lover who had come to life in her mind. In her dream he had rolled towards her; she recognised the pale skin of his chest and the dark line of hair running down the centre of his stomach. Her fingers had traced the line. He had pressed himself against her and she felt the throb of desire at the hardness of him. Her dream had felt so real it shocked her. Why did this lover visit her dreams? Why not sweet Etienne? The moths flapped in her face and she batted her eyes and cheeks and mouth, slapping herself in her anger. Why dream of a lover who had betrayed her? She could not bear to think of him.

But he didn't betray you, did he? her voices sneered. She hung her head. It was true. He had made no promises. It was she who conjured a life for them. When she knew a child was forming inside her again she had been overjoyed. She had imagined a future beyond the revolution, a new life, a new beginning. His games of duplicity had fooled her too. She had deceived herself that she could be a butterfly, instead of its plain, overlooked cousin.

Girardin spat powdery wings from her lips. She pushed a rag into her mouth, scraping the bitter taste from her tongue.

A sharp rap at her door startled her. She had to remember who she was: Louis Girardin, steward of the *Recherche*. She wiped the smeared moths from her face. Opening the door a crack, she was surprised to see the tall botanist at her door. Today he wore no coat, only a loose shirt over his breeches. There was something in his expression of distaste that made him look familiar, and the sensation unsettled her. Perhaps it was just the dream lingering, pulling up people from her past she wished to bury.

'Steward, these moths are an outrage! I cannot light a candle, so desperate are they to pile their fat bodies one upon the other and extinguish it. How can I work? Something must be done!'

She blinked. What did he expect her to do?

'You must speak to the General! The supplies are of inferior quality. He has been duped. For this species of moth to be emerging, the biscuit must've been on a journey before.'

Reluctantly, Girardin stepped out. He ushered her forwards and she complied, squinting against the flapping onslaught. What was she to say to the General? She climbed the stairs with the naturalist close behind and turned towards the stern. Sheep pens flanked either side of the gun deck and in the gloom she could see their round eyes watching her. A cow shook its head to clear the moths and stamped its foot, while another scratched its behind on one of the cannons.

The infestation of moths grew thicker near the stern of the boat. The savants' quarters were above the bread rooms where most of the ship's biscuit was stored. From behind the closed doors she heard a vehement oath, a shirt snapping in the air and the clatter of a shaving bowl, followed by more exasperated swearing.

'You see? We are housed in the worst possible location.'

Climbing the stairs to the quarterdeck, a gust of moths burst from the hatch behind her and fluttered upwards into the sails and out across the open sea. Perhaps they hope to reach Tenerife before us, she thought. Above her head, the telltales lay flaccid against the sails. She stood in front of the General's door and realised the savant was no longer with her.

'Come in!' the General replied in answer to her knock.

Girardin took a deep breath to steady herself. She wiped her hands against her tunic, then entered.

The General looked up from his desk. Captain d'Auribeau stood beside him. A lone moth followed her into the room. She focused on its urgent fluttering, knowing it to be in tune with her heartbeat. This was the first time she had been in the same room as their captain. Up close, he had an unsettling countenance, low eyebrows in a pale, pointed face, and a tic that made his features jump and jiggle for no known reason. He could not be much more than thirty years, but his ailments aged him.

The General waited expectantly.

The moth made a haphazard path up towards the window panes in the cabin's ceiling.

'We are receiving complaints, sir,' she stammered. 'About the quality of the stores.'

'Are we?' The General cocked his head. 'From whom, might I enquire?'

She saw a look pass between the two men.

In her anxiety she could not remember his name. 'A savant. The tall one.'

'Ah, Monsieur Labillardière,' the General said with a knowing smile. 'Of course.'

D'Auribeau clapped his hands together and twisted his palms apart with distaste. The moth was smeared across his hand. 'An old trick, to show a few good cases and supply the rest with second-rate wares. I'd have thought Captain Huon de Kermadec would be wise to such deceptions, a man of his experience.'

Girardin did not like the tone of his voice.

The captain inspected the remains of the moth on his palms before dusting it from his hands with exaggerated disgust. She saw his lips purse with satisfaction.

'The wine,' d'Auribeau continued, 'is so inferior that the crew almost refuse to drink it. They threaten the most foul punishment on those responsible.'

'I agree it is watered-down barrel scrapings passed off as Bordeaux,' said the General placatingly. 'The provisions supplied to us are a disappointment.'

'Captain Huon de Kermadec must feel this failure keenly.' D'Auribeau looked up to the moths dancing along the ceiling. 'The victualling was his responsibility.'

With his hands clasped behind his back, the captain had a look of a crow about him, Girardin thought. Bobbing and swaying with its wings folded away. She was suddenly reminded of her mother's stories of village crows, the hateful men or women that sent anonymous poison letters to their neighbours. Had she betrayed Captain Kermadec by coming to the General with this complaint? She thought of his kindness to her and felt ashamed.

The General looked at her directly. 'There is nothing that can be done until we resupply at Tenerife, but I shall write to inform Minister Fleurieu of this deception.'

Write to the minister! What had she done? Would Huon de Kermadec be censured?

'If the *Espérance* were not so sluggish we would have reached Santa Cruz port before now,' Captain d'Auribeau noted wryly.

'You cannot blame Captain Kermadec for these light and fickle winds.'

She thought she heard a note of admonishment in the General's voice, but as Captain d'Auribeau turned his face away from the General, she saw his lips purse again with self-satisfaction. She pictured Huon de Kermadec's flushed cheeks and slow spreading smile and knew she had helped to strike a blow against him. Feeling sickened, she made to leave.

A messenger at the door interrupted them. 'We have sighted the peak of Tenerife, sir!'

'Very good, Raoul!' the General replied. 'You see, Captain d'Auribeau? All will be well. We shall be enjoying a glass of Tenerife wine by lunchtime tomorrow.'

The aide pilot who had delivered the message stepped aside to let Girardin pass. He bent low in a bow of exaggerated courtesy, as one might for a lady of the court. The gesture startled her. When he rose up she caught the smirk upon his lips. He was looking at her with obvious interest beneath a heavy fringe of black hair. Her heart thumped. Again she felt the demons of the past chasing her. There was no way she could know this man, yet his bold look had the hint of the familiar and she began to doubt the invisibility of her disguise.

Chapter 11

Tenerife, Canary Islands, 13 October 1791

THE OARS GROANED AGAINST THE SIDES OF THE LONGBOAT as the six sailors swung their backs. Girardin sat in the bow, chewing her thumbnail. Directly ahead lay the town of Santa Cruz. Thick forests of palm wrapped the town in a vivid green blanket. A church tower of white and grey stone glistened in the sunlight, thrusting above the terracotta roofs. She could hear the bell tolling, calling the faithful to prayer. She shifted on the wooden thwart. Her feet were tangled in empty wicker cages and she kicked them free.

Traps of all sizes had been tossed into the boat by the two men sitting alongside her. The naturalist Labillardière wore his customary oversized black hat. It tapered outwards to a flat top designed to give the impression that the head beneath must bear a brain that was large and impressive indeed. She blamed him, fairly or not, for making her betray Huon de Kermadec. She felt complicit in d'Auribeau's attack on his abilities and it nagged her conscience. Labillardière, for his part, seemed oblivious to her scowl. He stared past her and up towards the peak of Tenerife, the mountain that loomed above the town.

The broad brim of his hat cast a shadow over his face, but she could see his features were strong: full lips, heavy eyebrows and large dark eyes. A feeling that she had met this man once before chafed at her. She knew his face, the timbre of his voice . . . but from where? After watching him through her eyelashes for some time, she gave up trying to remember. If he recognised her, he gave no sign. She pulled her own hat low to shield her face.

Beside her, the gardener Félix Lahaie rubbed his hands together. She saw his fingers were dry and cracked, with dirt ingrained, and they reminded her of her father's hands. Even long after Jean Girardin had left the garden beds of Versailles, the chapped and splintered skin had betrayed him. But she did not hold this similarity against him. Félix had a gentle pouchiness to his features and an amiable lip. She was inclined to like him. When he had climbed into the boat that morning he had winked at her. 'I am being allowed to go botanising with the savants.' He spoke freely as Labillardière had not yet arrived. Leaning forwards he tapped his nose. 'I must keep my own collections secret, they hate competition.' Girardin had returned a small smile and said nothing.

A golden crescent beach swept away to her right. The breeze was warm and fragrant, bringing the spicy, floral scent of land. Despite her nerves, she began to feel the stirrings of excitement. These would be her first steps on foreign shores. Félix caught her eye and grinned.

On the pier, two men from the *Espérance* were waiting for them. One wore a long brown coat and stood with his hands on his hips, while his servant held a parasol above both their heads.

'Claude Riche!' Labillardière called out to him and threw up a rope. The boat bumped against the wooden pier.

Claude Riche removed his hat in greeting and a spray of crimped, wiry hair bounced up. His greatcoat was appended with all manner of pockets. There were loops with vials, pincers and knives. A hammer and a flintlock pistol hung from a belt. On his back he wore a canvas pack onto which he had attached more hooks, rings, belts and buckles, and clipped an assortment of wicker cages like a human beast of burden. Girardin had never seen such outlandish garb. She heard the officers in the stern sniggering.

The sailors stowed the oars and scrambled up the steps, teasing and tripping over one another in their haste to be first to the alehouses along the docks. The officers were not far behind.

'Get back here!' Labillardière called after them, but the sailors must have lost their hearing because they pounded faster along the pier.

Girardin helped Félix unload their equipment. He told her they were to climb the peak and wouldn't be back for several days. She looked up to where the mountain had lost its tip in cloud. It seemed an impossible feat.

'Here,' she murmured. 'Take this.' She pulled a cold salmon pie from her bag.

He thanked her warmly. 'Did you bake this?'

She shrugged. 'It needs sage.'

Félix smiled, then nudged her with his elbow. 'Go on, don't be shy.' He nodded his head towards the town. 'Or they'll get the best ones.'

Girardin swallowed. She looked along the length of the pier. How well would her disguise carry her through this town? Was it too late to change her mind? She rolled her shoulders forwards, hollowing her chest. Félix gave her a cheery wave as she set off.

The dockyard whores had arranged themselves in battle lines and their fingers clawed her shoulders as she forced through their ranks. Gaunt faces pressed around her. The women wore black rags wound over their heads as veils. She heard them praying as they clutched their rosary beads and begged, offering up their bodies for another bite, another morsel of life.

Girardin escaped, ignoring the jeers of the sailors behind her. She walked quickly through the cobblestone streets, unsure of her way but feeling comforted by the stone buildings. This could be a European town, she thought, if it weren't for the coconut palms and banana plants. The people of Santa Cruz took no special note of another foreign sailor in customary loose white shirt and wide trousers, and with each step through the port town, her confidence grew. It felt good to have solid earth beneath her feet again. In her pocket she had the first of her wages and the coins felt weighty with promise.

She had thought long and hard about what she might buy. Nothing expensive—she had her future to save for—but she wanted something to show her son when she returned. *This is what I bought for you with my first wages.* She imagined herself presenting him with some toy she had found, some exotic Spanish treasure.

The street she walked up was lined with stalls selling trinkets and relics. Carved Madonnas gazed serenely down at her while the hawkers screamed in high-pitched Spanish, touting their wares. She shook her head. Each stall proclaimed to have the true finger of Christ, a bona fide splinter of the cross, but she wanted none of it. Keep your vengeful God, she thought and hurried past.

The street turned abruptly and Girardin found herself in an open plaza, facing a glaring white church at the far end. The brightness made her eyes water. Heat emanated from the cloistered plaza, the buildings on all sides blocking it from the cooling breeze. A forbidding belltower of grey and white stone rose above the terracotta-tiled roof, casting a narrow finger of shade. Girardin kept to the perimeter of the square, beneath a fringe of palm trees.

Here women clustered in groups, wearing coarse woollen cloaks, despite the suffocating heat, and broad-brimmed hats that sheltered their faces from the sun. Their children ran wild, chasing pigeons and stray dogs across the sun-baked cobbles. Girardin felt the eyes of the women watching her warily. It was a shocking thing, she found, to have someone look at you in fear. A matronly grandmother in a black dress wrapped her white, crocheted shawl tight around her, crossing her arms over her bosom as Girardin passed by.

Two elderly men sat cross-legged across from one another, duelling with chess pieces. She saw a small boy playing with a brightly painted wooden cup and ball. A *bilboquet*! Perfect, she thought. She would find one for Rémi. Her steps were quicker, lighter, as she passed in front of the church.

In the far corner of the plaza she came upon a statue of the Virgin Mary standing high on a pedestal. She paused at its base. Untouchable, Girardin thought, looking up at the Madonna. Incorruptible. The mother of Christ held out her arms to her, but Girardin turned away. She saw the dour grandmother staring at her.

A French uniform caught her eye. A sailor was crossing the plaza towards her. He did not creep around the edge as she had, but walked boldly in the open sun. Girardin felt a trickle of sweat bead down from her temple. The Frenchman took off his hat and flicked his dark fringe from his eyes. She recognised him as the pilot, Ange Raoul, and remembered his deferential bow to her at the General's cabin door.

'A tribute to the immaculate conception,' Raoul said, glancing up at the statue. 'Where's the fun in that?'

Girardin shuffled backwards. Raoul's features were sensous and full. A handsome man aware of his sexual power. Despite his smile, she felt his menace.

He advanced, forcing her to circle around the statue. 'I've been following you,' he said.

Girardin stumbled on the uneven cobbles.

'Young man on his first shore leave should be in a whorehouse, not looking up stone skirts.' He backed her towards the wall of the church, into the shadow of the belltower, his dark eyes intent. When her heels touched the stone wall, he raised his head, sniffing loudly, taking in the scent of her. Her eyes grew wide.

From behind, the Spanish grandmother charged at them, warbling abuse, smacking her walking stick on the stone and pointing to the sea. *Fuck off home*, she seemed to be saying. *Take your fighting and fornicating elsewhere. Godless French.* When Raoul turned, Girardin fled into the Iglesia de la Concepción.

Inside, the nave was blessedly cool and dark. Her eyes were slow to adjust. She let her heart's pounding slowly steady itself. She would be safe in here, she hoped. She pictured Raoul's arrogant stare, his flared nostrils. He suspected her sex and she was sure he had meant to confirm it.

No one followed her into the church. The doors stayed firmly closed against the heat and light. Peering around the grey stone pillars, she found empty church pews. She slid into one and knelt before a silver altar.

She was hit by powerful memories. It had been thirteen years since the funeral of her son, Jojo. After that, she had cursed God. He had stolen her darling boy like a thief in the night, cajoling, whispering false promises, dragging his soft cheek away from hers. God had heard her blasphemous thoughts and He punished her. He took Etienne. Who was she to question His plan, accuse Him of heartless barbarity?

Footsteps rang loudly on the stone floor. 'Santa Cruz de la Conquista—the Holy Cross of the Conquest,' a voice boomed in the space behind her.

Girardin jolted upright.

'I'm sorry, I didn't mean to scare you.'

She turned to see Monsieur Ventenat, the chaplain of the *Recherche*, walking forwards into the candlelight. His hands appeared chalky white against his flowing black robes. His bald head, naked without wig or hat to conceal the shape of his skull, disturbed her. It reminded her of death.

'God grant that our journey does not end in as much blood as these Spanish explorers have on their hands.' Ventenat knelt and genuflected before the altar. 'The noble savage, the perfect state of society.' He sighed heavily. 'I fear many will have cause to regret our coming among them.'

Girardin was confused by his melancholic words. She dropped her head and mumbled prayers for their safe passage. But she was thinking of Rémi. She had abandoned her son to the mercy of the Church even though she knew God had none left for her.

'Holy Father, who art in heaven . . .' The chaplain raised his voice so that it echoed in the cavernous space.

She wondered which of her sins had sealed her fate. Was it cursing God for taking her first son from her? Or before that, when she disobeyed her father and married Etienne with his seed already taking root in her belly?

Raising her eyes to the light streaming through the high windows she spoke silently to God. *Are you listening?* Her fists tightened beside her legs.

'Thy will be done on earth as it is in heaven,' Ventenat intoned.

You took one son from me. You will not take the other.

'Lead us not into temptation.'

Keep him safe, you judgemental fucker. She swore at God as easily as if she had spent her life at sea. *He is innocent.*

'And deliver us from evil,' Ventenat finished.

She stood abruptly. Even if Raoul was waiting for her, she couldn't stay in here a moment longer. She burst out into the plaza, feeling the eyes of God on her back. Running now, she sought out the narrow alleyways leading to the sea. Entering the church had been a mistake. She should not have let her anger overcome her. Foolish! She needed God on her side now. She had left her son in His care.

Two French sailors staggered out of the alehouse door and weaved across the path in front of her. She flattened herself against a wall. A Spanish soldier pursued them with his sword drawn. More of the town's guards began to rally in the street and she felt exposed. She ducked down a passageway, hoping to find her way back to the wharf.

In the alleyway, Raoul held a prostitute against the wall. Girardin gasped, skidding to a halt. The woman's black dress was pushed up her thighs and he thrust against her, kneading her breasts. The

Angelus bells of the church began to toll and the woman cried out, pleading with Raoul to let her pray. He pushed her back against the wall and she began to chant her prayers, closing her eyes, face upturned to God.

Girardin watched transfixed, unable to move away. Raoul cried out in satisfaction and let the woman fall to her knees. She held her rosary beads to her lips, tears streaking her face. 'Holy Mary, Mother of God, pray for us sinners, now and at the hour of our death,' she sobbed in Latin.

Raoul turned towards Girardin, the flap of his trousers gaping open. He made no effort to cover himself. Had he known she was there? Girardin stumbled back. He locked his eyes with hers as he slowly rebuttoned his trousers. He smiled. There was surely no mistaking the threat in his casual actions. Hold your nerve, she commanded herself.

'Pardon me, Monsieur,' she said, before turning on her heel. His laughter climbed the walls of the narrow alley.

Girardin broke into a skittish run that she forced herself to contain. Before her, the ship's officers were rounding up the drunken crew, pushing them towards the liberty boats. The church bells clanged and the Spanish townspeople collapsed to their knees, chanting the Angelus for the third time. She thought only of returning to the ship. This time the whores let her pass unmolested. She wrapped her hand around the key at her neck. Her cabin key. How quickly that dank, tight space in the heart of the ship had become her only sanctuary.

Chapter 12

GIRARDIN COUNTED THE BARRELS FOR A THIRD TIME. EACH TIME she had reached the same result. Six barrels of wine were missing. The holds were almost full and in a matter of days they would sail. How was she to explain this to the General?

She confronted Besnard in the galley. 'Some of the Tenerife wine is missing.'

He did not bother to look up. Both the chef and his assistant were chopping onions and carrots for soup, their backs turned to her. 'Not my problem.'

'You and I are the only ones with keys to the store!'

'Maybe you counted wrong.'

Girardin felt rage flush through her. She turned back to her ledger, disturbed that her shaking hand had blotted ink on the carefully ruled pages. She had read through the lists of her predecessor and assumed that his neat hand had turned to a scrawl because of the drink. Now she wondered if Thomas Besnard had driven him to the bottle.

'Where do you want these?' A voice startled her. A crewman stood in the galley holding two large cabbages out to her. She turned to her commis staff.

'I need you to assist me,' she said to them, raising her voice uncertainly above the noise of the fire. Besnard ignored her. The braid down his back swung with each jerk of his shoulder. The assistant, Luc, turned a bleary eye to look at her. He shrugged.

'The vegetable bins need to be scrubbed and cleaned,' she said.

'Do it yourself,' Besnard said.

She listened to the blade strike against the board, heard the oven door screech open and clang shut again. She felt torn by indecision, unable to move, at a loss as to how to gain authority over these men.

'Now, please,' she said, her voice too timid.

Besnard dropped his cleaver. He plucked the apron from around his neck and let it fall to the floor. 'I'm busy,' he said.

She stepped back to let him pass.

Her knees felt weak. Besnard pushed the crewman with the cabbages in front of him, swearing at the imbecile for interrupting him. As they moved away she saw the naturalist, Labillardière, watching her. How long had he been there? Had he witnessed her humiliation?

'*Laurus azorica*,' Labillardière said, holding out a bunch of leaves, 'the Canary Island bay tree. The gardener thought you might like them.'

She took the leaves and gripped them tight to disguise her shaking hands. 'Thank you,' she said.

'The salmon pie you provided for our journey was a lifesaver on the mountain.'

She was surprised, disconcerted by his praise. He looked vulnerable without his hat. She saw his dark hair was matted to his forehead and she felt more kindly disposed towards him for it.

He stood staring at her until she broke the awkward silence. 'How was it?' she asked.

'Moist and succulent, and the pastry had retained some of its crispness.'

'No, Monsieur, not the pie—the mountain.'

'Miserable. We spent a night behind a wall of cracked lava, like sleeping on broken glass in freezing temperatures. But the pie was delicious.'

'It was my late . . .' She stopped herself just in time. Her mouth dropped open. How easily she had almost betrayed herself. Oh, Etienne, she thought, I dare not think of you. 'It was my late mother's recipe,' she said, then added quickly before he noticed her distress: 'The peak of Tenerife, did you reach it?'

'Of course—at least, the gardener and I did. Claude Riche was seized with a spitting of blood and continual vomiting, being of weaker constitution.'

There was something in his unwitting arrogance that suddenly reminded her of where she had seen the botanist before. At the salon of Sophie de Condorcet! He had been invited to speak of his years of exploration through the Levant. Girardin remembered the tone of his voice, his irritation as he was asked many questions, each one interrupting his botanical tale. Where did he sleep in Lebanon? In shepherds' huts, of course. How did he travel through Syria? By foot or by donkey, of course. Did he fear for his life while nursing a plague-stricken monk? Of course not.

Would he remember her? Girardin pulled back from the lantern light. There was nothing in her state now, dressed as she was, to remind him of those days. And though her entrance at the salon that night had been late and clumsy, a plain girl who made no effort to speak would hardly have made an impression.

Labillardière had been introduced to the salon by his friend Jacques Hébert, who attended only rarely. It was said Hébert preferred the radical Club des Jacobins that met on rue Saint Honoré. But that night, he had looked like the cat with the cream, purring delightedly at the attention he was receiving for bringing such an enlightening speaker. She watched him ingratiate himself with the Marquis de Condorcet, Sophie's husband. Hébert's dark, shoulder-length hair was beginning to recede on his forehead, even though he could not have been more than thirty years old, and she saw he wore it long out of vanity, to sweep across his brow. His long, pointed nose dipped into the aroma of the marquis' best claret and gave an appreciative quiver.

'Weasel,' Olympe snarled. 'I do not trust him,' she whispered to Marie-Louise. 'Or any of his Jacobin friends.'

The explorer, Labillardière, looked ill at ease. The tall, stiff-shouldered man stood aloof at supper, pressed back against a brooding still life by a Dutch master: peasant-caught hare bent backward over the table, pewter tankards, a crust of bread. Marie-Louise could see he did not enjoy his audience at the salon. He declined a plate of elegant sweets. In his speech he had spoken of suffering. In Palestine, he had witnessed peasants with nothing to eat but the wild herbs plucked as soon as they emerged from the rocky earth. He had returned home to Alençon only to see people die of hunger in the street for want of bread.

The women pressed around him, wanting to know what the Turks and Arabs were like.

'The people of the Levant die of hunger and poverty just as our own countrymen do.' He looked to his friend, Hébert, and gestured with an impatient flick of his head.

Hébert pulled a cake from his mouth to speak. 'Equality for all men!'

'And women,' Olympe added amid the applause. But Labillardière had already left the room.

That night, Labillardière had looked at the men and women of the salon with contempt and Marie-Louise could see the hypocrisy reflected back at her. They gathered to discuss inequality and justice while they ate sumptuous suppers in gilded halls. They dressed in plain and simple fashions to show their contempt for the ancien régime, but they did nothing! Men like Labillardière and Hébert were men of action. Did it matter that the pamphlets Hébert published were cruel and fictitious? Did it matter if he told lies, if the result was to wake the citizens of France from their slumber? Perhaps others in the salon had the same sense that she'd that day. They were not doing enough. The world had to change and they had to do more.

Goosepimples spiked her skin. These memories chilled her. She wrapped her arms around herself to stop from shaking.

The naturalist was still speaking. Unaware of her distress, Labillardière was showing her the soles of his shoes, which had been torn apart by the lava.

'I am fascinated by the alpine boundary,' he said. 'We were surprised to find a delicate violet growing at the edge of the exposed volcanic summit. Beauty survives in the most unexpected of places.'

Besnard appeared behind him and shunted the botanist aside. 'Some of us have to work, not prance about picking flowers.'

Labillardière stared at the chef, his eyes narrowed and upper lip jagged in distaste. Then he bent forwards, leaning close to her ear. She flinched; her fear of recognition, however ludicrous, still lingered. He did not appear to notice. 'Your chef is selling extra rations of wine to the sailors,' he said in a low voice.

Girardin stood motionless. She held her breath while Labillardière spun on his heel and left the galley. She watched him dodge past the ship's boys as they mucked out the animal pens. Slowly, she released her breath. She waited, calming the beating of her heart. Then she turned to her chef.

'Give me your key,' she said.

Besnard snorted and ignored her.

She stepped closer, smelling the stale sweat in his tunic.

'Give me your key,' she said again.

'Don't be stupid. How am I supposed to cook without ingredients?'

'You will make a request to me and I will issue you the stores.'

'This is fucking outrageous!'

She raised her voice back. 'Fuck you! I can have you thrown off this ship and left behind in this syphilis-infested Spanish port. Do you understand me? Fuck it!'

They locked eyes for the first time. His were bloodshot.

'You cannot,' he spat.

'I am your superior, do not forget that!'

He swore. 'Wait till I tell Captain d'Auribeau you've been cooking delicacies for those republicans! Salt beef and biscuit, that's all he allows them.'

'Perhaps you can explain to him where the six barrels of Tenerife wine have gone!' She thrust out her hand again.

Besnard threw his keys at her. She caught them in her fingers.

Chapter 13

On the day they were to sail from Tenerife, Girardin inspected her storerooms for the last time. She had requested two crewmen to reorganise the hold and sort the rice and grain from the musket shot. All the crates and boxes of foodstuff were now labelled. She was pleased with their work. The fresh vegetables and fruit had been stowed. The belly of the ship was full to bursting.

From Besnard, she now had disgruntled obedience. She had overheard him speaking to Luc: 'There is a rumour that the steward is a relative of Fleurieu, the Minister of Marine. Best to let him think he is in charge.' She had allowed herself a satisfied smile.

Above her head a jar of juniper berries crashed to the floor. She leaped aside, cursing the plague of rats that swarmed through the ship, gnawing through her sacks and eating all the raisins. Climbing onto a tea chest, she thumped the shelves to chase the rats out of the store. A grumpy face popped out, and she jerked back in surprise. A pale-faced monkey with a cap of black hair pulled back its lips and bared its teeth.

'You rascal!'

The monkey launched across to the salted pork legs with a scream, and swung there waving an orange in its hand in triumph.

'Thief!'

The monkey peeled back its lips again, laughing at her.

She lunged and the monkey hurled itself to the floor, still clutching its prize. She threw herself into a tackle, sliding along the floor, catching hold of its tail. It squealed, turned, and pitched the orange at her head. She ducked, letting go of the monkey's tail and saw him sprint out between the legs of an officer standing in the doorway.

'Oh!' she cried, looking up from where she lay facing a pair of polished boots.

Captain Huon de Kermadec laughed with genuine delight. 'You bested Armand's capuchin. I am impressed. He is a notorious sneak.'

She scrambled to her feet, wiping her hands on her tunic, embarrassed to be found looking so foolish.

'The old sailor with the monkey,' she said, to cover her humiliation. 'I recognised him. Did you have him follow me onto the *Deux Frères*?'

Kermadec ducked his eyes and she noticed a spot of pink blooming on each cheek. 'Armand is a good man,' he said, avoiding her question. 'Sailed with him on the *Resolution*.'

'Does he know who I am?' she asked boldly. She set her jaw, aware that her breathing was too rapid, her voice harsher than intended. This man was a captain, her superior—she should not speak to him this way. But she was afraid that Armand might have loose lips, that he might have mentioned something to the pilot Raoul that made him suspicious of her sex and tempted him to follow her through the streets of this town.

Kermacec shook his head. 'He thinks you are my nephew. My sister's son.'

'Is he still watching me? Does he suspect?' She thought of the men playing cards, laying bets, losing their wages. What price would such information be worth? she wondered. Would her secret be sold to settle a gambler's debt?

'His eyesight is not so good.'

She thought of the hundred men working, eating and sleeping on the decks above. 'They must never know,' she said in a strained voice.

'You have nothing to fear from Armand. I swear to you.' Kermadec took her inquisition with good grace, but his eyebrows pulled into a confused frown. 'Has something happened? Do you fear for your safety?' He stepped towards her in the narrow space.

Should she tell him of her suspicions about Raoul? It concerned her that he had become friendly with Besnard, and the two of them had formed a gang of sorts with the butcher. The three men lounged together on the deck, smoking, playing cards and teasing the ship's boys. When Raoul's eyes fell on her, it made her feel like the smallest hen in the coop, the one that would be hounded and harried until pecked bare. She could not afford to show any weakness.

But what could Kermadec do? His attention would only put her at risk. Raoul had not laid a hand on her. How could she explain she was afraid of his snide swagger, his taunting sexuality, and a sense that he somehow knew exactly who she was?

She was being foolish, she scolded herself. Raoul was a bully testing a weaker man, that was all; she had let her imagination run away with her good sense.

Kermadec's gaze lingered on her face, as if searching for the truth. His concern touched something frozen inside her and she slid her eyes away.

'Soon we will sail for the Cape,' he said. 'A long sea journey of many weeks.'

Kermadec was still watching her. She saw the worry in his furrowed brow.

'If something has happened, something to make you doubt your safety, it is not too late to turn back, perhaps find a placement on a ship heading back to France. We could find another in this port to replace you.' He lowered his voice. 'I would not willingly put you in danger.'

This was her moment to withdraw. He was giving her the chance to return home. But it was too soon. She had nothing to offer her son, no way to raise him. She lifted her chin. 'I will be fine. No one suspects.'

His face relaxed into a smile. He looked relieved and it surprised her. The adventurous, boyish gleam returned to his eye. 'There is so much of this world I would love to show you.' He grinned. 'You will not regret it.'

She forced a smile to braven her spirit.

But when he stepped closer to her, she fell back. She felt the size of him looming over her, aware of the strength of his arms beneath his buttoned blue coat. He raised his hands, careful like a stablehand with a skittish mare, and bent to pick up the orange that had rolled between her feet. 'For you.'

She had made a fool of herself again. Kermadec did not mean to harm her. She took the orange and inhaled the tart freshness of the zest. Did he know that oranges were her favourite fruit? Idiot!

How could he know? What made her think of that? She was aware of the closeness of his body, the broadness of his stance. He had not stepped away. This giddiness was unsettling. Beautiful men always made her anxious, that was all.

'Then I will see you in Cape Town,' he said softly.

She nodded, voiceless, afraid of the way her heart had come to life in her chest.

Chapter 14

Latitude 5°30′ N, longitude 18°30′ W, Atlantic Ocean, 14 November 1791

For three slow weeks, the expedition suffered through bouts of calm and squalls of rain that soaked them to the skin. In the unrelenting wet heat, Girardin felt the constant itch and sting of sweat as the whalebone corset chafed against her skin. She had tightened it day by day until her chest was flat. The longing to remove the corset was countered by her fear of seeing what remained of her breasts.

Finally, she could bear it no longer and late one night, locked in her cabin, Girardin dared to pull at the laces of the corset. She felt the pressure ease and moaned with relief before scratching and wriggling to be free. The boned corset fell to the floor. Grey, sodden bandages covered her breasts and she winced as she peeled the final layers. The sudden stench forced her to cover her nose and mouth. She looked down. Her breasts were flat, nipples pressed inwards, and her skin was pale and soggy except where the corset had rubbed it red and left it dotted with pustules. She sucked breath between her teeth as she soaked a rag in vinegar and dabbed at the boils. Her milk had long dried up.

'Steward!'

A fist knocked violently on Girardin's cabin door. She scrabbled for her tunic.

'Citizen Girardin!' the voice called.

'Just one moment!' she snapped, throwing a blanket over the corset and bandages. Reluctantly, she unlocked her door.

'Help me find some cheesecloth from our stores,' Labillardière demanded.

Girardin stood still, blinking against the candlelight he held in front of his face.

'Be quick about it, or we will miss our chance!'

Grabbing her set of keys, Girardin led the naturalist down the stairs toward the storerooms. Beneath her armpits, she felt the pustules sting.

'How much do you need?' she asked, pulling out a length of the fabric. When she touched the muslin it felt creamy and soft against her skin, like a soothing caress. Labillardière spread his hands apart and she cut a length to match. He vanished without thanks. Finding herself alone, she quickly sliced off more muslin and tied it around her waist to hide beneath her shirt.

Overhead, she heard feet running along the deck. Light flashed down the hatch. Intrigued, she climbed up after Labillardière and found him at the rail with two men. The General was dressed as usual in his formal uniform, but beside him the rotund Lieutenant Rossel wore a hastily buttoned coat over his nightshirt. Without his wig, the lieutenant's dark hair was mussed by the rising wind.

Across the sea, black clouds bloomed along the horizon, smothering the stars. The freshening wind roughened the surface of the water.

Girardin shivered. Lightning cracked and she gasped as the whole expanse of the sea was lit by a sheet of green fire that swept towards their ship. All about them the sea sparked with a ghoulish light. Girardin crossed herself. Holy hell. Was this God or Satan coming for them?

'It's the electric fluid!' Lieutenant Rossel shouted over a clap of thunder.

The General agreed. 'It is always on the stormiest nights, when the atmosphere is charged with electric fluid, that the sea shines with this brightness.' He seemed calm, untroubled by the ghostly green light.

She saw Labillardière sneer. 'It is not the electric fluid that causes this luminosity. It is from animals.'

Rossel snorted. 'How could animals do that?'

Girardin edged closer to the men just as a pod of dolphins leapt through the waves and swirled the bright green lights into fantastic patterns. What was this supernatural substance? Was its beauty meant to lure men into the depths?

'*Tursiops truncatus*,' Labillardière said, unable to resist pointing and naming the dolphins as he passed behind her. 'I need to make a net.' He made for the stern of the ship with his field axe in hand.

'What on earth are you doing?' an outraged voice demanded. Captain d'Auribeau charged down the gangway towards her, chasing Labillardière.

'Proving a scientific theory,' Labillardière called over his shoulder. He had raised his field axe and was aiming it at the flagpole.

'This is insupportable!' d'Auribeau shrieked. 'You cannot take such liberties with my ship!'

The captain shoved Girardin aside. She fell against the rail as the ship rolled sideways, sliding head first over the luminous cauldron of the sea. She opened her mouth in terror, a strangled squeal slipping out, before she caught the rail in her hands. The glowing water surged beneath her. She pushed herself back into the ship, scrambling away from the edge, imagining herself flailing in the frothing green wake as the ship sailed away.

'I need a long thin pole,' said the naturalist, 'and this is perfect.'

'You will not touch His Majesty's flag-bearer!'

'Surely you have a replacement.'

'That is beside the point!' D'Auribeau grasped Labillardière's arm.

'Here! Will this suit?' said a voice behind them.

Girardin turned to see that Félix Lahaie had appeared on deck. He offered Labillardière a fishing rod that had been fashioned out of a broken broom.

Labillardière shrugged off d'Auribeau and replaced his axe in the belt on his hip. Adjusting his coat, he nodded his thanks to the gardener.

Captain d'Auribeau clasped his right arm behind his back as though to control its violent actions. The whole left side of his face was caught in a sudden palsy. Only Girardin saw his twisted face as he strode back past her.

Labillardière strapped a makeshift cheesecloth net to one end of the pole. 'Félix, take this and lean out the side. I'll hold your legs.'

She gasped, almost stopping them. She imagined green sea serpents waiting to rear up and snatch Félix as he dangled off the ship. She imagined him lost to the ghoulish water as she herself had almost been.

Félix took a step back, his fear plain on his face. 'Monsieur Labillardière, surely your greater height would be more advantageous to the task?' he countered.

'I'm surprised at you, Citizen Lahaie. I thought you were keen to show us your aptitude as a student of the natural sciences. There is nothing to be afraid of.'

Félix glanced at the General then back to Labillardière with eyes narrowed. Unwilling to appear lacking in sufficient zeal, he snatched the pole from Labillardière and submitted to being hoisted up and over the rail.

Lightning struck the ocean and the waves pulsed with green light. The wind rocked the ship and rattled the sheets against the mast. The first splatters of rain reached her face. Girardin couldn't bear to watch a moment longer.

She hurried back to her cabin and locked the door behind her. Stripping off her tunic, she took the fresh white muslin and began to wind it tight around her breasts. The cloth felt cool against the raw wounds. As the ship rolled in the storm and the winds began to howl, she took a knife and sliced along the ribs of the corset, dismantling it, leaving no trace of its former purpose. In the morning she would throw the whale bones back to the sea, like an offering.

The fresh squall that had brought the rain and the ghostly phosphorescence did not last, and by noon the following day the muggy heat had returned. The ship sagged in a breathless hollow and she found the crew lounging sluggish and dispirited on the deck. Girardin looked for the naturalists, uncertain if they had survived the ordeal of the previous night. She had expected to see them with the fishermen, but today the artist, Piron, was alone as he sketched the foreign fish.

The crew had strung washing lines across the deck, hoping for a drying breeze. She pushed through the sodden clothes, hanging limp like flensed skins, their cold arms draping around her neck as she made her way to the stern. They screened her from view as she pulled out the small bag of whale bones at her hip. Weighted with lead shot, the bones sank quickly, swallowed by the blue. She whispered her thanks to Madame d'Yauville for her gift.

A splash behind her made her turn. Two men were hitching an old sail over the side of the boat. Too late she realised what it was for. The men stripped naked.

'Better watch yourself or you'll be next.'

Girardin jumped at the voice at her shoulder. She turned to see Armand with his monkey sitting proudly on his shoulder.

She narrowed her eyes at the monkey, acknowledging the thief from her stores. It pulled back its lips at her.

'General makes us take more baths out to sea than I've ever had on land. It ain't natural, all this washing,' Armand grumbled, while his monkey picked through his greasy hair.

'Look who's come to join us, lads!' Raoul slid down the rigging, dangling his legs above her head. Her heart hammered, realising her danger. She had been so careful these past weeks. How could she have let herself be caught like this?

Girardin backed away, but found herself circled by the men.

'He doesn't shit with us, he doesn't shave with us,' Raoul called out. 'He doesn't even bathe with us.'

The men laughed.

'Afraid to show his nice white arse, perhaps?' the butcher suggested as he soaked a rag in vinegar and rubbed it under his armpits.

'Round you, he should be!' quipped a skinny boy with front teeth like tombstones. He snaked sideways to avoid the sting of the snapped rag.

'Jealous, are ya?' The butcher then tipped more vinegar onto the rag and began to rub his teeth.

Over the side of the ship, Girardin could hear the men singing as they soaped and splashed. She scanned the group around her, desperate to run but certain that such cowardice would be her undoing. She crossed her arms in front of her.

Raoul leaped to the deck. He stripped off his shirt and loosened his trousers. She ducked her eyes away as he swept a vinegar rag around his groin.

'The General likes to have us spick and span.' He tossed the rag at Girardin. It bounced off her chest.

'Leave the boy alone,' said Armand. 'All this washing doesn't do anyone any good.'

'But the General's favourite, surely he wants to see your flesh all pink and shiny.'

Girardin watched the men heave on the ropes and lift the sail from the water. Around her more men began to strip off. She took a step backwards, but the noose of men closed tighter.

'Louis Girardin!' a voice called from behind. Félix pushed through the sailors carrying a pail of sea water. 'You must see this.' He tugged her arm. She caught his eye and something passed between them, an acknowledgement. He was urging her to trust him. The gardener felt no kinship with these bullying men, she realised. She let him pull her from the ring of men.

'We'll soon see what you keep beneath those filthy rags, *Louis* Girardin,' Raoul jeered. 'Wait till we cross the line!'

She followed Félix below deck, her heart pounding, skin flushed. Raoul's final words bewildered her. Cross which line? The mousey smell of the sailors lingered with her. She had nearly lost everything. If they had exposed her, there would be no place of safety for her on this ship. Louis Girardin was her protection, worn like a greatcoat against foul weather. She could not survive this journey without him.

Félix led her to the great cabin and closed the door firmly behind them. She leaned back against the reassuring wood. When her eyes had adjusted to the gloom she saw that the great cabin had been transformed. The windows had been blocked and the room was lit by a single lantern. Every surface was covered in books or loose leaves of paper. Plant presses were piled on the floor. Books splayed open at her feet.

'They are even smaller than I predicted,' Labillardière said excitedly, catching the water from the dripping cheesecloth net into a glass dish. He and Ventenat were gathered around a brass instrument at the end of the table.

Félix smiled at her, beckoning her forwards. 'Would you like to look in the microscope?' he asked.

What were they looking at? The water in the dish looked clear, there was nothing in it. She took a step towards it, then faltered. Could they sense the sex of her if she stood among them? Félix nudged Ventenat out of the way and made room for her. The brass instrument waited, its eyepiece thrusting upwards, inviting curiosity.

Hesitantly, she approached the strange instrument. At first the view was blurred and she closed one eye and then the other. Félix turned a brass dial and suddenly her vision filled with rounded blobs, like fish eggs.

She drew back. The dish beneath the microscope held clear water. How could she possibly see those things? 'Are they alive?' she whispered.

'Minute animalcula, just as I hypothesised!' Labillardière swirled the small glass container. 'Look again.'

Félix blew out the lantern and the room went dark. A chill leaped down her nape. In the eyepiece, tiny sparks of greenish light twinkled all over the round, jellylike bodies. Girardin jumped back. The dish glowed green.

'It is the creatures themselves that release the light!' Labillardière bounced on his toes. 'When I pass this water through blotting paper they are captured, and the water no longer glows!'

Félix struck his flint to light a reed and the lantern flared to life again.

'And do you know what this discovery means, gentlemen?' Labillardière clapped his hands together. 'We are the first men in the world to have found the creatures that emit this ghostly phosphorence! Hundreds of sailors have seen the phenomena, but we have seen its genesis!'

'You mean these things are in the water all the time? In the sea water that we wash in?' Girardin looked to the pail Félix had set down, repulsed by the thought.

'Good question,' he said, enthused. 'Are they spread across the water's surface and only luminesce in the right conditions? Or do they float in big schools and we encounter them sporadically? That is what we must test. Citizen Lahaie, we will need your services again this evening to take more samples of the waters.'

'Surely, Citizen Labillardière,' Félix replied quickly, 'in the spirit of your egalitarian ideals, you might like the honour of taking the samples yourself?'

'My dear gardener, this is why you will never make a true savant. How many times have I told you that our sampling regime must be kept standard?'

The cabin door swung open behind her. Captain d'Auribeau in his tricorn hat was silhouetted against the daylight. 'What in the name of the King have you done to this room?' he roared.

'For a small man he has a very loud voice,' Félix whispered to Girardin.

'You have found us in the middle of a momentous discovery!' Labillardière announced.

'How are my officers supposed to eat and take their rest in here when you have filled every surface with your paraphernalia?' the captain demanded, unmoved.

The naturalists looked around them as though noticing for the first time the paper and drawings strewn across the dining table, the hand lenses and mineralogist's hammer carelessly placed among the china plates. At d'Auribeau's feet a large tome lay open displaying the reproductive system of a goat.

Girardin began to edge away from the dining table.

D'Auribeau stalked towards Labillardière, clutching his arm behind his back. 'You will clean this room now.'

'I'm afraid that's impossible. My colleagues and I are about to make our drawings of these amazing specimens. It is not convenient.'

'I will tell you when it is convenient!' d'Auribeau snapped. 'I am your commanding officer.'

'The pursuit of knowledge is a higher power than your own.'

The top of d'Auribeau's hat just reached the naturalist's chin, and he was forced to tilt his head back to fix Labillardière with his stare.

Backing towards the door, Girardin stumbled against a chair. A stack of books on the seat wobbled and she caught the journal perched on top. None of the men seemed to have noticed. She opened it. Would they miss an empty book? she wondered. Her thumb rubbed the deckled edges of the paper.

'Soon we will cross the equator,' d'Auribeau said. 'The navy has a special ceremony for men who have never crossed the line before.'

Girardin froze. Cross the line. Was this what Raoul had meant?

'We'll have you stripped naked, tarred and smeared with the scrapings from the pigsties and hens' coops, and then tossed into the ocean! I do love a good ritual, don't you?'

Her breath was trapped in her chest. Félix looked up and their eyes met. He stared, puzzled, as though he saw the naked fear in her.

She fled. Behind her, she could hear smashing glass and d'Auribeau's voice pierce like a splinter.

'Was that your momentous scientific discovery? How clumsy of me.'

Chapter 15

Latitude 1°30′ N, longitude 25°30′ W,
27 November 1791

GIRARDIN SLEPT LITTLE. HER THOUGHTS WHIRLED AROUND THE questions that frightened her most. Would she ever know a moment's safety again? She feared her deception would give even decent men an excuse for cruelty. Had she consigned herself to years of torture and rape? She listened to the rumble of snoring from the crew and the freshening wind that nudged the ship towards the equator. Her father was right; she was a foolish child, not capable of making her own decisions. What stupidity could outweigh this?

Abandoning her hammock, Girardin reached for the stolen journal. She smoothed her fingers along the crease in the centre of the page. The paper sighed beneath her stroke. She allowed her quill to hover above the page, afraid to make a mark on the unblemished skin. She formed the letters in large, careful strokes.

My darling son,

The words, were stark black on the creamy paper, judging her. What sort of mother abandons her child?

I have failed you.

The act of writing was becoming easier. She concentrated on the lines flowing from one letter to the next as she drew the ink across the paper. It was easier to make marks than to think about the meaning of her words.

I have nothing to leave you, except my story.

But what could she tell him?

The first time she'd formed a word out of letters had been with a stick in the gravel. A boy had showed her. She had caught him drawing in the path that her father had raked that morning. They were in the labyrinth, her favourite part of the gardens; the trellis walls with their overgrown creepers gave her plenty of places to hide. It was clear he was not one of the gardeners' children as his clothes marked him out as someone from the palace.

'You can't do that!' she whispered, looking over her shoulder to see if her father had seen the boy. The boy merely laughed, fearless, a high, ticklish sound. He scratched more figures in the path. She was both scared and thrilled at his daring. 'Can you teach me?' she asked with sudden boldness.

'Give me your name,' he said. With great care the boy traced symbols into the dusty gravel. 'Here you are.' He held out the stick. 'Copy what I have written.'

She felt the spark of illicit thrill when she clasped the stem. She began to trace the letters he had drawn, careful with each mysterious shape. When she was finished she stood back to admire the whole.

'My father says lessons would be wasted on me.'

'Well you can go to mine instead of me!' he offered cheerfully.

'I think they would notice the difference,' she scoffed.

'Not really, no one pays any attention to me—it's my brother that matters. How old are you?'

'Seven.'

'Exactly the same age as me. I will bring you some of my clothes! You can go to reading, writing and mathematics, and I will go to geography. That is the only subject I like. One day I will sail around the world. I am going to be an explorer!' He charged off around the circular base of a fountain, his arms spread wide.

Marie-Louise cringed, afraid the gardeners would hear them. Children were not supposed to play in the gardens, they all knew that. The gardens of Versailles were a mystery to families of the gardeners. The wall of the garden towered above the gardeners' shacks and none of the children were allowed through the gates. On summer nights, they watched fireworks fly above the wall and ran like rats around the base, looking for a way in.

When she found the hole in the garden wall, she told no one. Not one of her brothers or sisters and none of the other gardeners' children. She removed the blocks from the crumbling mortar and squeezed through, carefully rebuilding the hole behind her. The garden was not like anything she had imagined. It had no dirt. She had slipped through a portal from a world of muck and grime, of brown wood and grey stone, to this ordered fantasy, this crisp, green parkland. The statues had been scrubbed so that they shone white in the sunlight. The water of the fountains sparkled. The grass, flush with spring growth and neatly clipped, was luminous. The world as she understood it would never be the same again. This wall was so thin, she had touched the blocks with her fingertips to remind herself that it was real, but the difference from one side to the other had been staggering.

    Girardin slammed the journal shut. The candle stuttered with the sudden draft of air. There was no point in reliving old memories. She didn't want to think of Versailles and all that she had done there, especially now. Tomorrow she would be exposed, stripped naked with all the others who had not crossed the equator before. Tomorrow, she would have to fight.

Chapter 16

The equator, latitude 0°, 28 November 1791

It was still dark when she made her way to the galley. She took a knife from the block and cinched the drawstring of her trousers tight, trapping the handle against her hip. But with her first step, the knife slipped and pierced the leather of her shoe. Breathing deeply to calm herself, she took the knife and slid it into her trouser pocket, slicing along the seam. Then she strapped the knife blade against her thigh with a bandage of cheesecloth. She practised slipping her hand into her pocket and grasping the handle. For now it would have to do. She thought of the naturalists carrying their instruments in purpose-built pockets. If she survived the day she would sew a leather pouch on the inside of her trousers. If she survived the day.

Girardin prepared the General's breakfast as usual and listened to the ship begin to stir. The sailors rose early, singing with gusto, the air charged with anticipation. She walked solemnly past the animal pens, ignoring the jaunty whistle of the sailor shovelling manure into buckets. The chickens squawked and flapped as they were grasped by the feet and swung upside down, their feathers swept out beneath them. She didn't notice Besnard until he pushed his face into hers. He wore a wig made from an old mop and had coconut halves strapped to his chest. He arched his back and wiggled.

'Not crossed the line before, eh?'

Girardin gripped her tray. What would a man like Besnard do if he knew the truth: that a woman dared to act as one of them? Worse still, that she dared to be his master?

A young midshipman rushed up from below, catching her elbow by mistake and spinning her around, setting the plates rattling on her tray. She caught the apologetic grin of a clear-faced boy, Mérite de Saint-Méry, not yet twenty years. He cried out his apologies as he reeled away, scampering up the ratlines as though the rope net was a ladder. He laughed as he climbed into the tops. 'You'll have to catch me first, Raoul, if you want to tar and feather me!'

She whirled about to see Raoul standing behind her holding a sharpened trident.

'You'll be next.' He smirked. 'And don't think you can hide in the General's bed.'

Girardin ducked her burning face and hurried away. None of the naturalists had yet left their cabins and their doors were firmly closed. As she climbed the stairs to the quarterdeck, a roar erupted behind her. She saw a barrel thrown into a net, dunked into the ocean and hauled back out, dripping. She felt the shape of the knife pressing against her thigh.

D'Auribeau was with the General when she entered his cabin. Silently, she placed the coffee pot on the dining table and arranged the breakfast dishes. Neither man paid her any attention.

'Captain d'Auribeau, you forget we have civilians on board.'

'But, sir, the crew are expecting naval traditions to be observed. We have a duty to fulfil.' D'Auribeau tilted his head back, his jaw jutting forwards.

The General sighed. 'You know as well as I the difficulties we face in maintaining cordial relations between the officers and the savants. I fear our naval rituals will be misunderstood.'

'But those naturalists are insupportable! They treat you with the utmost disrespect.' His hands were crossed behind his back and Girardin watched as his fingers repeatedly stretched wide and then clenched into fists.

'There is a civilian chaplain on board! Captain d'Auribeau, think of what you say. These petty rituals can get out of hand when men find themselves unleashed. As much as we'd enjoy tumbling them from their pedestals, it is not worth risking eternal damnation!'

'We should never have let republicans on board this ship. They have no respect for authority, no respect for the King.'

The General held up a placating hand.

'They are revolutionaries!' d'Auribeau spat. 'We do not know what they might have done.'

Girardin dared not move, dared not breathe.

The General shook his head. 'These men are obsessed with plants, not politics.'

'Politics? You call the imprisonment of our King politics? It is treason!'

'Nevertheless, our King has tasked us with scientific investigation. We must suffer these savants. We must show them respect.'

D'Auribeau paced across the room, unable to hold himself still.

Girardin shrank away as he swung about. 'The crew have spent time preparing for the ceremony. They will not like this.'

Girardin poured the General's coffee with a shaking hand.

'Double their rations and give them bonus pay to spend in Cape Town.'

'I fear they may act rashly.' D'Auribeau lowered his voice. 'Perhaps mutinously.'

Girardin dropped the coffee cup into its saucer with a rolling clatter. A black tide sloshed over the sides of the white porcelain. She murmured apologies for the interruption. D'Auribeau kept his gaze fixed on the General but flicked an eyebrow in annoyance. Girardin steadied her hands on the tabletop. Would the captain's tactic work?

'Mutiny?' The General shook his head. 'I have more faith in my men.' His eyes drifted towards Girardin. She caught his gaze, hoping he could read her gratitude.

'General, you have given me captaincy of this ship and as such I must declare most forcibly that military rule should be upheld! We cannot allow these savants to run our expedition!'

'Captain,' the General snapped, 'you forget yourself. I am the leader of this expedition and it is for me to say how it should be run!'

The silence was complete. Girardin held her breath.

'Make the announcements,' the General said curtly.

D'Auribeau marched out through the cabin door and slammed it behind him. Girardin let her breath slowly seep out of her. Leaning against the wall, she closed her eyes.

'A brilliant navigator, that man,' the General said with a sigh. 'The best in all the French navy I would say. He has a rare talent for mathematics and astronomy. Diplomacy, however, is not his forte.

He does not yet realise that humiliation is a bitter pill which may be swallowed but never dissolved.'

Girardin heard the roar of disappointment from the deck and felt the smallness of the paring knife against her right thigh. How foolish her plan now looked. The ship had a crew of almost a hundred men; she never could have fought them off.

'Thank you,' she said shakily, 'you have saved me.'

The General gestured towards a chair. 'Sit.'

She wiped her hands down the front of her trousers and sat slowly, careful of the knife nestled against her thigh. Together they listened to the scuffles breaking out on deck. The booming voice of Lieutenant Rossel commanded order. Quickly the men were set to work.

'Best you stay in here awhile.'

Those kind eyes. That sad smile. The wrinkles in the soft skin beneath his eyelids seemed more pronounced today. Up close she saw beads of sweat streaked through the white powder he dabbed on his face to conceal the spots of age. His distinguished grey wig sat awkwardly upon his brow and she had an urge to reach up and push it into place. He looked like a man who should be in a country house bouncing grandchildren on his knee, somewhere far away from the tempestuous souls aboard this ship.

'I was brought up in a château,' he said unexpectedly. 'Massive place, built right on the edge of a river valley and so many rooms you could get lost in it for days. Problem was it had tiny windows, you could never get a decent view of anything. And it was miles from the sea. Try as I might, I could not get the stubborn monolith to move any closer.' His eyes twinkled. 'Come.' He stood up and opened the door to his private chamber.

Girardin's eyes widened. Was this the price of her safe passage?

'I want to show you why I have chosen this life.'

Obediently Girardin followed, but her hand slipped into her pocket and rested on the hilt of the knife. Her mouth was dry, her pulse loud in her ears. The General led her past his neatly folded bunk and out onto a small balcony at the stern of the ship.

'An uninterrupted view for miles around.' He spread his arms wide. The morning sun filtered through the hazy air and cast a creamy glow on the horizon. Far behind, the *Espérance* and her reflection appeared as an ink blot against the sky. Storm petrels swooped and reeled, scanning the ship's wake for food. Beneath their feet the water rushed past. 'And there is always somewhere to go.'

'And yet we are still trapped,' she ventured. 'Trapped on this ship.'

'Better to be trapped on a moving object than a stationary one!'

'Only if you are the one directing its route.'

'Very true.' He laughed. It was a rolling, gentle sound.

'How do you know where we are?' she asked. 'How do you navigate?'

The General leaned forwards. 'You want to know?' He looked sceptical.

She bristled. 'Yes.'

'Very well.' He grinned, as if amused that she would ask such a thing. He gestured for her to follow him back to his desk. 'Two things are important to remember. To find your place anywhere in the world you need latitude and longitude.' He took the globe and placed it in front of her. 'We need to know where we are up and down, and side to side. You have heard us speak of this?'

She nodded, looking at the plotted course of the *Recherche* on the chart on the wall.

The General continued, 'Remember that the earth is round and that it spins.' He flicked the globe so that the earth turned in front of her. 'Like a ballerina in a pirouette,' he said. 'She sees the lights of the auditorium swirl around her just as we see the lights of the sun and stars circle around us every day.'

He ran his finger along the line circling the middle of the globe. 'Today, we are here at the equator. This is the sun.' The General raised his fist. 'At noon today it will be directly over our heads.'

With the index finger of his left hand he traced the path of the ship on the globe, trailing down the belly of the earth. 'As we sail away from the equator towards the Cape we will look back at the sun; it will be behind us, not ahead.'

It took Girardin a moment to comprehend. Now when she looked back towards home, towards her son, she would have the sun in her face, not at her back.

The General continued. 'As we move further away, the angle changes, so at noon the sun will not be overhead, it will appear lower in the sky. With the Borda Circle, I measure the angle of the sun above the horizon and know how many degrees we are away from the equator. That is latitude: our position north or south of the line. At night we can take the same measurements with stars.'

Girardin frowned. She feared to show her stupidity, but also knew she may never get another chance to ask questions. 'But if latitude is measured in degrees, what distance is that?'

'It is a way for us to draw lines across the earth, and to put the globe onto sheets of paper.' He cupped his hands around the top of the globe. 'You see the lines converging here? They look like slices of a pie. It is because the earth is round that we can divide it into angles. Do you know that a circle has three hundred and sixty degrees?'

She did know this. But who had taught her? Certainly not her stepmother. Nor the nuns, who taught her to read and write well enough to make housekeeping lists. Besnard had already discovered her inadequacy. 'You write like a girl,' he had said, peering over her shoulder at the ledger. She had been shocked, forgetting that her education could betray her. Women were not taught to spell as men were and her written language was a female one. 'My mother taught me,' she had lied to him. In truth, she was fifteen when her father finally sent her to the Catholic convent, afraid her illiteracy reflected poorly on himself and her marriage prospects. By then he was a respected businessman, a worldly man.

The General was talking about Babylonian astronomers, but she pictured a boy scratching circles in the gravel paths. A boy she had met in the garden of Versailles where she was not supposed to be. She heard the squeal of her father's wheelbarrow. The boy had taught her about the magic formulas to measure circles.

The General continued, enthused by his lesson. 'If we draw a line right down through Paris, think of this first line as our prime meridian. Now all we need to know is how far east or west of it we are. That is our longitude. And for this I need two chronometers.' He pointed to the brass clocks on his desk. 'One I keep at the same time as Paris, the other I change to match our local time.'

'Time is different in two places?' This was something she had not thought of before. 'How can that be?'

'Time is measured by the passing of the sun through the sky. Or as we turn past the sun, if you remember the ballerina.' He pointed to the map on his wall, where the position of the *Recherche* had been marked with a black dot. 'When we reach the Cape—' he moved his finger forwards '—we will be an hour ahead of our friends in Paris because we greet the sun before them.'

She looked at the ticking chronometer, telling the time of Paris. In its brass cogs, time passed steadily. Unceasing. Unstoppable. Her son was growing older without her.

'The earth turns fifteen degrees each hour,' the General continued. 'If we are two hours ahead of Paris, we must be thirty degrees east of Paris.'

He pulled out a chair and sat. 'When I first joined the navy we had no reliable chronometers, no way of knowing where we were from east or west. We set sail into the unknown. That was true adventure.' He sounded wistful.

Girardin touched her finger to the globe. The equator, the imaginary line separating the old world from the new. Sharp as a knife edge, they teetered on it, in the middle of this ocean.

The General clapped his hands together. 'Enough. I have work to do and so have you. Alert the cooks to prepare for a feast. Tell the butcher to slaughter one of the cattle. The men need a diversion to take their minds off their disappointments. Tonight we will have music and dancing!'

Chapter 17

Latitude 35°40′ S, longitude 14°45′ W, 15 January 1792

'Look at that!' Félix cried. Girardin followed his finger to a spot in the choppy waves. She saw nothing.

A school of fish leaped into the air. Their fins spread like wings as they burst from the water in a flash of shiny colour, gliding above the waves with wings flared. Girardin spun about. The ship was surrounded by flying fish. What bizarre creatures! Fish that wanted to fly? Surely a cruel trick that God had played on them.

The naturalists danced along the rail in front of her, their faces turned upwards to the sky. Girardin looked up to see a flock of enormous white birds swooping down like angels. She jumped back. The heavy birds spread their wings above the water to slow their dive and scooped the flying fish into their mouths. A golden sack inflated beneath their long bills, trapping the fish inside. Amazed, she watched the birds plummet from the sky and pluck the hapless fish from the air. One of the birds landed on the water with the fish fighting inside the pouch, like bony elbows struggling to be free.

Girardin was used to the fleet, little storm petrels that followed the ship. The tropics had brought the black man-of-war bird with its bright red pouch, like a goitre, at its throat. She had once seen a trusting booby light down on a sailor's outstretched arm. But these huge, white birds with golden purses beneath their bills were like nothing she had seen before.

'*Pelecanus onocrotalus*,' Labillardière said excitedly, 'just as Linnaeus described it!'

'The great white pelican,' Félix translated.

Ventenat flapped past her in his long black robes, not yet changed after the morning's sermon. Eyes intent on the birds, he tripped on a coil of rope, fell sprawling to the deck, but righted himself before she could reach out. Even the sailors seemed excited watching these magnificent birds.

'The birds are a good sign,' Armand said. 'Land is near.' The monkey stood up on his shoulder, resting one hand on the old sailor's head, as if it too were searching for land along the horizon.

After crossing the line, the winds had blown strong and fair and both frigates made good speed. But for six weeks the winds blew only from the east, pushing them so far off course that the crew laid bets on when they would land in Brazil. Girardin had despaired of reaching the Cape before their supplies were exhausted. All the fresh meat and vegetables were gone and she conjured meal plans out of nothing at all. Soup with onions and oil. That was a dish her mother used to make for the family when they couldn't afford meat and vegetables. She remembered her mother complaining in hushed tones, 'What use is a garden if you can't grow any vegetables?' Once, she had seen her mother wish aloud for more carrots in front of her father and receive a smashed nose. Girardin counted the remaining bags of onions in her head, while the men grumbled that the broth was not nutritious.

Eventually the winds had turned westerly and pushed them hard and fast towards the African continent. The sound of the wind driving the ship forwards was a comfort to her. Each morning, Girardin scanned the horizon for land. Each morning, the relentless sea stretched in all directions, showing her that the two ships were utterly alone on this ocean.

At New Year, Girardin was overjoyed to see the *Espérance* draw alongside the *Recherche*. The officers and crew shouted out their greetings to one another. She saw Kermadec with his men, his smile broad, his arm raised. The ships met like two albatross on the wing, passing one another briefly in mid-air. She waved to the *Espérance* with a smile she couldn't hide from her face.

After that, the sightings of seabirds became more numerous and the sailors began to lay their bets, convinced that land was near. One day she saw a tiny bird flit past her ear. Its golden breast flashed. A wagtail! It stunned her to see this bird of the fields so far from home. She remembered them dancing around the ponds in the gardens at Versailles. Where are you going to little bird? she wondered. Seeming lost and fatigued from its long flight, she watched as it fluttered down to rest for a moment on the taffrail, then suffered itself to be taken in Labillardière's net.

Ange Raoul now spent most of his time aloft, locked in competition with his older brother Joseph over who would be the first to spy the Cape. Raoul had shown her no further aggression, given her no cause for alarm, but yet when he looked at her she felt uneasy in her skin, like a doe quivering at the scent of a wolf. He regarded her with the patience of a hunter and a smug familiarity, as though he knew exactly who she was.

A squeal from the starboard made her turn.

'Félix! A net!' Labillardière cried while drawing his pistol. 'Careful, don't scare it off.'

'Have you seen the size of its beak?' Félix squawked.

A pelican stood on the taffrail. It towered above the crewmen. Girardin was sure if she were standing on the deck beside it, she would be looking straight into its beady black eye. Puckered golden skin hung down at its throat, gently fluttering in the breeze. It ducked its bill down and surveyed the shipmates with easy nonchalance. Spreading its massive wings wide, it gave two strong flaps.

'My God, Ventenat, what would you say its wingspan is? Nearly three metres?'

'Yes, eight, perhaps nine feet!' Ventenat agreed.

Labillardière inched closer with his pistol held out in front of him.

Félix and Ventenat unravelled a seine net used for fishing and crept towards the pelican. Beside her, Armand's monkey leaped from his shoulder.

'No!' cried Armand as his pet trotted along the rail with its tail spiked into the air, intent on the intruder. Girardin watched the pelican. It waited until the monkey came within range then drew itself up tall and lashed out. The monkey squealed and twisted away just as the heavy beak snapped shut with the solid clap of an axe on wood. A gulp of air inflated the pouch and the monkey scampered across the deck and back up onto Armand's shoulder.

The pelican regarded them calmly.

'Throw the net now!' Labillardière commanded.

Girardin wanted to warn the pelican. *Flee, flee now. You can fly!* The filaments of the net glistened in the sunlight as Félix raised his arm. The pelican swung its head and gazed at him with a black-eyed stare.

'Shoot it first!' he cried.

'Don't be stupid, we'll lose it over the side!'

The pelican snapped its beak together and thrust its wings wide, baring its breast. Girardin imagined the shot bursting red upon its feathers. Saw it fall back and float upon the water. *Don't you know what will happen to you if you are caught here?* She flicked her arms at it, not caring if Labillardière saw her. The pelican turned its head to her. With a small hop backwards, it disappeared below the rail.

Labillardière ran to the side. 'You fools! You've lost it!'

The pelican flew low across the ocean, the black tips of its marvellous wings lightly brushing the water's surface. Girardin smiled.

Chapter 18

Cape Town, South Africa, 18 January 1792

When Table Mountain rose out of the sea before her, Girardin wept with relief. Out of this wide, endless ocean, the General had found the Cape. The Cape of Good Hope. Good Hope. Hope. She clung to the words. She had survived three months packed tight with these men, like salted fish in a barrel that had been set afloat. She wanted to feel solid earth beneath her feet, to smell the warm scent of land.

She swayed, feeling her seasickness return as she took her first steps onto the wharf. The boards seemed to buckle upwards and she tottered like a bandy-legged old salt. Around her supplies were being delivered, animals traded, barrels rolled loudly along the planks used as makeshift gangways. Soon she would have fresh beef and pork to feed the crew, and chickens and goats to load into pens. She halted, unable to take another step. There were too many people, too many bodies jostling for space. Everyone moved so quickly. Her shoes felt weighted to the wharf.

Behind her, Labillardière ran down the gangway. She watched him push aside the sailors carrying sacks of grain on their shoulders, and heard the men swear and curse at him. Labillardière bounded past her on the wharf and made straight for his friend Claude Riche, who was arguing with the surgeon from the *Espérance*, Denis Joannet. Girardin had met the chief surgeon for the first time just that morning when he sought her out in the galley.

'The air down here is foul.' Joannet had screwed up his face. 'It will bring fevers in the crew. Fumigation is what you need.' She began to tell him they smoked the tweendecks with gunpowder twice daily, but he had already turned away.

'The crew are like children frightened of medicines. Would you believe they accuse me of poisoning them? How dare they!'

He strolled around the galley, tapping his fingernail thoughtfully against the canisters of treacle, juniper extract and malt barley.

'While we are in port these men will practise the excesses of debauchery in all manner of evil places.' He shuddered and lifted a jar of treacle from the shelf. 'A spoonful of this should disguise the taste of mercury.'

He leaned in close to her, so close that Girardin could see the hairs sprouting from the tip of his nose and the splintered red veins on his cheeks. 'Syphilis,' he said. 'Will the navy ever be rid of this scourge of the seas?' His breath of pickled walnuts was strong in her face.

Joannet had pocketed the jar of treacle as he left.

Now Girardin watched the surgeon tussle with Claude Riche over a cage trap. She thought Joannet had the advantage. He was shorter and stouter. He dug his toes into the wharf and leaned his weight against the bamboo cage. Loyal Michel Sirot, Riche's servant, flapped about beside them, beating Joannet with his parasol like a maid punishing the dust from a floor rug. She smiled. They are children, she thought; children who had not been taught to share. Labillardière rushed between the men. From this distance, Girardin could not hear the altercation, but she could see Labillardière wrench the cage away from Joannet. Words floated across to her. *Pseudoscience. Profession. Respect.* The surgeon straightened his coat and shouldered a canvas pack before stalking away.

Girardin felt the muscles in her legs begin to relax. Her breathing slowed and became more regular. She let the push and pull of the dockyards wash around her like waves. She was amazed at the freedom her clothes gave to her. You are fortunate, she told herself, to have made it this far. A mouse limped along the wharf, missing a hind foot. It stopped and sniffed the air, its whiskers throbbing. You are like me, little friend, she thought. Both of us small and brown and unnoticed, and yet still afraid. A sailor dropped a sack of rice and a loose board jumped. Girardin saw a pink tail disappear over the side.

Girardin walked. Placing one unsteady foot in front of the other, she left the wharf and made it to the flagstones of the quay. Her stomach rolled. She kept walking and soon she felt dry-packed earth beneath her soles. She heard voices in many languages: Dutch, Portuguese, French and English. Chickens screeched and flapped. In the marketplace, the crowds were disorientating. Random noises alarmed her. She stumbled and put her hand against the flank of a cow to steady herself and felt the annoyed swatch of its tail strike her. Like the marketplace in Brest, the air stank of oily fish and oysters going bad in the sun. She was reminded of the boy with the stack of papers being pushed into the muck of the street. What news was there of home? she wondered.

'Have you ever seen a more sickening sight?' She turned at the familiar voice, squinting up at Labillardière. She followed his gaze. The ship docked alongside the *Recherche* had begun to offload its cargo.

'How many are there?' Girardin whispered.

'Near four hundred would be my estimate.'

The Negro men and women shuffled from the ship. Heavy manacles bound their ankles and kept them close together. They were emaciated and could barely stand. Girardin had never seen black people before, never seen the people of Africa. The manacles dug into their flesh, and she saw the streaks of fresh red blood over crusted black. When the chain of women was pulled apart from the chain of men, their warbled cries to one another grew frantic. The sound was deafening, and Girardin felt the busy marketplace pause and turn to look.

The women wailed, heedless of the swift canes on their flesh. They were pushed through the streets. Girardin stared at the manacles around their ankles as they were shunted past. She could not meet the eyes of these women. She wrung the fabric of her tunic in her hands. While she could hide within her clothing, these people could not hide their skin. She smelled them. It nearly made her retch. Their legs were smeared with shit, and urine had stained their rags. The townspeople drew back, holding their handkerchiefs to cover their mouths, screwing their faces in disgust.

'These slaves have been forced to stand in their own excrement since Mozambique!' the naturalist cried, looking around him, accusing anyone who would meet his gaze. Girardin felt the power in Labillardière's muscular frame as he stiffened with anger. 'You people should feel ashamed of yourselves!'

The slaves bore the marks of the cane, bloodied welts on their shoulders, backs and heads. Their faces were bewildered, distraught. What did they think was happening to them? The men and women were herded into separate pens.

'I caught one of the traders boasting that he could purchase three blacks for the price of one handsome dog,' said Labillardière. She saw that he was trembling. His anger reminded her of Olympe. Her friend would not stand idly by if she were here. Olympe would add her voice to his condemnation.

'The practice of slavery is an abomination!' Olympe had cried out from a table in the middle of Etienne's café. 'We writers must do all in our power to condemn it.' Back then, Marie-Louise did not know her name and it would be many years before they became friends. She was amazed by this beautiful woman sitting openly at a table with her male companions, her voice loud and unconcerned. Her showy white headdress towered above all, gleaming like silver satin.

A group of men stood and slapped their napkins onto the table, pulling their eyebrows into frowns and making a display of their exit. Women should not be seen eating in public.

Marie-Louise hovered at the kitchen door, uncertain. She looked quickly to Etienne but he was too busy in the kitchen to notice the woman in the centre of their café.

'I am going to write a play,' she told her companions. *L'Esclavage des Noirs.*'

'No one will put on a play about slavery,' the man beside her scoffed. He caught Marie-Louise's eye and gestured for coffee.

'You must give them names. That is the key. These Negroes could be you or I if they have names. I will not write about slavery, I will write about two slaves, Zamore and Mirza. It will be a love story.'

As Marie-Louise poured them coffee, the man shook his head. 'It will not make any difference; the practice is too important for the economy.'

Olympe had arched her brow and gave her fan an annoyed flick. 'It is the doing of the thing that matters. We must do something.'

Marie-Louise was secretly pleased to see this remarkable woman come more frequently to the café. The customers eventually grew used to her and ceased to complain. Olympe de Gouges, the eccentric woman playwright. They ignored her or treated her with disdain. Olympe did not care. Marie-Louise loved it when she swept into the room, wearing her opinions like her mode of dress, audacious and bizarre.

'It is only colour that separates the African from the European. If they are animals then so are we,' she had exclaimed, oblivious to the startled glances of her friends. 'Colour is the beauty of nature. Do you treat your brown chicken any different from the white?'

But Girardin was afraid to speak out as Labillardière had done. She was not as brave as Olympe de Gouges.

In the marketplace, the auctioneer's voice rose above the cries of the Africans. Girardin recognised the singsong rise and fall of the business at hand. The men and women, held in separate saleyards, screamed in terror. Girardin knew this would be the last they saw of each other. Husbands and wives, brothers and sisters, mothers and sons.

The marketplace resumed its daily business and she heard the people around her complaining of the racket. Did they not know what it was like to lose the ones you loved?

The auctioneer's gavel slammed on wood. She started. The slaves were lined up before their owners, their feet and wrists still bound. What kind of life awaits them, she wondered, in these masters' homes?

After Etienne's death, Marie-Louise had had no choice but to seek her father's protection. She had lost her husband and let his café fall into ruin. Jean Girardin had suffered her return, even though everyone knew that a widow under one's roof brought bad luck. Still grieving, Marie-Louise was slow to realise that her life was no longer her own. Her father stripped her of her married name, Lesserteur, and reinstated her as Marie-Louise Girardin. He chose the clothes she wore, the books she read, even the needlepoint patterns to occupy her days. Since she had no funds of her own she could not send or receive a letter without him knowing. He permitted her no friendships. From her stepmother, she was entreated not to cause any further embarrassment. She could do nothing but wait for her father to find her another husband.

'No man should have complete domination over another,' said Labillardière, clenching his fists. 'It makes beasts of both.'

Nor any man over a woman, Girardin heard Olympe whisper in her ear.

Chapter 19

'La Pérouse has been sighted!'

'In the Admiralty Islands.'

'By an English captain.'

The rumours had circled the *Recherche* faster than a terrier chasing its tail. Captain Hunter, an English officer aboard the Dutch ship *Waaksamheyd*, had recently visited Cape Town and left behind news that he had seen islanders with French uniforms near New Guinea. But Captain Hunter's ship had left port the same day as their arrival in Cape Town and the rumours could not be confirmed.

Girardin pictured Kermadec's large map open on his desk in his library in Brest and the tiny dots of islands in the vast expanse of ocean. Back then, she had thought the mission ridiculous, that they were fishing for raindrops. But now it seemed there was hope La Pérouse and his men might be found. It warmed her heart to think of it. If a mission as impossible as this could succeed, it gave her hope that she too could be reunited with her son.

She slipped her thumb under the cuff of her sleeve and felt the raised ridge of her burn. It reassured her, this touchstone, to remind herself of Rémi. She dug her thumb into the burn, consoling herself that the matching scar he carried was a promise she would return. But the further she sailed from France, the more distant and unreal her old life seemed. Her son would be six months old. Six months! The recognition of it made her gasp.

Félix looked up from his work. She faked a sneeze. It was not hard to believe with all the pollen dancing in the air. Today, Girardin was with the naturalists in the great cabin. They were preoccupied with a heavy haul of plants from their explorations at the Cape. Blooms of irises, lilacs and orchids were strewn across the table. On return from each of their sampling trips the naturalists came back to the ship to catalogue and preserve their specimens. Félix was plucking seeds from spent flowerheads with his tweezers and placing each one carefully in a partitioned wooden tray. An ornate tin and copper chest lay open before him, and the wooden trays fitted neatly inside. He was collecting the seeds of his future, she thought, watching him pull the fine threads from the flower and lay each one in its nest.

With the officers housed ashore in Cape Town, the naturalists' books and papers were once again spread across the cabin. Dozens of jars filled with butterflies lined the walls and drying flower stems hung from the ceiling. Out of loneliness or boredom, Girardin found herself drawn to the naturalists. She hovered close, like a bee to nectar, and they accepted her without question.

The chaplain passed her another sheet of paper. 'It is an art and a science,' he told her. He arranged the plant specimens attractively with their flowers opened out and leaves flipped to display the detail of both sides. Using his tweezers, he spread the petals of the iris before she placed the paper on top. He had shown Girardin how to place the sheets within the press. She carefully lined up the sheets of paper and laid the wooden slab across the top, turning the baton to tighten the straps around the collection. With each turn she couldn't help but think of the bandages wound tight around her own pressed and flattened breasts.

The artist, Piron, sat at one end of the table, half hidden by a mound of fluffy pink proteas. 'The General will change our course now, you mark my words,' he said, shaking his paintbrush at Labillardière.

'Pah! What evidence do we have?' said Labillardière, not looking up from his microscope. 'Some second-hand reports of natives wearing pieces of red and blue clothing and gesticulating that they want to be shaved? Am I the only one among us who thinks a finger scraped across a throat and directed at an Englishman may have been misconstrued?' He made the quick, sharp motion to prove his point.

'But we must investigate,' Girardin blurted. 'This is a rescue mission.'

'That is not my mission.'

She shook her head, exasperated. She did not understand him. It heartened her that the savant could care so much about the plight of slaves, but that he could care so little about their lost countrymen puzzled and frustrated her.

'If we change our course, I will leave the expedition,' Labillardière declared.

Félix snorted. 'Good. I will have your cabin.' He winked at Girardin.

'The needs of the naturalists always come last. It is becoming intolerable. Claude Riche and I will no longer stand for it.'

'So melodramatic,' wailed Félix, clutching his hands in front of his heart.

Girardin hid her smile.

'It is a point of principle.'

'You would give up your chance of new discoveries?' Girardin did not believe it.

'There is no country in the world where one finds as many interesting plants in so small an area,' said Labillardière, selecting another flower from the pile beside him. 'I should be very happy to stay here and explore further.'

Félix mouthed to her, 'No, he will not.'

Without warning, the door to the great cabin swung open. Girardin yelped with surprise. Piron swore as he knocked his jar of brushes and the murky water spilled across his illustration.

'Does no one knock?' Labillardière muttered.

Captain d'Auribeau entered, followed by the General. He raised his eyebrows at the mounds of flowering plants piled on the table and the flower stems strung upside down from the beams, but made no comment.

'Ah, Citizen d'Entrecasteaux!' Labillardière said, not bothering to rise from his microscope. 'Perfect timing.'

She saw Captain d'Auribeau bristle at the impertinent address and the General put a hand on his arm to quell him.

Labillardière stood and stretched, exaggerating his full height beside the diminutive captain. He reached into his jacket pocket and produced a letter, solemnly handing it to the General. 'As trained professionals and head of our respective areas of natural history on this expedition, Citizen Riche and myself demand that all collections be handed over to us for proper scientific evaluation, or else we shall be forced to tender our resignations.'

The General stared at him. 'But surely, Monsieur Labillardière, the enthusiasms of the men should be encouraged. Natural history belongs to all. Is it not for the good of science that knowledge is shared?'

'Science is a careful, considered matter undertaken by learned savants—not a free for all! Many of the officers and crew have begun their own collections and even the surgeon Joannet fancies himself a botanist and wishes to join our collecting. This fever of pseudoscience is unconscionable!'

To Girardin, the General looked weary, like a father tired of settling the petty squabbles of his children. He regarded the savant from beneath his brows. 'You would abandon your chance to explore in lands where no other savant has been?'

Labillardière swallowed. 'Of course.'

'We should sail without them,' d'Auribeau declared. 'He admits there are others capable of collecting these plants and shells. Leave them behind and let us concentrate our efforts on geographical discoveries.'

Labillardière looked pale.

The General sighed. 'I will consider the matter. We have few days remaining in this port, so if you wish to collect more flowers—' his gaze lingered on the fluffy proteas '—I suggest you make the most of the opportunity.'

The General turned stiffly to Girardin. 'The cook said I would find you here.'

She coloured, feeling guilty without knowing why.

'We need to discuss the search for La Pérouse,' he said.

'Foolish,' Labillardière couldn't help but observe. 'Another long sea journey without opportunity for botanising.'

'Enough! What consequence is this to you if you have resigned your post?' said d'Auribeau.

Labillardière's mouth opened and shut. For the first time Girardin saw him speechless.

'Come,' the General said to her. 'We have need of your opinion.'

Flustered, she passed a wilting specimen to Ventenat and wiped her hands on her tunic. With a glance at Félix for reassurance, she followed.

'And clean this cabin up!' d'Auribeau snarled as he slammed the door behind him.

In the General's cabin, Girardin saw that the officers of both ships had been called to the meeting. All heads turned to face her. She scanned the sea of blue frockcoats and white-cap wigs for Captain Kermadec, seeking his encouraging smile. She stepped forwards. Ahead of her were the observatory trio: stout Rossel, sparrow-like Beautemps-Beaupré and the fiddle player, Saint-Aignan. The surgeons—Joannet from the *Espérance* and Renard from the *Recherche*—stood close together. The lieutenants of both ships were introduced, but their names were lost to her as soon as they were uttered. She failed to find Kermadec in the crowd.

Captain d'Auribeau took his place before the map on the General's wall. 'You have heard the rumours?' d'Auribeau asked, without looking at her.

Did he mean of La Pérouse? She was afraid to speak.

The General smiled gently. 'We have need of your advice. If we investigate this sighting in the Admiralties, we must deviate from the King's plan. We would head north to Timor immediately and abandon the charting of the southern coast of New Holland.'

The observatory trio stirred. She glanced across at Beautemps-Beaupré. The young cartographer looked distraught.

'How long will our supplies last?' Captain d'Auribeau asked her.

Girardin swallowed. She looked at the map upon the wall. Where was Timor? She had no idea. Where could they restock? Dare she ask or would that expose her ignorance? The men stared at her expectantly.

'The holds have been refilled with dried vegetables, grain and biscuit,' she murmured.

The General cupped a hand to his ear. 'Speak up.'

Girardin cleared her throat. 'The fresh vegetables will not last long if we are heading north to the tropics.'

D'Auribeau waved his arm with irritation. 'How long can we feed the men on this ship?'

Girardin thought of the long journey from Tenerife to Cape Town. 'Three months,' she said, 'if we can make our own flour for bread. Perhaps more if we ration the salted meat.'

The men exchanged glances. Girardin felt light-headed. What if she were wrong? What if she had condemned them all to starvation?

'Captain Kermadec,' said the General, 'would you conduct a thorough investigation of our stocks?'

'And do it properly this time,' d'Auribeau muttered beneath his breath.

A chair scraped back, and she saw Kermadec rise at the back of the room, head bent beneath the low ceiling of the cabin. Relief flushed through her at the sight of him. Her heart thrummed. It was only relief, she told herself, to see a friend among these stern men.

He gestured to the door for her to join him. 'Let us consult your records.'

As they left the General's cabin, she felt his hand press against the small of her back. It was there for only a moment, but long enough for her to feel the heat of it.

'My . . . My ledger is in my cabin,' she stammered.

'I am sorry I could not come and find you before now. Damn Claude Riche and his demands. He bickers constantly with the surgeon Joannet. And now the savants all threaten to leave the expedition! They vex me greatly. I wish they would leave and relieve me of my headaches!'

She thought of Labillardière and his disdain of the search for La Pérouse. 'Do you believe this rumour?' she asked.

'We have to believe it.' He smiled down at her. 'Hope keeps one alive.'

They continued in silence to her cabin door. She fumbled with her key. For a moment she thought Kermadec might follow her into her cabin where they would be alone and out of sight. Her breath shortened. But Kermadec waited outside, respecting her privacy. She opened her neatly ruled ledger and ran her finger down each column, the names of foodstuffs, the numbers of barrels and crates. The ordered lists calmed her. Never in her life had such responsibility fallen on her shoulders.

'To the holds,' Kermadec said, lifting a lantern from the wall.

The air below deck was moist and hot. As they climbed down the rope ladder, she was pleased to see the holds were fully laden. The supplies were neatly stacked. The ship was ready.

'You have a system,' he said, noticing the date marked on a barrel.

'So I know how long each one will last.'

The space was small and cramped and she had to stand uncomfortably close to him.

'May I?' he asked, reaching out. She had wrapped her arms around her ledger, holding it against her like a breastplate. He lifted the ledger from her grasp. Removed of her armour, she felt exposed, with no shield to cover her heart. She quickly crossed her arms.

Propping the book open on a crate, Kermadec smiled as he followed her careful ticks along the margin. "Flour, grain and beans. You have checked each delivery?'

She nodded. Of course.

'Impressive,' Kermadec said.

She smiled at his praise, but turned her face into the darkness.

'Three months,' he said. 'How sure are you that these supplies will last three months?'

'It is an estimate only, not a calculation. What does your steward say?'

'My steward! I do not trust his counsel. He is either a negligent fool or a cunning deceiver.' Kermadec covered his mouth with his fist, suppressing a cough. She heard the rattle in his chest as he breathed deep.

'A deceiver? You suspect your steward is a thief?'

'A profiteer. I suspect he sells our supplies to the crew, but I have no proof. He may simply be wasteful. I shall watch him closely on this next leg of the journey.'

He dipped his hand into an open sack of shiny red beans, letting them sift between his fingers. They glittered like jewels.

'Will three months of supplies be enough to change course for the Admiralty Islands?' she asked.

'Maybe, if the winds are kind to us.'

'And if they are not?'

He didn't answer. He looked at her directly, his warm brown eyes intent on hers. The golden lamplight flickered and leaped across his face. She didn't like the way her heart was flittering. She didn't trust herself.

'I have feared for you these last months,' Kermadec said in a low voice. 'I have chastised myself for suggesting this journey.'

A confusion of emotions surprised her. He had feared for her. Did that mean he cared for her? The voices in her head laughed at her. *Stupid girl. He means he feared you could not do your job.* She blushed, ashamed of her stupidity.

'Crossing the line, I thought I had condemned you.' His brow was furrowed, his eyes deep with concern.

'I am well,' she said, mustering a confidence she didn't feel.

Seized by a coughing fit Kermadec crumpled over, holding a handkerchief to his mouth. Girardin reached out instinctively, but stalled her hand. A cough like this was not good. She knew that much. She remembered pressing her hand to Jojo's back, feeling the violence of the spasms in his tiny chest.

'The air below these decks is not good for my lungs,' he wheezed, easing himself upright. 'I find it doesn't have any air in it.' He smiled and wiped his face, folding his handkerchief. His breath rattled. 'Do not look so alarmed!' he said with a laugh. 'I am not in mortal danger. It is just a cough. The curse of all sailors. Come, let us take your records up on deck where I can breathe.' When he edged past her, he was careful not to let any part of their bodies collide.

'Captain Kermadec,' she called after him, 'if we find La Pérouse in the Admiralties, will we go home?'

The look he gave her was hard to read. Sadness, pity, disappointment? 'Eventually,' he said.

Part Three

Rechercher: to seek

Chapter 20

Indian Ocean, latitude 34°37′ S, longitude 42°24′ E, 5 March 1792

GIRARDIN SAT ON THE DECK WITH HER LEGS DANGLING OVER THE side of the ship. The air was still, the sea flat and monotonous. All was quiet and muted without the wind and waves. Beside her, Piron leaned against the rail and sketched Armand as he slept, mouth hanging open, clay pipe fallen to his chest. In this breathless heat, there was no sign of his monkey. With a small stick of charcoal Piron drew the creases of Armand's weathered face, the grey stubble underneath his jaw. She marvelled at his quick, sure movements, bringing simple lines into life.

The ship rocked gently, barely moving. Slow ripples lapped against her sides. Even the sailors kept their voices hushed. They must know, Girardin thought, what trouble we are in. I have consigned us to starvation. We'll never make it to Timor in three months.

Almost three weeks had passed since leaving Cape Town and they had progressed no further north. Each day she carefully measured out the flour and told Besnard to cut the meat into smaller portions. He reminded her that Magellan had lost two hundred men for want of fresh food. The winds nudged them continually to the east instead of north. Or, worse, fell away to nothing.

Loud footsteps interrupted the silence. Piron looked up from his sketchbook as a long shadow was cast across the page.

'You really cannot draw figures,' said Labillardière, studying Piron's sketch of the reclining sailor. 'The proportions of his limbs are completely wrong.'

'Are you still here?' Piron said. 'I thought we'd left you in Cape Town with the others.' The artist winked at Girardin.

For the past three weeks, Labillardière had been sulking in his cabin. He had threatened to leave the expedition, protesting at the surgeon Joannet thinking himself one of the savants. It surprised Girardin that a professed revolutionary should be as zealous as any nobleman in his protection of his privileges. Labillardière was a man content to show his command of knowledge, his mind a compendium of Latin names, but he was reluctant to share in the pursuit of it.

And yet, no one liked to be thought dispensible, she thought. How would the carpenters, the cook, the smith react if their craft was usurped by amateurs? For Labillardière, recognition meant everything. Being a botanist, being a learned savant, she realised, was Labillardière's entire identity.

In the end, the General had declared all collections to belong to the expedition, not individuals, which pleased no one. A mineralogist and an artist from the *Espérance* disembarked, along with the *Recherche*'s astronomer. Only Félix was overjoyed that he now had his own cabin.

Armand suddenly snorted, waking himself with a confused frown. Squinting at Girardin, he said, 'I wouldn't sit like that if I were you.'

'Why not?' she asked.

'I lost two mates that way.'

'What foolish story is this?' Labillardière said.

'We were sitting here at the bow, our legs over the side, bare feet treading the breeze. I turned my head away for a moment, to share a joke with a young lad, and when I looked back, me mate Thierry was gone. Vanished.' The sailor snapped his fingers and opened his eyes wide. 'Sitting right where you are, right there.'

Girardin shifted uneasily.

'Barely had time to screech out an oath or two, when she did it again! All I saw was one long tentacle.' He raised a forefinger and wiggled it in front of Girardin's face. 'Poor lad never stood a chance. She sucked him down head first!'

Girardin pulled her knees up to her chest.

'I don't mind telling you, I moved faster than a galley rat and scuttled under a longboat. I were too afraid to move or call out a warning. And then she were upon us, all arms of slimy, reeking terror, like something from the firepits of hell! She climbed the rigging, threatnin' to drag us under into her whirlpool lair. Gonna tip us up and throw all hundred souls into her open maw. I saw it in her eye, that hunting eye. She feeds on men's souls.' The last word rattled in the old sailor's throat until his voice faded to silence.

'Pure fantasy,' scoffed Labillardière. 'How much brandy have you had?'

'Go on,' urged Piron.

'Not much more to tell. Some quick wits slashed her greedy tentacles from our mast and sent her reeling back to her hole at the bottom of the ocean. I still remember it curling and fizzing with its venomous magic on our deck.'

'What was it?' breathed Girardin.

'Hallucination,' said Labillardière.

'The Kraken,' said Armand, showing the whites of his eyes.

'You say it has eight arms?' said Piron, kneeling on the deck with his sketchbook in front of him.

'Aye, eight long, muscular things they were, all covered in suckers the size of saucers.' Armand held two hands in a ring shape in front of his face.

'Tentacles? You mean, like an octopus?' said Piron.

'Aye! That's right, like an octopus, but a colossus. Not like any octopus I seen before. Had one great big eye, the size of a wine-barrel lid, and it looked right at me.'

'A Cyclops?' Girardin asked, remembering the Greek myths.

'Well, maybe it had two eyes,' the old sailor conceded, 'but I only saw the one.'

Piron sketched rapidly, wrapping tentacles around the frigate's sails. Girardin noticed the blue ink tentacle curling around Armand's wrist. On his forearm a crude bulbous head and huge eye stared out at her. Armand carried his adventures inked on his arms. She saw tattoed serpents, sharks and palm trees. She turned her wrist to expose the blazing red brand on her own arm, understanding the need to mark your skin with memories.

'We'll be seeing her soon enough, no doubt,' Armand said, crossing his arms.

Piron looked up from his sketch.

'What do you mean?' Girardin asked.

'Idiotic nonsense,' said Labillardière.

Armand ignored him, relishing his tale. 'She lives in the southern seas, needs the icy waters to calm her voracious bloodlust. She sits among the whales, gorging on their offspring.'

'But we're going north,' said Girardin. 'To the Admiralties.' To La Pérouse, she thought. And then home.

'Not for long. Mark my words, we'll be turning south. Sailing through such shrieking storms and fierce tempests that you wish to God he would take you then and there. Across oceans that drop away beneath your feet as suddenly as they rear up to swallow you. And she'll be waiting for us.' The old sailor ran his tongue across his yellow teeth. 'I can feel it in my bones.'

Chapter 21

Latitude 35° S, longitude 44° E, 6 March 1792

THE GENERAL ABANDONED HIS ATTEMPT AT A NORTHWARD course. When the announcement was made to turn east and take the southern route below New Holland instead of north to Timor, Girardin slumped with the relief of it. The responsibility for their supplies lasting until they reached Timor was no longer hers to bear.

Almost as soon as the ships turned, the winds turned against them. In the night, a southerly gale rose and she listened to its agonised wail. Lying in her hammock, Girardin pressed her hands over her ears. Her dreams were filled with writhing tentacles; she saw them snaking through cracks in the wood and splintering the hull. She woke to a shattering crack that rocked the ship. When morning came, she saw the windmill had been wrenched from its footing in the night. Their means of making flour was now shredded across the ocean behind them. Labillardière blamed the ferocity of the wind, but in her mind's eye a long tentacle wrapped itself around the stem.

'The Kraken,' she whispered to Félix.

'These sailors will fill your head with superstition and there will be no room left for reason. Learn to think!' Labillardière cried in exasperation.

Félix and Girardin exchanged glances.

For weeks the ships slogged into headwinds, making little progress. All the sailors were spooked by the fickle, unnatural winds. They came upon an island covered in flame that turned the sky copper and the clouds thunderous as it burned. Out of the corner of her eye, she saw Armand flick his fingers to ward off evil.

God is toying with us, she thought. He is like a boy, blowing a walnut shell boat in a puddle. When we try to go north He blows us east, when we go east, He blows us back. When she turned her face forwards, she felt God's cold breath on her cheeks.

Even the General cursed their luck. 'These fiendish winds turn against us. If we were to go west now, I believe the winds would turn to spite us!'

We are trapped in His whirlpool lair, Girardin thought, remembering the words of the old sailor. He will keep us here in the belly of the world, turning us around and around for eternity. He will not let us find La Pérouse. He will not let me return home for my son. What good are my wages trapped here at the bottom of the world? She looked into the swirling fathoms of blue water. Or lost at the bottom of the ocean?

'We still have the chance to map the southern coast of New Holland,' said Lieutenant Rossel, casting a look at Beautemps-Beaupré, who paced along the deck, desperate for a sight of the great continent.

It annoyed her, this talk of mapping coasts. How long would that take? Shouldn't the rescue of La Pérouse take precedence above all else? She had studied the map in the General's cabin. Great lengths of the coastline of New Holland were unknown. Only a thin dotted line suggested a sweeping boundary between sea and land, terminating in a curl of solid ink, like a misplaced hair, marking the coast of Van Diemen's Land.

The General said nothing. He stared out at the empty horizon, squinting into the blasted wind.

'There has never been an expedition such as this,' cried d'Auribeau, his voice cracking in a moment of despair. 'We are expected to look urgently for our lost compatriot and at the same time make detailed charts of foreign shores.'

'And more importantly,' interrupted Labillardière, 'make biological discoveries for the betterment of France.'

Girardin saw d'Auribeau scowl.

Beautemps-Beaupré started when the General placed a hand on his shoulder. 'Forgive me, son. We must abandon the search for New Holland's coast and sail deeper south.'

The expedition set a course for Adventure Bay in Van Diemen's Land. There, the General assured her, they would find wood and water, fish and birds aplenty. The explorers Tasman, Furneaux and Cook had all been there before them. Girardin was relieved, both by the promise of supplies and the decision to search for La Pérouse.

As the old sailor had promised, the turn south brought them into the westerly wind. A snarling, roaring, icy wind. She turned up the collar of her greatcoat against its bite. The gales blew them towards

Van Diemen's Land at a pace so far unmatched in her experience. The two ships were flung across the southern ocean like stones skipped over puddles.

The wind brought storms: some drenched them in freezing water; others swept along the horizon, threatening violence. For days on end the wind blew without pause. The chaplain abandoned his attempts at Sunday sermons on the deck, as his words, along with the pages from his Bible, were whipped away with the wind.

But tonight the sea glowed with phosphorescence and the wind had calmed. After so long with the rattles, whistles and clanging of the wind through the ship, Girardin found the breathlessness eerie. What did the ocean have in store for them? By now she had begun to think of the southern ocean as a living creature, a predator. She did not trust this offering of peace.

The atmosphere was loaded with electric fluid. Félix paced the deck alongside her, anxious that this calm did not bode well. Together they watched a thunderstorm gather on the horizon. Before long, a wind began to circle them, gusting first from the west and then the east. It ruffled the surface of the luminous water. It whispered and ran away. It teased and taunted them.

And then it came directly at them, blowing ghostly fireballs from the phosphoric waves. The wind grew bolder and the ship rolled in the swell. A sudden crack of lightning struck the ocean alongside them.

Girardin yelped in fright.

'Fire!' someone screamed. 'We've been hit!'

'It's St Elmo!' Armand cried.

Girardin looked up to see a blue fire at the top of the mast. It hissed like a cornered cat, back arched and hairs spiked along its back. The wind attacked with a shriek, extinguishing the ghoulish sparks by tearing the main topsail free of the mast. She saw the shredded canvas whipped into the air before being sucked down into the waves. A piece of shattered mast bounced upon the deck and hurtled towards them. She pulled Félix down as the splintered chunk sailed above their heads and crashed through the rail of the ship.

Captain d'Auribeau screeched commands and the sailors hauled on ropes. Waves flooded the deck. The ship tilted bow-down over the crest of a huge wave and a wall of water filled the sky. No sooner had the ship levelled out than it began to rise again, climbing the next gigantic wave. Girardin glimpsed the *Espérance* bob to the top of a wave, tiny and fragile against the immense sea, before falling away from sight.

A tide of sea water rushed around her, carrying pieces of the broken mast. One smashed into her knee, knocking her down. She slid along the deck towards the stern, unable to stop herself, just as the surgeon, Pierre Renard, leaped into the longboat.

She scrambled to her feet outside Labillardière's cabin. Félix caught up with her and they both tumbled inside.

'What are you doing in here?' roared Labillardière. He was cowering on his bed in the corner, still fully clothed and with a rug wrapped around him.

'Helping to protect the specimens.' Félix stepped nimbly out of the path of a small writing desk that slid across the floor.

'The specimens are all in the great cabin, where you should be!'

Girardin flattened herself against the wall as a chair sailed past her and smashed against the door.

The ship ached and moaned as if the wind and waves were tearing it apart. 'When will this end?' Girardin whispered.

Labillardière looked up at the barometer on his wall. 'The mercury has fallen by six lines.'

Girardin took this as a bad sign. She felt the ship ride the summit of another wave and then suddenly slip sideways, pitching her stomach. She covered her head, imagining a huge wave rearing over them.

A deathly clanging sounded against the hull.

'The Kraken!' she cried.

'The mizzen chains . . .' Labillardière said, before an almighty crash swallowed his words. The ship bucked as though it had struck a rock and threw them sprawling to the cabin floor. Water poured through the cracks in the panelling of the walls. All three ran for the door.

In the corridor she was hit by a foaming torrent rushing down from the topdeck. Animals screamed and Girardin felt her feet wash out from under her. Helpless, she rode the water, hitting the legs of wide-eyed calves and feeling the sharp hooves of the goats climb across her back. Salt water filled her nostrils and burned the back of her throat. She raised her head above the water for a mouthful of air before she hit the hull, trapping a kid goat behind her. It struggled to free itself and stamped on her injured knee in its escape.

She cried out at the burst of pain.

A chain of men began to pass buckets through the hatch to the deck. They needed help. She should help. Instead, she curled up tight, shivering as the cold water soaked through her clothes, her teeth rattling in her mouth. The ice water sloshed backwards and forwards, carrying straw and animal dung with it.

'The surgeon—has anyone seen the surgeon?' a voice called down the line of men swinging buckets to one another.

'Renard, the surgeon, is he here?' Lieutenant Rossel waded through the swamped deck.

Girardin struggled to her feet, balancing on her good leg. 'Check the longboats,' she called, grimacing against the pain in her knee. 'What has happened?'

'It's the General,' Rossel grunted.

Chapter 22

Eddystone Point, Van Diemen's Land, 20 April 1792

A NIGHT AND A DAY HAD PASSED SINCE THE STORM AND GIRARDIN was still forbidden to see the General. Renard had restricted his visitors. She made broth as instructed by the doctor for the General's breakfast, lunch and dinner, but she was not allowed to serve him. Renard delivered his meals. She realised she missed her time with him. One of the pleasures of her day was sitting with him while he took his breakfast. She missed watching him plot their course on the map with careful precision. Each day she could check for herself how far they had come. She liked to see the chronometer, the brass clock held in its wooden box, ticking the time in Paris like a heartbeat. It reminded her that her son was waiting for her on the other side of the world.

Renard assured her the General was recovering, but she wanted to see for herself that he was not grievously harmed by his fall. Surely his health would improve with the care and attention of those who loved him? She saw the barrel organ being splintered into kindling for the galley ovens. The General had been thrown against it in the storm and his ribs broken.

Her knee ached. It had swollen to twice its normal thickness and the cold had stiffened it, forcing her to walk with a swinging gait. The westerly gales continued to push them hard and fast towards Adventure Bay in Van Diemen's Land. The wind whistled in a constant whine and chilled her through. The old sailor, Armand, scared her with tales of the savages who threw rocks and spears at Marion du Fresne's ships and would not let them drop anchor. Their ship needed urgent repairs after the storm. What if they too were turned away?

If only she could speak with the General.

He would hate this enforced confinement. Each day without fail, he had taken a turn about the deck and loved to see the crew busy in their occupations. It was his motto: no man should be idle.

On the third day after his accident, she watched Renard leave the General's cabin to take his own lunch and she seized her chance. She had expected to find him confined to bed, but was relieved to see him at his desk, surrounded by his charts. He turned, smiled, and looked pleased to see her. And pleased to see the meat upon her tray.

'Thank the Lord above! No more soup. Renard must think me quite recovered.'

Girardin flushed.

The General rose with difficulty. It made her sad to see him so reduced, shuffling towards her with his hand clamped to his side. He looked his age and more. She turned to fill his brandy glass from the sideboard.

Behind her, the General set about cutting through the salt pork, wincing with every twist of his torso. His face was pale and droplets of sweat had formed along his upper lip. Girardin felt shame. She had defied Renard for selfish purposes and now she had caused the General harm. She went to him, reaching for his knife. 'Let me.'

The General flicked at Girardin's hands. 'Stop fussing. I do not need a nurse to cut my food for me.'

'The surgeon—' she began.

'Yes, the surgeon.' He nodded. 'He confines me to my cabin while our ship is slowly torn to pieces by this interminable wind, but he does not say that I should be treated as a child!'

She bit her lip, knowing his words were born of pain and frustration. She should not have come. A twinge stabbed her knee and she gripped the edge of the dining table.

The General looked into her face. 'You have been injured,' he said. 'Please sit.'

Girardin hesitated.

'Sit!'

She sank into a chair, easing her leg straight out in front of her. Together they listened to the whine of a fresh squall. She felt the ship tilt beneath her. The sensation was nauseating.

The General pushed his plate away, abandoning the stringy meat. 'We have travelled the whole breadth of New Holland in just three weeks,' he said. 'They have sighted the Eddystone this morning. We shall soon be in Van Diemen's Land.'

'What should we expect?' she asked. 'I mean, by way of resupply.'

The General winced, and pressed his hand to his ribs. 'Not much by way of trade. The natives here are reticent.' He paused. 'We know little of them.'

'What if we are chased away, not allowed to make our ships' repairs?'

'You think of Marion du Fresne?' He swallowed his brandy. 'Do not trouble yourself.'

Girardin chewed her lip.

They were interrupted by a messenger. 'A signal from the *Espérance*, sir. Captain Kermadec requests an audience with you.'

'What is the problem?'

'We are having difficulties locating Adventure Bay. He doubts our direction.'

The General muttered beneath his breath. He groaned and pushed himself upright. As Girardin rose to take his elbow, he slapped her hand away. He took a chart from his desk and pulled the cabin door open.

Girardin followed him to the quarterdeck, shivering and wishing she had thought to bring her greatcoat. Misty clouds touched the ocean and then swirled away like the legs of grey-stockinged ballerinas. If Van Diemen's Land was ahead, she could not see it. There was no sun, no horizon, no means to tell where they were in the world. The sea and sky were grey. Behind them she caught a glimpse of the Eddystone, a tower of rock stained white by the mess of birds. Albatross and gannets careened around it. This chimney of rock was their only point of reference, and the clouds dipped and swirled like a veil across it.

Lieutenant Rossel put down his spyglass. 'We thought we had Tasman Head a moment ago, sir.' Lieutenant Saint-Aignan held the logbook and compass while Captain d'Auribeau had the helm.

'Surely you capable men do not need the assistance of an injured old man to find your way?'

A gust of wind blasted through the ship. Ahead the mist lifted to reveal fluted cliffs soaring up into the cloud. Waves roared as they crashed against rocks and boomed in the sea caves. The veil of mist fell once again to conceal the treacherous coast.

'Adventure Bay lies ahead,' said Rossel with certainty. 'We have seen the passage.'

The signalman rushed up the steps of the quarterdeck. 'Sir! Captain Kermadec does not think this is Adventure Bay! We are east of the Eddystone.'

Captain d'Auribeau uttered a disparaging snort. 'He cannot read his maps. We are west of the Eddystone.'

The General took the logbook from Saint-Aignan. 'The last bearing had the Eddystone south of us at nineteen degrees to the east, not west. Kermadec is correct.' He raised an eyebrow to Captain d'Auribeau.

'The lieutenant may have written east, but he called the bearing to the west!' d'Auribeau snapped.

Saint-Aignan turned pink. He blinked rapidly. 'I—I misspoke, perhaps. I do not remember.'

'We are here,' the General interrupted, jabbing the map. 'South Cape.'

To Girardin, it seemed that the sea lifted them on ever-higher swells, ever closer to the obscured cliffs. The southerly blew hard behind them. The mist parted and Girardin saw the passage, an opening in the rock, perhaps the entrance to a bay, perhaps not. It was impossible to know what lay ahead.

Silence.

After so many weeks in violent storms, the soundlessness of the bay stuffed her ears with wool. It stole the words from men's lips.

The quiet bay was domed by mist, a massive cathedral vault that demanded hushed voices.

The plop of the lead line as it hit the water's surface broke the silence. The line reached the end of the reel with a snap. 'Still no bottom, sir!'

D'Auribeau ordered the longboats to row the *Recherche* deeper into the bay.

Girardin watched the men bend their backs to the oars and the rope between the ship and the boats grow taut. The thought of having to turn back out into the wind and waves if they could not find anchor here made her feel sick to her stomach. The *Espérance*, still under sail and catching the last of the breezes in the middle of the bay, sailed boldly past them. Girardin saw d'Auribeau snarl as her stern disappeared in the mist.

'Twenty-five fathoms! We have found the bottom!' A cheer rang out as the sounding was called.

'Too deep,' the General muttered. He winced and pressed a hand to his rib. 'Prepare the men to turn us about. We will have to resume our search for Adventure Bay.'

D'Auribeau cast a look at the darkening sky. 'But, sir, one more sounding, I entreat you!'

Girardin knew every man on board was wrung out and exhausted. Sailors sat on the spars above waiting for the order to furl the sails. The officers watched the General with anxious faces.

'Very well. Row us deeper.'

The *Recherche* inched forwards. From the bow, a sailor tossed the lead line and counted the knots on the rope as it slid through his hands. 'Fourteen fathoms!' he cried, reeling in the line. 'Fourteen fathoms and sandy bottom!'

A safe anchorage. Girardin pushed through to the bow. She couldn't quite believe it. The sailor showed her the tallow beneath the lead weight and she touched the grains of sand with her own fingers.

That night, Girardin lay in her hammock in utter stillness. For once her bed did not swing. The timbers did not creak and moan. Peace. Here they had found a bay where no European ship had ventured before. The thought was fantastical. What would her father think if he knew? She, Marie-Louise Girardin, the girl who was once forbidden to leave her father's house, had come all the way to the bottom corner of the world.

Chapter 23

Recherche Bay, Van Diemen's Land, 21 April 1792

AT DAYBREAK, GIRARDIN HAD HER FIRST GLIMPSE OF THE harbour they had named Recherche Bay. The trees reached out to her, reflected in the still waters of the bay and rising above a crisp white rim of beach. After so long without the colour green she gorged herself, delighting in the myriad shades of the foliage. Shades of green tinged with grey and blue and ochre and crimson, so unfamiliar, so different from the uniform green of home. Here, even the water was another shade of dark green. She watched a ripple distort the reflection of the trees. She breathed deep, taking in the scent of wet leaves and forest floor, banishing the salt. The strangeness was enticing and terrifying in equal measure. Green was the colour of spring, of new life, hope. But it was also the colour of fear.

At the bow, she caught sight of Raoul among the queue of men at the seats of ease, those crude planks of wood extending from the bow and serving as a lavatory. No other sailor gave her the creeping shivers like this man. She did not trust his knowing smirk. In truth, he frightened her.

The General came up silently behind her and placed a hand on her shoulder. She started in surprise. She was aware of the crew watching them. Of Raoul. She heard the men laughing and turned her face to the shore.

'Like stone columns in a cathedral, don't you think? So straight and true, and reaching up to impossible heights,' he said.

The trunks of the tallest trees were bare, thrusting confidently skywards, their tops lost in the morning mist. These trees looked like no cathedral she had been in. Girardin remembered the cathedral of Saint-Louis at Versailles, with its stern row of arching columns. Many years ago she had walked beneath them, about to marry Etienne Lesserteur, in a dress hastily made to disguise her belly.

'An amphitheatre of nature,' the General said. 'Here at the ends of the earth, in this solitary harbour, we could be separated from the rest of the universe.' He spread his arms wide and Girardin was relieved to feel his hand lifted from her shoulder.

When she glanced towards the bow, she saw Raoul watching her from beneath his black fringe. She stepped back, hoping to make her escape below, but Labillardière appeared from behind, trapping her between him and the General.

'Have you ever seen trees such as these?' the General asked him. 'Astonishing. They must be a hundred and fifty feet high!'

'I estimate fifty metres in height,' Labillardière agreed. 'Those trees look like myrtle but are a prodigious size. These are ancient forests, the like of which we no longer encounter in Europe.'

'Raw nature in all its vigour and yet at the same time wasting away. This is life! See there, trees as old as the world, loosened by age from their roots, covered in blankets of moss and supported by the shoulders of the strong young trees beside them.'

Girardin wondered if the General imagined his captains at his side.

'Some saplings are only waiting for the oldest trees to fall,' Labillardière said ominously. Girardin pictured Captain d'Auribeau lurking in the shadow of a tall tree.

'Have you ever been to the gardens of Versailles?' the General asked Labillardière.

At the mention of the gardens, Girardin tensed.

'Twice,' Labillardière replied, 'but I shall never return. They have destroyed the botanical gardens! The glasshouses, the collections, all ripped out to make way for the Queen's latest fancy. An English picturesque garden! The loss to scientific inquiry is unsupportable.'

'I used to think the gardens so beautiful. The avenues, the bosques, the grand canal. Hedges in fantastic patterns. Topiary in impossible shapes. But what we are missing! Raw nature offers the imagination something more imposing, more vivid than the pretty embellishments practised by civilised man. Don't you agree?'

'The royal gardens are nature bound and dominated by man,' murmured Labillardière.

Girardin pictured herself removing the crumbling bricks of the garden wall. She remembered her first look at that ordered world of clipped green lawns. So different from this dark tangle of wild forest. Here each tree grew over the top of another, crowded together, their limbs entwined. The early sun caught the naked branches at the tops of the trees, exposing their sensuous bends like dancers' arms in an exotic painting. Here there was energy, movement, but no respite, no space. She had the sense that if she were to walk in this forest she would be swallowed up.

In the bow, she saw Raoul had taken his place at the seats of ease. She edged closer to the General, hiding from his view.

The General sighed. 'It seems a pity that it will be necessary for us to let the first axe fall in this forest.'

'These trees will make excellent masts,' Labillardière noted.

'Our ship has taken a battering. It may take us weeks to repair her. No man will be idle, be they carpenters or sailors. There is much to be done.'

Girardin felt Labillardière stiffen at her side.

'It is imperative that we have time to collect specimens and complete our taxonomical investigations,' he said. 'This species will likely be of great economic importance to France.'

The General held up his hand placatingly. 'You will have time to go ashore to do your botanising. But the needs of the ship come first.'

'And what of the needs of your geographers, Citizen d'Entrecasteaux?' Labillardière flicked his hand at Lieutenant Rossel and Beautemps-Beaupré, who were overseeing the lowering of the yawl. The boat was being loaded with equipment to set up an observatory on land. 'I see they have priority.'

'They go to witness the eclipse of Jupiter's moons. This is a unique opportunity to make measures of longitude.' The General's tone grew sharp. 'There will be sufficient time for your excursions.'

Girardin sidled out from between them.

'But no men left to help with our surveys.' The naturalist's voice was sour.

'Monsieur Labillardière, you may apply for volunteers to assist you in your endeavours as before. If no man chooses to accompany you, then that is perhaps more your fault than mine.' The General took his leave with a curt nod of his head.

Girardin felt her buttocks press against a coil of rope. She had backed herself against the mast. The General passed by without a look in her direction. Labillardière drummed his fingers on the taffrail and watched Lieutenant Rossel as he lowered more of the observatory equipment into the ship's boat. On shore, tents were being erected, a forge built and washing lines strung along the beach. Soon the men would be busy with repairs. Labillardière slammed his fist on the rail and turned. Too late, she dropped her eyes to avoid his gaze.

'Steward, I trust you are not afraid of adventure.'

Girardin opened her mouth to protest but no sound emerged.

'Good. We will journey to the interior just as soon as a boat becomes available.'

Accompany the naturalists into that forest? No, she couldn't do it. What if they became lost and could not find their way back to the ship? Who knew what creatures might live among those tangled roots?

Labillardière left her before she found her voice.

She would have to make her excuses. She almost called out to bring him back, but she dared not draw attention to herself.

'You won't catch me volunteerin' to go shooting birds and chopping trees,' Armand leaned out from the ratlines above her head with a bucket of tar in his hand. He raised his eyelids to show the whites of his eyes. 'Savages.'

Girardin shook her head. She promised herself she wouldn't listen to any more of his doom tales. He had scared her witless on the crossing of the southern ocean. Last night he had told her of Marion du Fresne being killed and eaten by the New Zealanders.

'Scared of the savages?' a voice called out from the bow of the boat. 'Or scared to get out from beneath the General's nightshirt?'

Girardin turned to see Raoul wipe his arse with the ragged end of a knotted rope. She snapped her head away. She heard the men around him laugh.

She stood her ground as Raoul stalked towards her. 'With your fresh face and fine wrists—' he snatched one of her hands '—you're nothing but a girl.'

'You can't let him talk to you like that, lad!' Armand growled.

Girardin tugged her hand free.

'In my day, no man would take an insult like that to his honour. Defend your reputation, boy!' Armand called down.

Raoul laughed. 'This wet chicken? There is no way he would fight me!'

The old sailor scaled down the ratlines and slammed his tin of tar on the deck. 'He is calling you a coward. I've run men through for less than that!' Armand pushed his face into hers. His blue-filmed eyes were shining. 'This rascal needs to be taught some manners. Challenge him to a duel!'

'What say you, *Louis*?' Raoul took the frayed rope from the ablutions pail and slapped it against her chest. A fleck of soiled water landed on her lip. Disgust flooded through her.

She spat on his foot. 'Tomorrow,' she said without thinking. Anger pulsed in her throat.

Armand crowed with delight. 'I'll make the arrangements! Get yourself a second, Monsieur Raoul. Tomorrow at first light we will meet on this savage shore!'

Chapter 24

Port du Nord, Recherche Bay

GIRARDIN PACED OUTSIDE THE CHAPLAIN'S DOOR. IT WAS DARK, but she saw his lantern light glow beneath it. The corridor was empty. She took a deep breath and tapped on the door. She heard a chair drawn back inside and feet shuffling towards her. When Ventenat drew open the door she saw him blink with surprise. He wore a nightcap over his bald head and a blanket wrapped around his shoulders. She stepped into his cabin before she could lose her nerve.

'Forgive my intrusion,' she mumbled. Her eyes darted around the room. Beside the desk was a large dresser with a drawer pulled open. Rows of insects were splayed and pinned to a board, each one pierced through the heart. She stared at the tiny shining daggers. Ventenat nudged the drawer shut when he saw her looking.

'An interest of mine,' he said with a small chuckle. 'No need to tell Labillardière.' He clasped his hands in front of him and inclined his head. 'How can I be of assistance?'

Her mouth was dry. She stared at him. Could he help her? She touched her chest, wondering how easily a rapier might run her through.

'Does God forgive?' she blurted.

'Have you come for confession?' He gestured for her to sit, but she could not.

'No, not confession.' She wrung her hands. 'When I die, will my death be payment enough for my sins?' Her voice was high and strained. She saw the confusion on the chaplain's face. 'Will those I love be safe from His condemnation?'

'If you will confess—' he began.

'I cannot.' This had been a mistake. What had she thought he would say? That if she went to her death willingly God would be assuaged, that what she had done would be forgiven? She fled from the room.

Of her own eternal damnation she was assured, but now she was thinking of her son. She had left him in the care of the Church. Her hands were shaking when she put her key to her cabin door. The crew were already in their hammocks and she did not linger. She bolted the door behind her.

What have I to leave him? she wondered, opening her chest of belongings. A spare tunic, a heel of soap, a purloined bandage. Perhaps the knife she had stolen and strapped to her thigh. Nothing worthy of sending home to her people. Nothing that spoke to her son. *How will he ever know that I meant to return for him?*

She searched for her journal. At first she had hidden it in the grain, attached to a piece of string, but the mealworm had begun to nibble at the edges of the pages. Then she had prised a floorboard loose to make a secret cache. But fearing this hiding place would be too easily found, she had placed the journal in a tin box and buried it deep within a chest of tea leaves.

For all this preoccupation with the safety of her journal, she had yet to write another word on its waiting pages.

Now, she set it upon her desk and took up a quill.

To my dearest son,

Forgive me, I am not a brave woman. I have done a foolish thing. Many foolish things. Tomorrow I face my death and I do not go easily to it. They tell me to set my affairs in order, and I must explain why I have abandoned you.

Her hand stalled. How could she explain? What was done was done. No good would come of writing it down for others to find. She closed the journal.

Sleep, when it finally came to her, was fitful and brief. In the darkness of her waking hours she thought of the skewered beetles in the chaplain's drawer. She touched a point on her breastbone and remembered the time when a stick had pierced her skin there and left a bruise that had stayed with her for weeks. She had not thought about that day for many years. She huddled in her hammock with her blanket wrapped around her and kneaded the imaginary lump with her fingers.

'No, you hold it like this.' The boy snatched the yew stick out of Marie-Louise's hand and wobbled it between his thumb and forefinger. 'Balance it like you are presenting a rose to your mother, not gripping an axe to chop down a tree.' He folded her hand around the stick.

'Put your feet like this.'

'You look like a rooster.'

The boy ignored her. 'Always salute your opponent.'

She raised the yew sword to her forehead and curled her left arm behind her even though she felt like a teapot.

'En garde.'

They held their stick swords aloft, facing each other. The boy shuffled forwards and Marie-Louise burst into laughter.

'Look, if you can't take this seriously, I'm not going to teach you anymore!' The boy slapped the stick against a copper leopard. The sound reverberated around the bosquet and Marie-Louise snapped her head back, listening for her father. But the high trellis walls, dense with creepers and moss, kept them safe in the labyrinth.

'Sshh.' Marie-Louise put a finger to her lips.

The boy lunged forwards and Marie-Louise squealed, forgetting what he had told her about how to parry and riposte. The point of his stick struck her chest above her heart.

'You see,' he said. 'These lessons could save your life.'

Chapter 25

The first knock at her door was timid.

'Steward!' hissed a voice.

She opened the door to the gap-toothed smile of her second. He had combed his hair, shaved his whiskers and dressed in his best coat for the occasion, and had a sword hanging at each hip. She pressed her hand to her breastbone. Would she remember what she had once been taught? This was madness. How could two children playing with sticks help her now?

Slowly, she pulled on her frockcoat over her best white shirt. Armand put a finger to his lips and she followed him silently towards the deck. The air was crisp and the night retreating. She walked as though condemned. Rumours had spread and men nodded in silent tribute as she passed. She could not meet their eye. The custom of duelling may have been outlawed, but here the tradition was still respected. Yesterday, Girardin had dismissed the thought of going to the General—far better to die in this charade of honour than to live with the consequences of her shame. There would be no peace for her if she did not meet Raoul on this beach. And yet as she passed the copper urinal, she rapped her knuckles against it, setting it ringing, almost as if she hoped to draw the attention of the officer of the watch. Armand whirled around, listening. They waited, but no officer appeared. Perhaps his silence had been bought, she thought glumly.

The boats were lowered at the side of the ship and Raoul was already waiting, his face shadowed by his hat, his cloak pulled high. Girardin faltered, her heart falling into her stomach. She wiped her palms on her coat and tried to be calm. Do not shame yourself, she thought. Meet your death with dignity.

In the boat, she recognised the butcher and the blacksmith, a big German named Fitz. Armand nudged her with his elbow. She climbed down the rope ladder and then clung for a moment, her fingers curled around the rough coir.

'Hurry up,' hissed Armand, and as she stepped down, the boat lurched beneath her feet.

Armand unhitched the rope swiftly—too swiftly. She wondered where his squalling monkey was today. Armand had not yet begun to climb down the ladder. It occurred to her that she could still scramble back up and seek the General's protection. But even as she thought it she knew such action would condemn her. She looked up again. Armand seemed to be waiting; had he had a change of heart? Suddenly a figure appeared beside him. Girardin glimpsed a uniform beneath a dark coat and her heart squeezed hard. Am I saved?

'You took your time,' Armand growled. Both men climbed down into the boat.

The midshipman turned and flashed a smile at Girardin. 'Never one to miss a duel!' It was Mérite de Saint-Méry. He wore no wig and his brown hair had fallen loose of its braid. She remembered him running away from Raoul on the day they crossed the line. A hot-headed boy by all accounts. Not her saviour.

'Quiet! Do you want to get us all court-martialled?' Raoul spoke for the first time. She was pleased to hear the strain in his voice. She couldn't see his face in the darkness. The two opponents sat at either end of the boat. She kept her eyes fixed on the bald head of the butcher as he swung backwards and forwards on the end of the oar. Her stomach surged and swelled even though the sea was calm. With only two men rowing it seemed to take an age for the dark shore to inch towards them.

Be strong, her mother whispered in her thoughts. Girardin remembered her mother kneeling beside her when she was a young child, consoling her. 'Your father named you Marie-Louise, but I gave you your middle name,' her mother had said, dabbing salve onto the welts on the back of her legs. 'Victoire. It was your grandmother's name. She was a survivor and you will be too. Always remember that.' But Girardin did not feel victorious now. She felt like she was being rowed across the water to her death.

The gentle waves parted with a sigh as the bow of the boat wedged itself into the sand. Climbing out, Girardin felt the cold water bite at her ankles. She staggered onto the beach. Onto an exotic land. She had no time to marvel at it. All six of them tugged on the ropes to haul the boat safely onto shore. The grains of sand beneath her feet were the colour of ground-up bones.

They followed the blacksmith to his forge. Armand drew Girardin to one side, rubbing his gnarled hands together in a motion that was either nervous or excited, she could not tell.

'Don't worry, lad,' he said out of the corner of his mouth, his clay pipe clamped between the gap in his teeth. 'If ye should stumble, I'll be here to run the rascal through!'

'My thanks,' Girardin muttered wryly.

He dropped into an elaborate bow before gravely removing her coat and folding it across his arm. The hairs on her nape pricked as though cold fingers had circled around her neck. Armand handed her the sword. She took the hilt and balanced it between her thumb and forefinger just as the boy in the gardens of Versailles had shown her. Her hand trembled and the vibration travelled to the tip of the fine blade, causing it to arc wildly. Armand wrapped his hand around her wrist and pointed the blade away.

'Courage, lad, courage.' He thumped a fist to his heart.

Mérite had marked the en-garde lines into the sand. 'We don't have much time. We have to return to the ship before the change of watch and it's almost dawn.'

Girardin looked up to the spreading glow along the horizon. The early rays caught the edges of the purple clouds and turned them flaming orange. A fittingly dramatic sky under which to die, she thought.

'Gentlemen . . .' Mérite cleared his throat. 'We stand here today to settle a dispute of honour in the noblest tradition. Monsieur Louis Girardin desires reparation from Monsieur Ange Raoul. Let the matter be settled on first blood. Salute.'

Girardin raised her sword to her forehead and looked back down to her feet. *Put your ankles together*, the boy had said. *Point your right foot to the north and your other to the west.* Girardin held her lips clamped into a tight white line. Go to your death well, she thought.

'Come now,' Raoul purred. 'I have no desire to maim one of our fairer sex. One word and we can end this now. Let us kiss and make up.' He pursed his fleshy lips.

Blood pumped into her face. Beside her, Armand howled curses. 'Don't let the bully win!' Girardin only dimly heard him above the pounding in her ears. Ange Raoul stood before her in the half-light, head thrown back in laughter, a shadow man, a faceless man. He could've been any one of the men who had betrayed her.

'En garde!' Mérite cried, impatient to begin.

She moved her left foot back and sank her weight down. Now that the moment had come she felt steady. Her breathing slowed, and she felt the weight of the sword in her hand. *Balance it like you are presenting a rose to your mother*, the boy had said. This is for you, Maman, Girardin thought as she lunged.

Raoul parried her thrust easily with a flick of his wrist and a shriek of steel against steel. He did not return the strike. Instead, she saw the glint of his teeth. 'You are content to die for your secret then,' he whispered.

Girardin scuttled back on the sand. Raoul danced forwards with his sword outstretched and Girardin forgot her stance and fled backwards into the darkness of the trees.

'Ha, you see? A coward!' Raoul called after her.

Girardin felt the strength of the trunk against her back. It was smooth and stripped of bark. It was solid and would not bend. She turned her head and saw the face of a child. A dark child with hooded eyes. They shared a look of shock. Girardin blinked and looked again but the girl had disappeared without a sound, as though she had never been there. A girl about the same age as I was, she thought, playing in the garden of Versailles.

Pushing herself from the tree, Girardin walked slowly back into the open. *Imagine you hold a stick instead of a sword in your hand*, a voice told her. *Imagine you are back in the labyrinth at Versailles. Remember yourself as you were then. You were once brave. Remember, remember.* This voice seemed to think she could fight.

She raised her sword in her right hand and curled her left beside her ear.

Raoul assumed the stance without a word. He leapt, striking the sand with his heel, bouncing forwards and then back. Girardin matched his feint. Both swords flicked out like lizards' tongues tasting the air, but they did not touch.

Raoul advanced again and the swords clashed. Parrying his strikes was instinctual, but she could not return his attack; he sliced her sword away before she could lunge. *Too slow*, the boy's voice screamed in her ear. *Remember the positions, have your hand ready to strike when you parry his blade!* Instead she slashed at his rapier, shuffling backwards on the sand, aware that Raoul was smiling as he pushed her towards the trees. He was playing with her, she realised, like a cat torturing a mouse.

Girardin ducked sideways and spun out of his range. This was foolish. How could she compete with a trained swordsman? A girl who had learned to duel by playing with sticks in the garden of the King! Every fibre of her body screamed for her to run. She glanced into the dark forest and wondered how far she would get climbing through the tangled limbs before he tracked her down.

Taut-lipped, she raised her sword once again.

Raoul tossed back his fringe, his gaze intent, hungry. 'Admit your secret and this foolishness can be over.'

She should throw down her sword, admit her sex, plead for their silence. At least then she might survive long enough to return to her son. Yet she did not speak.

Raoul launched his attack, driving her backwards until her spine pressed against a tree. Their blades slid together, hilt to hilt. His face close to hers. 'Don't make me hurt you, Marie-Louise Girardin.'

Her head jerked back. He knew her name. How could he know her name? It was a guess, that was all—he could not know. He meant to frighten her.

'I am Louis Girardin.'

'Such dedication to your disguise.' He smirked. 'Our mutual friend would be impressed.'

Her eyes widened. He knew someone from her past. She forced herself to look at his features—the cleft of his chin, the full lips, the long, dark eyelashes—but her memory failed her. She did not recognise this man.

'We could come to an agreement,' he suggested, raising one eyebrow, inclining his head towards the men. 'To both our benefit.'

He meant to keep her as his whore and sell her to each of the men in turn. Her breath was rapid. She saw the heavy shapes of the butcher and the smith and imagined them pinning her to the sand.

She twisted away from him. 'No.'

Raoul renewed his attack, backing her towards the sea. Her wrist ached with the effort of absorbing each blow. Her swollen knee began to throb. I could end this, she thought. I could still survive this day if I submit to him. If I let him be my master.

In that moment, Girardin saw her chance. She stepped quickly to the left and Raoul's blade whizzed past her chest. She stood tall, no longer backing away, and stretched out her arm. Raoul reared back in surprise. She saw the flare of his nostrils as his head tilted back. The tip of her sword licked at his chin. A streak of red bloomed on his shirt.

'First blood!' Armand cried. Girardin turned to see him leaping about, hands raised over his head like his monkey. Dazed, she felt the sounds of the alien forest rush back into her head. She heard Mérite declare the duel over. Somehow, by some miracle, she had survived. Her head slumped forwards.

'Watch out!' Mérite cried.

She threw her arm up to shield herself as Raoul lashed out. No longer laughing, his face was brutal. She saw the flash of silver as the blade swept downwards across her upper arm. Blood sprayed, splattering the sand. Girardin sank to her knees, gasping as she landed. Strangely, she felt no pain in her arm, only in her knee.

Mérite rushed to her side and pressed a hand to her wound. She saw blood gush between his fingers. Armand charged at Raoul and knocked his sword from his hand.

Mérite whispered, 'We'll get you to the surgeon.'

'No,' she gasped. 'Félix, take me to Félix.' Then the pain tore across her arm and she began to scream.

Chapter 26

'What have you done?' Félix hissed at Mérite. Girardin was draped across his shoulder. 'How could you let this happen?'

Mérite had bound her arm with fabric torn from his own shirt. 'Can you fix the wound?'

Together they carried Girardin between them. Her head lolled forwards. She clenched her teeth against the pain. At the door of Labillardière's cabin she heard Félix send Mérite away before he dragged her inside.

'Quick, he has lost a lot of blood.'

Girardin noticed the whole right side of her shirt and trousers were soaked in blood.

Labillardière demanded to know what had happened.

'A duel,' Félix spat in distaste. He rounded on her. 'Do you know how foolish you have been? Do you know how many men die in useless contests of honour?'

'I think he is well aware,' Labillardière said, pulling Félix out of the way. He removed the bandage Mérite had tied around her wound. 'We must take your shirt off.'

'No!' Girardin pleaded, her mouth dry. 'Cut the sleeve.'

Labillardière reached to take a blade from his desk. With two neat incisions, he tore the sleeve away from her arm. Looking down, she saw the wound gape open. It didn't look real, this pulpy mess with dark oozing liquid, the flesh so vivid red. The workings of her body were laid bare. She could see through to the bone. This is all we are, she thought while panting at the pain, no different from any other beast. She closed her eyes. Gently, Labillardière's fingers pressed the sides of the wound together. She cried out. The pain felt like a jabbing knife.

'It will have to be stitched.'

Girardin's eyes snapped open. She saw a puckered water vessel made of dried kelp on Labillardière's desk. The seaweed had been punctured by some sharp implement and sewn into a carrier. The folds had hardened into ridges. She groaned.

'Here, take this.' He thrust a bottle of brandy beneath her nose. 'Drink one mouthful now and two after.'

Labillardière gathered a long needle and some waxed thread. 'Look away,' he commanded.

Girardin felt his fingers gently pressing her skin and then she jerked forwards at the first bite of the needle. Labillardière pushed her back against the wall. She gritted her teeth and thought of the white-hot pain of childbirth. The pain could not be worse than that and she had survived. She had survived a lot of things.

When he was finished, he handed her the bottle again and she gulped and coughed. She felt tears leak from the corners of her eyes without permission. She cradled her arm. She was safe now, she told herself. She had survived.

Labillardière lifted her thin arm and wrapped a bandage around the wound. 'It will scar.'

Girardin lay back on the bed. The brandy burned in her stomach and her arm throbbed. Beads of sweat dripped from her forehead. Labillardière stood with his arms folded, staring down at her.

'You won't say anything?' she grunted, breathing heavily.

'Duelling is punishable by court martial.'

She closed her eyes.

She woke hours later with a sharp stench in her nostrils. Confused, she registered the strange surroundings, feeling the ache in her arm, and remembered she was in Labillardière's cabin. The botanist had gone but Félix sat at his desk, pouring yellow powder into small vials. Girardin struggled upright. 'What is that smell?'

Félix turned towards her in surprise. 'You're awake. Good. It's seal excrement.'

'What are you doing?'

'The pigments can be used in painting. Labillardière's idea.'

'It stinks.'

'Indeed, that's why I'm doing it here in his cabin and not mine.' Félix smiled. 'How are you feeling?'

'Terrible.'

'Naturally.'

Suddenly she remembered her duties. 'What time is it?' Girardin swung her legs over the side of the bed. 'The General's meals!'

'All taken care of,' Félix said, pushing her back down on the bunk. 'We have told him you are ill with fever.'

Girardin wiped sweat from her brow. The pain eased when she raised her arm. She lay back and let the ship rock her gently from side to side.

Into the World

Waking some time later, she heard voices arguing in whispers. 'We cannot leave her here. One of us will have to stay.'

In her groggy state, Girardin thought they had said 'her'.

Labillardière continued. 'I cannot pass up this opportunity to go ashore. You will have to be the one to stay. I will be gone for five days, maybe more.'

Félix mumbled something that she couldn't hear.

'Go plant a garden, then! Always blathering about your precious collections of seeds—ask if you may take the steward for an assistant.'

'Won't she need the dressing changed?' Félix asked.

That time she was sure Félix had said 'she'.

Girardin felt an urgent need to urinate. She had to return to her cabin. Getting unsteadily to her feet, she launched herself at the door before either man could stop her.

Chapter 27

THE MORNING WAS GENTLE AND THE WATER PLACID BENEATH the rowers' oars as Girardin returned to shore. On her lap she carried a bag of laundry, hoping to find a private moment to wash her bloodied trousers in the sea. The shirt she had worn was ruined, already torn up into bandages. A week had passed since the duel and her wound still ached, but the seepage was mostly clear and free of blood and there was no sign of infection.

Beside her, Félix held his satchel of seeds on his knees. His gardening implements were stowed between their feet. Félix had treated her no differently after she left Labillardière's cabin, and she began to wonder if she had imagined the words between the naturalists, imagined they had guessed her sex. Perhaps her fevered state had made her paranoid. Perhaps. When Félix asked her to help him plant his garden she had not hesitated. She wanted to repay him for the friendship he had shown her.

A large bird with a long curling neck and black plumage glided beside them, keeping pace with the boat. It looked identical to the white swans that had graced the canals at Versailles, but here at the bottom of the world everything was the opposite. Black instead of white. She watched it turn towards their boat, dip its regal orange beak and stare at her, before a loud boom shattered the morning stillness. She jerked back in her seat, knocking her bad arm against Félix.

Joannet stood in the longboat from the *Espérance* with a musket raised. The swan bobbed in a pool of spreading blood.

As the boat drew closer to the shore, she could hear the blacksmith at the forge and she scanned the men at work along the beach. Thankfully, Raoul was not among them. He knew her name. As impossible as it seemed, he knew her. His smugness made sense to her now. She had scoured her memories, turning them over and over. Had he seen her at Etienne's café? But that was so long ago, why would he remember her? Then after Etienne died she had rarely appeared in public. Had she met him at the salon of Sophie de Condorcet, perhaps? But what would a sailor in the King's navy be doing at a meeting of revolutionaries? At her father's house, then? Had he once known Jean Girardin?

Regardless of how he knew her name, his face that day had told her everything she needed to know. She had shamed him. What had begun as a game for him, taunting her for his amusement, had now become a matter of retribution. She would need to be more wary than ever before.

Coming into shore, she heard the thudding of an axe, the rhythmic screeching of the saw. Over in the laundry yards, the men were standing naked in the waves, singing as they scrubbed themselves clean. Who would be next to challenge her? she wondered. Would her defiance be enough?

As she stepped onto this beach for a second time, the sand squeaked beneath her feet. Before, she had not noticed this strange squawking when she walked. She knelt and dug her fingers into the fine white sand, wondering at the life of each grain, where it had come from and what tides had carried it to this shore.

Her previous landfalls at the ports of Santa Cruz and Cape Town had not prepared her for this moment. Here there was no reassuring mark of a European hand: no wharves, no homes, no streets, no order that she recognised—only the wall of forest, looking down on her.

At a shout behind her, she turned to see a gigantic tree felled. The vibration as it struck the earth travelled through all the bones of her body.

Ahead, Félix had disappeared into the undergrowth.

'Wait!' she called, hurrying after him.

Here the forest seemed less dark than down by the forge, the trees less thick around the middle, their roots less sprawling. The forest floor was dry and patterned with long thin leaves in colours of peach and apricot. A strong scent filled her nose, like walking into a perfumerie. It was so different from anything she had experienced before. The hard leaves scratched against her as she followed after Félix.

'Watch out for snakes,' he said over his shoulder. She froze. Strewn around her were thin branches and long strips of bark curled across the ground. She placed her feet cautiously, flinching at every crackle beneath the dried leaves.

High overhead a creature screamed. Girardin twirled about, searching for the source of the fearful noise. Its cry leaped through the branches, never staying still long enough for her to see what manner of creature made the harsh call. Sometimes ahead, sometimes behind, the creature stayed with them as they walked, while Girardin tried not to imagine talons sinking into the flesh of her shoulders.

It was a relief to finally reach the clearing Félix had made for his garden. Girardin threw her bag of laundry to the ground. He had cleared an area of roughly twenty feet long and wide, scraping the dry topsoil, leaves and small plants to the sides. She dug her toe into the hard clay base. 'You mean to get vegetables to grow in this?' she said incredulously.

Félix looked miffed. 'I am the top student of the Jardin le Roi, recommended by André Thouin himself. I can make a garden anywhere.'

She screwed up her nose doubtfully and spat into the dust.

But when Félix picked up his hoe and sank it into the dry earth, she did too. Together they set about loosening the soil. Each time she hit a hard patch of earth the vibration tore at the stitches in her arm. Soon, she was sweating hard despite the cool air.

By the afternoon they had separated the garden into four beds, and her sleeve was now soaked with fresh blood.

As Félix sprinkled his chervil, parsley and chicory seeds into the plots, Girardin stood back and wiped the sweat from her forehead. She was glad to help him. If he knew she was a woman, he gave no sign. Even alone in the forest with him, she felt safe.

Behind her, she heard the thump of footsteps. Quickly, Girardin brought her hoe in front of her. A fern frond shook. She ducked down and saw a, thick-furred animal watching her, its nostrils quivering in its pointed face. It was the size of a small dog, but it reminded her of a squirrel with its small chest, forearms and large round end. Suddenly it bounced. She fell back, amazed to see the creature spring from its cord-like tail. Each quick hop sounded like a heavy man's footfall. She stood up, about to call out to Félix, when another bounding creature crashed into the back of the first, clutching it beneath its arms. The male began thrusting with its strong hind limbs. Girardin covered her mouth. The thrusting continued, with the female looking warily at Girardin, holding her gaze.

She turned to Félix. She knew he would be excited to see these unusual creatures. He was bent over his plot, scattering potato seeds. Beside her, the thrusting continued. Tiny black fingers dug into the fur of the female, holding her firm. Girardin saw Félix stand and brush the dirt from his hands. She walked towards him and said nothing.

When they returned to shore to meet the boat later that afternoon, the beach was deserted. The forge was still. The carpenters and the laundrymen had already returned to the ship. Only two figures were waiting on the sand. As they drew closer she was surprised to see Labillardière and Ventenat returned from their explorations. Ventenat sat among the bags of plant specimens, his clothes unkempt and dirty, scratching at red welts on his face and arms. He looked up and grimaced at Girardin, and she noticed one of his teeth was missing.

'What happened to you?' she asked.

Labillardière answered for him. 'He fell into an ants' nest.'

'They were very large ants,' said Ventenat.

A light rain began to fall. Girardin walked down to the water's edge and crouched in the shallows. She splashed salt water over the fresh blood on her sleeve and clenched her jaw against the sting. The skin had swelled and closed around the stitches and she would have to ask Labillardière to cut them free. She took to the bloodstains in her clothing with soap and a stiff-bristled brush. In the failing light she couldn't tell if it made any difference. Perhaps the stain, like her scar, would stay with her as a mark of remembrance. A reminder of what she had overcome.

Looking up, she saw lanterns floating across the still water, solemn beacons in the grey mist. The sailors were rowing out to collect them.

'At last!' Ventenat stood up and stamped his feet to warm himself.

Behind them, a party of officers emerged from the bush with Captain d'Auribeau at their head. She quickly wrung her blood-stained trousers and returned them to her bag. The officers stood together in neat formation, spaced as regularly as the gold buttons on their blue coats. Despite the dense bush they had pushed through, their white breeches were clean and their tricorn hats firmly placed. Girardin recognised the observatory trio, Rossel, Saint-Aignan and Beautemps-Beaupré. Standing in the rear was the midshipman Mérite. She hadn't seen him since the duel. Protectively, she crossed her arms, covering her wound with her palm.

The naturalists sprawled on the beach, their clothing smeared with dirt, their shirts untucked. She inched towards them.

Labillardière called to Rossel, 'I hear you failed to get your instruments ready in time to see the eclipse of Jupiter's satellites.'

The group ignored his taunt.

'Shame. Such a rare phenomenon. One would have thought it worthy of better preparation.'

'The weather was cloudy,' snapped Rossel.

Girardin helped the naturalists gather up their collections and move to greet the boat as it landed. She did not look at Mérite.

'Not so fast,' d'Auribeau called out. 'Officers have right of passage before civilians.'

'We were here first,' Labillardière exclaimed.

'Shame,' replied d'Auribeau, 'hope your wait was not too long.'

'You know very well that we have been on an arduous trek for many days with poor provisions while you and your officers have dined on freshly caught fish and the sea parsley that we have collected for you!'

'No need to lose your temper with me, Monsieur. It is the natural order of things that needs to be upheld. Where would we be if our betters were not afforded the privileges that their rank demands?'

'We would have revolution, Citizen d'Auribeau!'

The word churned her stomach. There was no escape from it, she thought, watching the two men face off. Even here, so many miles from home, the revolution had followed them.

'On this ship naval discipline must prevail, not your revolutionary fantasies, Monsieur Labillardière.' D'Auribeau pushed past the naturalist.

The officers began to board the pinnace and she stepped back to let them pass. Only Beautemps-Beaupré had the good grace to look ashamed.

A hand clasped her elbow and Mérite pulled her to one side. 'I am relieved to see you recovered,' he said in a low voice.

He searched her face intently. She was close enough to see the beginnings of a moustache growing above his top lip. She made no reply.

'Word has spread and your bravery is known. Raoul has accepted defeat. Do not expect harm from him.'

She saw the earnest look on his young face. My God, he believed it.

'I hope our General would not hear of this,' he paused, his voice dropping lower still. 'Of my part in this incident.'

She shook her elbow free. His concern was not for her but for his own career. She saw Félix watching them, alert.

'Your boat is leaving,' she said.

'You can come with us.'

'There are injured men here.' She pointed to the chaplain, whose lip had swelled to twice its natural size.

Mérite glanced at d'Auribeau and looked pained. His face told her he would not disobey.

She turned her back on him.

Girardin sank down to her haunches alongside the naturalists as they sat among their collections, the rain falling on their shoulders. The boat launched and she watched the dark shapes of the officers' tricorn hats vanish into the mist. She felt her flare of temper slowly dampen.

'It won't be long,' Félix said, nodding to himself.

But hours passed and there was still no sign of a return boat. Once again, her swollen knee had stiffened in the cold. Her arm throbbed. Behind her, Labillardière paced the shore and cursed d'Auribeau for holding the sailors back from returning to collect them.

As the rain grew heavier, Girardin helped the men drag their bags and bundles into the base of a burnt-out tree. Inside she found it larger than it looked, at least four feet wide with the remains of a cooking fire at the centre. She helped Labillardière urge it into life.

Félix made fire brands to signal the ship.

'It is no use, they mean to keep us here overnight for our impertinence,' said Labillardière.

'Your impertinence,' Félix said forlornly, waving the brand above his head.

Girardin moved closer to the fire. She peered out through the holes in the blackened trunk to the dark forest. Surely the General would not leave them to the mercy of whatever strange creatures lurked here? Eyes were watching them from the bush, she was convinced of it. Were they animal or human? Threatening or wary? She remembered the face of the girl hiding in the shadows of the trees. Had she imagined her?

Labillardière rummaged in his bag and produced a large skull. 'Some sort of carnivore,' he said to her, pointing to its teeth. 'We heard the cry of a leopard-like creature one night.' He seemed not to notice her petrified expression. 'How is your wound?' he asked.

'Sore.'

'Good. You only have yourself to blame for such foolishness.' He stabbed at the coals. 'We have no food left to share. For the last two days we have had nothing but four mealy biscuits to sustain ourselves.'

She drew her legs up towards her chest and wrapped her arms around her knees. The fierce ants that Ventenat had disturbed crawled all around her feet, as long as her thumbnail and with giant jaws.

'I see the boat!' Félix cried, running down to greet it.

'You took your time,' Labillardière sniped as he climbed into the pinnace, setting it rocking. The men rowed in silence, ignoring the naturalists as the rain dripped from their ears.

The General and Captain d'Auribeau were waiting on deck when they returned. The sight of the two men looking down from the ship as she climbed the rope ladder made her unaccountably nervous. She felt like a child with something to hide. The General's face was stern.

'Citizen d'Entrecasteaux!' Labillardière cried out as he climbed aboard. 'The treatment we have received at the hands of this captain is deplorable. Once again the needs of the savants on this expedition are relegated to that of mere civilian passengers on a joy ride around the world. Our rights as integral members of this mission have been completely ignored.'

'Monsieur!' The General's voice cut through the tirade. His cheeks were flushed and his eyes livid. 'Monsieur! You think yourself above your own democratic ideals! I have tolerated quite enough of your self-importance. The needs of the crew are paramount. They must have their dinner. There was no conspiracy. I will not allow their health to be affected by ungrateful spoiled children! You, sir, should be ashamed of your behaviour.'

Labillardière was stunned into silence. The General was breathing hard, his nostrils sucking air. Girardin had never seen him so out of temper and it scared her. D'Auribeau had clasped his twitching arm behind his back and his smile was smug.

Then she saw the plant presses lined up along the deck. Girardin stared at them, confused. The edges of the papers were wet from the rain and already the ink had begun to run, blurring the carefully transcribed names of thousands of specimens.

'Oh no,' she murmured.

Labillardière followed her gaze. 'What have you done?' He turned on d'Auribeau.

'The great cabin has been returned to the sole use of the officers.'

The naturalists rushed to drag the presses beneath cover.

'Imbecile,' Labillardière fumed. 'Our collections will rot away before we even return to France!'

The General caught Girardin's arm, holding her back from helping them. She winced as the stitches pulled across her wound. He narrowed his eyes at her. 'You should be careful spending time with those men,' he warned. 'Their ideals, their passions, are dangerous.'

She knew he did not mean their collecting of flowers and beetles. They were republicans, supporters of the revolution, and they were not afraid who knew it. She saw concern as well as anger in his eyes. It shamed her. After all she had done in the name of the revolution, the General was afraid she would be led astray by botanists.

Félix called to her. 'Help us!' He struggled to pull the presses into the dry bread rooms.

Her eyes followed the General as he climbed the stairs to his cabin.

'Be careful whose side you choose,' Captain d'Auribeau hissed in her ear as he left.

The naturalists tugged at the sodden presses. Her friends needed her help. Félix stared at her, rain dripping from the curls of his hair, his arms cradling his treasured box of seeds. She saw his wide-eyed dismay as she slowly backed away.

Chapter 28

GIRARDIN PLUCKED FEATHERS FROM A PARTRIDGE. SHE WRENCHED the feathers from the bird's pimpled skin, holding it up by its feet. The ship was ready to depart and she was eager to leave this bay.

The General's words of warning had remained with her. She was afraid to disappoint him, so when the naturalists came to ask if they might leave the presses near the oven to dry, she let Besnard refuse them. When they asked for her help with their researches in the forest, she was too busy. She pulled the stitches from her arm herself. She must distance herself from the naturalists. The General would protect her on this ship, not them. She could not risk being labelled a revolutionary; her position here was precarious enough. She had her son to think of, she told herself, swallowing her guilt. She avoided Félix, knowing she could not bear the look of betrayal in his gaze.

Word of her duel had spread throughout the ship just as Mérite had said, and some measure of grudging admiration was now afforded to Louis Girardin. Armand beamed and winked whenever she came near. Raoul had been sent ashore, first to aid the carpenters in felling trees and then to join the hunting parties. She hid when the hunters arrived back, bringing their partridges, ducks, parrots, turtle doves and swans for her to pluck and salt. He had not confronted her again in the four weeks it took to repair the ship.

The ships' departure had been delayed as the General sent exploration parties on ahead. There was talk of an undiscovered channel to the north, and the thought of a virgin strait conquered by the passage of a ship between two shores had excited all the men. Olympe would be amused, Girardin thought, with a sad smile.

Girardin stroked the snowy plumage of a heron, lying with neck bent on her workbench. Olympe would not abandon her friends to save herself. She had no fear of what others thought of her. Girardin pictured her friend, her white wig lending her height among the black hats. Olympe de Gouges had stood to face the National Assembly in a gallery crowded with men.

'Man, are you capable of being just?' Olympe cried out.

'Giving rights of citizenhood to a man's wife?' replied one of the assembly. 'What next, an education for the man's hound?'

Laughter filled the chamber. They warmed their throats at her expense! Marie-Louise's cheeks flamed on behalf of her friend. They thought her mad. She had yanked on Olympe's arm, urging her to sit. 'What are they afraid of?' Olympe had whispered into her ear.

Girardin knew Olympe would still be fighting now. The revolution was just the beginning. Olympe was determined that not just men but women too would be treated as equal citizens in the new regime. Olympe fought for everyone. She fought for slaves, for peasants, for whores, even for bastard children, when no one else thought to question the right of a man to deny the existence of his child, without blame, without consequence. A bastard child was worthless. Gutter-born. Waste.

The sudden welling of emotion threatened to swallow her. The yearning when it came to her was utterly debilitating. She dropped onto her hands and knees. She was panting, a keening sound, like a freshening squall, building in her throat. Would she ever hold her child again? Would she ever hear her son's footsteps? Feel him wrap his arms around her?

It will pass, she told herself. It will pass.

She was alone in the galley. The floor was littered with feathers. All morning she had been preserving fish and fowls. Among the soft feathers, she knelt on grains of hard white salt that had spilled over the floorboards, like frozen salty tears.

Distantly, she wondered if anyone would find her like this, but she was incapable of moving. Of caring. She pressed the heels of her hands into the sharp lumps of salt. She felt the stabs of pain and was glad of it.

There were no tears with this pain, no release. It closed her over like a clam. It stayed within her, like a hard, pearlescent tumour.

Kermadec found her. She heard him cry out, felt his arms wrap around her and lift her to her feet. Girardin pushed away from him, using the barrel of salted fish to hold herself upright. She waited for the numbness to seep back into her. It always did. The fish stared back at her, their eyes already beginning to cloud.

'I'm alright,' she said, gesturing for him to back away.

'What has happened?'

'Nothing.'

'Tell me.'

She shook her head. 'You won't understand.'

'Has someone hurt you?'

She drew a deep breath and held it, on the brink of confession. Her breath rushed out. 'I miss my son.'

Kermadec fell silent. She closed her eyes, letting her head sag. She heard him step back, retreating. He would go now. He would leave her be.

'Let me show you this,' he said.

She raised her head.

'I found it in my library.' He unrolled a map along the bench. 'It's of the Admiralty Islands,' he said, his voice rising in excitement. 'There is Vendola Island.' He stabbed his finger at the island above New Guinea. 'Where Captain Hunter said he saw La Pérouse.'

'Rumours,' she said softly.

'We will make a stop in New Caledonia to resupply, and then continue onwards to the Admiralties. It will not be long now.'

Suddenly he reached for her hand. She was startled, but did not draw away. His grip was warm and firm.

'We will find him,' Kermadec assured her.

He meant La Pérouse, but she thought only of her son.

The ships left Recherche Bay in late May, passing through the newly discovered strait and out to the open sea. The breeze was fresh on her face as the ship surged ahead towards the islands of the Pacific. Gannets reeled overhead and dolphins played in the waves alongside the ship. Yet she could not shake a feeling of dread. When she looked up, Raoul lay stretched out on the spars like a panther content to wait.

Chapter 29

New Caledonia, 20 June 1792

GIRARDIN HEARD GUNSHOTS. SHE WAS IN A MOB OF WOMEN. THEY carried pitchforks and splintered brooms. She was pushed and elbowed and she tried to move her feet but they were stuck. She looked down and saw the hands of a palace guard around her ankles.

She woke at the sound of cannon fire. It took her a moment to orientate herself. Her bed was swinging. The nightmare was a familiar one, but it always left her nauseous and confused. The cannon boomed. The signal cannon. Warning shots! She swung her legs to the floor, dressing quickly. The dregs of her dream, horror and guilt, swilled in her stomach.

Outside, a bell began to clang. 'All hands on deck!'

She looked at her hands. What use was she on deck? What did she know of sailing? A fist thudded on her door. She left her cabin and followed the men as they scrambled up the stairs.

The wind battered her face. She narrowed her eyes against its sting. Looking down, the waves swirled and foamed like washing waters. All about the ship, wave-beaten rock circled them. To the north, south, east and west, the reefs had drawn a noose around them.

'Welcome to New Caledonia,' said Labillardière. She looked about for Félix, realising now how much she needed his gentle, reassuring smile. But with a hundred men on deck, she caught no glimpse of him. She stayed close by the naturalist's side.

The wind whistled through the masts, snapping the sheets against the wood. Ventenat appeared on deck wearing his black cassock. He tripped and sprawled on the wet deck. She stuck out her hand to help him upright. He thanked her with his gaze, and she felt ashamed once again at how she had avoided these men during the past weeks. He clasped the cross around his neck, chanting loudly for their safe deliverance. She hoped God would listen to him, as she could not pray for herself.

'Chaplain, be quiet, for heaven's sake!' cried Lieutenant Rossel from the helm. He ordered the crew to trim the sails on the starboard tack. Ventenat silently crossed himself.

The sails went slack and Lieutenant Rossel swore.

'What's happening?' she asked.

'The tack failed,' said Labillardière.

'Where is Captain d'Auribeau?'

'Where do you think? Incapacitated. Under the care of the surgeon's opiates.'

Their captain had been in bed since the previous day, suffering with his spasms and delirium, a frequent affliction that she knew Labillardière suspected was an addiction to laudanum. At the helm, Rossel's wig had been snatched by the wind and tendrils of his curling dark hair flew upright. His face was blotched red. He began to call the manoeuvre again.

Ahead the *Espérance* was caught within the same reefs. From this distance it looked as though the ship was almost upon the rocks. She gripped the rail, taut with fear for Kermadec. She imagined the ship listing, picked up by a freak wave and dashed upon the reef. Like a painting of a shipwreck, she saw the men falling from the rigging, pictured the captain remaining at the helm.

Beside her Ventenat whispered his prayers. He smiled grimly at her. 'God will save us.'

She thought of La Pérouse and his ships. He was supposed to have sailed this same route past the reefs of New Caledonia. Had they become stranded here? Had they too prayed to God to save them?

She could imagine now the fate of La Pérouse and his crew. She saw their ships splintered on these reefs, the men forced to bake in the tropical sun, their skin peeling from them, their lips caked in salt. How long would their provisions have lasted, their water? Would they have risked swimming to shore and been plucked off by sharks or other monstrous creatures?

Rossel called the commands to complete the tack. She gripped the rail. It was taking forever to execute this turn. The wind snapped at the loosened sails and a rope flew free. Rossel swore again and sent for the General. For a second time, the tack had failed. Girardin felt the waves lift them ever closer to the reefs.

She did not want to die here. The realisation startled her. She wanted to live. Only a matter of weeks ago she had been prepared to sacrifice her life to God if it would help to save her son. What had changed? Did she not trust God to uphold his side of the bargain?

As soon as the General emerged from his cabin, Rossel called for another officer to take his place at the helm. 'I have an appalling headache,' he declared by way of excuse.

'He cannot handle the ship in these conditions,' said Labillardière, realisation dawning. 'He doesn't know what to do.'

Lieutenant Saint-Aignan looked up in terror when he heard his name called. Girardin had rarely seen him at the wheel. Did he have sufficient experience with ship-handling? He climbed the quarter-deck slowly and took his place beside the General. All the crew were silent, waiting for his commands. Girardin held her breath.

'Look about for something to cling on to when we go down,' observed Labillardière. Girardin had not missed his mordant wit in the weeks she had been avoiding him. She wished that she had Félix at her side now.

'What are your instructions for the crew, Lieutenant Saint-Agnan?' the General asked calmly.

Saint-Aignan's long face was pale. He cleared his throat. Then he began to shout.

Girardin heard the litany of orders and watched in horror as the ship swung about, but stalled before they had fully turned. The sails went slack.

'He has forgotten to have the jibs brought down,' Armand muttered from behind her.

'I cannot watch,' said Ventenat. 'We surely don't have room to fail again.'

Girardin kept her eye trained on the *Espérance* ahead. She remembered the feel of Kermadec's arms around her waist, lifting her from the floor. He would not let his men die on these reefs. The *Espérance* tacked.

A cheer rang out from the crew. 'She has found a passage through!'

Girardin watched as Kermadec's ship slipped through the jaws of the reef and ran clear into the open ocean. She felt a burst of exhilaration. He had survived. Tears welled in her eyes. All they had to do was follow his lead.

At the helm of the *Recherche*, Lieutenant Saint-Aignan doubled over, clutching his stomach, assailed by a sudden malaise.

'The depth of talent on this ship seems woefully inadequate,' Labillardière noted.

'Save your low-flying knives,' Armand spat. 'We're not dead yet.'

The General called to the surgeon. 'Monsieur Renard, kindly fetch our captain from his bedchamber; Lieutenant Saint-Aignan has been struck ill and must be relieved from his post.'

Girardin turned to Armand. 'What's happening?' she demanded. 'Why does the General not take the helm?'

The General stood impassive, no sign of emotion in his countenance. Did he not see the deadly peril they were facing?

Armand snorted. 'There are proper ways of doing things.'

'But we could be wrecked!'

Armand looked at her with ill-disguised contempt. 'If he makes every decision for them, they'll never learn to use their wings.'

The rolling waves lifted and dropped the ship, nudging them ever closer to the reef. Once again, she felt the power of God in each swell, like a boy slapping the surface of a puddle to overturn a walnut shell. He could sink them, or save them. She looked towards the *Espérance* in despair. Whatever we do now will make no difference, she thought. We are in God's hands.

Captain d'Auribeau staggered to the quarterdeck. For once, she felt sorry for him, pulled from his sickbed only to face certain death. He looked dazed. Palsy crippled the whole left side of his body.

Labillardière scowled. 'The General will let us all perish at the hands of this drug addict.'

'Seems to me he wants to teach you a lesson in respect,' growled Armand.

D'Auribeau took the helm. He spun the wheel and turned their bow towards the reef. The *Recherche* picked up speed. They surged at the reef.

'What's he doing?' Girardin cried.

'Saving our lives,' Armand grunted. 'Lend a hand, for God's sake.'

Girardin took her place among the seamen. She gripped a rope. All around her the sailors and soldiers, civilians and officers stood ready. The carpenters and cooks stood shoulder to shoulder with gunners and sailmakers. All hands. Together.

She licked her dry lips. She felt the wind whisper around her neck, her ears, against her cheek. Her feet were planted and she could feel every movement of the ship through her soles, her knees, her hips, her core, like a message. She felt the skittish mood of the ship as she rode the waves ever faster towards the reef.

'Ease the foresheet!' d'Auribeau commanded.

The orders were called and when the men about her hauled, she hauled. When they eased, she eased. When they made fast, she made fast. She had no time to look at the waves crashing on the reef. The ship turned quickly and surely, like an albatross catching the wind, gliding through the gap and out to join the *Espérance* on the other side.

She looked up in surprise.

'God has saved us,' Ventenat said, his pale face sweating.

Armand belayed a rope about a pin, looping and twisting the rope with a flourish. 'Good ship-handling saved you,' he said matter-of-factly.

Girardin sank to her knees and turned up her palms. Fat, glowing blisters were beginning to throb. These hands had helped to save them. She unfurled her fingers, feeling them stretch and sting. She had helped to save herself.

Chapter 30

Latitude 17°57′ S, longitude 160°21′ E, 2 July 1792

THE EXPEDITION SAILED ON PAST NEW CALEDONIA. THE REEFS had proved impenetrable and they could not find a way through to reach the coast. They had no fresh supplies of food to sustain them. The crew complained to her of heartburn, pains in their guts and ulcers in their mouths. They blamed the salted provisions. Girardin saw her ankles swell and red pinpricks spread over her lower legs. She told no one. By now, her menses passed with a twist of pain and an ache in her back, but little or no blood. Perhaps it was the poor diet after so many months at sea, but Girardin took it as yet another sign she was not fit to be a mother.

Girardin lit a candle to mark the first birthday of her son. As she replaced the glass to shield the naked flame, it stuttered as if she was starving it of air. The thin flame was all she had to offer him. She regretted fleeing from Raoul in Tenerife before she had found some small trinket to spend her first wages on. It would have cheered her to pretend she had a present for him. Instead, her son would spend his first anniversary of life in a foundling hospital or in the basement of a church. In her nightmares, the children lay in darkness on sour mattresses, forbidden to get up, pressed tight against one another. A slant of grey light filtered through a high window. She imagined them fed only on thin oat water. The nuns' hands were kept tucked away beneath grey robes, never touching the babies, as if they carried sin on their skin. She tortured herself with these visions, rubbing her thumb across the burn on her forearm.

But was Rémi still with the nuns? Perhaps he had been sent to the countryside, as Olympe had hoped. When the winds were blowing fair and strong and the sails were full, she allowed herself these fancies. Olympe had said there were women who were so well fed they had breast milk to spare for foundlings. The church paid these women, the *nourrices*, to nurse the babies. It must be in their interests to keep the babies well fed and healthy, to keep them alive. Yes, in the country there would be more food than the city. Surely no one would die of hunger in the country. The fullness of the sails reminded her of milk-white breasts.

This thought sustained her, but it terrified her also. How would she ever find him again? Even if they found La Pérouse's ships in these islands and turned for home, where would she begin? *One son dead and the other abandoned*, sneered a voice in her head. *Better left with those who know how to mother an infant*. Girardin had no answer for the needling voice. She didn't know how she would keep her son alive.

By late July the ships had found anchorage in Carteret Harbour in New Ireland, close to the Admiralty Islands, where they would begin their search for La Pérouse.

Girardin pressed her swollen gums. The pressure relieved the pain momentarily, but it did nothing to stop them bleeding. She swilled water around her mouth and spat over the side. It tasted foul.

'Can they not collect it further upstream?' she asked one sailor as he rolled a barrel along the deck.

'This whole place is a swamp,' he grunted.

The wood that was brought on board was infested with scorpions, the water was putrid and the supply of coconuts meagre. When Labillardière found the trees had been cut down to claim the nuts he was furious. 'This is short-sighted insanity! If I hadn't intervened they would have cut down all the palms along the shore.'

Girardin shrugged, holding the strange fruit in her hands. 'The men are lethargic, sickly. The coconut water will revive them.' She spoke more confidently than she felt. 'Joannet says so.'

'Do you know how long a palm tree takes to grow?'

'Of course not.'

'How can we destroy its potential to feed so many without knowledge of what we are doing?'

She had no answer. All she knew was that they needed fresh food urgently. She tapped at the the coconut's outer casing, wondering how to break it.

'For pity's sake, give me that!' Labillardière took out his machete and sliced clean through the base of the husk, nicking a hole in the hard inner nut and splashing water onto the deck. He held it up to her. 'There. But it will take more than a few coconuts to save us.'

He was right of course, but it was something to sustain them while they searched the Admiralties. The General had told her that they could resupply fully at the port of Amboyna in the Dutch East Indies. By then, we will have rescued La Pérouse and his men, she thought, her mood lifting. By then, we will be preparing for the journey home.

She tipped the coconut towards her lips and tasted coconut water for the first time. It was sweet, surprising and delicious. The juice splashed down her chin. It had been so long since she had tasted sweetness.

'Refreshing, isn't it?'

Kermadec was watching her. It was a shock to see him after so many weeks and she felt unmasked. She remembered her weakness at Recherche Bay, and his kindness. It meant nothing, she had told herself many times; he meant only to reassure you.

'Wait until you taste papaya, melon and bananas. Pineapple! I have so much to show you yet. We cannot turn for home until I have seen you taste pineapple. It would be good for my soul.'

His smile was broad and his cheeks glowed. It was impossible not to be uplifted by his presence. She offered him a cautious smile in return.

'I wanted to give you something,' he said, pulling a cylindrical object from beneath his vest. 'My father gave it to me when I was a boy. It's a Dutch telescope.' He held it out to her, balanced in the palm of his hand. The telescope was just four inches long and made of tin with gilt decoration.

'For me?' she said. 'But your father gave it to you.'

'He regretted that when I ran away to sea! Take it. It would give me pleasure to know you have it with you.'

She lifted it to her eye. The palm trees along the shore blurred and jumped before her, their coconuts close enough to reach out and touch. She drew back, amazed. She imagined showing it to her son, letting him have this same feeling of elation. Magical.

'I cannot accept this.' She handed it back. 'I have nothing to give you in return.' She could not be beholden to him. She could not let herself be in his debt.

'Take it,' he urged, pressing it into her palm. 'For our search.'

She studied his earnest face. Did he mean for La Pérouse or something more?

'It catches the light,' Kermadec said, 'to bring things that are far away closer to you.'

Chapter 31

The Admiralty Islands, 28 July 1792

UNDER LEADEN SKIES, THE SHIPS BEGAN THEIR SEARCH OF THE Admiralty Islands, setting a course for Vendola Island. The atmosphere crackled with expectation. Before long, they came upon an archipelago of tiny islands, dots of white sand with few palms, each one circled by a reef. When Girardin looked over the side of the ship the clear blue water seemed bottomless.

Hopes were high among the crew. Wagers were being laid. She was tempted to lay her own bet, as if putting her coins down would tilt the odds in favour of La Pérouse's rescue. The telescope pressed against her thigh in a pocket she had sewn to hold the cherished gift. Looking through its eyepiece gave her a pulse of sacrilegious joy. She had the feeling of besting God, of seeing further than he intended her to.

'Where did you get that?'

She turned to see Félix watching her. It startled her to find him suddenly so close.

'A friend,' she said, slipping the telescope back into her pocket. He raised his eyebrows.

Her cheeks felt hot. She had spent so little time with the naturalists since leaving Recherche Bay. They must know she had been avoiding them. The General's warning had frightened her and she could not risk falling from his favour. Yet she felt guilty, remembering the naturalists' care of her when she had been wounded. Few others had shown her friendship. She looked for Félix again, but he had moved away.

A cry from the tops brought men running to the bow.

'Wreckage!' She heard the word repeated down through the ship. She took out her telescope, but the image in her eyepiece leaped about. Perhaps there, on the beach, was the eviscerated hull of a ship? The men pressed around her, leaning over the rail, but she could not imagine how these islands, with their barren white-hot sand and few coconut palms, could sustain a shipload of men. If this wreckage was one of La Pérouse's ships, the *Astrolabe* or the *Boussole*, would they find only bones remaining?

They sailed closer to the island and the men fell silent. She held her breath. Was rescue truly possible? Would they soon be going home? She could see spars of wood rising from the sand, half sunken in the ocean. The wood was bare and bleached, picked clean. But as they inched closer still, the hull of the supposed wreckage became clear. Drowned trees had beached upon the reefs and their branches protruded from the ocean like the ribs of fallen frigates. She watched the illusion shatter as they sailed past.

Many times that afternoon, she saw the spectre of these ghost ships stranded on the reefs. As the sky blackened and a downpour of lukewarm water doused the decks, Girardin gave up hope and went back to her duties.

When Vendola Island was finally sighted it was not at all what she expected. The hillside slopes were cultivated with coconut plantations and terraced root crops. Smoke rose from fires in thatched huts. Here there was a village. Here there was hope of survival, she thought with growing excitement. With food and shelter the men might still be alive.

Two young officers rushed past Girardin, elbowing one another as they raced for the glory of rescue. She recognised Mérite who was first to reach the rail, and Saint-Aignan, holding his violin high above his head. Stout Lieutenant Rossel followed behind, pushing aside Mérite and choosing only Saint-Aignan to accompany him into the pinnace. The rowers took up the oars. Mérite slapped the rail in annoyance as the boat rowed off to shore without him.

Her first glimpse of the natives was terrifying. The islanders of Vendola surged across the reefs and launched their canoes. Girardin was shocked at their speed; she imagined the ships being invaded by these fearsome men.

'They know of European ships,' Labillardière said, coming to stand beside her.

The *Espérance* lowered a boat and she identified the tall frame of Captain Kermadec stepping into it. Soon both boats were trapped in a flotilla of canoes and unable to reach the shore. Trading began in earnest. She could see coconuts and spears tossed into the boats. Girardin winced as some of the islanders beat others with cudgels and forced them to relinquish the traded nails and axes to their chiefs.

'Even among the noble savage,' Labillardière said sadly, 'taxes leave the poor with nothing and their chiefs with all.'

The rowers set to the oars once again and pushed through the entourage of canoes, heading for the shore. Girardin took up her telescope. The boats landed on the beach and the islanders swarmed around them. Did she see a flash of blue? A red cloth? A stumbling man dash out and fall upon the sands? She found the women, standing back beneath the coconut palms, holding their children behind them. Then Kermadec loomed in and out of her wavering gaze, speaking with a group of the woolly-haired men.

'Give me that,' ordered Labillardière. He plucked the telescope from her hand and put it to his eye. Without it she could only see dark shapes.

'Fools!' Labillardière cried. 'They are coming back. Why would they return so soon when the islanders still have coconuts to trade?'

'They return because we all want to know what has become of La Pérouse!' Girardin snapped at him, frustrated by his lack of sympathy. 'Can you not see how important this is?'

Labillardière tilted his head as he looked down at her. 'You really think there is a chance La Pérouse can be found?' He barked out a laugh, casting his eyes around the anxious faces of the men about them. 'Oh, this is precious.'

'You are impossible!' she cried. 'We are on a rescue mission. We have to find La Pérouse and go home!' She felt the men beside them turn to stare. Her voice sounded high and screeching, like a market woman selling cod. She could not afford to lose her temper.

'Look around you. Do you see space set aside for bringing men home? Even if half the complement of La Pérouse's crew had survived, where do you think we would put them?'

Girardin snatched her telescope back from him, her hands shaking too much to put it to her eye.

'This is not a rescue mission,' continued Labillardière. 'Not even the National Assembly thinks that. This is a scientific expedition. I just wish the General would stop this foolishness and admit it.'

As she watched the boats returning from the shore, she saw Kermadec turn to her and shake his head.

For weeks they searched the Admiralty Islands. At each new island encounter, Saint-Aignan would play his violin, hoping to draw the natives out to meet them. As the days passed without success, even his more buoyant tunes had a note of despair. Girardin could no longer bear to watch him standing tall in the bow, his fiddle cradled against his cheek.

The trading too had been a disappointment. The islanders would only part with a few coconuts and the sailors grumbled at the lack of fresh food. The rash on her lower legs had turned black, like a sooty mould creeping on her skin. The sailors did not like to mention the scurvy sickness, but she knew they all suffered. On Armand's arm she had seen a pus-coloured lump the size of a pullet's egg. Labillardière blamed the torrential rains. Joannet urged her to dose the wine and brandy with preparations of cinchona bark. The General assured her that rest would revive them all, once they reached the Moluccas, the Spice Islands.

Everyone aboard felt subdued by the failure here. She had pinned her hopes on finding La Pérouse and returning home, but now she felt disillusioned, uncertain of their future. She had no opportunity to speak with Kermadec, but she imagined he felt this disappointment as keenly as she did. She turned the telescope over and over in her hands, wondering at the meaning of his gift.

In the falling light, the ships anchored at the last island of the Admiralties. Here the islanders were fishing offshore and would not come out to meet them. She watched with little expectation as the General launched a paper lantern on a floating plank to arouse their curiosity. The weather was so calm and the sea so smooth that the lantern remained alight, floating on the dark water. The islanders seemed spooked by the ghostly apparition; they chanted loudly and quit their fishing grounds.

The candle glowed for many hours in the still night, while Saint-Aignan played his soulful chords. It reminded her of the candle she had lit to mark her son's birthday. To Girardin, it seemed to be a message, a final goodbye.

La Pérouse was not here. They had gambled on a rumour and lost.

Chapter 32

Amboyna, Molucca Islands, 6 September 1792

THE PORT OF AMBOYNA IN THE HEART OF THE SPICE ISLANDS WAS a jolt to her senses. The scent of cloves and wood smoke drifted in the still morning air. Wooden crates, stamped with the insignia of the Dutch East India Company, were stacked on the wharves. Malaysian fishing junks and canoes jostled for space among the Dutch ships. Trading had begun and voices yelped in strange, high-pitched languages. Fish were being smoked and dried. Exotic fruits of brilliant yellows and bright crimson were piled on mats. Armand pointed to the cartload of yams being tipped onto the wharf, while his monkey hopped up and down on his shoulders and screeched. Here at long last, she thought, they would be able to rest and restock.

The little colonial town was encircled by gardens of fruit trees. High on a hill, a crumbling Dutch fort looked down over the pointed roofs of huts and solid wooden homes. In the centre of the town she saw a Calvinist chapel, and in the western quarter the sweeping bird-wing shape of a Chinese pagoda. To the north she glimpsed the tiered pyramid roof of a Malay mosque. The scene was like a painting on a decorative panel, like something she had once seen on a noblewoman's dressing screen.

'Cloves and nutmeg,' the General said as they watched the bales being loaded onto a ship. 'The Dutch have monopoly on trade. We must persuade them we are not here to steal their precious spice plants.'

It had been a shock to learn that foreign ships were not permitted to dock here. She counted eighteen brigs and sloops in the port, all under Dutch colours. The General prepared to set off to persuade the governor that their mission was not a commercial voyage. Girardin chewed her thumbnail.

'For God's sake, nobody mention we have botanists on board,' the General said to his lieutenants as they climbed into the boat. But he winked at her as they drew away.

Girardin longed to know what the General intended to do now. Would they continue the search for La Pérouse? He was yet to reveal their next destination. Whenever she asked about their route, all he would say was: 'To Amboyna. There we will find all the supplies we need.' But for what? she had wondered. For a journey home?

When the General returned to the ship, he was smiling. 'Children, you are going ashore!' he announced, spreading his arms wide.

The crew cheered. Someone cried out, 'We will behave like little angels!' She doubted it, most strongly.

Within a week almost all the officers had taken rooms in the town. Girardin watched the naturalists load up their cages and presses onto the back of a truculent donkey. They made a fine nativity scene, she thought, the chaplain hauling on the donkey's lead, Labillardière striding ahead, his tall hat visible above the crowd on the bustling street, and Félix struggling behind beneath the weight of his pack. Ventenat pulled the lead with all his might while the donkey's neck stretched out straight, its toes digging into the dirt street. She smiled to see its stubborness. Félix put down his pack and shouldered the rump of the donkey. It charged, the rope went slack, and Ventenat toppled onto his back. She sniggered as the donkey cantered up the street. But when the naturalists finally disappeared from sight, her smile faded and she felt an unexpected pang of loss at being left behind. This time they had not asked her to join them in their researches.

Girardin was to stay on board to supervise the loading of supplies and to help Besnard prepare dinner for the crew. By day the sailors scurried into the brothels and alehouses, but at night they returned to the ship, like rats to their nests, ordered by Joannet to avoid the worst excesses of debauchery. As the days passed, she grew impatient. The climate was hot and muggy and every afternoon the rain fell like ropes. She itched to leave the ship and explore the town, but the constant arrival of flour and biscuit and meat kept her days filled. Besnard ignored her.

No longer able to speak with the General now that he had lodgings ashore, she felt isolated and uncertain. She wrote letters to Olympe in her journal, for comfort. She wrote to her son, asking him to forgive her. She felt the urgency stronger than she had before, a dread that the longer they delayed the harder it would be to find her boy. The false reports of La Pérouse in the Admiralties had been a diversion from the King's instructions. What would the General decide to do?

Other doubts plagued her moments alone. When would Raoul speak out? He knew her name, knew she was a woman. A sly word in Besnard's ear would be all it took to reveal her secret. Why did he keep silent? Or did he mean to seek his own revenge? She knew he would not forget her shaming him on the beach in Van Diemen's Land. Girardin removed her wages from their hiding place in her cabin and sewed the coins into the hem of her tunic. If he came for her, she would be ready to run.

Today, Besnard had leave to take his turn at the alehouses ashore, and she was alone in the galley. The ship was unusually quiet.

A cough behind her made her swing about.

Captain Kermadec smiled at her. His hands were clasped behind his back.

'You startled me,' she said, heart pounding.

'I would like your opinion on something.'

She raised her eyebrows.

'But you must close your eyes.'

'Why?'

'Trust me.'

She stared at him for a moment, then let her eyelids fall closed.

It was disorientating to be plunged into sudden darkness in the cramped galley. Sounds grew louder. She heard the animals chewing in their stalls, their teeth grinding the fresh hay. She smelled the musky lanolin of the sheep's wool. In the distance, strange booms and thumps echoed from the loading docks. The ship swayed gently on its mooring.

'Now hold out your hands.'

She wanted to trust him, but she hesitated. Even in the darkness, she was aware of the shape of him, standing just an arm's length away. She stretched out her hands.

The weight of the fruit surprised her. Spines pricked her palms, sending curious tingles across her skin. The rough surface was too hard for her nails to puncture. As she circled her hands up towards the neck, her finger struck a thorn.

'Ouch!' She opened her eyes.

She snorted. The pineapple was a ridiculous fruit. It wore a top knot of barbed fronds curling outwards like a jester's cap and its skin was puckered into circles of green and gold, like a turtle's shell.

'Smell it,' he urged her.

She pressed the fruit to her nose. The scent was indescribable, completely unfamiliar, an absolute novelty. When he took it from her, the scent lingered in her nostrils.

He cut through the length of it. When it fell open the fruit was creamy golden, a shade of yellow that reminded her of buttercups. He quartered it, trimmed out the heart, and offered her a golden wedge.

She touched the fruit to her lips and that alone was a burst of sweetness. Juice exploded in her mouth. She tugged on the fibres of the flesh with her teeth.

'This is so good,' she said, her voice husky.

Kermadec laughed. He looked thrilled as she took another bite. The juice dripped from her chin and she had to use her forearms to clean her face. Kermadec fell about with laughter.

For the first time in such a long time, she laughed freely. She didn't care that she looked foolish. She took another piece, then another, letting the juice spill down her shirt.

When it was finished, her lips were stinging and her tongue felt raw. Fibres of the fruit were caught in her teeth. She wiped the juice from her mouth with the back of her hand. They stood facing one another, all laughter gone.

'Steward!' a voice called from above.

Their eyes widened. They both felt it, she was sure, this guilt at being found together. They had crossed some boundary into suspicion.

'Steward!' The voice belonged to Joannet. They heard his footsteps heavy on the stairs.

There was no need to be ashamed. They had done nothing but eat fruit together. 'Quick,' she whispered, pushing Kermadec behind the oven. She hid beside him, her body pressed against him hip to hip.

'Monsieur Girardin!' Joannet called as he entered the galley. He tutted and tsked at the remains of the dripping pineapple. 'Too much fruit will bring on illness.'

She shared a look with Kermadec. 'Go,' she mouthed to him. He winked in return.

Girardin stepped out, wiping her hands on her tunic. 'Joannet, how can I help you?' She watched Kermadec sidle around the back of the oven, away from the surgeon, and make his silent escape.

'Ah, there you are!' Joannet frowned at her from beneath his heavy eyebrows. 'You are requested to go ashore,' he said. 'One of the naturalists has fallen gravely ill.'

Chapter 33

Girardin hurried behind Joannet through the spice-scented streets. The smell of nutmeg invaded her nostrils, making her sneeze. She passed garden plots and spreading trees heavy with fragrant flowers. Green vegetables were growing in the alleyways and on rooftops and even the cracks in the walls seem to sprout some fruiting or flowering plant. But she took no joy in this garden paradise, this prodigious display of life.

'Who is ill?' she asked the chief surgeon.

Joannet shrugged. 'The messenger did not say.'

The sun beat down on the crown of her head. She had forgotten her hat in her haste, taking time only to remove her journal from the ship, wanting to keep it close beside her. Here the Malay people wore woven conical hats to shade themselves or scarves across their heads. They crowded the streets, standing, walking and sitting cross-legged with items of trade displayed on mats in front of them. A group of Dutch women wearing long black dresses and white bonnets to protect the whiteness of their skin, clustered together like nuns. Instinctively, Girardin crossed the street to avoid their scrutiny.

Sweat made her skin clammy and dripped between her breasts. She could still smell pineapple juice. It had soaked through her shirt, her bindings, perhaps even her skin. She had let her guard down with Kermadec and her cheeks flushed at the memory. She had forgotten what it was like to lose yourself in laughter, to be as giddy as a foal, and now her chest ached at the reminder.

'How much further?' she asked

'Not far.' Joannet sidestepped a pile of manure.

Girardin thought of Félix's kindness to her from the first moment they met. She thought of Labillardière, his brusque arrogance, but his tender fingers mending the gash on her arm in Van Diemen's Land. And clumsy Ventenat, with his secret passion for colourful beetles and his faith that God would look after them all. Their friendship had sustained her on the long sea voyages and given her a measure of safety, and yet she had abandoned them to keep in the General's good graces, to please the royalist officers. She saw the wounded expression on Félix's face and was disgusted with herself.

Joannet stopped outside a house built in a medieval style with lime plaster and dark wood. The upper storey jutted out above the street and she felt the oppressive weight of it as she stood beneath.

'The General leased the house from a Dutch family who have gone to replant the nutmeg plantations of Banda Island after a hurricane.' Joannet gave a gleeful chuckle as he rapped on the door. 'The Dutch ripped the spice plants out of every other island in the East Indies to keep their stranglehold on trade. I bet they regret that now!'

'The General?' she said. 'The General is here with the naturalists?'

'And Captain Kermadec.'

She stilled, listening to the thump of her heart. Smelling pineapple.

'D'Auribeau played a prank on the naturalists. He pretended to be Labillardière and took over their arranged lodgings. I found it very amusing.' He rapped again on the door. 'The General took pity on them.'

This time the door swung back and the strangest man Girardin had ever seen stood before them. He wore a footman's uniform and his woolly hair was dusty white, but it was not a powdered wig. His nose was broad and his lips full, like the slaves she had seen in Cape Town, but his skin was a sickly, almost chalky white. She found she wanted to reach out and scratch his face, as though he had merely covered himself in powder.

'An albino Negro!' Joannet cried with delight. 'Well, I never. The things you see.'

He was still shaking his head as Girardin followed him into the dark house.

Two more servants materialised in the gloom. These were Malay men with short flat hair that shone like raven's feathers. One took her by the hand and led her up the stairs.

The fetid stench of the invalid's room hit her with force. The window shutters were drawn and the room barely lit by yellow candlelight. A figure vomited noisily into a wooden pail as she entered. She couldn't see who it was. Girardin stepped closer to the bed. The invalid collapsed back and stared upwards, mouth falling open. Some of his teeth were missing. Ventenat. She remembered his fall into the ants' nest in Van Diemen's Land. Girardin felt a stab of relief, and was instantly ashamed.

Labillardière came around the bed to meet her. 'His symptoms are alarming and he is in great pain,' he said in a low voice. 'We fear to leave him alone.'

Félix stepped out from a dark corner of the room. 'Will you help us?' he asked. She met his eye, relieved to see him, but fearing he must think her a coward. 'There is no one else we can ask.'

'Get some air in here,' Joannet ordered. But the piercing shard of light when the shutters were opened caused Ventenat to cry out in pain. Girardin jumped back in shock when an attack of hiccups convulsed the sick man's body.

'Too much fruit,' declared Joannet. He turned to her with a self-righteous eye. She licked the taste of pineapple from her lips as though it could betray her. 'And imbibing the crude spirits and fermented liquors,' he continued. 'That's the cause of dysentery.'

Girardin ground her teeth. How dare he suggest the chaplain was a debauched drunkard? She took a seat by Ventenat's bedside, noticing his face had become waxy, almost corpse-like.

'These putrid fevers are highly contagious,' Joannet said in his booming voice. 'We must cut off as much communication with others as possible, as one would separate a mangy dog from the pack.'

Girardin could only hope that Ventenat was protected by his delirium. She dunked a cloth in a pail of juniper water and wrung it hard.

'And in the case of a mortal outcome—' Joannet dropped his voice to a loud whisper '—everything this man has touched should be burned.'

Félix burst forward, his lips set in thin white lines, and pushed the surgeon from the room.

'Vinegar,' Joannet yelled as the door closed behind him. 'Fumigate the room with vinegar.'

Félix turned to her, while Ventenat groaned on the bed.

'Will you stay?' Félix asked. 'Will you help us care for him?'

She blinked tears from her eyes, relieved he still trusted her enough to ask. 'Of course,' she said.

Girardin held a bucket as the chaplain leaned over the side of the bed to vomit up the broth she had made him. She helped him crouch over the pail when the spasms clenched his bowels. Each evacuation left him more disorientated and feeble. He called out for his brother. Girardin squeezed his hand and sang to him, trying not to think of her first son, Jojo, and the night when the fevers came to take him from her.

Labillardière relieved her at midnight. One of the servants, the albino Negro, gestured that she should take his own bed for the night. Girardin declined his offer, assuring him she could sleep in a chair, but he became insistent. Labillardière shrugged. 'The man has offered you something of his own free will. How often does he get to exercise that which we take for granted?'

'What do you mean?' She was too tired to puzzle over Labillardière's words.

'The servants are slaves,' he said with disgust. 'Leased to us along with the house.'

Slaves. A commodity that could be bought and sold, traded away from their friends and family as readily as the crates of cloves and nutmeg. She felt sick. She stared at the man's wrists. She could not imagine him as one of those shackled men on the dock at Cape Town. She wondered if he had children he would never see again.

He tugged her sleeve. His insistence only increased her sense of guilt. Now it seemed churlish to resist and Girardin accepted the man's generosity with profuse thanks. She followed him to his cupboard-sized room and stretched out on the thin mattress, laying her head on her journal. All those words that nestled inside the pages were messages of love to her son that she could not bear to be without.

The straw mattress was lumpy and crawled with biting insects that niggled their way through her clothes to her skin. But she was safe inside a house, on solid land. And somewhere inside these same walls, she thought, Captain Kermadec was also spending the night.

Chapter 34

VENTENAT'S CONDITION REMAINED UNCHANGED THROUGH THE next day. By nightfall, a room had been prepared for her. Its floors had been swept and mopped, the rugs beaten and all the surfaces wiped, but its musty smell caught at the back of her throat. This room had not been opened for many years.

In the centre of the room was a magnificent bed. The coverlet was silk and intricately stitched in gold, green and blue. Girardin longed to stretch out flat on the mattress, to feel its solid weight beneath her. The walls were whitewashed and empty of any paintings. Dark mahogany furniture of both Dutch and Oriental style decorated the room. Beneath the window stood a small writing table, each carved leg ending in the shape of a human hand balancing upon a globe. She would write to Olympe, she decided, thinking of the letters she had written in her journal, telling her about the power of the ocean waves and the beauty of the snow-white albatross. Let her know that she was safe. From this port there must be a ship that could take a letter home.

Girardin took a seat in front of the washstand and mirror where the servants had left a basin of tepid water for her to wash and a knife for her to shave. She looked long at her reflection. It was the first time she had seen herself in nearly a year. Pulling back her lips, she bared her teeth and gently probed at her gums; they felt swollen and tender. She took one of her front teeth between her fingers and felt it move forwards and backwards, wondering briefly what price her teeth might have fetched in the Paris slums. She grew afraid to wiggle it further lest it fall to the basin in front of her.

Her hair had grown and it curled around her ears in an alarmingly feminine manner. She picked up the razor beside the basin and drew its blade along her scalp, scraping from the crown of her head towards the fringe. The greasy clumps came away in her hands as though her hair were falling out at the roots. When she was done, she took stock of her reflection once more. The near bald head and plain face that confronted her was no more masculine than before. She looked like a street girl who had sold her hair to eat. And something about the smallness of her head, the curve at the back of her neck, reminded her of a vulnerable child. A baby.

She wept.

She wept until her shoulders were weak and her head was heavy on her arms. When her tears had dried, she dipped a rag into the tepid water of the basin and wiped it across her cheeks. Tears would not help her. She wiped around the base of her neck. She knew she stank. How long had it been since she had dabbed perfume on her skin?

Dragging a chair across the floor, Girardin wedged its back underneath the doorknob. Sure that no one could disturb her, and with the windows shuttered, she began to strip off her clothes. Loosening the drawstring, she let her trousers fall to the floor. Even in the dim candlelight, the black rash on her lower legs repulsed her. She pulled her tunic over her head and slowly unbound the grey bandage from her breasts. Not daring to look she closed her eyes and felt the pulpy, clammy skin. It was tender beneath her fingertips. Girardin washed quickly. She dosed the water with vinegar and dragged a wet rag underneath her armpits, around her breasts and between her legs. She pulled a starched nightgown over her head and it fell stiffly to her ankles, covering her completely.

A sense of relaxation, almost happiness, spread through her. She had missed these elements of her former life. A thick mattress, clean sheets. What luxury! She sat on the bed and ran her fingers across the embroidered coverlet, feeling the richness in each stitch. A person of wealth must have owned this bedspread. Girardin felt sure this room had once belonged to a woman. At the end of the bed stood a large wardrobe. She should not look in it, she told herself sternly. It was not her business to poke around in other people's possessions.

She tugged open the mahogany doors and released the cloying scent of musty fabric. She sneezed. As she had suspected, the wardrobe was filled with a woman's gowns. But these gowns were not like those worn here by the Dutch women. They preferred simple dark dresses fastened to the neck, while these gowns were sumptuous and decadent, a reminder of the ancien régime. Sky-blue satins, golden yellows, silks the colour of summer peaches. These gowns belonged to another world, as alien to this island as she was. These skirts could once have swept around the great ballrooms of Europe, perhaps even the court of Versailles. She reached out to stroke the slippery material. This shade of pale blue had been a favourite of Olympe and it reminded her of the day Olympe de Gouges stepped back into her life.

Marie-Louise was preoccupied with a parasol that was refusing to open and did not see Olympe rushing for her carriage. The two women collided in a swirl of fabric.

Marie-Louise recognised her instantly. A towering headdress of silver-white curls. Large, dark eyes in a complexion of soft snow. The other woman's rosebud lips opened to exclaim, 'Madame Lesserteur!'

Marie-Louise nodded but did not correct the mistake. By her father's decree she was once again Mademoiselle Girardin.

Olympe de Gouges immediately offered her condolences and expressed her sadness that she could no longer visit Café Lesserteur on her travels to Versailles. In another woman the forthrightness would've been an attempt to wound or the worst of manners, but Marie-Louise saw no malice in Olympe's moist eyes. It had been five years since the death of her husband and Marie-Louise was grateful to have Etienne come to life again for a moment in their memories.

Olympe de Gouge was speaking: 'Do you ever visit Paris?'

Marie-Louise shook her head sadly and looked down at her feet. The stitching on the toe of her left shoe was beginning to unravel. She concentrated hard on the little yellow thread.

'You must come to see the production of my play! *L'Esclavage des Noirs.*'

'My father . . .'

'Yes, bring your father.'

Marie-Louise looked up to meet Olympe's eye. She could not explain that her father would not countenance her friendship with a woman playwright. Respectable families considered Olympe de Gouges to be little more than a prostitute to debase herself so in public. Simply standing here unaccompanied in the street and talking to this woman was arousing whispers that would no doubt arrive back at her father's doorstep.

A slight rise and fall of Olympe's eyebrows was the only sign she made to show she understood. 'Well, I do hope we can see you in Paris sometime soon.' She inclined her head in farewell and turned towards her waiting carriage.

'I hope so too!' Marie-Louise blurted out, suddenly desperate to stall Olympe. Her hand shot out and gripped the fabric of her skirt.

Olympe paused and turned back. This elegant woman seemed to stare at Marie-Louise for the longest time, appraising her. Marie-Louise knew her waif-like body barely filled the bodice of the dress that had been once belonged to her sister. She felt the pinch of her shoes and the weight of her headdress, which was sliding off-kilter and tilting her neck at an uncomfortable angle.

Finally, Olympe smiled. 'Sophie de Condorcet! No one, not even your father, would disapprove of your visiting the wife of the noble Marquis de Condorcet! Sophie will send you an invitation to her salon. All the most exciting thinkers attend our gatherings. You shall join our circle!'

Marie-Louise beamed back. Standing in the glow of that beatific smile and the infectious enthusiasm, she could imagine no difficulty with the plan. It was only later, after Olympe had bundled up her skirts, climbed into her carriage and waved farewell with a cheerful flick of her fan, that Marie-Louise began to doubt. Waiting for her stepmother with a light rain beginning to fall and her parasol jammed shut, she realised her own folly. She would've laughed at herself if she did not feel so wretched. Her father would never let her attend meetings of learned men and women whose education, values and politics were so different from his own. Even if the Marquis de Condorcet were an aristocrat.

But she had been wrong. Olympe de Gouges had been a better reader of his character than his own daughter. Jean Girardin had seen the chance to further his own ambitions in the connections that his daughter might make. When the invitation arrived, her stepmother had squealed with joy.

The dress her father had given her was green taffeta. It fitted well, having been made to measure rather than handed down. She had stood in front of the Hôtel des Monnaies on the banks of the Seine, gazing up at the severe façade, too afraid to enter. Inside were the rooms of Sophie de Condorcet and her husband, the Marquis. The words of her stepmother lingered with her. 'Remember your duty to your father. He could be a man of influence, a burgher of Versailles. Be a dutiful child and think of all he has done for you.'

Marie-Louise clutched her fan tightly in one hand. To her mortification, the hostess of the salon was informally dressed in a simple shift with a loose scarf wrapped around her shoulders. Marie-Louise felt outdated and awkward in her hooped pomposity. All the more ridiculous to be emulating the ancien régime, she thought, given her humble beginnings. Sophie wore her hair long and loose. She welcomed Marie-Louise warmly with a kiss on each cheek. The Marquis was much older man than his pretty wife; he wore no wig and his silvered hair was receeding. She noticed his face powder was erratically applied and mostly rubbed off.

Marie-Louise said little, but absorbed much. She met men and women who were witty, sardonic and fearless. They discussed the philosophy of Voltaire and his nemesis Rousseau. They challenged the rules of society and they duelled with one another, turning their words into swords. They saw what was wrong in the world and were prepared to speak it. It was here she learned that the nobility and clergy did not pay tax; only the Third Estate, the workers and peasants of France, contributed to the coffers.

'A nobleman may be utterly and constitutionally mad,' one said.

'Or a murderer,' another interrupted.

'But he must not, under any circumstance, demean himself by using his talents in literature . . .'

'Or law!'

'Or science.'

'Or any productive means of supporting himself and his family—he must not work for a living,' the man said with exaggerated disgust, 'for he will immediately lose the privilege of his noble birth and be forced to pay tax the same as any snivelling peasant.'

'Quite right,' agreed another speaker, his voice laced with sarcasm. 'That is the natural order of things.'

Beside Marie-Louise, Olympe shot to her feet. 'You men mock our system of governance and deny that man is superior by virtue of a noble birth alone, and I support you. But I say to you, what of women? Should we not challenge what is thought to be the natural order of things?'

A man with a weasel-like face, pointed chin and eyes too close together put up his hand. 'We have heard you too many times, Madame. Outspoken women are tiresome.'

Some of the men snickered, and Marie-Louise felt heat radiate from her gut. The last time she had seen this man attend the salon was when he had brought his friend the botanist. He was enjoying the attention.

Olympe's gorge was up. 'Why must we be denounced as whores if we dare raise our heads from the affairs of the home to that of our homeland?' she challenged him. 'Why are we not allowed to speak?'

A man with a wig of chestnut curls interjected. 'I must agree with Rousseau that motherhood is a woman's highest responsibility and her greatest gift to mankind. Outside the home, a woman loses her greatest radiance.'

Marie-Louise thought of the long hours she spent in her room in her father's house. Its window faced into the courtyard. All she could see of the world was a distant patch of sky.

'You fear us having ideas—ideas above our role in life, ideas that you cannot control,' Olympe continued.

'You are meddling in things your mind is not capable of comprehending,' the weasel-faced man explained to Olympe. 'Stick to breeding.'

'I comprehend freedom, Jacques Hébert, you vulgar man,' she spat back, losing her temper.

Marie-Louise saw him smile in triumph, revelling in Olympe's loss of self-control as if it proved his superiority.

The Marquis himself interrupted. 'It will be France's eternal loss if we do not extend the equal right of democracy for all women as well as all men.' He smiled at Olympe. Marie-Louise was grateful for his support. The Marquis was an extraordinary man.

But the chestnut-wigged man disagreed. 'Women are happiest in their domestic realm. They have their fathers and husbands to speak for them. It is against their nature to go beyond their sphere.'

'Like a domestic animal,' Olympe said under her breath as she took her seat.

Marie-Louise cleared her throat. She had never dared to speak her mind at the salon before. 'I wonder,' she said softly, 'why it is necessary to go to such lengths to suppress a woman's curiosity?' Her voice was small and hesitant. 'Why confine her to the house, deny her education, control the things she is allowed to learn and do and say? Why is that necessary, if it is against her nature to be curious about the world?'

Olympe de Gouges beamed pure sunlight at her.

Jacques Hébert was smirking, one eyebrow jumping with delight. He had looked at her with such naked curiosity, she could not help but feel that she had bared too much.

Girardin ran her fingers down the sky-blue satin and stretched out the full skirt. With dismay, she saw the dress hung in shreds, eaten by moths. She reached for another. Crowded black bodies hibernated between the folds. She squealed. Hundreds of cockroaches began to squirm in the light and run for cover. One darted across her hand and up the sleeve of her smock. She beat at her arm and felt them crawl across her bare feet. Leaping onto the bed, she watched in horror as the shiny, armoured bodies scuttled out in waves from the wardrobe.

Chapter 35

GIRARDIN JOINED THE NATURALISTS IN A SILENT VIGIL AS Ventenat's condition slowly worsened. Labillardière kept his hand on Ventenat's wrist, monitoring the rapidity of his pulse. Sweat beaded on the chaplain's forehead and soon his face was dripping. Girardin wrung out the scrap of linen she had used to bathe him, feeling sure his time was near. She looked across the bed at Félix and was surprised to see him smiling.

'The sweats are a good sign, are they not?' Félix asked.

'I feel his pulse quicken,' Labillardière confirmed.

To Girardin, Ventenat looked as near to death as before. A Malay doctor arrived to tend the invalid and Girardin left the room. She felt certain there was little to be done for the chaplain now. In her final glimpse back, she saw Ventenat's sharp nose as prominent as a gravestone.

The hallway was dark and she reached out her fingers to feel her way along the rough plaster. Three nights had passed and she had seen no sign of Kermadec. Only the General had come to visit Ventenat. Slits of light squinted through the shuttered windows at the end of the corridor. Joannet told her the General had taken rooms on the lower floors. She felt her way down the staircase.

On the ground floor, she heard raised voices coming from a salon.

Girardin stepped softly on the flagstones, careful not to let her heels fall. She was alone in the dim corridor, but she checked again, glancing over her shoulder, before she pressed her ear to the door.

'We must go back to search for him!' It was Kermadec's voice.

Next she recognised the sly tone of d'Auribeau, but couldn't make out what he had said.

'We have a duty to investigate the Friendly Isles as soon as we are able,' urged Kermadec.

'We shall, we shall.' The General, placating. She imagined him clapping a hand to Kermadec's shoulder to reassure him.

'But not until we have completed the King's instructions.' That was d'Auribeau.

'The Friendly Isles, New Caledonia, the Solomons, these are the locations of La Pérouse's itinerary we should explore. Not the southern coast of New Holland!'

She heard footsteps, pacing.

'Mapping the unknown coast is crucial to our mission,' d'Auribeau responded calmly.

'How long will that take? Another year? How many men might die for our negligence?' The footfalls were louder now, coming towards her. She sprang back into the shadows.

Kermadec burst out through the doors and strode down the corridor away from her. He did not turn, he did not look back, and she did not have the nerve to follow him.

Ventenat began to recover. Whether from the onset of the critical sweats, as Labillardière maintained, or from the healing hands of the Malay doctor, Girardin couldn't say for sure. It was a miracle.

As the days passed, she was relieved to see Ventenat slowly but surely recover his strength. Soon he was well enough to leave his sickbed and sit with her on the shady verandah, looking out over the kitchen garden with its drooping fruit trees and leafy green vegetables. It was a joy to hear the parrots crashing and screeching in the trees, so full of life. She was content to sit and breathe in the fragrant air. Here even the bark of the trees exhaled perfume. But Ventenat seemed much changed after his illness. It worried her that he jerked with nervous tics and his thoughts would sometimes drift away like tendrils of smoke that couldn't be caught.

Each afternoon they watched the rain clouds gather above the distant hills.

'There would be a sign, don't you think?' Ventenat said, his Bible shuddering on his knee. 'So close to death, there should've been a sign.'

She reached for his hand, but she could not be the one to reassure him in his faith.

The General gave her permission to stay in the house rather than return to the ship. Although she feared to think what mess Besnard might make of her stores, she was relieved. Happily, she took over some of the duties of the Malay cook, making some of the General's favourite dishes. At first the kitchen staff were wary of her and she couldn't look at them without thinking of them as slaves. It tortured her to think they might have children they would never see again. But surprisingly the kitchen was a place of laughter. The cook was a good-humoured woman with creases around her eyes from when she smiled, like lines of sunlight. She was quick to hug and console the younger kitchen staff. The servants soon welcomed Girardin, both men and women taking her by the hand to show her around the house, and she slowly came to realise they had formed their own family.

As the weeks passed her own health began to improve. The black rash on her legs faded. The sores in her mouth and the burning in her stomach eased. Her injured knee and arm no longer ached. When alone with the General she tried to turn the conversation towards the next phase of their voyage, but he would not be drawn on the subject. Captain Kermadec spent his days engaged with provisioning the ships. The closeness of their moment in the galley now seemed as distant as a half-remembered dream. In the house, he did not seek her out.

Félix and Labillardière now felt secure enough in their friend's state of health to go on excursions into the forests. Claude Riche told them he had seen a lizard with wings that flew between the trees and Félix had been eager to see this flying dragon for himself. They were gone for several days at a time, returning only to catalogue and store the specimens they had collected. When they were absent, the household was peaceful. But when they returned, the house was fraught with argument.

'But slaves, Citizen d'Entrecasteaux! How can you buy slaves from these Dutch masters for our expedition when you know they have been stolen from their homes?'

Girardin stood against the wall in the dining room. Labillardière had returned to the house unexpectedly when the General was entertaining the officers at his table. The revelation that the General had purchased men to join their crew had shocked her. It was bad enough that they had slaves to wait on them in this house, but worse still to participate in the practice.

'The slaves come from Ceram and the Moluccas where the prisoners of war were formerly eaten! Now the prisoners are sold as slaves instead. Which evil would you prefer, Monsieur Labillardière?'

'One abomination does not excuse the other.'

She glanced around at the other servants, the small Malaysian men with their round, pleasant faces. She was glad they could not understand the language.

The General sighed. 'The systems of governance here are unjust, but we cannot change the world, Monsieur Labillardière. We have enough to concern ourselves with on this voyage.'

Girardin sought out Captain Kermadec, but he would not meet her eye. Did he know about this? Had he been the one to buy the men?

Labillardière continued, 'You agree the domination of these people is reprehensible, and yet you support the very institution that keeps our own people in similar chains of bondage.'

Lieutenant Rossel snorted. 'You cannot compare the situation here, where the commerce is built on slaves, with that of our homeland. Preposterous!'

'A noble class that does no work and pays no tax. A corrupt clergy...' Labillardière paused to glance at Ventenat, who gestured for him to carry on. 'A corrupt clergy plucked from the wastrel and demented sons of nobility who abuse and exploit their flock. We do not reward talent and merit—we crush it! You are right, Citizen Rossel: it is preposterous to compare the two systems of governance. The leaders of our homeland are far worse tyrants and they have already been judged and found wanting!'

'And what of duty, Monsieur?' Captain d'Auribeau said coldly. 'You speak of your rights but not your responsibilities. We are the children of the monarchy. Would you speak as disrespectfully to your own father, insist that you know best how to run his household and push an old man out on the street? What hope does a society have if those are its principles?'

'What hope does a society have if it accepts governance purely by an accident of birth? We are children no longer, Citizen. The Enlightenment has taught us to think for ourselves. We can use our intellect and reason. We can reject tyranny!'

'When we return to France, our King will be reunited with his throne and your revolutionary friends tied to the palace gates by their entrails!' With a clatter of dishes, both Labillardière and d'Auribeau stood, stiff-backed and bristling.

'When we return to France the King will be dead!'

Girardin gasped. A shocked silence stilled the table. Then Kermadec shot to his feet, challenging Labillardière to recant his words. She had never seen him look so furious. She pressed herself back against the wall.

'Gentlemen! Please sit!' the General commanded sternly above the din.

Labillardière's nostrils flared, but he took his seat with exaggerated annoyance. The officers followed suit, eyeing him as though he were a wild animal they needed to tame.

'Monsieur Labillardière, you forget you are on a mission in the name of our King,' said the General.

Labillardière snorted. 'In name only. The monarchy is no more. The people are the true rulers of France.'

'You would not be here on this voyage if it were not for the passion of our King. We are his servants. Our search for La Pérouse, our discoveries of geography and natural history, are all for his glory, not your own. You had better hope that your premonition is not correct, Monsieur. For if the King falls, then I predict your precious National Assembly will tear themselves apart to seize power from one another and our beloved country with it!'

'I have greater hope that reason will prevail.'

'No doubt you do. But I have greater experience in the virtues and vices of man.'

Girardin was trembling. The officers were lined along one side of the table, the naturalists on the other. She looked at Kermadec, whose face had flushed bright red above his white cravat. Even the General was breathing hard. She knew now that if these men ever discovered what she had done for the revolution, all was lost.

Chapter 36

GIRARDIN STRETCHED OUT ON HER BED IN THE AFTERNOON HEAT, listening to the shrill pulse of insects outside the windows. Her journal lay on the pillow beside her. She had been writing to Olympe, pouring her anxiety into the ink until it eased her heart. She would have to burn those pages. The letter she would send to Olympe was a simple note. She had sealed it, hoping to place it with a Dutch ship, not knowing if it would ever reach her friend's hand. She closed her eyes. Tomorrow, she would return to the *Recherche*. Tomorrow she would be gone from this house and all its reminders of revolution.

When she met Jacques Hébert again, months after his argument with Olympe, it was at a ball. He singled her out. She recognised him as the writer, the Jacobin pamphleteer who had shown such naked interest in her that night at the salon. At the ball, he wore a wig of tight curls pushed too far back on his head and it aged him. His nose was too long and his face too narrow for her taste. But when he asked her to dance, she found she could not refuse.

'You appear to be a most curious woman,' he whispered in her ear as he passed her in the contredanse.

She had felt a blush spread across her chest.

'You are perfect,' he said to her on the next turn, 'for what I have in mind.'

The intensity of his gaze excited her.

'I see you are brave. You are strong. You are enlightened.'

With each circuit of the dance, she walked taller and with more grace. She thought her partner grew in charm in the different light. When he smiled at her his face was transformed. When Olympe flicked her fan and frowned from the corner of the room, Marie-Louise ignored her. She felt the fierce thrill of being chosen.

When they left the floor, Hébert steered her away from Olympe. He took her outside, into the cool night air.

'A spy!' she exclaimed when he told her what he wanted of her.

'An informant,' he said, glancing over his shoulder. 'To be my eyes and ears in the palace of Versailles, to watch the pigs at their trough.'

Her eyes grew wide. He was offering her the chance to act. To be someone of significance. Someone who made a difference.

'Knowledge is power,' he said, clenching his fists.

'My father would never allow it.'

'Leave your father to me. We will tell him you have been chosen as a companion to a noblewoman from a family of influence.' He grinned and she saw that he had the measure of her father perfectly.

She pictured the walls of her father's house, the enclosed courtyard with cracks in the plaster like ropes she could not climb. Her breath quickened. She had found a way out.

'Tell no one what I have said. None of your friends, not even Olympe de Gouges. What I ask of you requires the utmost secrecy. Can I trust you?'

She had smiled up at him, eager as a pup. 'Yes,' she said.

A knock at Girardin's door startled her to her feet.

Huon de Kermadec pushed the door wide. 'I hope you don't mind, but I saw your door ajar.'

She forgot she had cracked it open for the breeze. She glanced back at her bed as though she had left Marie-Louise lying there in her ball gown, trembling, at the moment her life was changed forever.

He followed the direction of her gaze, and she felt her cheeks warm. Kermadec wore his white shirt loosely tucked, the weather too hot for jacket and cravat. Golden hairs curled on his damp chest. The sight was so intimate she quickly looked away.

'Your hair,' he said. 'I almost did not recognise you at the General's table.'

She reached up. It had grown back fine and clean, fuzzing her head like flocked velvet.

'I have news to share with you,' he said.

'The General's decision?' Her heart thumped.

He nodded, his face sad. 'We will chart the unknown coast of New Holland. I am sorry.'

She spun away from him. It was as she had expected, but the realisation of the extra months, perhaps years, at sea sent her spirits plummeting. She should never have come on this journey.

Crossing the room, she pushed her window shutters open, but now the heavy scent of spice was too sickly for her. The town stretched out below her, with its uneasy mix of Oriental and European houses. A knot of Dutch women in their black dresses and white caps stared up at her from the street, pinch-faced. She gulped the wet air.

He followed her to the window and she could sense him standing close behind her.

'We will find La Pérouse,' Kermadec said, his voice full of certainty. 'It will just take a little longer.'

She worried her thumb under the cuff of her sleeve, searching for the familiar raised skin of her burn. She felt nothing. Startled, she pulled her sleeve back, terrified that the mark might have worn away to nothing. The scar was now a smooth red weal on her pale arm.

'We will find him,' he murmured, his breath a whisper against the nape of her neck. Were all men full of false promises? She slid sideways, putting a writing desk between them.

'Did you know about the purchase of the slaves?' she said, her voice sharp, wanting to wound.

'They are volunteers,' he said, guarded. 'They seek escape from this place.'

The irony was not lost on her. Had she not used the expedition herself to run away? Her fingers tapped the surface of the writing desk where the servants had polished the lacquer so well that she could see herself reflected. 'We should pay them for their service,' she snapped.

'We will,' he said, moving close to her. 'And when they leave us they will be free men.'

He was standing directly in front of her. He smelled of warm cologne and fresh sweat. She stared at the rise and fall of his chest. He reached out and caught her hands in his and pulled her gently towards him. She resisted, afraid to let herself soften.

'Louis!' a voice called from the stair. 'Louis Girardin!'

Girardin jumped back as Félix burst through the doorway. His eyes followed her sudden movement.

'We brought you a present,' he said, dangling a green lizard by its long tail. 'Like a chameleon,' he added lamely, 'it changes colours.' He lifted it up in his hands.

The lizard stared at her with an all-knowing eye.

Chapter 37

HER RETURN TO THE SHIP WAS DIZZYING. GIRARDIN EDGED between mounds of potatoes, yams and different kinds of melons, carrying her lizard in a bamboo cage. The ship was overflowing with food and livestock. Great quantities of banana leaves adorned the stern. She saw the old sailor, Armand, smuggle a piglet beneath his shirt and disappear below deck. She struggled past makeshift corrals crammed with goats and hogs. A stag stomped his foot, nostrils flaring. She caught the defiant look in his eye as he tossed his wide, impressive antlers. Beside him, a doe quivered in her stall. The stag and its breeding mate were to be released on New Holland, intended to supply future mariners with fresh meat.

Besnard confronted her. "Bout time you showed your face.'

'What is that?' she said, pointing to the gaily-coloured bird perched on his shoulder. She felt queasy watching the parrot kiss his lips, searching for the seed the chef held between his teeth. Looking around, she saw that almost every sailor aboard had adopted the fashion. The air was filled with the piercing shrieks of their birds.

'And that?' He jabbed a finger at her lizard in its bamboo cage. She ignored him, lifting the cage high as she sidled past.

After weeks of space and solitude, this shambolic frenzy squeezed the breath from her. She fought her way through the press of men and beasts, anxious to reach her cabin.

The vapours below deck reminded her that she faced another long sea voyage. Another year at least before they turned for home. Think of your wages, she consoled herself. She had survived the southern ocean once before and she had no choice but to endure it now.

When she reached her cabin, Girardin locked herself in. She hung the cage from a hook and pulled apart a piece of ship's biscuit to feed the grubs to the lizard. Its eyes darted around the cabin. 'Your new home,' she said. The familiar boundaries both comforted and oppressed her. She lit a candle.

She was pleased to be leaving Amboyna, and yet she was not. She was pleased to be far from Captain Kermadec, and yet she was not. She could not settle, remembering how easy it would have been to let herself fall.

An eerie wailing, like a woman's haunted cry, drew her back on deck. It serenaded the ships as they departed from the Dutch East Indies. The soulful voice travelled across the water and sent shivers down her arms. The sailors grew quiet. She saw Armand cross himself. 'It's an omen.'

'It's the bamboo.' Labillardière appeared at her elbow. He pointed to a river mouth where tall stakes of bamboo had been driven into the ground. 'The natives drill a hole through each segment and the wind whistles a tune. We came across it on our travels.'

'Sounds like the devil's work to me,' the old sailor said with a contemptuous sniff.

Labillardière ignored him. 'I hear we are to abandon La Pérouse and travel to the southern ocean once again.'

Girardin refused to be baited. 'The General must have good reason. He follows the King's orders.'

'The General thinks of his legacy. He wishes to be remembered on the charts of history,' scoffed Labillardière.

'And are you so different?' she asked. 'Do you not wish to be remembered long after your death in the names of the plants you have discovered?'

Labillardière thumped his fist against the rail. 'Look around you. Look at the oak boards beneath our feet, the fibres of these ropes, the cotton of your shirt. Where would we be without plants and the discovery of their uses? Look here—' he scrabbled around in his knapsack and held up a candle '—the gum of the tree *Dammara alba*. The natives roll it into candles wrapped with sago leaves. It burns with no wick and no smoke for three hours! This is the sort of discovery we should be taking back to France. But instead the efforts of the naturalists are pushed aside in favour of the stargazers and the mariners. I cannot reason with him. We have all seen what lucrative trade the spices make. But he cannot see that our researches should be of equal, if not greater, import than mere cartography!'

'But there will be opportunities, surely, when we stop for water?' She thought of Kermadec without meaning to. The next time she would see him would be on Timor, when the ships were to resupply with water.

'Mark my words, the needs of the savants will be the lowest priority.'

In the following days, her lizard dined on the explosion of cockroaches that had stowed away with the wood. It roamed about Girardin's cabin, crunching their shiny bodies into its mouth. The cockroaches could not be contained and they made their way through linen, books and papers, even draining the ink from inkwells. Her lizard and its appetite was in great demand and welcome in every cabin. '*Lacerta amboinensis*,' Labillardière declared it to be, 'sailfin lizard. The female of the species.' He had snapped his book closed. But Girardin named her Passepartout after the master key that passes everywhere.

While her lizard thrived, the sailors' parrots succumbed to convulsions and died within days of leaving Amboyna. Secretly, Girardin was thankful for the respite from their fierce shrieks. Besnard was distraught.

The goats were next to perish for want of better food.

The scheduled visit to Timor for water was abandoned. Light and fickle breezes forced the ships to veer out deeper into the ocean in search of stronger winds. Labillardière was proved right. He was denied his chance to explore and Girardin now realised she would not see Captain Kermadec for many more months.

As the weeks passed she replayed all the moments she had spent alone with Huon de Kermadec, the feel of his hand on the small of her back, the strength of his arms as he pulled her to her feet, the shock of his hands drawing her in to him. Had she remembered their connection to be more than it was? Had he only meant to give her comfort?

At night, Girardin tried to banish him from her thoughts, but the fantasies remained. She imagined Kermadec with his arm resting across her shoulders, smiling at her. They were standing in a field and her son was running through the long grass towards her. There were flowers in the field, and a goat. Her son was now a small boy. He had a shock of white-blond hair.

With Kermadec, she could raise her boy. With Kermadec they could be a family. The thought was there, like a dormant seed, waiting for water.

What was she doing? How could she allow herself to feel this way? God punishes you whenever you dare to hope for something better, she reminded herself.

To make matters worse her body began to burn and ache for touch. Each night a throb settled between her legs. She denied herself in punishment, knowing the feelings would pass. But she dreamed of the weight of a man lying on her, his hardness. She felt his wet lips on hers and the sudden suck of her lower lip into his mouth, and her loins kicked in response. She woke to the pulsing sensation and felt shame and anger—anger that her body had betrayed her yet again.

During the day, she paced the deck. The tightness of the ship pressed on her spirits. Now that they had lost sight of land, there was nothing but the distant shape of the *Espérance* to fix her eyes on. Beside her, the stag shook his head and snorted in his corral. He lunged from left to right. She saw holes in the planks where his hooves had turned for days on end.

It was time to forget this foolishness. Kermadec meant nothing by his attentions. Did she honestly believe that he would want her? A captain of a ship, no less! But she took out his gift to her, the telescope, and found the *Espérance* through its eyepiece.

She turned at the crack of splintering wood.

The stag had burst from his pen. His hooves slipped on the deck, striking buckets and coils of rope. She watched as the magnificent animal twisted away from the hands that reached for him. The doe, still confined in her corral, whirled around. Sailors scattered as the stag lowered his head and charged towards the stern. His leap was weightless, he hovered in mid-air with the ship moving out from beneath him, and then he was swimming, strong and hard, nostrils flared above the water. The cry of the doe tore her ears and Girardin turned to see the deer staring back at her, wide-eyed and trembling.

The stag held his antlers valiantly above the waves. Could he smell land? she wondered. They had sailed for days without sight of it. How long could he swim? He did not hesitate nor waver in his direction. What of the sharks?

He would rather take his chance of freedom, Girardin realised, than stay constrained a moment longer.

Chapter 38

Cape Leeuwin, New Holland, 5 December 1792

THIRST.

A kind of madness, an obsessive need, gripped her. She fought it. She understood why men had been caught drinking from the stagnant rain gauges. She must drink! She took a small mouthful of mud-tasting brine and let it trickle down her throat. The water from Amboyna had turned putrid and the rations had been cut to one small bottle a day.

She began to dream of the fountains of Versailles. Of falling into the pools, of splashing at the feet of Apollo's horses, of drinking from his spouting horns. She remembered the wet juice of an orange. The boy had plucked one from the tree, casually dropping the peel to the ground. She had been shocked. 'The oranges are to be looked at, not eaten,' her father had told her. 'The King will know if we take one.' All the gardeners knew the consequences if they were caught with stolen fruit. The boy held out a piece of orange to her and she took it. An explosion of juice filled her mouth, sweet and tart. Now she thought of the taste of pineapple.

The southern coast of New Holland was devastatingly dry and barren. Her excitement at seeing land again after two months of ocean voyage evaporated as they commenced the slow and careful running survey. The entire coastline was bare and arid, with only sparse and feeble shrubs. Tremulous lines of smoke rose from the fires of the land's inhabitants. There were no trees. No rivers. No hope, she thought, of finding water. Girardin swallowed, tasting dust.

The sky above the continent was stained a brownish yellow. She had never seen a sky like it, as if no amount of fresh wind could cleanse the air of its ancient history. The warm wind blew softly from the land, scented with particles of smoke and clay. Girardin licked her chapped lips, taking a sip of muddy water that barely moistened her mouth.

During the windless days they baked under a hot sun. But the nights were cold and Passepartout suffered, slumping into torpor. Labillardière advised her to take the lizard into the sun each morning to reinvigorate her limbs. She had kept close to the naturalists during this leg of the voyage, protected once again by their oddity. Today, Félix sat cross-legged on the deck with Passepartout crawling around his neck, feeding her cockroaches from a jar. Ventenat was splayed out beside him, lying on his back in his black robes, his arms and legs spread out wide like a starfish. 'Taking in God's rays,' he murmured. 'One must be open to His messages.' The sailors gave them all a wide berth.

Labillardière stretched and yawned with exaggeration as the mapmakers came near. 'Geography is staggeringly tedious,' he said and fell back to the deck with a loud snore.

Girardin saw a curl of hair come loose from Beautemps-Beaupré's careful combing.

Labillardière thumped his arm across his forehead. 'No man of true intelligence could bear it.'

'Ignore him,' Rossel said, holding back Saint-Aignan as he aimed a kick at the naturalist's leg.

The trio continued taking their bearings and drawing their profiles of the coastline. Each slow day was the same. The ships communicated only by flag signal and she saw nothing of Captain Kermadec. A dry ache had lodged in the base of her throat. Her gaze wandered to the *Espérance* again and again as if the frequency of her glances might bring the ship closer.

This rugged coastline was her enemy. It kept them from finding water and it kept her from Kermadec. Both ships now struggled through an archipelago of islands. The puzzle of rock islets and low hummocks confounded their every turn. The round backs of the islands reminded her of turtle shells that seemed to rise out of the water in front of them whenever a promising channel opened up.

Sharks had been spotted in the wake of the ships. One tall, dark fin had been following them since Cape Leeuwin. 'Are you waiting for us to founder on these rocks?' she asked it as the grey shape passed beneath the ship. It was monstrously large. Labillardière called it *Squalus carcharias*. The sailors called it the Angel of Death. The beast came close enough to raise its small eye above the water and show its white throat and belly to her. Large enough to be a man-eater, Labillardière had said, showing her an illustration from Buffon's encyclopedia of its mouthful of saw-like teeth.

Captain d'Auribeau passed behind her as he circled about the ship. He kept his jacket buttoned tight across his white shirt, his chin high and his tricorn low on his brow. His presence on deck gave her a chill, like catching a glimpse of a shark's fin from the corner of your eye. She watched him call up to the pilot, Ange Raoul. It unsettled her that d'Auribeau seemed to pay particular attention to him, to single him out for favour. The two men would parade about the deck in the evenings, heads bent together in whispered conversation. She wondered what it was they discussed so earnestly. She had suffered no further taunts or threats from Raoul; he had told no one of her secret, but she remained wary of him. She felt safest when he was on lookout in the tops, and was thankful that the tall masts put that distance between them.

A cold wind rose from the south-west, whispering around her ears. Above her head the sheets began to hum in the freshening wind. She could no longer smell dust and smoke from the land. When she turned her face, she felt the bite of the southern ocean, and it spiked her flesh with shivers.

Captain d'Auribeau raised his eyeglass. 'The *Espérance* is in trouble.'

Girardin swung back towards Kermadec's ship. The *Espérance*'s sails were ghostly white.

'She's being blown into the islands.'

The *Espérance* tilted to her side under the power of the wind.

Curse this coast, this parched coast, Girardin thought, gripping the rail. Shipwreck here would be certain death.

'They are turning!'

The *Espérance* seemed to turn towards the chain of islands, not away from them. She fumbled for her telescope.

'They are taking in the mainsails, running under foresail only,' Rossel cried from the helm. 'Turning crosswind.'

'I think they have seen a way through!' Raoul called down.

'A risky manoeuvre,' said d'Auribeau. 'Kermadec must spread the mainsail at the height of the blast to make the gap.'

The sailors around her fell silent. Girardin bit hard on her lip as the mainsail on the *Espérance* was raised. The chain of islands looked impassable. They would be stricken on the bare rocks, she was sure of it. The squall growled behind her and she waited for the gust to hit the *Espérance*. The sail snapped tight like a filled wineskin, but did not split.

'She is through!'

Girardin breathed again. He was alive.

Chapter 39

Espérance Bay, New Holland, 9 December 1792

'A LUCKY FIND,' SAID HUON DE KERMADEC AS HE CLIMBED ABOARD the *Recherche*. 'A port of providence.'

Girardin ducked behind a mast. From there she could watch him without being seen. Her mouth was papery, even more so than usual in this dry heat, and she could feel her heart throbbing in her throat. Even if she had a chance to speak with him, she wondered what she would think of to say.

'We shall name her Espérance Bay!' the General declared.

'A fortunate discovery,' d'Auribeau acknowledged reluctantly, 'but only if it provides us with the water we urgently need.'

The bay that Kermadec had chanced upon was expansive. The beach was stark white, the sea a shade of bright blue that hurt her eyes, and the dunes behind were covered in scraggly bushes. The hills were low and desolate. They had scant hope of finding anything much to sustain them, she thought, but it hardly mattered. At least both ships were safe and anchored.

In Kermadec's face she saw the strain of the past months. He had dark circles beneath his eyes and his cheeks had hollowed. He had lost weight since leaving Amboyna. She heard his wheezing cough as Rossel came to congratulate him and saw the solicitous hand that the General placed on his shoulder. Straightening up, he looked around the ship. She held her breath. Was he looking for her?

The General ushered Kermadec and his officers towards his cabin. Would he seek her out? Of course not. She shook her head. Her palms were clammy and her heart as jumpy as a girl with her first infatuation. This was impossible, she scolded herself. She had imagined more between them than could possibly exist.

Labillardière gripped her arm. 'There you are! Why are you hiding here? Come on, the boat is leaving for shore. Now is our chance.'

'What?'

Félix grinned, throwing a pack on his back.

She looked back to Kermadec, desperation stark on her face. What if she missed her chance to speak with him? She caught Ventenat watching her. His face was lined with sorrow and understanding. He touched her hand. 'That kind of thirst is madness.'

The shoreline of Observatory Island was marked by low cliffs and white-stained rocks where seals wallowed, unconcerned by the approach of their boat. Along the shore, she watched strange birds with their wings held stiff at their sides plunge into the water one after the other. They stumbled over the rocks as though their legs were bound together at the knees.

'What are those creatures?' Girardin asked.

'Penguins,' Labillardière said, taking aim with his pistol and dispatching one.

Birds that can't fly, she thought with astonishment. Birds that had learned to swim.

The boat surged towards the shore on the crest of a wave. 'There is no place to land,' Labillardière noted. 'We will have to leap.'

Girardin turned to him in fright.

Ventanat tapped her shoulder. 'Look there!' A grey shape glided beneath the the boat. Her stomach dropped. She heard a sailor mutter, 'The Angel is with us.' The fin of the great white shark pierced the waves like a knife blade. She gasped. 'It has followed us into the bay.'

Ventenat looked oddly gleeful.

Labillardière tossed his pack onto a low cliff. He waited till the boat was lifted to the top of a surge, then he thrust his long limbs out and landed safe on the rocks. Girardin felt ill. There was no way she could do that. She scanned the waves for the shark, but its fin had disappeared below the water.

Félix grasped the collecting cages and threw them across the gap.

'Hurry up,' the coxswain grunted.

'Come on,' Félix urged her. 'You next.'

'I cannot,' she said, her face white.

He held out his hand to her, but she could not prise her fingers from her seat.

Félix gave a curt nod, and on the count of three he jumped. He landed spread-eagle on the rocks beneath the cliff, then hauled himself up to join Labillardière. She looked down into the swirling waters, the long strands of seaweed tossed about by the waves.

The boat drifted with the current along the shore and the oarsmen grunted as they rowed out again to make a final approach. On the cliff, Labillardière and Félix were two small black shapes against the bright sky. Girardin felt a hand at her back. Ventenat stood. 'We'll do it together.'

'No, I can't.' She remembered the doe that had been too afraid to leap. She saw her wet and quivering nostrils, the size of her eyes.

Ventenat nodded and wrapped his coat tight about him.

'Last chance,' the coxswain said as they turned the boat about.

Ventenat was already standing at the stern, balancing on the edge of the boat. His black coat-tails flapped around his thin legs, trousers soaked by the sea spray. It had been barely three months since the chaplain had lain gravely ill; surely he was not well enough for such heroic feats. She looked for the shark circling the boat. 'Do not risk yourself!' she called.

Ventenat pushed his tall hat down firmly on his head. The boat rose up on a wave and Félix cried out for the chaplain to jump. Ventenat turned to Girardin. 'Pray for me,' he said and simply stepped from the boat into the water.

Girardin screamed. The coxswain swore numerous violent oaths, all blasphemous. Ventenat disappeared into the weeds and then popped up between the rocks, carried by the swirling current along the cliffs and spinning like a children's top. He had lost his black hat and his head looked like polished bone, his arms were splayed out at his sides.

'Row!' the coxswain screamed. Ventenat was dragged back out to sea by a retreating wave. Girardin imagined the leap of that giant shark, with its pointed nose and gleaming white belly.

'Take this.' The coxswain passed her a grappling hook. The men rowed hard towards the cliff face. The languorous seals raised their heads but did not move. The boat was so close now Girardin could smell their ammonia stench.

'Can he swim?' she called.

The coxswain barked a laugh showing the idiocy of her question. What if he could? How would that help him now?

Ventenat lay with arms and legs oustretched, face turned up to God. The next wave brought him rushing towards them.

'Lean out, lad!' The coxswain swung hard on the rudder and manoeuvred the boat between Ventenat and the rocks. She snagged his arm with the hook and hauled. As he drew close, she wrapped her arms around his chest. The weight of the water in his clothes sucked him down. With a guttural cry, she wedged her knees against the side of the boat and pulled, managing to heave his chest across the gunnel. Water gushed from his open mouth. The grey skin of his face was pulled taut. She bundled him onto the floor of the boat.

He coughed and spewed more sea water. 'You saved me,' he gasped, pulling her face close to his. 'God would've let me drown.'

Chapter 40

On her return to the ship, all was in turmoil. No one appeared to notice the drenched and miserable chaplain draped over her shoulder. Claude Riche was missing.

'What on earth possessed Kermadec to let that cursed savant loose on the continent?' Captain d'Auribeau raged about the deck. 'Does he not know how to keep his men in check?'

Kermadec had already returned to his ship to deal with the disaster, and she had missed her chance to speak with him.

She helped Ventenat to his cabin. He thanked her, professed himself recovered and lay down in his hammock, still soaking wet. She covered him with a blanket.

'I am testing Him,' he said through clattering teeth.

'Enough,' she scolded him. 'No more.'

The image of Ventenat swirling in the water would not leave her. They had so nearly lost him to the Angel of Death, and now calamity had struck again. Search parties had been sent but found no trace of Riche. Girardin thought of the pale, freckled naturalist with his coat of many pockets and his wiry spray of hair. She learned he had gone into the barren dunes alone, looking for the remains of a petrified forest the water parties had seen. Not even his servant had gone with him. He was utterly alone.

At dusk, the boats were sent back out to leave supplies for Riche in the hopes he would return to shore in the night.

By morning, the biscuit, brandy and firearm left for Riche were untouched.

Félix and Labillardière returned cold and hungry from a night out on the exposed rock. In the panic they had been overlooked and the boat parties had forgotten to return for them. Félix told her they were forced to broil the penguins for their dinner.

Labillardière was eager to join the search for his friend, but the General would not allow it, afraid he would become lost as well. She watched as the boat returned to shore spooking a mob of bizarre creatures on the beach. The animals bounded away, springing on their long legs and tails. These creatures shared the same peculiar hopping movement as those she had seen in Van Diemen's Land, but these were much larger, their bodies tall and muscular. When they stopped and turned back, she saw their faces looked like long-snouted hares with prominent ears twitching.

'Kangarous,' Labillardiere said, with evident longing to get closer.

The day passed slowly. Girardin walked the deck, noticing the damaged wood where the stag's hooves had bored into the planks. They would have released the deer here on New Holland. The stag and hind, Adam and Eve, the first of a herd meant to sustain the explorers of the future. But when the stag chose to flee, the butcher had sharpened his knives. What use was a doe without her mate alone on this continent? They had dined on venison.

She saw the anxious looks passing between the General and his officers. The rumours began to spread, mutterings about how long they could afford to wait. No reliable source of water had yet been found to resupply the ships for their journey.

As the sun set on another day, the search parties returned having seen no sign of Claude Riche. Not even Riche's own dog was able to track him down. She imagined him blistering in the heat by day and shivering under his coat at night. Perhaps he had a lump of sugar or a scrap of biscuit left to sustain him. Had he found a trickle of water?

Girardin stood at the bow, watching the sky burn orange above the horizon. The dunes were blackening in the falling light, and the pinprick glow of distant fires gleamed like animal eyes in the darkness. It was dusk, the hour between dog and wolf. Girardin imagined Riche's horror, alone in this savage land. Did he listen to the freakish night sounds and wonder whether he would spend the rest of his days here, in this land as desolate and foreign to him as the moon?

A movement caught her eye. Captain Kermadec approached her, a slow smile spreading across his face.

She gasped. She had spent so long wishing she could speak with him, and now he was here, standing in front of her. She flushed with an unfamiliar sensation of delight.

'May I join you?' he asked.

She nodded, smiling like a fool, but helpless to stop herself.

He moved to stand beside her at the rail, his arm just touching hers.

'I have missed you,' he said softly.

She closed her eyes. Gently, he laid his hand over her hand. She held her breath for several hard beats of her heart.

His hand was warm and his palm surprisingly soft, but when she opened her eyes she saw it was a sailor's hand, scarred like all the others with cuts and burns and mended bones. Hesitantly, she touched his thumb, running her finger along a silver scar. 'How did you get this?'

'You imagine some daring deed of seamanship, perhaps?' He smiled down at her. 'My sister pushed a desk onto my hand. I was six. She was a menace for our governess. We both were.'

Girardin returned his smile, but the mention of a governess only served to expose the chasm between their worlds.

'Your poor mother,' she said, imagining the small boy taking his cut hand, streaming with blood, to her lap.

'My mother, God bless her, had passed. Only my father had to suffer us.'

'Forgive me.' She had spoken carelessly again and cursed her thoughtless tongue.

'There is nothing to forgive.' He squeezed her hand. 'You were not to know.'

We have that one thing in common, she thought. We were both motherless children.

They stood together in the darkness, arms touching, listening to the waves lap against the hull of the ship. She felt her tension ease, and she leaned against him. For the first time in such a very long while, she let someone take her weight.

The foreign constellations crept into the night sky. Was Riche looking up at the stars too, she wondered, terrified that he might never see the North Star again, never find his way home?

'Can you imagine what he must be thinking?' she said, finding her voice. 'Out there.' The sky had coloured to Indian ink and the land was black.

Kermadec sighed. 'Damned Riche. A torment from the very start.' She felt him stiffen. 'These savants will be the ruin of us.'

She frowned, remembering the rumours. 'Is it true, what they say? That you would leave him behind?'

'I fear he is dead and fallen down some dry crevasse. That is why we cannot find him.'

'We don't know that!' She pulled away from him.

'You're right. But how long can I risk my men? We cannot survive this coast if we do not find water. Each day we lose here condemns us all.'

'But to abandon him? To leave him here with no way home? What if he lives? What if he watches us sail away from him?' Her voice grew frantic. She couldn't believe that he would sacrifice one of his men, that he could discard Riche so easily.

'I do not do this lightly.'

He must know that she did not only think of Riche. She had left her son in similar desolation, alone and afraid, on a dark slab of stone.

'We cannot abandon him. I beg you, one more day.'

'One more day,' he said, pulling her close, his lips against the crown of her head. 'I promise you.'

She felt the shock of his embrace, but let herself be comforted by the strength of it. She squeezed her eyes closed, trying to quell the voices in her mind. *You left your child. You do not deserve happiness.*

She lingered on the deck, watching as Kermadec's men rowed him back to his ship. In the east, a fat golden moon rose above the ocean. It looked to be kissing the water goodbye.

In the darkness she heard a hooting laugh. It came from above. She looked up into the rigging. She saw nothing: no movement, no shape.

'Come down and show yourself!' she said bravely to the blackness.

Raoul shifted into the moonlight, crowing like a cock who had seen the dawn light before any other.

'How dare you spy on me?' Her voice came out as a squeak.

His laugh was a long, low rumble. 'Oh, Marie-Louise. Did you think you were the only spy on this ship?'

She fled the deck, fear nettling her skin, and memories chasing at her heels.

To be a spy for the revolution! Marie-Louise had found the idea thrilling. Hébert had collected her from her father's house, arriving in a carriage wearing the silk culottes and tight-curled wig of the aristocracy, and leaving behind the story that the powerful and influential family of Noailles would look kindly on the Girardin family—and their business—for the benefit of Marie-Louise's company.

'It would be no small thing to win a contract to supply wine for one of the largest families at court,' hinted Hébert.

'It is said they occupy an entire wing of the palace,' her stepmother said, wide-eyed with greed.

'Madame Marguerite de Noailles is newly wed into the family and requires a companion. No one too young or pretty, you understand.' Hébert had looked knowingly at Jean Girardin. 'No one likely to turn her new husband's head.'

Marie-Louise pretended she had not heard. She did not care what he said. She was excited. Just three short steps from her father's house into Hébert's waiting carriage and she would be gone forever.

As the horses lurched away, she did not look back.

He took her to a rented room where she could change out of her best taffeta and into her new clothes. Worn clothes. A dust-coloured apron over a faded red dress. Her throat was dry.

'Just follow what the others do. You'll soon learn.' He smiled reassuringly.

She nodded.

'You will be superb,' he said, lifting her chin gently with his finger. 'I know it.'

She walked alone towards the palace, her letter of employment sweaty in her fist. The avenue was long, the gates shining golden in the distance. Her heart quickened. She was on her own now. And there was no going back.

The next morning she watched the search parties leave the ship for the final time. Today, Labillardière had been allowed to join the search. Raoul too was among the men. His words from the night before tormented her. What did he mean by accusing her of spying? Could he truly know what she had done? She paced the deck, hoping to jostle her memories. There had been so many people at Versailles, so many more than she had imagined. The palace was full of courtiers and their servants. All their faces swam before her; how could she possibly remember?

Girardin went about her tasks in an agitated state of suspense. By the middle of the day the sun was baking. Girardin peered towards the shoreline. It hurt her eyes to look at the shimmering salt-crusted dunes. She splashed drops of muddy water onto her tongue, ignoring the taste of it. Nothing moved on the shore.

At dinner, the search parties returned.

'Did you find him?' she called out.

'No,' replied Labillardière, climbing aboard.

Girardin slumped. We will sail away. We will leave him stranded in this barren place at the bottom of the world, dreaming of the family he will never see again.

Labillardière had a strange smile on his face. 'He found us.'

'What?' Girardin looked around her for confirmation. She saw the men's smiles. Saw Mérite leap up onto the taffrail, balancing like an acrobat with his arms spread wide, his face shining. 'Riche has been saved!'

'Where did you find him?' she asked Labillardière.

'As I said, we did not find him. But look . . .' He rummaged in his pack and carefully unravelled a piece of canvas. He held up a plant stem with tubular red flowers, each shaped like a wizened hand encased in a velvet mitten. 'I discovered this. A flower with the soft paws of a kangarou. A species entirely new to science!'

She clenched her jaw. He was truly impossible. 'But what of Riche?' she cried.

'We saw no sign on our travels. We returned to our rendezvous in a state of grave apprehension for his life.'

'The other search party then?'

'They found his pistol, a handkerchief and some botanical notes, that was all. We were beaten at last; even I was convinced of the death of our unfortunate companion. There were tears of despair and exhaustion. Riche's servant was distraught. Such dreadful wailing when he saw that we were making to depart! The poor man fell to the ground, overcome by tears. It was some moments before we realised they were tears of joy. Claude Riche had come stumbling through the bushes! He arrived just at the moment we were due to depart.'

Girardin felt the hairs of her nape rise.

'Incredible!' Félix clapped his hands.

'He saw our ships from a distant hill and tortured himself with the thought we would leave before he reached the coast.'

Girardin looked toward the *Espérance*. We did not leave him, she thought. We did not maroon him here with no hope of return. Whatever else she had to fear in the coming journey, she would not have his abandonment on her conscience.

Chapter 41

Port du Sud, Recherche Bay, Van Diemen's Land, 22 January 1793

AT THE FIRST TOUCH OF SAND BENEATH HER FEET, GIRARDIN stumbled and sank to her knees. She gripped the fine sand in her fist. Van Diemen's Land at long last. Safety. Fresh water.

After leaving Espérance Bay, the ships had tracked along a sheer rock face of white limestone. No land could be seen beyond the cliff. No birds rose from it. No smoke. From west to east the wall looked endless, with no change in elevation, and no inlet or stream or river to break their thirst. Weeks passed until there was scarcely any water left in the ship's hold. Each day was the same, a slow charting of the coast. Each morning she rose to see the wall's blank white face.

When the *Espérance* had signalled her distress on New Year's Day, d'Auribeau convinced the General to ignore it. Girardin had been shocked. The signal was a code; it meant supplies were critical and Kermadec had only enough water to sail to Van Diemen's Land.

She thought of Kermadec's suspicion that his steward was stealing rations. Was that why they had so few barrels left? Had the steward sold their water? She'd heard rumours that the *Espérance* had no more water for making bread and that their rudder needed urgent repairs. For three more days the General continued the running survey of the coast. She watched each day pass in agitation, thinking of the anxiety Kermadec and his crew would be feeling. Did they think their commander was punishing them? D'Auribeau pressed the General to continue, to keep looking for the supposed strait between New Holland and Van Diemen's Land. But the wall of limestone and the headwinds were relentless. Even the *Recherche* was desperately short of water. The coffee ration had been cut for all but the officers, sending Labillardière into a rage at the injustice and causing one of the officers to hurl a jug of wine at his head. She was tearful when the General finally made the call to turn away from that coastline and return to Recherche Bay in Van Diemen's Land where she knew they would find water.

Girardin heard splashing. She pushed herself upright and followed the sound of men singing. At the rivulet she rushed forwards, wading into the water. She cupped her hand and scooped up the cold water, drinking noisily. The water was tea-stained but fresh and she couldn't remember when she had tasted better. She gulped it, not caring if the water spilled down her shirt. She felt like plunging beneath the surface, soaking and scrubbing the dry dust from her pores. She dunked her head and scrubbed the roots of her hair. A wooden barrel bounced over fallen logs and splashed into the creek beside her, drenching her. The sailor made no apology as he shoved it downstream to the waiting boat crews.

'Your captain?' she asked, hoping her voice would not betray her nervousness. Droplets of water dripped from her nose and chin. The sailor pointed behind him.

Girardin picked her way alongside the rivulet until she saw Kermadec standing beneath the shade of the paperbark trees. With the luxury of observing him unnoticed, she could let her heartbeat slowly settle. He was thinner than he had been five weeks ago and his long back was rounded as he rested on a staff of wood.

Girardin squared her shoulders and stepped forwards.

He turned, recognised her, and smiled. With relief she saw his eyes were shining.

He inclined his head to her. 'It is good to see you.'

'And you,' Girardin murmured, biting her lip.

She was close enough to hear his chest rattle as he took a deep breath. 'It is good to see you,' he repeated.

Girardin steadied her hands by clasping her elbows. They were awkward together. These weeks apart had changed something between them. She wanted to reach out to him, but held back. Below, she heard the men splashing in the creek, their songs, whistles and laughter reaching up to them. 'I bring a message from the General,' she said. 'He hopes you will dine with his officers this evening.'

'Ha! A fine evening that would be. Shall we listen to Captain d'Auribeau's snide remarks on the quality of our supplies? Will I watch him curl his lip and declare that this water my men have collected for him tastes of stagnant marshes?'

She was startled at the anger in his voice. His tone was bitter. It had the chill of the southerly wind.

'And will I suffer as the General laments his lost chance of charting the unknown southern coast?' He thumped the staff into the dry dirt.

She ached for him. That awful coast had changed him.

Kermadec raised his chin. 'I know my errors; I do not need them explained to me. Please tell the General I must dine with my own officers.'

Girardin felt her throat close tightly as she swallowed. 'But when will I see you again?'

He was silent, his jaw grinding. The desperation of her question hung in the air between them. She was close enough that, if he chose to, he could reach out and touch her.

'How are your provisions aboard the *Recherche*?' he asked finally.

She cleared her throat. She could not tell him the flour purchased in Amboyna was stale and rancid. 'As good as can be expected.'

'Fresh fish will hearten the men. Have the sailors been fishing?'

Girardin nodded. Why was he asking her this? An awkward silence grew between them.

Girardin looked to the beach, where a boat from the *Espérance* was drawing in to shore. She watched as Claude Riche stepped from the boat. His servant held a parasol above his head to shield him from the sun. The parasol was frilled and beaded like the one she had once owned.

'How is Monsieur Riche?' she asked.

'A great vexation,' he said harshly. 'He insists on continuing his researches even though he is unwell.'

The surgeon, Joannet, followed from the boat, weighed down with his own collecting paraphernalia. She watched as Riche's loyal servant stuck out his foot to trip him on the sand. She sniggered and turned to Kermadec, but he wasn't smiling.

'I find their petty jealousies no longer amuse me.'

She frowned, uncertain how to mend this strangeness between them. She turned her face to the beach. Two seagulls hooked their wings over the onshore wind, stalled in mid-air.

She heard rustling in the forest behind them. Labillardière and Félix crashed through the undergrowth.

'Oh!' Félix cried, looking between her and Kermadec. 'There you are. We are going to visit my garden!' He held up an empty pack to her. 'Come and help us with the harvest.'

She flicked her eyes towards Kermadec. He regarded the arrival of the gardener as he would a hair in his soup.

'Will you join us?' Félix asked her again, waving the sack.

She had failed them in Espérance Bay. Her courage had failed her. She wanted to help them now, but she glanced at Captain Kermadec and shook her head.

Félix looked crestfallen.

A third man in an officer's uniform burst through the ferns behind them. She recognised the midshipman Mérite, and remembered the last time she had set foot on this land, feeling a twinge of pain in the sword wound on her arm.

'What are you doing here?' Labillardière seemed surprised to see Mérite had followed them.

'General's orders.' Mérite grinned. 'Wants someone to keep an eye on you all.'

'The General sends a boy to babysit us.'

Girardin saw a pistol hanging at Mérite's hip.

'After what happened with Claude Riche, he doesn't trust you to keep to your word.'

Labillardière turned his back and set off into the forest.

'The garden is this way,' Félix called to him, pointing northwards along the beach.

'We must take advantage of every moment that is offered us,' Labillardière said, disappearing behind the ferns.

Félix muttered to himself and set off purposefully along the beach. After he had gone ten feet, he turned, hands on hips, and noticed that no one was following. 'This way!' he called again.

She could hear Labillardière slashing through the ferns, heading deeper into the forest away from him.

'Well, I suppose just a small detour,' mumbled Félix.

Mérite caught her eye and shrugged. He followed the naturalists into the forest and the brief whirlwind of activity moved on without her. The ferns closed together behind them. The glade beside the creek returned to silence.

'Do not trust those savants,' Kermadec growled.

She blanched, shocked by his coldness. 'They are my friends.'

'They are revolutionaries,' he said with disgust. 'I have heard the way they speak about our King.' He pressed his handkerchief to his lips and his breath wheezed. 'I do not want you consorting with them.'

She drew back. He meant to control her. She thought of her father and his careful inspection of all her invitations. She had thought Kermadec a different sort of man. Perhaps she had been wrong.

'They are harmless,' she said, her voice soft and steady.

'Harmless? Riche nearly killed us all with his selfishness!' His voice rang out in the clearing.

But her blood was pumping in her ears. She made her decision. 'Félix!' she cried out. 'Monsieur Lahaie!'

She turned away from Kermadec and pushed through the undergrowth in search of the naturalists. The bracken snatched at her legs. Her cheeks burned. She felt humiliated and furious, if only for the thoughts she'd let run rampant. Kermadec was no different from other men. He had meant to sleep with her, that was all; he meant to do nothing more than relieve an itch. She had imagined a life with him, imagined they would marry and she could reclaim her son. The lie of it burned in her chest. The sound of his hacking cough behind her did not check her stride.

Chapter 42

Hours later, as the straps of her pack sliced into her shoulders and the leather of her boots rubbed her toes raw, they still had not reached Félix's garden. The sea was so far behind them she could no longer hear it. After being cramped on the boat for so many months, she was unused to walking such distances or carrying a pack that was heavy with the plants Labillardière had collected. As her flare of temper at Kermadec cooled, she regretted her hasty decision. Each step rubbed her blisters. The roots and vines snagged her feet and she swore aloud in frustration.

Confused by the sudden change in Kermadec, Girardin tried not to let her thoughts dwell on him. But his coldness hurt her. Had she truly misread his intentions? She clambered over a fallen log and the deceptive wood gave way beneath her, piercing her palm with splinters. She swore again. Perhaps he had only meant to protect her from the naturalists and their foolish obsessions, she thought, pulling the spines of wood from her hand. It was not like him to lash out like that. Kermadec was hurt by the General's treatment of him and angry with Claude Riche for risking all his men; surely that was the root of his dislike for the savants. Too late she realised she was thinking of him again.

The excitement of walking in this strange land had lessened with each painful step. At first she breathed its novelty, delighting in the strange scents and sounds. It felt good to set out on solid earth, to feel the living forest growing all around her. Sunlight glinted through the leaves of the tall eucalyptus and she squinted into the sparking light. It reminded her of crystal chandeliers. The tall trees began to take on the appearance of towering ballroom pillars and the voluminous tree ferns became the spreading skirts of dancing women. She felt dizzy, seeing flapping feathers and fans. It was how she had imagined her return to Versailles would be when Hébert had seduced her with his flattery at the ball. This same feeling of excitement, of setting forth on an adventure. She had not thought of the danger. She had wanted to see inside the palace and walk its gilded halls. All through her childhood, the palace had glimmered, golden and untouchable.

In reality, her introduction to the palace was not glamorous. Each morning, Marie-Louise opened a window and aimed the contents of a chamber-pot at a shallow drain running through the raked gravel below. Hébert had found her a place not as a companion, but as a chambermaid to Marguerite de Noailles. She emptied pots, swept ashes and gossiped with the servants of the courtiers in the urine-doused stairwells.

From the palace windows, she could see out along the avenues of the gardens to the woods beyond. She could see the bosques she once played in as a child. Far below her, the gardeners trimmed the trees into tight shapes, tucking their roots into clay pots. The men looked so small from her attic window, so insignificant. She watched them on their knees, clipping the lawns so that not one blade of grass was out of place. If she had seen her father from this height, perhaps he would not have seemed so terrifying.

She had become the eyes and ears for the revolution as Hébert had asked her to be, but in her first months at the palace she had not even seen the King.

'But what do you want me to do?' she demanded of Hébert when they met secretly in the streets of Versailles.

'Be patient, my sweet cuckoo,' he had said, lifting her chin with the tip of his finger. 'Your time will come.'

'Stand back!' Mérite called to Girardin, snapping her out of the past.

A long black snake glided in front of her boot. Terror pinned her to the forest floor. The snake wound itself through the leaves, like a piece of rope that had come to life, able to propel itself without legs or wings. It reared up to look at her.

Mérite aimed his pistol and fired.

'What have you done?' Labillardière bashed through the undergrowth. The snake's body had been ripped apart by the blast. 'Imbecile! A needless death that provides neither opportunity for scientific inquiry nor contributes to our dinner.'

'It was a snake,' offered Mérite, as though this was sufficient explanation.

She stared at the pieces of the snake, her own legs losing rigidity. She squatted down. One careless step in this land could kill a person. The strips of fallen leaves and bark scattered over the forest floor could camouflage any number of malevolent creatures.

Félix took her elbow and helped her to her feet. Labillardière led them out of the trees and down into a wide, flat marsh. She was relieved to be out of the tight, dense forest. The grasses looked soft and inviting, and copper-coloured butterflies danced around her legs. But as she pushed through the waving grasses, she felt the sharp, pointed barbs pierce the cotton of her trousers. Here, too, nothing was as harmless as it seemed.

At the edge of the marsh a large lake appeared before her. Clouds scudded across its surface as if the sky had turned upon itself. Gratefully, she cupped a handful of the clear water, but when she slurped it into her mouth it was warm and salty. She spat it out. Not even the water could be trusted.

'How far are we from the garden?' Félix called out to Labillardière.

Labillardière consulted his compass and looked up at the sinking sun. 'If we follow the edge of this lagoon we should find fresh water,' he answered obliquely. 'We can camp there for the night.'

Girardin let her head fall forwards. The day's march had begun to take its toll and now she would have to spend a night out under the stars, unprotected from the beasts lurking in these black forests. Her temper had made her foolish. She should've returned to the ship. The General would be furious with her.

'Don't worry,' Mérite said. 'We will be safe.'

She thought of Riche.

Later that evening, huddled around a fire built to ward off the cold night, Girardin began to shake. They had walked along the edge of the lagoon for several more hours before they found a rivulet and finally camped beneath the shelter of the trees. They ate foraged oysters and ship's biscuit toasted on the fire to singe the weevils. She lay down with her head resting on her pack, not caring if she crushed their prized specimens. Her hip dug into the earth as she turned her back to the warmth of the fire. She hadn't brought a coat or a blanket. Kermadec was right: the naturalists could not be trusted. Even a simple visit to a garden became an ordeal. She shivered. The voices of the men murmured behind her. The fire crackled and spat. Finally, exhaustion claimed her.

Sometime later she woke to the urgent pressure of her bladder. She heard snoring, and rose, stiff and aching. It was dark and the fire had died away to embers. As she moved through the forest, the dry twigs and leaves cracked under her feet. She stepped cautiously, seeing snakes slithering in the shadows out of the corner of her eye. When she turned her head, they disappeared, and she realised they existed only in the fever of her imagination. The urge to pee trumped her hallucination and she squatted among the bracken. The relief was immediate. She breathed out, long and loud. Her head tilted back and she looked up to the boughs of the tall trees above her. They reached out to each other, like bare arms glowing in the moonlight. For a moment, she was filled with stillness and peace. Beneath their embrace she felt insulated from the world.

Back at the campsite, she lay down alongside the softly snoring men.

In the morning, when she woke to the scent of wood smoke and the hazy mauve light of dawn, Félix and Labillardière were gone.

Chapter 43

'Mérite!' Girardin shook his shoulder.

He grumbled and rolled away from her.

'They've left us!'

Mérite raised his head to scan the campsite. 'They do this. Get up and go off botanising at the peep of dawn. They'll be back, expecting us to have a fire going and breakfast ready.' He let his head drop again.

She crouched beside the grey embers of the fire. The invisible birds screeched above her. The trees that had seemed to shelter her in the night now exposed their bare trunks to the morning light, like shanks of bone protruding from meat.

Behind her the branches cracked and shook. She whirled about. Some animal from the lagoon was crashing through the undergrowth. Girardin had barely time to kick Mérite's leg before Félix and Labillardière blundered into the campsite.

Félix rummaged through Mérite's belongings and pulled out his pistol.

'A party of savages,' Labillardière explained.

Mérite scrambled to his feet.

'About one hundred of them!' cried Félix, hastily ramming a bullet and powder into the muzzle. 'Armed with spears.'

'Possibly a group of forty,' Labillardière amended. 'Mostly fishing. But with only this pruning hook to defend ourselves, we thought it prudent to retreat and avail ourselves of your flintlock.'

'Are you sure?' Girardin breathed.

'Of course we're sure—they're following us!' Félix said, aiming the pistol at a nearby tree.

'Nonsense, we were careful not to let them see us.'

'How long have we got?'

The gun in Félix's hand boomed and a patch of dirt leaped into the air.

'Give me that! Do you want to scare them off?' Labillardière snatched the pistol from Félix.

'Yes, that's exactly what I want to do!'

'Be calm, everyone, we cannot lose this opportunity to communicate with the inhabitants.'

All three turned to Labillardière. 'What?'

'We must return to the lagoon.'

'He's insane,' Félix cried. 'Ignore him. Let him go and be slaughtered. The General has said we are to avoid any incidents that might end badly for them or us. It's in the King's orders, apparently.'

'We are also on a scientific expedition,' Labillardière argued. 'We are here to observe, to learn, to record our interactions.'

'I'm here to grow vegetables!'

'The gardener wishes to return to his patch,' Labillardière sneered. 'Those who wish to join him are free to do so. But might I remind you all that I carry the only compass. And my path is back to the lagoon.' Labillardière stowed the pistol at his hip and pushed through the grasses at the edge of the clearing.

Girardin had a sour, metallic taste in her mouth. She glanced at Mérite, who shrugged in return. They followed Labillardière as he picked a path through the shrubs. She could hear Félix muttering curses as he followed behind. The grasses poked at her legs and caught around her ankles. She tripped and stumbled into Labillardière, who had come to a halt in front of her. A group of naked men stood before them.

Her mouth fell open in astonishment.

Behind the men were women and children. So many children! The children peeked out from behind the adults, staring in wide-eyed wonder. It had been so long since she had seen a child, and now she remembered the boy on the street in Tenerife, playing with the ball and cup. That seemed an age ago. She crouched down slowly, unable to stop herself smiling at the children.

The people of Van Diemen's Land were the strangest she had ever seen. She counted seven adult men and eight women. All were naked. The nakedness of the men did not disturb her as much as that of the women. The women astounded Girardin. They had no modesty, made no attempt to cover their sagging breasts and private parts. Instead, animal skins, like the kangarou, were draped across their shoulders or rolled around their middles. The women had shaved heads, like hers, and the men had rubbed orange clay into their hair, which hung clumped and matted around their faces.

'Félix,' Labillardière said as the gardener joined them, 'time to put the tea on. We have company.'

Labillardière reached slowly into his pack and she saw the native men grow tense. They murmured to one another. Cautiously, he pulled out a piece of ship's biscuit and advanced to the eldest man of the group, taking a bite first and then holding it out to him. She held her breath. Hesitantly, the native man took it and nibbled at the edge. When Labillardière stuck out his hand in greeting, the elder clasped it in return, stooping forwards and then taking his left leg and extending it back beyond his body. Girardin and Mérite exchanged astonished glances. When the old man straightened up again, his face was lit with a pleasing smile.

The children ran towards them. Girardin was soon surrounded by them. They giggled as they touched her clothes and stroked her skin. She resisted the urge to wrap them in her arms.

A small boy aged perhaps nine or ten offered Girardin a string of whelks that he wore tied around his head. She had never seen shells so beautiful. They were tiny and pale, but iridescent, so they glowed purple and green as she turned them over in her palm. They sparkled like the phosphorescence on the sea. This would be a perfect gift for her son. She imagined tying them around Rémi's head as this boy had done, like a crown. She beamed at the boy, sorry she could not tell him how much this strand of shells meant to her. In return, she tugged the red kerchief from her neck and knotted it around the crown of his head. He gave her a look of such joy that tears spilled shamelessly onto her cheeks. He ran off, calling to his friends, and she tied the string of whelks around her neck, feeling the points of the shells prickle her skin.

Labillardière invited the party to the campsite, where they boiled water for tea and offered sago to their guests. Girardin had never seen the naturalist look so hospitable. He began to pull off layers of clothes and rifled through the packs, generously offering shirts, both his and Félix's, to the natives. A young woman examined herself in a brocaded waistcoat in much the same manner that a European gentleman might if he were trying on a waistcoat at a tailor's.

A group of girls had climbed a tree and crouched in the limbs above. Labillardière called up to them. 'Trade,' he said, dangling a pair of pantaloons at a girl with a kangarou skin draped across her shoulders.

The girl promptly leaped from the tree and ran away into the woods.

Her relatives called to her, gesturing for her to return, seemingly embarrassed by the girl's refusal. The skin must signify something important for her, Girardin thought, for she was the only one of the young girls wearing such a thing. Labillardière did not understand. He called out to her again. Girardin wished he would leave it be. Only the women were wearing skins like that, tied like slings across their breasts. Girardin felt a sudden lurch. Perhaps that was how they kept their babies close.

The adults pleaded with the girl, calling her out from the forest. To Girardin's surprise, the girl reappeared, and with good grace exchanged the skin for the trousers. The cotton pants dangled uselessly in her hands.

Labillardière mimed the action of putting on his trousers, but the girl still looked confused. The adults and older children gathered to watch in silent consideration. Girardin felt her nervousness return. It seemed a poor trade. The kangarou skin had been so important to the girl. Everyone seemed to be holding their breath. A misunderstanding now could still be fatal.

'May we help you to dress?' Labillardière enquired of the girl, taking the trousers from her hand and gesturing for Félix to attend.

The girl stood facing Félix and gently placed her hands on his shoulders to steady herself. She lifted one foot and waited. Félix looked embarrassed. He cast his eyes about to anywhere other than the naked girl leaning against him. Labillardière quickly knelt and rolled the trouser leg, muttering apologies as he eased her leg into the garment. The girl understood and stepped down, raising her other leg and submitting herself fully to Labillardière's attempts to dress her. She was so vulnerable and yet so trusting; Girardin swallowed hard against the lump in her throat.

After a while the women begin to gather up the children. With sadness, Girardin searched among the children for the little boy who wore her kerchief on his head. She waved to him and he warbled back with a luminescent smile of strong white teeth. As they filed off into the forest, a child tripped and began to wail. A man picked up the child and consoled it with gentle caresses, kissing the child's tears away. It shocked her to see a man treat a child with such tenderness, to be unconcerned that his actions might make him seem as soft as a woman.

One by one, the women and children and then the men disappeared back into the forest. Silence descended quickly and completely.

Girardin felt light-headed. She looked at Félix; he was smiling and humming softly to himself. Labillardière was grinning as he packed up the campsite. The children had made them all happy. For those brief moments, she had felt joy. She was dizzy with the warmth of it, and surprised that she was capable of feeling such lightness once again.

Suddenly a young man came back through the trees brandishing a spear twice the length of a man. Her breath caught in her throat. She had a vision of Ventenat's beetles, each one stuck through the middle. She put her hands to her stomach. Silently, the men had retrieved their weapons from the forest and now surrounded them. Beside her, the naturalists stood still and quiet. Mérite reached for the pistol hanging from Labillardière's belt.

Labillardière put out a hand to stall him.

The boy with the spear came up to Girardin and took her hand. His skin was nutmeg brown but he had rubbed charcoal all over his body as if to darken himself further. She saw the vein at his wrist throbbing as strongly as her own. On his shoulders, raised welts were carved vertically into his skin. He tugged her hand, urging her to follow him. She cast a frightened glance at Félix. But the young man at her side smiled and briefly their eyes met. For a moment she shared the gaze of this otherworldly boy. Gently, he pulled her arm again and she followed him.

As the party moved off, the savages hurried ahead to clear bracken and fallen branches from the path. They held back vegetation to let them all pass unscratched, despite the fact their own naked skin was exposed to the sharp sticks and barbs. Girardin found this solicitous treatment startling. Labillardière protested, but the natives ignored him. The boy beside her guided her down a slope, taking her elbow to support her.

'What is the meaning of this?' she asked. 'They treat us like royalty.'

'They treat us like invalids,' Labillardière said, shaking off the offer of assistance to climb over a log.

After they had walked for some time, one of the men gestured at Girardin to sit. '*Medi, medi.*'

She sank down gratefully. Mérite sat beside her. 'Do you think we are the first white people these savages have seen?' he asked.

She leaned against the base of a tree, watching the boy with the spear dig pieces of ship's biscuit from his teeth. She had wondered the same.

'*Tangara,*' the natives said a few minutes later, urging them upright.

In this way they had continued for half a day. Every hour they were forced to rest.

Mérite turned and whispered to Girardin, 'They are leading us somewhere.'

She looked at the sharpened spear of the long-limbed youth beside her. He smiled back at her.

Labillardière consulted his compass and turned towards a rough path, but the savages halted him and urged him down another. Mérite nudged Girardin and caught her eye meaningfully.

'Where are they leading us?' she called to Labillardière.

'To the site of our gardener's magnificent garden.' His tone sarcastic. 'We shall soon see what prodigious growth has occurred in the year since our last visit.'

Félix rushed past her. 'Quick, before they damage the vegetables!'

'I suspected as much.' Labillardière scuffed the dry earth and sneered at the pitiful vegetables.

'Here's the sorrel.' Félix pointed.

'Prepubescent leaves at best! Why didn't you dig your seeds into the moist humus near the rivulet we have just passed? Surely the cresses should've been planted on its banks? Is this ignorance, stupidity or forgetfulness?'

Girardin saw Félix wilt. He cradled a shrunken cabbage in his hands. 'Perhaps the potatoes?' he said hopefully.

Labillardière dug up a worm-eaten nugget. 'Hardly a demonstration of the beneficence of our mother country.'

Beside her one of the native men knelt on the dry soil. He wrapped his finger around a seedling and pulled. A malformed and shrunken radish sprouted from the base. Then he pointed to each of the herbs struggling to survive among the wiry bracken.

'Remarkable!' Labillardière enthused. 'He distinguishes the foreign specimens perfectly!' He began to pronounce the names of the plants to his new student.

Félix looked wretched. He unearthed a few more shrunken potatoes. 'It was the drought,' he murmured.

Girardin patted his shoulder. She remembered digging her hoe into the dry clay. Feeling the hardness of the earth jar her wounded arm. Now, only the strong stems of the bracken ferns seemed to benefit from the turned earth. The failure of the garden was not a surprise, but it saddened her to see Félix so downhearted.

'It needed your care,' she said to him. 'That is all. We cannot expect to leave a garden without its gardener.'

His smile was glum but grateful.

From Félix's garden, the savages led them safely through the forest and out to the beach. She blinked in the sunlight. The glare of the white sand stung her eyes after so long in the shade of the forest. She knelt down on the dune, relieved to see the ships anchored in the bay. She had survived her first night under the stars and returned unscathed.

Mérite signalled the ship by firing his pistol into the air. The savages scattered in alarm, but they soon returned, racing each other along the shore. Targets were set. She watched the young man who had guided her through the forest throw his spinning spear a hundred yards distant and reach his mark. He trotted back towards them, taking the opportunity to leap over a massive tree trunk that had fallen across the beach.

'If I were not fatigued from our exertions, I would gladly enter this contest,' Labillardière said. 'A tolerably fit European would have the advantage over these savages in agility.'

Girardin smiled to herself. She tilted her head back. The sun was warm on her throat. She felt the grains of sand under her palms. Félix had built an imaginary fire and was demonstrating how to cook his potatoes in the embers. The men watched him with unmistakable scepticism.

The boy who had thrown the spear came to sit cross-legged on the sand beside her. He smelled of the clay in his hair and the smoky charcoal blackening his skin. He was startling. It was not the otherness of him that surprised her, but the sameness. She pointed to the welts on his chest, and he proudly picked up a shell and mimed a slicing action. She winced and rolled up her sleeve where the ragged scar from her own rite of passage on this shore was stark red against her white muscle. The young man nodded.

Mérite jogged up to them. He was breathless from racing some of the boys along the beach. He had a wild look in his eye and his hair was loose. She thought she had never seen someone who looked so alive.

He reached for her hand. 'Come on!' Without thinking, she let him pull her up. Mérite looped his arm through hers. The native boy leaped to his feet and copied Mérite, taking her other arm. She saw his dark muscle against her white sleeve. He flashed his strong teeth at her.

'Félix, put down those sorrowful potatoes,' Mérite called. 'Link arms and dance a jig with our hosts!' Mérite capered away to the left, pulling her off balance and together they laughed and sang and twirled around Félix's imaginary fire.

When the boat eventually arrived for them, she was reluctant to leave. Labillardière encouraged the men to come aboard the ship, but they would not step into the water. She felt a great sadness to be leaving them so soon. She watched the boy with his spear backing away from the waves. How strange and precious this fleeting moment of connection had been. Reluctantly, she climbed into the boat after Félix.

'I feel ashamed,' Mérite said to her.

She looked across at him.

'I thought they meant us harm, but instead they offered us friendship.'

She had misjudged this young officer. A year ago, she had thought him reckless and over-confident, caring for no one but himself. But now she saw something else in his eyes.

'How fortunate are we?' he said. 'To be here. At this moment.'

She felt the pulse of the waves beneath her like the rhythm of a heartbeat. Had she let guilt and fear make her dead to beauty and wonder?

'We shared tea and biscuits with savages!' He laughed with delight.

The thought was fantastical. She grinned. Her heart pounded with a burst of emotion. Today I have danced with savages! How many others at home safe in their beds can say the same?

As the boat passed through the breaking waves, she turned back to see the natives watching them from the water's edge. She raised her hand in farewell and heard an answering shout of joy from the young man with the spear.

In that moment, she wished she had thought to ask his name.

Chapter 44

BY THE NEXT MORNING, THE NEWS HAD SPREAD THROUGHOUT the ship of the encounter with the people of Van Diemen's Land and almost all the men wanted to go in search of them. The holds were raided for supplies of red kerchiefs, mirrors, beads and other trinkets meant as gifts. Saint-Aignan hurried past Girardin carrying his violin. Piron climbed into a boat holding his box of charcoals beneath his arm. Two parties were forming, one led by Labillardière and the other by d'Auribeau.

Girardin watched the boats leave. The General was to meet Huon de Kermadec this morning. She went below decks, determined not to be seen waiting for his arrival. She rattled through the pans, added salt to the barrels of pork and chased the monkey from the stores, but as she heard the *Espérance*'s boat bump against their ship, she couldn't stop herself from climbing back into the morning sun. She was just in time to see Kermadec duck into the General's cabin.

A gob of black oakum splattered on the deck at her feet and a voice called out a belated warning from above. She swore back. The expletives rolled off her tongue as easily now as if she had been taught to curse from a baby. She scanned the deck. It felt wide and spacious with both boats launched. The *Recherche* was almost deserted. Only a few sailors remained to tar and grease the sheets. She took a deep breath to steady herself, then strode towards the quarterdeck.

What are you doing? she scolded herself, while inventing a hundred reasons to knock at the General's door.

At the base of the stairs, she paused. The door of the General's cabin was closed. On the poop deck above his cabin, the splintered remains of the windmill stood as a monument to the fury of the southern ocean. Up there would be a skylight window that provided daylight to the General's dining room. Many evenings she had spent gazing at the moon and stars through the distorted whorls of glass as she waited to serve the General's table. But without a specific duty to perform she could not be caught on the poop deck; that was an area reserved for officers only. Casting a glance behind her she saw the observatory trio of Rossel, Saint-Aignan and Beautemps-Beaupré in the bow, clustered around their charts, their backs toward her, heads bent.

Swiftly, she climbed the steps, crept past the window box and lay beside the base of the ruined windmill, her heart hammering into the oak boards. What was she doing? Why risk discovery just for a glimpse of a man who had no genuine interest in her?

She raised her head and peered through the panes of glass. She saw no shapes, no movement. Rising to her knees she changed position, dismayed to see the fresh tar smeared across her clothing. She still could not see Captain Kermadec.

Raised voices drifted upwards from the stern. They are outside in the gallery, she thought. Inching forwards, she hid behind the base of the windmill.

'If you take up the matter with Fleurieu, I will be forced to defend myself!' Kermadec was saying.

Girardin could not hear the General's reply.

'You are mistaken,' Kermadec continued. 'Unlike others, I have not forgotten the primary aim of our mission. We are to rescue La Pérouse. The King, the people of France, demand this of us. For heaven's sake, Bruni, the man is our friend!'

The General raised his voice. 'The King instructed us to explore the southern coast of New Holland. He made it clear that we are to chart these waters for France. We failed in our mission. We failed in our mission because the *Espérance* was poorly provisioned. In good conscience, I must report this in my letter to the minister. Captain d'Auribeau—'

'Captain d'Auribeau is most anxious that the blame for any failings should not spatter his boots, I am certain,' Kermadec interrupted. 'And who will take the blame if we fail to find our compatriot? We should not have attempted the circumnavigation.'

'The King—'

'Do you fulfil the King's ambition or your own?'

Girardin shifted her weight. It pained her to hear them argue. She should not be here. This was foolish. She pushed herself up to a crouch.

'What have we here?' a voice as thin as a wire snare whispered above her.

She looked up.

Raoul dropped onto the deck as lightly as a cat. 'Not supposed to be up here, are you?' he said softly, placing a finger to his pursed lips at the sound of coughing below. 'Eavesdropping.'

She scanned the deserted deck. He had her trapped behind the splintered windmill. She crouched, waiting for him to move, waiting for a chance to spring away.

'You want to know something amusing?' He cocked an eyebrow. 'Captain d'Auribeau has asked me to report anyone acting suspiciously. He believes we have a republican spy on the ship.' He laughed and her spine went cold.

'Keep away from me.'

'Or what—you'll cry out? I think not.' He gestured towards the arguing voices below. 'Not if you want to keep your shameful secrets.'

She turned to flee but he struck her down from behind, slamming her chin on the deck and pressing her face into the tar between the boards. Her nose spouted blood and her breath bubbled out in sharp painful gasps. His knee on her back skewered her sternum to the deck. She felt him tearing at the cords around her waist. The knife hidden in her trousers pressed into her thigh, trapped beneath her. Raoul said nothing as he tore her clothing. She squeezed her eyes closed, waiting for the moment when he would shift his weight back to unbutton his trousers and she would have a chance to go for her knife. But he knelt on her elbow, pinning her down. Her scream came unconsciously as the full weight of his body descended on her arm.

He picked her head up by her hair. 'I know who you are, Marie-Louise. I know you were Hébert's bitch. So if you want to protect your secret from your beloved captain, you'll stay quiet.'

She smelled the vinegar stench of his breath. She heard the door of the General's cabin slam and footsteps disappear. They hadn't heard her scream. Kermadec was leaving. There would be no rescue. She squirmed and kicked out, but Raoul laughed and shifted his knee to her thigh. Then as he tugged once more at her trousers she felt his hands leave her body. She heard a surprised grunt followed by a roar of pain. The weight of his body left her back. She turned to see the fingers of the monkey pressing into his eyesockets. It clamped its teeth on his ear. Raoul ripped at the monkey and flung it into the ocean. Blood streamed down his neck. Girardin gripped her knife and scrambled over the side of the boat.

Chapter 45

Resting her toes on a narrow ledge above the gallery of the General's cabin, Girardin waited for the shaking in her legs to subside. Behind her, the angry squeals of the monkey announced it had found its way to the anchor chain and climbed out of the water. She could not see Raoul.

Sidling around the side away from the stern, she made her way back into the ship. Lieutenant Rossel charged down the deck towards her like a bull. He swept his gaze over her tar-smeared shirt and bleeding nose and shook his head. 'Clean yourself up, steward, fighting is a fool's game. Someone call your mother a whore, did they?'

Girardin mumbled something in a thick voice, but Rossel had already passed and was climbing the steps to the General's cabin. She looked at her tar-blackened hands, thankful he hadn't noticed the knife she clutched in her right palm.

In her cabin, Girardin barricaded the door with the crates of ship's biscuit. She curled up in the corner of her room, nursing her throbbing elbow. Her face mangled with tar and blood, her nose engorged, she knew she looked like a monster.

He knows about Hébert. She dragged a blanket down on top of her. How could he know? She closed her eyes, willing herself to find his face in her memories. Who was Ange Raoul? A royalist spy? An informer? It was possible she had been seen with Hébert when they met in the streets of Versailles. Hébert would be known to the King's men for his republican newspaper, for his inflammatory pamphlets. Raoul could have seen her in Hébert's carriage or followed her from one of the rooms he rented. He could have been watching her at the palace. The thought sent pinpricks of terror through to her fingertips.

Girardin spat blood onto the cabin floor. Leaning back against the wall she felt her face throb and swell. She remembered his crowing laugh in Espérance Bay. He had watched her with Kermadec and knew he had this knowledge over her. Hébert was right. Knowledge was power. All Raoul needed was the right moment to strike.

He could be lurking outside in the messroom. He could be watching her door even now, waiting for her to come out. It would take no effort at all to push her back into her cabin; then who would hear her screams? And it would not stop at that. Once he knew she dared not go to the General, she would be his to take whenever he chose.

Much later, Besnard banged on her door. 'The baker says we are running out of flour!' She heard him curse and stomp away when she didn't respond.

Her face had swelled and her skin felt taut, but she pulled the blanket off her shoulders. She could not stay locked in her cabin forever. She pushed the crates away from the door. Holding the knife out in front of her, she pictured her path. A few short strides and then she would be at the stairs.

Besnard was gone when she reached the galley, but the monkey was waiting for her. It had been grooming the salt from its fur and a lick of hair stood straight up on top of its head. It regarded her with large, serious eyes, its expression clear: I do something for you, you do something for me.

Girardin rummaged in a barrel. 'There's no fruit left.' She tossed it a stale bun. 'Come back tonight. There'll be something better for you then.' The monkey scurried off with its prize, as if pleased with their understanding.

Girardin pinched her nose against a fresh gush of blood and slid down to the floor, leaning her back against the oven, still warm from the morning's baking. She closed her eyes. She remembered how powerless she felt beneath Raoul's weight. The terror as he tore at her clothes. She scrambled for a pail and vomited into the scraps.

Girardin wiped her face and bloodied nose with a cloth. She pushed herself off her knees and stepped cautiously from behind the oven. She left the galley, walking out past the animal pens and into the middle of the open deck. From there she could see Raoul hanging from the rigging, his arm flung out and pointing to the shore. She forced herself to keep her eyes on him, almost daring him to look at her. He accused her of spying, so a spy she would be. If she had to stay aboard this ship with him then she would be the hunter—let him be the prey.

Raoul jumped down from the rigging. Her gut lurched, the flush of bravery immediately extinguished. He held out his hand to Captain d'Auribeau to help him climb aboard. She watched Raoul speak in the captain's ear. What was he telling him? she wondered. If Raoul knew all about her past, why hadn't he exposed her already?

She felt the bump of another boat hitting the ship. Ropes were thrown out. The voices of the men rose in an excited gabble. Piron climbed over the side of the ship, clad only in his underwear, his naked skin smeared with black charcoal. She lost sight of Raoul again. She crouched down behind a coil of rope, afraid to be found so exposed. The goats shied away from her as she ducked into their sheltered stalls beneath the gangway. She crept along, like a rat shuffling through the straw.

All the sailors had climbed on board. The General stood in the middle of the two excited groups, each vying to impress him with their tales. Saint-Aignan stormed red-faced out of the crowd, holding his violin. She froze among the cattle, and he passed inches from her hiding place. 'Lively tunes,' he muttered to himself. 'Next time I will play more lively tunes.'

'Saint-Aignan!' Labillardière called after him. 'Tell the General how much the natives enjoyed your concert.'

'Fuck off,' St Aignan swore back at him.

'Excellent taste in music. The entire group showed their appreciation by stuffing their fingers in their ears.'

As the men roared with laughter she crept closer, climbing in among the sheep, smelling their greasy lanolin. She knelt in their manure. Their bodies pressed against her and she felt them quake, suspicious of her intentions.

She overheard snatches of conversations.

'They wouldn't take any of our food. Not even sugar for their babies. I saw one mother take it straight out of the infant's mouth!'

'The women dive for abalone and lobsters while the men sit around the fire. They act like they're afraid of the sea!'

'It's a disgrace!'

What freedom this superstitious fear of the water must give these women, Girardin thought, if the men were not able to swim at all. For how many generations had mothers taught their daughters to escape into the ocean?

'The women disappeared beneath the waves for an age—longer than I could hold a breath.'

'I thought for sure they'd be caught in the seaweed and drowned.'

'Or eaten by sharks!' another said.

'But no! Each time they returned with baskets full of seafood to broil on the coals.'

Girardin pictured these fearless hunters with their shorn heads, sagging breasts and stretched stomachs. The rope-like muscles in their arms and legs. These women would not abandon their children. They gathered the food for their family. To feed themselves and their children they were dependent on no man.

'The women are completely naked,' a sailor was saying to his rapt audience, 'and sit with their legs spread. All they do by way of modesty is bend one knee and curl a foot in front of their private parts!'

Then she heard Ventenat raise his voice, addressing d'Auribeau. 'I merely said that the practice of polygamy was observed.'

'It is true,' Labillardière confirmed. 'The man we met made intimate gestures to indicate that the two women by his side were his wives. Perhaps the husband of one of the women was dead and her children fatherless, as it is not the normal practice. The other women took pains to make that clear to us.'

'But, chaplain, you have said you find these people to be in a perfect state of society. How can you, a man of God, condone polygamy?' d'Auribeau challenged Ventenat.

'Can we not observe without passing judgement?' the chaplain snapped. 'In this harsh and unforgiving world, is it so wrong if the hard business of providing food for the family is shared by two women?'

'It is against nature. A child should be raised by a man and his wife. That is the natural order of things.'

Girardin was tired of the discussion. Against nature? What was meant by that? It angered her, this talk of the natural order. Had they not seen the variety of nature in their travels? Had they not seen the fish that could fly, the birds that could swim? In France, unwanted newborns could be torn to pieces by dogs in the streets. Bastard babies whose fathers would not claim them, who considered them an embarrassment. Whose idea of nature was that? Who were the true savages? Heat flushed through her. Would she have had to give up her baby in a society such as this? For certain, she would not be half a world away from her home, disguised and wretched.

Ventenat turned away from d'Auribeau, twisting his hands and muttering as he passed her in the stalls, 'He is Tartuffe! The nasty, pious fraud.'

Labillardière called to the General: 'These people wondered where our women were. It seemed unnatural to them that we should be without them.'

'Dragged us into the bushes to check our manhood!' a young sailor cried out.

'No man without a beard was safe!' another cried.

'Once they stripped me naked, the women were more than satisfied.' One of the sailors thrust out his hips to a chorus of laughter.

'Shame Louis Girardin was not among us!'

Girardin recoiled at the mention of her name.

'Then they'd have found what they were looking for!'

The men were laughing. From her hiding place, she stared at their open mouths and yellow teeth. She saw their fleshy wet tongues. Every man had heard what the sailor said.

'Where is he? Louis Girardin, where are you?' another man called out.

Girardin shrank back among the sheep.

'He'll not come ashore again now! If he did, then we'd know the truth of his sex!'

The sheep bleated, turning angrily. Girardin crept back in the cramped stall. They knew. They all knew the truth. How could she be safe from any of them?

Chapter 46

As the days passed, Girardin kept to her cabin as much as she could. More than ever before, she wanted to speak with Kermadec. She needed to be off this ship, away from Raoul, away from all of them. She passed many nights without sleep, churning over her doubts and fears. Kermadec had been so cold and distant to her when they last met. Could she still turn to him for help? She lay awake in her hammock, watching Passepartout swing in her cage. At last she made her decision: she would ask the General if she could transfer to the *Espérance*.

But the following morning a throng of men blocked the General's door. They lined the gangway and filled the quarterdeck. 'Get out of my way,' she ordered, struggling with his breakfast tray. D'Auribeau had announced that the rations of bread were to be cut for the crew, but not for the officers. Now the sailors were refusing to sail.

The men barricaded the door while the General met with the ringleaders. A hand snatched the bread roll from the plate and she watched as it was torn to pieces in front of her. Bread. Once again it came to this. She stepped back, sensing anarchy.

Ventenat had mounted the quarterdeck like it was his pulpit. 'Bread! We had a king that would not give us bread, while he dined on towers of meat and sweets! Why should we suffer this injustice here while those in France are free?'

She had never seen Ventenat like this. His eyes were wide and wild. He looked terrifying in his black robes with bald and shining head. How did he know about the towers of food? She remembered those tall platters stacked three feet high like women's headdresses, each one striving to be taller than the last. Towers of eggs. Towers of crayfish in glasses of champagne. The platters were paraded through the hallways on the way to the dining room, while the courtiers salivated, waiting for their chance to devour the leftovers. She had only once seen the table fully laden, and even then it was just for a moment. She had rushed to find her mistress with a message, but Madame Marguerite de Noailles, having danced from conversation to conversation to gain a prime position near the dining room doors, was in no mood to lose her place. She had swung her wide panniers and pushed Marie-Louise away with her glare. The doors opened wide and Marie-Louise felt herself bathed in light. She saw white walls with golden decorated panels, cornices and mirrors. A chandelier illuminated a dining table crowded with heavy dishes that appeared untouched. Then the King and Queen swept through. In her surprise, Marie-Louise forgot to curtsey as those around her instantly dropped. The King caught her eye and her mouth fell open before she threw herself to the parquet floor. Would he have recognised her? she wondered. Surely not after all these years. She would not have recognised him as the boy in the labyrinth, his girth now so round and his face so full of jowls.

It seemed a lifetime ago, those days at Versailles with the nobility all squabbling for the ear of the King. Living among rumours. Listening at doors. Learning to be invisible. And now her past was determined to catch her out.

'Ventenat!' Mérite cried. 'Get down from there!'

She watched as the sailors closed against him. Then, above his head, she saw a tricolour rosette had been tied to the stair. Its red, white and blue tails fluttered in the fresh breeze. She stared at it, stunned. Mérite pulled his rapier and leaped for the banister, striking the rosette down with his sword. She watched the rosette spin in circles as it fell. It hit the deck and Mérite pounced, pinning it through the heart.

She remembered wearing the tricolour like this. The symbol of the revolution. Marie-Louise had slipped out of the palace gates and pinned a tricolour cockade to her breast. The ribbon flapped ostentatiously as she walked. It was not safe to be on the streets without showing your patriotism to the republic of France. To be seen in the fashions of the ancien régime was to invite vitriole. Courtiers who wore white handkerchiefs to show their support for the King had been spat at, their faces slashed by fingernails, and beaten by mobs. This was 1789 and the Bastille had already fallen. The tide was turning against the King.

She walked quickly to her rendezvous with Hébert, her cap tied close around her face. She avoided Rue Satori, afraid her father or stepmother might see her. Turning a corner, she glimpsed Hébert's mustard-coloured carriage stopped in the street and saw a man she recognised as the Duc d'Orléans stepping out of it. A member of the royal family. The wind snatched at the ribbons of her cockade.

She fell back from the corner. Why would Hébert be meeting with the duke?

Before long she heard the rattle of the carriage on the cobblestones. She waited. The horses turned the corner and a footman leaped down to open the carriage door. Jacques Hébert leaned out to her.

'You still keep a carriage,' she said. 'I would've thought such a thing an extravagance of the aristocracy.' She climbed inside, saying nothing of the duke.

Hébert smiled. 'I find it necessary,' he said, lifting her hand and pressing his lips to her palm, 'for privacy.'

She withdrew her hand, tucking it beneath her skirts, ashamed that her face grew warm.

'To business then,' he said, handing her a roll of sheets. 'Distribute these. Tip them down the stairwells. Scatter them in the corridors. Let them know what we think of the Austrian whore.'

Marie-Louise unrolled the pamphlets and saw a drawing of the Queen with her legs spread, being pleasured by her lap dogs. Her eyes grew wide. She rolled it closed.

'Something the matter?' he said, his voice soft.

'What do you need me for?' she blurted. 'You don't need me to spy on the Queen—you print stories in your pamphlets that are worse than anything I tell you.'

'Careful, Madame. Are you not a patriot?'

She drew back, horrified that she had given him the wrong impression and eager to prove herself worthy. 'You mistake me! I meant that tales of gluttony and infidelity could be gleaned from listening to the servants' gossip in the markets. I want to do more!' She had put a hand to her heart, holding the ribbons of her rosette.

'All in good time,' he had murmured, reaching across to stroke her thigh.

A shout broke into her thoughts. Girardin ducked as a shoe flew past her head. Fights were breaking out among the sailors, between the republicans and those still loyal to the King. The men pushed and shoved, hurling insults. A wild punch threw the butcher into her, sending the breakfast tray spinning from her hands. She fell beneath him, his weight smothering her. She struggled out from under the heavy man and pushed herself up onto her hands and knees, wheezing, the wind knocked out of her. She heard Mérite send one of the brawling men below deck and cut the brandy allowance of both.

When she looked up, Captain Kermadec had boarded the *Recherche*. He stood tall and his cheeks were flushed red. She noticed his sword was drawn. Three of his officers fanned out behind him. He didn't utter a word.

Slowly, he walked among the sailors. His silence cowed them. The men were wary, expecting punishment. He forced each to meet his gaze. He stopped when he saw the tricolour rosette pinned to the deck. Tugging the sword from the wood, he thrust the rosette high and spun about.

'For shame.' His voice resonated deep and low.

All the men ducked their eyes. Nearby, she heard the teeth of a sailor grinding in his jaw and watched the muscles of his cheek bulge. She saw men spit upon the deck.

Kermadec removed the rosette from the rapier and crushed it in his hand. Girardin felt a crumpling sensation within her.

'Is it mutiny you intend? Do you care so little for your General?' Kermadec's disgust was plain. 'This man who has been a father to us all?'

Not one man moved or spoke.

'Get about your work.'

The direct order broke the mob apart. Subdued, the men shuffled away.

Girardin fled below deck, recognising in herself the desire to obey an authoritative voice.

The galley was deserted. She sank down behind the ovens, hidden from view. She could not confess to Kermadec, she knew that now. He would think her a traitor to the King. She wrapped her arms around herself. Raoul would keep his power over her.

At a cough behind her, Girardin scrambled to her feet. Captain Kermadec stood at the galley door. Her heart thudded against her ribs. The pain of their last meeting was like an icy finger pressing her sternum, pushing her away from him.

'Is it true that there is not enough flour for bread?' he asked, his expression unreadable.

She stepped forwards. 'The flour will not last till Java.'

As the lantern light caught her face, Kermadec gasped. 'What has happened to you?'

She remembered her split lip, realising her half-closed eye must be blackening. She relived the moment of her face hitting the planks of the deck, the weight of Raoul pinning her down. 'An altercation.'

'You are not safe!' He stepped towards her. 'I should never have convinced you to take on this role. I am a fool.'

She could not speak.

He tilted her head and gently touched her swollen lip.

'Tell me who did this.'

She shook her head. It was safest to say nothing. She could not risk giving Raoul the opportunity to speak.

'I came to apologise,' he said. 'I was not myself when we last met.'

She felt the tightness in her chest begin to unfurl.

'D'Auribeau plots against me. When we return to France, my career will be over. I fear I have given you cause to hope—' he swallowed '—for something more between us.'

She turned away from him, humiliated.

'No, please listen.' He caught her arm. 'I thought to distance myself from you, but I failed. I could not suppress my feelings. I am as helpless as driftwood pulled by the tide.'

'I do not cause you such turmoil willingly,' she said, incensed. 'I want nothing from you.'

'But I want to be with you.'

Her heart kicked. She slowly turned to him, searching his face for the truth.

Had he forgotten that she was a woman without family, without reputation, with only the coins sewn into the hem of her tunic to call her own? She had nothing. She was nothing.

'Unless we find La Pérouse, there will be no way to resurrect my reputation,' he said. 'I will be ruined. I will have nothing to offer you.'

It did not matter to her that he had no future in the King's navy. Couldn't he see that? She pictured again the scene of a grassy field and the flash of her son's white hair in the sun. All she wanted was to turn for home.

'We will look for La Pérouse together,' she said, linking his hands in hers. 'Let me be your steward on the *Espérance*.'

His eyes glistened. 'I would like that more than you know.'

She beamed at him, even though it hurt her face to smile. To be safe with Kermadec on his ship. Her heart felt like sunshine.

But his face clouded. 'I doubt the General will allow it. Our friendship,' he faltered. 'We are not on the best terms.' She felt the distance between them return and the darkness of her doubts and fears. She dropped his hands and the sunlight drained from her face.

D'Auribeau appeared in the doorway. 'Captain Kermadec, your negligence with our supplies haunts us still.'

Kermadec swung around, flustered and without retort.

'The General has been forced to capitulate. Five ounces of flour for all, officers and crew alike.'

Girardin breathed deep, relieved the General understood. Whether royalist or republican, all they had to rely on was one another. When we run out of bread, she thought, at least we will all run out together.

D'Auribeau looked from Kermadec to her and back, his eyebrow rising. 'We sail for the Friendly Isles in the morning, captain,' he said. 'I should think you would want to return to matters on your own ship.'

Chapter 47

Tongatabou, Friendly Isles, 23 March 1793

NOTHING IN THE SAILORS' TALES HAD PREPARED HER FOR THE scale of their reception in the Friendly Isles. The islanders surged out from shore in outrigger canoes loaded with produce. Piglets were carried beneath armpits, their ears pulled to create a squealing siren. Girardin stared, amazed and terrified by the sheer number of craft now bearing down on them.

Canoes clunked against the side of the ship. The islanders tossed bundles of fruit up to the waiting sailors then pulled themselves on board. Two men cried out to Girardin, grinning and pointing to the women that paddled with them.

'*Mitzi, mitzi!*' the women called, before dropping their paddles and scaling the ropes at the side of the ship.

The officers thrust open their windows and helped them through.

More canoes arrived. Now there was music. Girardin felt the joyful madness whirl around her. Saint-Aignan dashed for his violin. The sailors danced jigs with the islanders, while Rossel screamed orders above the din. Hatchets were traded for hogs. Clubs of bone and polished wood were demonstrated in fierce displays. Piglets chased poultry across the deck. A canoe under sail guided the ships through the deepest channel, and somehow the whole floating market of ships and canoes found safe anchorage.

Not since Amboyna had Girardin seen such an abundance of fresh fruit and vegetables. Pawpaw, coconuts and yams. The sights and scents were mouth-watering. Huge green-skinned fruits studded with spikes were soon piled into a pyramid on deck.

'What's this?' Besnard picked one up and sniffed.

'Breadfruit,' Labillardière replied.

A grunt from Besnard. 'What am I supposed to do with it?'

'Roast it like potatoes.'

Besnard narrowed his eyes. 'I'll boil it then.'

Labillardière shrugged. 'Suit yourself. The natives bury it beneath the ground to ferment it.' But Besnard had already left. The naturalist turned instead to Girardin. 'I don't think our cook likes me.'

'No one likes you,' Girardin said without thinking.

Labillardière merely nodded.

Girardin felt hopeful. These islanders knew of visiting ships. Her expectations of finding La Pérouse here in the Friendly Isles were high. This was his last known destination. Five years before, he had stopped in Botany Bay on the east coast of New Holland to repair his ships, take water and send word back to France. Then his ships set sail for Tongatabou and vanished.

She looked across to the *Espérance*. In the month since leaving Van Diemen's Land, the General and Captain Kermadec had remained distant. Neither man had set foot on the other's ship. But at least the General now seemed fully focused on their mission to find La

Pérouse. Passing the northernmost tip of New Zealand, he would not let Labillardière go ashore, and the naturalist had to be content with trading flax from a visiting canoe. As they journeyed north, she was heartened to hear the General name a group of islands after Kermadec. Perhaps he felt he had treated his friend poorly after all and meant to make amends. It had dismayed her, though, to learn that Captain d'Auribeau had named one of the islands after Raoul.

On the quarterdeck, the General gave orders to halt the trading. Amid the mayhem, an important man, a warrior chief, climbed on board the ship. Chief Feenou was the largest man she had ever seen. Great rolls of fat folded over one another around his middle. Scars of battle were inscribed across his broad chest. His woolly hair was dusted white like a European wig.

Chief Feenou announced the imminent arrival of the supreme chief of the Friendly Isles, King Toobou, and Girardin felt confident a king would know if La Pérouse had been here. She watched in fascination as a retinue of musicians came aboard before the King and set up a drumming beat. One magnificent warrior with an oiled chest put a conch shell to his lips and sent a haunting note across the water.

King Toobou's entourage of warriors were astonishing. They stood like trees, so large in every limb, so broad, so tall. Even their hands were enormous. If not for their warm smiles, Girardin would have been terrified of them. The French sailors looked small and poorly fed by comparison, their skin sallow and grey alongside the shining strength of these men.

King Toobou was even rounder in girth than Chief Feenou, and wore what looked like a straw mat fastened about his waist by a belt of cloth. He brought a gift of the papery tapa cloth decorated with brown inks that, when rolled out, stretched from bow to stern.

Girardin watched as Toobou presented a crown of brilliant red feathers to the General with great ceremony. In return, the General gave a red coat to Toobou and a blue one to Feenou. The warriors admired the coats and put them on, unperturbed that they could not button them closed. Toobou and his chiefs sat themselves in a circle upon the deck and the General, his crown of feathers perched awkwardly upon his wig, urged his officers to join them.

At this conference, Girardin hoped the General would begin to question the King about La Pérouse. She wanted to get closer, to hear what was being said. She would bring them refreshments. Wine, perhaps, or some brandy. Turning towards the bow, she slid past the bare arms and breasts of the islanders, smelling the pungent coconut oil smeared over the women's bodies and through their hair. A mirror flashed sunlight in her eye, gifts used to tempt the women, and she pushed a sailor away from her.

Blocking her path was a grey-haired islander. He squatted on the deck with a young girl, perhaps his granddaughter, beside him. She looked no more than ten years old. He called out to Girardin, offering her the girl. Girardin paused, shocked, uncertain of his intentions. She thought of her sisters; she thought of herself at that age. The girl looked back at her mildly, continuing to play with a handful of glass beads in front of her.

Girardin continued to the stairs. Beneath the deck, the darkened mess was crowded with naked limbs. The air was thick with grunting, any thought of privacy abandoned. It smelled of sex and sweat. She made for the stores. Besnard stood with his back against the door, his pants around his ankles. A girl with long black hair tied back with a new red ribbon bobbed at his crotch. Girardin gasped. Besnard's head was thrown back, his flabby cheeks blowing, breath whinnying through his nose. She fled.

The sudden call of a conch shell, like a warning, drew her back on deck. Chief Feenou and King Toobou were running along the gangway to the bow of the boat, coat-tails flapping behind. From the shore, a magnificent double-storey canoe had launched and was approaching swiftly. Toobou and Feenou promptly swept up the tails of their new coats and tumbled over the rail into their waiting canoes. Girardin stared in amazement. What did this mean? Had they lost their chance to interview the King of these islands? Was this an attack? The General looked about him in open astonishment. The remaining islanders threw themselves prostrate to the deck as a short, plump woman nearing fifty years of age was helped aboard the ship.

Queen Tineh sat beside the General at his table, nibbling sugared bananas. Girardin took a place close behind. The Queen's hair was cut short and rubbed all over with a reddish powder. By contrast, her attendants had flowing black hair, thick and shining. These women were even more beautiful than the islanders who had first come aboard the ship, and were not tempted by beads and baubles. They had ignored the sailors' lewd suggestions, their expressions calm and regal as they were shown about the ship. The sailors had been shamed into silence.

All the officers of the *Recherche* had crammed into the General's cabin with the Queen's warriors and her ladies-in-waiting. Labillardière had spread a vocabulary list from Cook's journal across his lap. The Queen and the General communicated in a hybrid mix of English, Tongan and French.

When Queen Tineh was told of King Toobou's ungracious exit, she snorted. 'They owe their positions to me. They hate to show their subservience.'

'King Toobou is your husband?' the General asked.

She looked revolted. 'My mother's brother.'

Girardin itched to know when the General would ask about La Pérouse. She had stood for hours through this dinner and he had not mentioned their lost compatriot once. They had been entertained by a song from the Queen's beautiful ladies-in-waiting that had lasted half an hour and consisted of only two words. The men had been captivated by the sensual movements of their arms. Girardin had stifled her yawns. Not to be outdone, Saint-Aignan then played tunes on both the German guitar and bird organ, both of which, she was surprised to find, he could play passably.

The General turned to the Queen. 'Do you remember the visits of the English navigators?' he asked her.

Girardin sharpened her attention.

Queen Tineh seemed to indicate she did, mentioning the names of Cook and Bligh.

'Have you seen any other ships, any Europeans dressed like us, in the French manner?'

Girardin wished she could see the Queen's face. La Pérouse had to have come here. If not, then where else could they look?

The Queen shook her head.

The General picked up a knife. 'Any cutlery marked like this?' he pressed.

Queen Tineh stood abruptly and Girardin leaped back. Had she taken offence?

The Queen wrapped her empty plate in a napkin and gestured to her ladies to gather the presents she had been given. Girardin watched as they also stowed the plates and cutlery in their belts. She turned to the General. He looked as shocked as her, but he stood and bowed deeply.

The Queen said, 'We will host a feast in your honour in five days' time on my island of Pangaïmatoo. If you wish, you may sleep with me.'

Stammering his thanks, the General managed to nod and shake his head simultaneously. Girardin saw Lieutenant Rossel stifle a grin with his hand.

'You offer me great kindness. Your accommodation is, no doubt, far more comfortable than this ship, but I am afraid I cannot leave my men. I hope you understand?'

The Queen shrugged, cast a glance over the assembled press of men, and turned her back.

Girardin waited till all the Queen's retinue and the officers had filed out from the cabin and she was alone. The table had been stripped not only of food but also of plates and cutlery. Not even the salt and pepper shakers remained. They had taken everything. She sank into a chair. She had hoped to hear news of survivors, imagined their countrymen building a ship from their wreckage on some nearby shore, intending to sail home. But the General's cautious questioning had been fruitless.

She had expected too much. She had let herself imagine their quest would end here. Her son would be a toddler now, perhaps even walking if someone—she hoped—had taken the time to encourage him. The fantasy of her reunion with her son came uninvited to her mind, Kermadec by her side, Rémi running across a field towards her.

So much depended on them finding La Pérouse. She could not rely on the General's hesitant interviews with the Queen.

She spread her hands across the empty table. A spark of excitement propelled her forwards. If La Pérouse had been here, there must surely be objects of French design left on these islands. Whether by trade or theft, there would some item—a plate, a cup—by which to identify the presence of Frenchmen among the islanders. Here was her chance to act. She would find these men. And she would take them home.

Chapter 48

WHEN THE DAY OF THE QUEEN'S FEAST CAME, GIRARDIN TOOK her chance to go ashore with the naturalists. She sat beside Félix in the boat, leaning out over the gunwale to marvel at the colourful fish darting away from the oars. The sea was so clear she could see down to the great gardens of coral branching out in magnificent shapes beneath them. Like trees crystallised in coloured sugar, she thought, as their boat passed above. Along the beach, palm trees waved their fronds in a beckoning rhythm with the wind, enticing her ashore.

A trading tent had been erected and thousands of islanders came to barter. They were taking on board more than six hundred coconuts a day. The butcher strung up the carcasses of the hogs almost as soon as they were traded. This truly was a kingdom of plenty, she thought, seeing the islanders queuing patiently with their produce. If La Pérouse and his men had been marooned somewhere in these islands, there would surely be survivors.

The rowers pulled the boat up on mudflats. Piglets snuffled in the mud, munching on seaweed and rooting out crabs and shellfish. Here, the native chickens were a novelty; skinny blue hens with orange feet strutted past her. She felt something crawl across her bare foot. Looking closely, she realised the beach was alive with walking shells.

'A hermit crab,' Labillardière told her, plucking the shell from the sand and overturning it in her hand. The protruding legs quickly disappeared and then some moments later re-emerged to flip itself over. Amazed, Girardin repeated the trick. 'They use discarded shells to make their homes.'

She placed the crab gently on the wet sand. Motionless, it looked the same as all the other abandoned shells. If only it were so easy to disappear. She thought of her own disguises, the cloaks she had worn, the houses she had lived in. She was still looking for the shell that fitted her so completely.

Preparations for the feast in the General's honour were well underway. There was music and laughter. Islanders carried long bamboo poles across their shoulders with fish and fruits dangling from each end. The mounds of food were stacked into pyramids. Smoke from cooking fires drifted lazily through the palms.

'Citizen Riche!' called Ventenat, waving. The naturalist stood amid a pile of collecting cages in the shade of a palm tree with his servant, Michel. So a party from the *Espérance* had already landed. She craned her neck to see if she could recognise Kermadec among the men.

'Monsieur Riche, is your captain coming to the feast today?' she asked, contriving to walk beside him along the beach.

'He has not been well.'

'Not well?' She hoped her voice did not betray her emotion.

'Bedridden.' Riche sniffed. 'We both suffer from consumption, yet I am able to continue my researches.'

Consumption.

What did she know of consumption? The diseases of the lungs were not helped by this hot and moist air, she knew that much. His health would surely improve if they turned for home. She felt even more anxious to begin her search for evidence of La Pérouse.

She went with the naturalists as they set off on their explorations, hoping to find a village in which to look for items that might have come from a French ship. Labillardière led them away from the feast intending to circle the island. As the morning grew older, the sun hotter and her throat drier, they crossed beaches of burning white sand and waded through waist-deep tidal channels. Riche, who had boasted of his fortitude, began to tire and his cough returned. He trailed behind the group with his servant scolding him for his stubbornness.

Up ahead, Girardin heard laughter and voices warbling over one another. She quickened her step. Circular huts made of woven and thatched fronds were dotted in clearings through the palms. A group of women sat outside a large hut, shaded by the coconut palms. Excited, Girardin approached the women and saw they were grinding coconut flesh into paste on a large flat stone.

Labillardière halted before the open doorway of the largest hut.

'Surely the basic laws of hospitality will extend to foreigners?' Riche said hopefully.

The sand radiated heat all around her. From the cool shade of the hut, a chief welcomed them with a broad smile and gestured for them to enter. The respite from the beating sun was immediate. As her eyes grew accustomed to the shade, Girardin looked up to admire the intricate ceiling of woven palm fronds. She collided with Félix who had stopped, staring at the back of the hut. She heard grunting. There on the mud floor was one of their crew, his hips thrusting, his body pinning a woman to the ground. The man looked up and tossed his fringe from his face. She recognised Raoul.

Unconcerned, the chief stood and gestured with cupped hands towards his mouth, offering them a drink of coconut water.

The sound of Raoul's grunting on top of the girl continued.

Horrified, Girardin backed away then turned and ran from the hut.

Outside, the women stopped pounding the coconut flesh to stare at her.

Girardin reeled about. She could not return to the ship; Raoul might follow her. I must pull myself together, she thought. I cannot let them see me like this. She remembered the pain of Raoul's knee on her back. She heard his words in her ear: *Hébert's bitch*. He could ruin everything for her if he chose. Turning towards the ocean she let the slight breeze cool her face.

She heard the naturalists talking as they too left the hut.

'One of the prettiest girls on the island,' Ventenat was saying.

'Is she his daughter or his wife?'

The women called to the naturalists to sit with them. They offered coconut water to drink. Félix brought her some of the pudding that the women had been preparing on a hot stone. Even though her throat burned with bile, she took it. The pudding was soft and sweet and delicious. She followed Félix back to the group, but sat apart from them, her back against a palm tree. She kept her eyes on the women as they mixed breadfruit with the coconut flesh, grinding it against the stone.

The women began to question Labillardière using explicit gestures and Girardin watched him squirm as he attempted to answer their queries.

'Are French women not taboo *mitzi mitzi*?' one woman asked. She seemed to be wondering if French men could sleep with other men's women at home as they did here.

'Our women would not give their favours so freely,' Labillardière spluttered.

Ventenat put a hand on his arm, urging him not to cause offence.

'How many wives does a man have?' another woman asked.

'Only one.'

The women laughed.

'What about *eguis*, chiefs?'

'Still only one. Marriage is between one man and one woman.'

They screamed with laughter.

Affronted, Labillardière began to explain that even the kings of Europe, the *egui lais*, had just one wife apiece.

'Imagine if Louis had more than one woman to meddle in the affairs of state,' Riche muttered.

Out of the corner of her eye, Girardin saw Raoul strut out from the hut. She tensed. The chief followed him out and a transaction occurred. Was it the knife he had held to her throat in Van Diemen's Land that he now gave to the chief? She forced herself to meet his eye. He flicked his greasy swatch of hair from his forehead. Raising his chin, he sucked a deep breath through his nostrils, as though smelling her out, just as he had done in Tenerife. She jerked back. He laughed and sauntered along the beach away from them.

The young woman came out of the chief's hut and took her place around the fire with the others. Girardin studied her face. She looked younger than the other women, but whether she was the daughter or wife of the chief, Girardin could not say. She seemed unconcerned by what had happened in the hut. Did she mind that she could be gifted to a sailor for the price of a knife? The woman picked up her coconut shell and resumed scraping it, the blade making a hollow scratching sound. Are they as free as they seem? Girardin wondered. She watched them laugh as they worked. Do these women choose their lovers? Or are they traded between families, just the same as French women?

She listened to the rhythmic scrape of knife blade on stone as the women worked. She watched the knives moving with their hands, seeing the tarnished blades from this wet heat. The staghorn handles.

'The knives!' she shouted, leaping to her feet.

Félix fell back, startled.

'Trade something for them.'

She held out a handkerchief and gestured to a knife, but the women drew back, tucking the knives away beneath their thighs. The steel was too valuable to them.

'Where did you get them?' she demanded. There were no deer in these isles. These were knives of French manufacture.

'What's the matter?' Félix asked her. 'You're scaring them.'

'The knives could be from La Pérouse. Don't you see? Some French sailors have been here before.' She turned back to the women. 'Who gave you these knives?'

The women started to call out in frightened voices.

'Sit down!' Labillardière growled at her. 'Do you mean to get us killed?'

Girardin felt in her pocket and pulled out her own knife. She showed them the gleaming blade. 'Trade! Trade!' she cried.

The woman who had been with Raoul in the hut seemed to understand. Sunlight glinted on the clean blade. Her own was dull and tarnished with blooms of rust. Girardin saw her considering, weighing up the trade, wondering if this could be some trick.

Girardin crouched before her, trying to smile encouragingly, careful not to scare her further. She was surprised at the steadiness of her hand as she held out her blade. 'Please,' she said. 'I would not deceive you.'

The woman nodded and the stag-horn knife was passed into Girardin's hand.

Chapter 49

THE FEAST IN THE GENERAL'S HONOUR HAD BEGUN BY THE TIME Girardin and the naturalists had circled back to the festivities. Troops of dancers wearing crowns of flowers and spiked green fronds beat their drums. Men's oiled thighs gleamed as they stomped the earth and women sang and swayed. Girardin scanned the crowd for Captain Kermadec.

Pigs were stretched and crackling over fires. Through the smoke, she could see the General sitting on a raised dais beside Queen Tineh, flanked by pyramids of pineapple and breadfruit. But she could not see Kermadec. The stag-horn knife was now safe in the leather pouch against her leg. She was certain this was a sign La Pérouse and his men had been here and desperate to show Kermadec what she had found. Worry tugged at her heart. Was he too ill to attend the feast? Or had he kept away because of his argument with the General?

A hand touched her elbow. She spun around. Kermadec smiled.

She laughed with pure joy. He seemed well. 'Are you recovered?' she asked. 'Claude Riche said you were suffering . . .' She could not bear to say the word 'consumption', not wanting to hear the condition be confirmed. 'He said you were unwell.'

'Come,' he said, drawing her away from the smoky feast, his breathing hoarse. 'I am better for seeing you. I had begun to fear you had not come ashore.'

She walked with him along the beach, the music slowly fading behind them. When they stopped beneath the shade of a spreading frangipani tree, she felt the throb of the drumbeat in the sand.

'I have found something,' she said in a rush. 'Something of La Pérouse.' She pulled the knife from her pouch.

Kermadec turned it over in his hand. She stared at him, waiting for him to speak. 'It has a stag-horn handle. It is from Thiers, the knife town, don't you think?'

'It could be French,' he agreed. 'The silver ferrule is more intricate than the English type. Where did you get it?'

'A woman in a village. She would not tell me who gave it to her. Do you think we should investigate?' She was excited, expectant, but Kermadec only shrugged.

'Take it to the General. It must be his decision.' He returned the knife to her.

She searched his face. Had he lost faith they would find La Pérouse here after all? The beach was deserted. Everyone was at the feast. She caught his hand. 'What is wrong?'

His smile was sad. 'It seems I have had my fill of ocean adventure. Each day I dream of our return to France.' He plucked a flower from the frangipani tree and twirled it between his fingers, pure white petals with a golden heart. 'I dream that when we return, we can be together. And we will find your son.'

The lump in her throat was too large for her to swallow. This was all she had dared to hope for.

'I wish we had more time,' he murmured. He looked back at the *Espérance*, anchored a cable length from shore. 'My boat will be here soon.'

'Don't go,' she said, suddenly desperate that they should not be apart.

He bent his head and kissed her. His lips were soft but urgent, and she tasted the sweet creaminess of coconut. He reached for her, circling his arms around her waist, lifting her to her toes. Her body responded. She leaned into him, pressing her thighs, groin, stomach hard against his, wanting this closeness, this bond to hold them here forever. But she knew what a risk she ran, being seen like this with him. She broke away from his kiss.

'It is too dangerous,' she whispered. Already she could see groups of sailors gathering at the shore.

He touched his forehead to hers and she linked arms with him, not wanting to let him go. 'I will ask the General if I can be with you.'

A shout rang out. They turned. Sailors were sprinting along the beach towards them, chasing a group of fleeing islanders. 'Thieves!'

'What's happening?' She recognised the smith of the *Recherche*, Fitz, charging ahead with his pistol raised. He caught up to the islanders at the water's edge. She watched him standing alone, ringed by powerful young men shouting and waving their clubs. Fitz swore loudly and fired his pistol, but the priming had fallen out. As he fumbled with the gun, an islander stepped forwards and split open the smith's skull with his club.

Girardin screamed.

Kermadec ran for the smith, calling towards the *Espérance*. She followed him out of the shadow of the frangipani tree and onto the baking sand. Within moments, all the islanders had set upon the smith, beating him till they imagined him dead. They stripped his clothing from his body. Girardin stared in mute horror, mouth open, unable to move her throat, her chest, not even to breathe. How quickly her bliss had turned to terror. She knew she should do something, anything, but to her shame she thought of nothing but her own safety. Booming cannon fire scattered the assassins. Thank God! The *Espérance* had seen their distress. They launched a boat.

The islanders sprinted towards her. The sailors took off in chase. She stood rooted in the sand, watching them run at her. What had happened to the kind faces and bountiful smiles? Was this to be her end, after all she had endured? To be massacred on these islands that had once seemed so welcoming?

Blood splattered across her face as one of the sailors had his teeth bludgeoned out by a club. A musket fired. The islander with the club lay dead on the sand. A double canoe surged through the waves to the shore. The islanders on board shouted, and she wondered if they would see the dead man beside her and retaliate. She saw Kermadec, alone, unarmed, moving towards the smith. She found her courage and ran to him.

Kermadec bent over Fitz, hauling the near-naked man to his feet. Blood streaked from a gaping hole in his forehead, but he could walk. He was still alive. She took one of Fitz's arms across her shoulder.

'Let's get him to the boat,' Kermadec said as the *Espérance*'s pinnace neared the shore.

Lieutenant Trobriand stood in the bow. 'Seize them!' he cried, pointing to the double canoe that had arrived moments before.

The *Espérance*'s men gathered pikes and sabres and leaped from the boat. Kermadec screamed at Trobriand to call back his men. The islanders on the canoe shouted to one another, confused. Most jumped into the water, but one man, dressed like a chief, stood defiant. Trobriand aimed his musket at the man and fired. The islander tumbled backwards with a shot through his breast.

'No!' Girardin cried.

A woman and her daughter ran out onto the beach, wailing. They began to beat at their own chests with their fists, crying out in grief. The girl wept over her father, rocking backwards and forwards, slapping herself about the head. These people were innocent; they'd had nothing to do with the attack on the smith. Girardin hung her head in shame before the dead man's wife, who screamed at the French with no fear for herself. Girardin shared a stricken look with Kermadec. An innocent life taken by French hands. An innocent life taken out of vengeance. What retribution would the islanders seek in return?

Chapter 50

GIRARDIN STOOD BESIDE THE GENERAL ON THE BALCONY OF HIS cabin, watching as the glowing fires multiplied along the shore, creating a ring of fire spreading out along the coast.

'There are more by the hour,' said the General.

Girardin nodded. The orange lights flickered through the trees. Dark figures passed in front of a large bonfire on the beach. People were gathering along the shoreline. Drums thumped out a coded message, booming out in sorrow or in anger. Was their intent to mourn the loss of the chief, or to rid the islands of her visitors?

'A disaster! What was Kermadec thinking to let his men act like that?'

'It all happened so fast,' she said, defending him.

'The man was a chief!' When he raised his glass to his lips to take a mouthful of brandy, she saw his hand was shaking.

It was late, well after midnight, and Girardin shivered despite the warm tropical air. The scent of frangipani mingled with wood smoke was becoming sickening.

The General took a deep breath. 'It was a matter of great importance to me that our expedition cause no bloodshed, and I have failed.'

He took another gulp of brandy, tilting his head back.

'How is the smith?' she asked.

'Renard does not hold out much hope. The injury to the man's skull is severe.'

'But what provoked the attack? Hasn't the trading been beneficial?'

The General shrugged. 'I fear these gifts we bring are a curse. They excite jealousies in men. And when all must be relinquished to the chiefs, it invites dishonesty.'

The General returned his brandy glass to the rail and it balanced there, delicate cut-glass catching the candlelight. She longed to pull it to safety.

'These people cannot be trusted.' The General pinched the bridge of his nose. 'They steal everything that's not pinned down and sometimes things that are. They would prise the bolts from our ship if we did not watch them. We must be away from here. It is no longer safe.'

'So soon?' she asked, shocked. 'But what of La Pérouse?'

'I do not think he has been here. They can count the number of yam harvests between Cook's visits. They know the contours of their coasts better than our best mapmaker. If there had been a shipwreck on these shores, I am sure they would know of it.'

'But what if his visit here does not paint them in a good light?' She looked back to the fires along the shore, remembering the crack of the club hitting the smith's skull.

'Then we must be even more cautious in our questioning.'

She reached for the knife in its leather pouch. Surely the General would not give up so easily. He had barely investigated these waters.

'I have this,' she said, drawing out the stag-horn knife to show him. 'I traded for it with an island woman. I think one of La Pérouse's men might have given it to her.'

The General did not answer at first. He took the knife, holding it up in the lamplight spilling from his cabin.

'There is no mark,' he said doubtfully. 'It could be English.'

'But worth investigating?' She had hoped he would be more enthusiastic seeing it as proof that La Pérouse had been here.

'The bayonets and hatchets I have seen are all of English manufacture. Even the coins are all English. We would expect to see much more of French design if La Pérouse had been here. One knife proves nothing.' He handed it back to her.

But Girardin could not give up so easily. They couldn't let this opportunity go to waste. 'It is French,' she said, and stowed it in her leather pouch. 'Captain Kermadec thinks so.'

'Ha!' He slammed his fist against the rail, making the brandy glass jump closer to the edge. 'What makes you think it was not from one of our men?' he growled.

She pictured Raoul then, his hips grinding into the girl beneath him on the dirt floor of the hut. The self-satisfied grin. Each thrust a threat to her.

'The blade,' she said. 'The blade is tarnished from this tropical air. One of our men would have kept it cleaned and dry.'

'Prostitution here is rife! Perhaps a sailor swapped an old blunt knife for the pleasures of some eager woman. The girls here will spread their legs for nothing more than glass beads and red cloth.'

She drew back, surprised at the harshness of his tone.

'This place is tainted with sex,' he said, his voice strained. 'This place is a lure. A lure with shapely curves and sickly scents. She is the pitcher plant. Deceitful. She draws us into her pendulous trap with the promise of delight. We have been fools. We are the fly on the edge of her lip. A tiny fly about to dive into her hungry mouth.'

The way he spoke startled her. The General seized the brandy bottle and refilled his glass almost to the brim. She had never seen him drink like this.

'Îles des Amis,' he scoffed. 'We must leave.'

The beating of the island drums thumped in her chest. 'Where will we go?'

'New Caledonia,' he said firmly. 'La Pérouse must have chosen to resupply in New Caledonia rather than here. Tomorrow we will dismantle the trading tent. I have made my decision.'

She turned her gaze towards the *Espérance*; the lamplights burned bright in her rigging like a beacon. She chewed her lip. Now was her chance to ask for a transfer to be with Kermadec. To be free of Raoul. If the General meant what he said, tomorrow might be too late. She had to speak now.

'I beg a favour from you,' she blurted, breathing quickly. 'I am not safe on this ship. The men suspect my true sex.'

The General turned his head, the look in his eye something she did not recognise; direct, intense, like the fires along the dark shore were reflected in them.

She swallowed. 'May I transfer to the *Espérance*?'

He swung about, knocking his glass with his elbow. She watched it topple from the rail and listened, breath stalled, for the inevitable splash at the end of its fall.

'You think a sickly, bedridden captain would serve you better?'

She winced. He had never spoken like this before. Never spoken such harsh words against his friend. She had insulted him.

'Foolish girl. Why do you think you have survived this journey unmolested?'

She flinched from him. He snatched her hand and pressed it to his lips. She stared, disbelieving. He pushed her backwards into his cabin, his breath doused with brandy.

'You are safe because the men believe you to be my whore.'

'Please, no,' she said, squeezing her eyes closed. She felt his hand lift her shirt.

'This place, this cursed place,' he mumbled into her hair.

'I love you,' she whispered, tears flowing. 'You are a father to me. Do not do this.'

She felt his arms tighten around her. He was shaking. Nothing could be the same between them now.

'Let me go to the *Espérance*,' she pleaded.

'No!' he roared, pushing her away. 'You will not go to him.'

She ran for the door.

'Your duty is to the *Recherche*!' she heard him cry out behind her. 'Your duty is to me.'

Girardin sat on the floor of her cabin, cradling Passepartout on her lap. She stroked the mottled brown skin. To the eye the lizard skin appeared coarse and hard, but beneath her fingers she felt how easily it might tear.

She had been blind. The General was right. Of course they believed her to belong to him. The sailors all suspected, but no man had challenged her since that first landing in Recherche Bay. Did she think the men left her alone out of grudging respect for her duties? That if she kept them fed she would be safe? Even if that were so, there would be no such security if she joined the *Espérance*. There she would be the outsider—unknown, unproven, a curiosity. She shuddered. Was the chance to be with Kermadec worth the risk?

Her friendship with the General was broken.

Once, she would have blamed herself. No more. Her mistake was to think the General was different from other men. She had respected him. He had reminded her of the kindly Marquis de Condorcet, who believed women could be more than they were allowed to be. He was the father she had longed for. But now the General had fallen in her esteem. She saw that he was no different from these tribal chiefs taking everything for their own.

Outside the sun would be rising. Soon they would face the anger of the islanders over their slain chief. She remembered the warning beat of the drums from the night before. But what filled her most with dread was the thought of seeing the General again.

Girardin moved through the ship in a daze, carrying the General's breakfast tray pressed against her ribs. Across the water, several canoes approached. She watched them come closer, her fear a dull thud in her chest. She expected reprisals, but when they drew up to the ship, there were women, not warriors, in the boats.

The daily rituals had resumed. Sailors whistled and cheered, helping the island women aboard on one side while d'Auribeau chased them from the other. She saw the captain slap a young boy's hands from the rail, and the boy merely backflipped with a gleeful shout into the water. If these people bore them malice, she saw no sign.

She climbed the quarterdeck and hovered outside the General's cabin, afraid to enter. The naturalists were nearby, having constructed a coffin-shaped box on part of the quarterdeck.

'Asexual reproduction is the only way,' Labillardière announced to Félix. He had filled the box with mulch to grow breadfruit plants. 'The natives take cuttings from the best fruit-bearing trees.'

Félix sniffed. 'I will put my faith in seeds.'

'They will return to wild type.'

'You are jealous. Mine have sprouted and yours have not.'

She stood listening to their bickering and staring at the General's door. What could she say to him? There was no going back to the way they had been before. And now she had lost her chance to go to Kermadec. The memory of his kiss was an ache.

D'Auribeau climbed the stairs and pushed her aside as he raged at Labillardière for commandeering space on the quarterdeck to grow plants.

'Do you not care about the starvation of our people?' Labillardière shouted at the captain's retreating back. 'He is a fool. These breadfruit could feed so many!'

On the deck below, Piron was sketching a beautiful island woman. The girl was naked to her waist and a crowd of sailors gathered to give her rings and beads. Piron did not notice his charcoals being stolen. Ventenat lost another pair of tweezers from his pocket. The soldiers sat on their rapiers, afraid they would be snatched from their scabbards. The islanders sensed this ship of treasures was about to leave.

She looked to the General's door. She remembered the brandy on his breath, his hands reaching for her, the anger when he thought she had chosen Kermadec over him. These islanders steal, she thought, because they fear if they do not take what they desire, another man might have it.

She knocked and waited.

He answered.

She pushed the door open. 'Your tray,' she murmured.

The General remained at his desk, bent over his charts. He did not turn to face her. The chronometer ticked loudly. 'Leave it,' he said.

Her heart was pounding. She knew her face was red. Her eyes felt full.

A cry rang out and a messenger appeared. 'The rudder chains have been stolen.'

The General roared in frustration. 'Let us be away before they take the teeth from our heads!'

Chapter 51

New Caledonia, 18 April 1793

THE COAST OF NEW CALEDONIA PROVED JUST AS TREACHEROUS as it had the year before. This time, the ships sailed along the eastern coast, looking for a way to break through the reef. It seemed as impenetrable as the rift between her and the General. He rarely left his cabin. He did not speak when she delivered his dinner. He would not meet her eye. It took three days of careful tacking in violent winds along the uncharted coast to find a break through the reef. She had hoped he would come out onto the deck to celebrate, but his door remained closed. Eleven days had passed since they'd left the Friendly Isles. The chasm between them grew wider with each passing day.

Once inside the reef, the ships sailed into the tranquil waters of the lagoon. Mountainous slopes rose steeply out of the sea and torrents of fresh water tumbled through the lush forests. Rainbows shimmered in the mist. It would be beautiful, Girardin thought, if I did not feel so wretched.

'Captain Cook spoke highly of the people here,' Labillardière told her when the ships were safely anchored in Balade Harbour. 'There were plentiful supplies to furnish his ships.'

'La Pérouse must also have come to this harbour,' Félix said encouragingly. 'There is no other way through this reef.'

She smiled at them. Both men meant to cheer her, to lift her spirits. Despite these calm waters, she felt brittle. She looked across the mirrored water to the *Espérance*. The peace between the two ships had been fractured.

Through her telescope, she ran her eye along the shore. She saw no remains of a French ship, no signs of life, only a forest of palms behind the wide crescent of beach, reaching up to a jagged mountain ridge. The crew gathered along the taffrail, waving red kerchiefs and flashing mirrors, remembering the women of Tongatabou. Smoke from cooking fires curled above the forest, but no people gathered on the beach and no canoes were launched from the shore. Girardin frowned. Why are they not coming out to trade?

Eventually, a party of four canoes ventured towards the ships, carrying both men and women. The sailors grew excited, and they began calling lewd boasts to the women as the canoes drew near. But the women, bare-breasted with only a narrow girdle of fringed bark over their hips, would not come aboard. The men climbed onto the ship with obvious trepidation. They huddled together in silence, naked but for the sheaths of bark wrapped around their penises. She saw the marks of violence on their skin. Several had eyes missing. All the islanders were extremely thin and lank with protruding ribs, a sharp contrast to the muscular men of the Friendly Isles.

This was so different from their arrival in Tongatabou. She looked to the General's door, expecting him to emerge to question these men. La Pérouse must have visited this harbour, surely. But the General's door remained closed.

Lieutenant Rossel held up some coconuts and yams and mimed for the islanders to bring some to the ship.

The natives immediately became animated and offered all the clubs and darts they carried in exchange for the coconuts. They sucked in their bellies and rubbed their hands on them, moaning in an unmistakable expression of hunger.

Girardin was shocked. Lieutenant Rossel caught her eye, his face grave. She looked to the General's door, feeling desolate.

'What has happened in the twenty years since Cook was here?' Labillardière wondered aloud.

The sailors muttered to one another, peevish and disgruntled by the lack of women. How soon would they turn their lupine eyes on her? She was eager to be away from the ship. If the General would not mount a search party for La Pérouse, she would find her own way to shore.

'Come on,' Girardin urged Labillardière. 'Let's explore this anchorage.'

When Girardin jumped barefoot from the boat into the water, her feet sank into coarse sand. She pushed her toes into the amber grains and scoured the soles of her feet, feeling the dirt and dead skin slough away. She wished she could strip naked, lie in these gentle waters and scrub herself clean. The memory of her encounter with the General had left her feeling soiled.

The rowers turned the longboat back towards the ship without coming in to land. The sight of the scarred men, their missing eyes and spear wounds, had spooked them all. There was violence here.

A party of armed soldiers had joined the naturalists on the shore.

'Wait!' a voice called from the boat.

She raised a hand to shade her eyes. Someone stood up in the boat, setting it rocking. Mérite jumped over the side into waist-deep water, holding his boots in one hand and a musket above his head. He splashed past her, grinning. 'I have changed my mind!'

'Must he always come with us?' Félix muttered. She noted the sneer of his upper lip with surprise.

'You may join us on the condition that you shoot no snakes,' Labillardière told the midshipman. 'If you must kill any, have the decency to break their necks so that we may learn from them.'

'With my bare hands, I suppose?'

'Preferably,' Félix replied.

Girardin waded ashore, following a tiny, transparent crab onto the beach. Only when it scuttled sideways did it reveal itself. When it stopped still, it vanished into the sand. A useful trick, she thought. This crab knew what it felt like to hide all the time. To creep and pause, to hover unseen. Did it know the danger of a life spent being invisible? she wondered. That it was possible to forget how to exist? The crab was so light and insubstantial it left no trace of its footsteps in the wet sand.

Girardin listened to the eerie creak and pop of a stand of bamboo. Plants with sabre-like fronds lined the forest edge like a barricade. A large black crow watched them from a branch. Its mocking cry of alarm seemed to reverberate through the palms, picked up and copied by invisible compatriots, but it did not leave its perch. It ducked its beak and cracked open an egg from the nest it was pillaging.

'Look here,' cried Labillardière. 'Masked lapwings! The same as we have seen in New Holland. This one feigns a broken wing to lead us away from its nest.' Girardin watched as the bird limped and dragged its wing along the beach. 'I have read of this deceit but not yet seen it!' Labillardière raced to follow the bird.

'This way,' she snapped. She had no wish to be reminded of what risks a mother might take to save its child. She straightened her back. Leading the way, she parted the dense foliage.

As they moved through the coconut palms and deeper into the forest, thick spiderwebs stretched across the tracks. She saw insects and birds hanging trapped in the sticky silk. Mérite now walked in front, slashing at the webs with his sword. Wisps of silk clung to their clothes. She saw a long-legged spider with a bulbous abdomen crawl across Félix's shoulder. Sandflies buzzed about them, attacking any exposed skin. Her skin was soon pockmarked with red welts where she had scratched furiously at the bites.

Girardin could not shake the feeling they were being followed. Each touch of a spider's web felt like a hand trailing along her neck. Every cracking branch made her leap. The soldiers slashed at the forest like it was an enemy.

Tendrils of smoke reached them through the trees. The smell of wood smoke was strong. Girardin stopped suddenly at the sight of a family group clustered around a fire. The men and women stood, motioning to the foreigners to join them. Cautiously, she approached. These people were emaciated, just as the men who had come out to the ship had been. The women's breasts hung low and thin. Only their hair seemed vibrant and full of life, black haloes frizzed around their faces.

Children ran through the undergrowth and climbed through the trees. She crouched, watching them pluck enormous spiders from the bushes and collect them in an earthen jug. The boys tipped them onto the coals and cooked them till crisp. She winced as they munched the delicacy with squeals of delight. Labillardière had to be quick to barter for one of the spiders before it was blackened on the coals. 'I shall call it *Aranea edulis*, after the Latin for edible,' he said.

Mérite traded a piece of salted pork for a spider with one of the children. 'Tastes like hazelnuts,' he said, having difficulty swallowing. The boy took a small bite of the pork and immediately spat it out.

'I do not like this,' she whispered to Félix. 'They have no food to trade.'

As far as she could tell the family had no items of French manufacture, no steel or iron, no pieces of clothing. Their language was incomprehensible. Labillardière had begun collecting a new vocabulary.

'Ask them if they have seen men like us,' she said to him. 'Five years ago.'

Labillardière could get no coherent answers from them.

The party climbed higher into the mountainous interior. To Girardin's surprise there were signs of cultivation on the slopes, but it seemed the crops had failed and been abandoned. Soon the plant life became sparse and the terrain rocky. A bracing wind blew along the crest of the mountain, chilling her and making her forget the tropical heat below. Thankfully, the mosquitoes no longer plagued them. From the summit of the mountain she could see the line of reefs running along both sides of the island. To the west she saw the violent breakers that had prevented them from landing here the year before. Far below, the tiny shapes of the *Recherche* and *Espérance* looked like toy ships.

The sound of a falling rock made her turn. Crouching below the track were a man and a boy, watching her. They were little more than skin and bone, their limbs even more wasted than the natives from the coast, their sunken eyes wary.

'They are eating stone,' she whispered, seeing them pick up rocks to gnaw upon.

'Steatite,' said Labillardière, collecting lumps of the soft greenish rock and putting them in Félix's pack. 'Perhaps it fills their stomachs.'

A boy held out the shoots of a hibiscus plant for one of the soldiers to try. The gesture of hospitality touched her. They were starving and yet they offered their food. The soldier chewed briefly and then spat it out, complaining of the bitter taste. Instantly the boy swept up the chewed shoot and put it in his own mouth.

As the party continued southwards along the ridge, Labillardière called out and pointed to a lush, cultivated valley with plantations of coconut palms and columns of smoke rising from a village. Girardin grew hopeful. Perhaps this settlement would have food to trade and some sign that a French ship had anchored here.

It took some hours for them to reach the hamlet. She was excited to see plantations of yams and sweet potatoes. But to her horror, the village was empty, the huts smouldering and blackened, and the coconut palms hacked down. She heard Félix cry out in shock. Burnt bones lay in piles. She saw long bones like those of a leg, a cage of ribs, the unmistakable curve of a skull.

She covered her mouth. 'What has happened here?'

Labillardière stroked the trunk of a beheaded coconut palm. 'Vengeance has triumphed over reason.'

Shaking, she turned away from the smoked bones. Funeral pyres or totems of warning? They left the burning village quickly, following the valley down towards the sea. A nervousness stole over her. No one spoke as they hacked and slashed their way through the thickening forest.

She smelled the charred meat before they came to it. Like pig meat. In a small clearing, a family was seated around a fire. Girardin blinked, covering her eyes against the sting of the smoke. She heard Labillardière decline their offer to share the meal.

An elderly man was tearing at a joint of meat with his teeth. He gnawed at the ligaments, the bone almost cleaned. Labillardière gestured for the bone and, graciously, the man passed it to him.

'As I suspected. The natives here are anthropophagi. This is the pelvic bone of a child.'

'No!' She could not believe it. Cannibals! She staggered back.

To confirm it, Labillardière gestured to parts of his body and then his mouth. The old man grinned and pointed to the thighs of a boy, smacking his lips together and whistling between his teeth. '*Kapareck!*' he said, squeezing the muscles of Mérite's arms with obvious admiration and desire.

She looked into the fire. The elbow joint of a child's arm blistered among the coals.

She vomited into the lush undergrowth.

The soldiers all drew their weapons, closing ranks.

'They only eat their enemies,' Labillardière said dismissively, his tone accusing them of overreacting.

Wiping her hand across her mouth, Girardin saw Félix scattering his seeds half-heartedly.

'God willing these atrocious people will make use of this harvest.'

Girardin felt dizzy. Sweat was slick on her face in the humid forest. 'I can't breathe,' she whispered to him. 'We have to leave this place.'

It horrified her now to think what remains of La Pérouse's men they might find. She thought of the piles of burnt bones. What traces would even remain to be found?

Labillardière wrapped the pelvic bone and stowed it in his pack. 'We need to show the General,' he said, noticing her look of disgust.

They hurried through the forest towards the coast, startled by sudden noises; the screech of a bird, the secretive creak of the tree limbs rubbing against one another. She expected a club to fall on her head at any moment, to be dragged by the feet across the earth and hoisted up into some tree to hang upside down, waiting to be hacked apart like a hog.

At length she heard children's laughter through the trees.

'A village,' Labillardière said.

She shared a worried glance with Félix. 'Perhaps we should skirt around it?' she suggested.

'And miss your chance to question the inhabitants about La Pérouse?' Labillardière raised a sardonic eyebrow.

Girardin walked stoutly through the village. The inhabitants rushed from their huts to greet them, unarmed and displaying genuine curiosity. They received the glass beads presented to them with squeals of joy. Girardin scanned the smiling faces. Few young men were present; the villagers were mostly women, children and the elderly, and all had wounds on their bodies. Around the village, part skeletons hung from palisades. Girardin forced herself to look at the heads of victims driven onto spiked fence posts. They were all shrunken and blackened. How would she know if any of these men were French?

The villagers beckoned to her. They wanted to show her their homes, but she held back. Skeletons twisted in the breeze—whether warning or decoration, she could not tell. A small girl with her hair bound in tight knots took her hand and eagerly pulled her into one of the conical huts. Once her eyes had adjusted to the shade, Girardin saw the neatly swept dirt floor with woven mats spread about. The central pole of the circular room was carved with intricate patterns. She cast her gaze about uneasily, looking for anything that might be French in origin, but fearful of what she might find. She saw wooden utensils and woven fans and some knives carved from bone, but nothing steel or silver. She left the hut feeling relief. She realised she did not want to find traces of the Frenchmen. To be stranded in this place would be appalling. Unimaginable.

Outside, one of the elders was demonstrating the use of an instrument made of a flat green rock polished to a cutting edge. Félix lay on the ground, cursing Làbillardière. 'I shall never forgive you for this,' he said. Smiling, the elder mimed slicing open Félix's belly. Félix cried out involuntarily. The man re-enacted hauling out Félix's intestines and throwing them away. He sliced off his genitals and passed them to an imaginary victor.

Girardin began to laugh. It was too much. She felt distanced from her own body. Was she truly watching these cheerful islanders demonstrate their grotesque butchery? The elder continued the pantomime, parting Félix's shoulders, hips and knee joints while the other villagers played the part of combatants taking pieces of the victim home to their families for dinner.

Her mouth was dry. Girardin mimed sipping water and the children ran to fetch it for her, grinning up at her as she quenched her thirst. She was anxious to return to the ship. These smiling cannibals confounded her.

They filed out from the village with the children chasing along behind them. Labillardière stopped suddenly in front of her, taking out his notebook. 'Evidence of a great corruption of morals,' he muttered.

For the price of an iron nail, a girl was lifting her fringed girdle to show a soldier what lay beneath. The girl demanded a nail from each of the soldiers as they passed and insisted on payment before satisfying their curiosity.

'This you find reprehensible?' Girardin could not help but snort in derision. 'After all you have seen of these cannibals, this girl's actions offend you most?'

She pushed past the queuing soldiers, afraid that she would reveal more of herself and her past than she dared.

What did Labillardière know of his friend Jacques Hébert? What would the high moralist think of what his friend had asked her to do?

'It is merely a question of distraction,' Hébert had said to her as the carriage bounced and jolted through the streets. 'Think of it as a necessary deception.'

'I am not sure I understand your meaning.'

He had tilted his head. 'Come now, Marie-Louise, you have been a married woman. I am sure I do not need to spell it out.'

How fitting that Hébert should come to mind in this barbaric land.

Chapter 52

Balade Harbour

EARLY THE NEXT MORNING, THE GENERAL CAME TO THE GALLEY. Girardin stared at him, a tray of freshly baked bread held in the space between them. Her mouth dropped open.

He held up a hand to stop her from speaking. 'I have been a fool,' he said softly. 'A delusioned old fool.'

The tray began to shake, the breadrolls shifting towards the edge. She placed it down.

'I spoke carelessly,' she said.

'No,' he said with a shake of his head. 'Do not apologise. My actions were unforgiveable. I am ashamed. I acted as if it was my right to take you for my own, like some feudal lord. I despise men like that. I grieve that I almost became one.'

She met his eye and saw only sadness.

'Come,' he said, gesturing for her to follow. 'Before there are too many prying eyes and ears.'

Hastily, she removed her apron and dusted her hands.

Two sailors rowed them across the bay. The sun had not yet risen, but the night sky glowed a brilliant blue and the last of the stars faded one by one from view. Girardin could feel her stomach sway with each pull of the oars. The General remained silent as the men rowed and she could not ask why he was bringing her to the *Espérance*. Her mind reeled with possibilities. Had Kermadec asked for her? Was she to be transferred after all? The boat collided gently with the hull of the ship—this ship she had travelled alongside for so long and so far without ever setting foot on board.

The officers of the watch stood to attention when they recognised the General coming on board. Joannet met them, his face grave. He drew her aside. 'We must discuss the matter of our supplies. This harbour has been most disappointing.' His jowls wobbled as he shook his head. Girardin frowned. Had she been brought here only to talk about coconuts and bananas?

On deck, the sailors were splicing worn ropes and mending sails. Their silence as they watched her pass was disconcerting. She took heart that the General led her straight towards the captain's cabin.

Kermadec's cabin was a replica of his library at his home in Brest; the walls were lined with books. It took her back to the night she had first met him. The armchairs, the side tables, even the pictures reminded her of that night. She saw the gilt-framed painting of two ships cresting the waves that had been above his mantelpiece. All that was needed to re-create the illusion of his library was a roaring fire and the man himself, stretched out in an armchair before it.

She looked around, confused. He was not here.

Pinned to the wall was the map that Kermadec had first showed her. In his library, he had pointed to those dots of islands lost in the middle of a blank expanse, and now she was here among them, so far from home.

She heard a cough. A heavy, wet cough. Eyes wide, she turned to the General. A curtain separated the study from the sleeping chamber and, quietly, the General drew it aside.

Kermadec lay cramped in his cot. Too long for it, his knees poked out; he looked like a skeleton folded on the bed. For a moment, her heart was afraid to beat, as if it were trapped in a cage of thorns. Then, with a guttural moan, she collapsed to her knees beside him.

Kermadec opened his eyes and tried to smile at the sight of her. She clasped his hand, gripping his fingers tightly. Translucent skin stretched over the prominent bones of his knuckles.

'I didn't know,' she whispered.

He nodded.

The General helped Kermadec to sit up. She stood back, noticing the bucket at the head of his bed, marked with thick black stains.

'My friend, forgive me,' the General said, his voice cracking. 'I should never have pushed for you to make this journey with me. I had no right to ask this of you.' The powder on his cheeks was streaked with tears. 'And I have not treated you well.'

'We make the best of the choices offered to us,' Kermadec whispered hoarsely. She saw he strained to suppress the need to cough. 'Who among us has not made mistakes? There is nothing to be gained from regret.'

As a coughing fit racked his body and the General held a crumpled handkerchief to Kermadec's mouth, Girardin wiped her eyes with the back of her hand. She struggled to understand how he had declined so quickly. We must turn for home, we must go back, she thought. He can still be saved.

She squeezed his hand. 'We will not be in this anchorage much longer. Just until we have enough water.' She waited for the General to reassure them, wanting him to confirm they would sail for France as soon as they were able, but he remained silent. *We need to sail north immediately*, she wanted to say, *for the sake of his health*. We need to get far away from this humid, cloying air filled with the smoke of charred flesh.

'And what of La Pérouse?' Kermadec asked.

She shook her head. 'No trace.'

'A blessing and a curse,' he said sadly. 'I would not like to be marooned here. If I should die here in this barbarous land, promise me you will give me a Christian burial somewhere these heathen cannibals will not be able to find me!'

Girardin shared a stricken glance with the General.

As Kermadec turned his face to the wall and drifted off to sleep, Girardin listened to the labour in each breath.

'He will recover,' the General said to her as the boat rowed them back to the *Recherche*.

Her voice was choked in her gullet, and she could not agree.

Each day the General collected her in the hour before dawn and they would be rowed across to the *Espérance* to sit with Kermadec until he tired. Sometimes they read plays, sometimes poetry. Sometimes the General would tell them stories of his adventures, tales that both of them already knew well. All three feigned an optimism they did not feel.

The stay in Balade Harbour had been a disaster. The watering hole that Cook had used had dried up in this season and the crew were forced to travel great distances inland to collect water, at risk of being set upon by the cannibals. A few coconuts were all they had traded in the way of food and, worse still, she knew their supplies were diminishing as the sailors stole food to trade for sex. Trading would be conducted peacefully on board, but then the departing islanders might turn and pelt the ship with stones, their edges sharp enough to take out an eye.

By the end of the week, relations with the natives of Balade Harbour had turned violent, with more skirmishes breaking out. The water and wood parties had been attacked for their axes and the fishermen for their fishing net, leaving wounded on both sides. Labillardière still spent his days exploring the forests, but Girardin refused to set foot on land again. 'It is safe,' he assured her. 'We are not their enemies. We do not intend to stay.'

She was silent. They see us shoot their birds, take their water and chop down trees to mend our boats. We give nothing in exchange for that. She saw that no one, neither the officers nor the naturalists, understood. It did not occur to any of them to offer payment for their trespasses. To take the necessities of life from this land was as natural to them as breathing.

Two weeks passed in this way, until one morning, the General did not call for her. On deck she saw immediately one of the boats was absent. The General had left for the *Espérance* without her.

All day she worried herself into a frantic state. Why had the General left her behind? She picked at the thought until it became an open wound.

It was late afternoon when an ensign came from the *Espérance* to collect her.

'Is your captain well?' she asked him, but the man would not commit to an answer.

As the sailors rowed her between the ships, she watched the tropical clouds grow fat and full with moisture and darken to a purple bruise.

She entered Kermadec's cabin alone and found him dressed in full naval uniform and seated at his table.

'You are better!'

He smiled gently. 'Come sit with me.'

On the table in front of him were some of his books, sheets of paper and a quill. 'I want to give you this.' Kermadec pushed a leather-bound volume towards her.

It was a book on mathematics. She frowned as she slowly read the title aloud. '*Principes Mathématiques de la Philosophie Naturelle*. A Translation and Commentary of Isaac Newton's Principia Mathematica? You want me to have this?'

He chuckled. It was a wet sound that did nothing to cheer her. 'I don't understand it either. It is by a woman of formidable intellect, Émilie du Châtelet. I think you will find her an inspiration. Promise me one day you will ask the General about her. I believe she once beat him soundly and most profitably at the card table.'

'I cannot take this. Your books are precious to you.' She turned to see the bookshelves behind her were almost empty.

'Clearing the decks. Making it easier for our dear friend d'Auribeau to move in.'

'Do not say such things!' she snapped. 'How can you jest?'

'How can I not?'

He signed the paper he was writing on and folded it decisively. 'The rest I will leave for Bruni to take back to France's libraries.

But I wish to give my dearest friends something of mine to keep close to them.'

'What do you mean? You are speaking nonsense. The General has seen how ill you are. He must let us go home—he must!'

'D'Entrecasteaux is a man of duty. He knows his duty to the King and he will not falter.' He picked up her hand and kissed it. 'You must find La Pérouse for me, and make all this suffering worthwhile.'

'We will find him together,' she sobbed, her tears falling freely.

'Don't cry, please don't cry—not when I no longer have strength to hold you in my arms and comfort you.'

She pressed the back of her hand to her eyes. He must be mistaken. She would speak with Joannet. He looked so much improved.

Gently, he kissed the tears from her cheeks and touched his lips to her mouth. 'You are extraordinary,' he said. 'I have never known a woman like you. I think I have loved you from the very beginning.'

'You are not leaving me.' Her voice was a growl, a threat.

'I have made my peace with life. My only regret is that I will not be with you when you find your son.'

Sorrow centred in her throat with the pain of a knife blade. She couldn't breathe. She wanted to wail her grief and rage at the world. But instead, she got up from the table and wrapped her arms around him, holding him.

'Will you lie with me?' he asked. His eyelids were heavy, his smile soft. 'I want to stretch out, I want to lie down flat.'

She took the mattress from his cot and laid it on the floor. When he lay down, Huon de Kermadec let out a long groan as if the last air of his lungs had been expelled. He flexed and pointed his toes, and smiled with childish delight. She lay down beside him, unable to speak, touching her head to his shoulder.

'It is the simple things,' he said, taking her hand in his. 'In the end, it is the simple things that matter.'

Chapter 53

Islot Pouidou, New Caledonia, 7 May 1793

THE FUNERAL FOR CAPTAIN JEAN-MICHEL HUON DE KERMADEC was held according to his wishes. Under the cover of darkness, his men began to dig in the sand of a low, flat islot. She learned he had chosen the place himself, an inconspicuous smudge of white sand separated from the mainland of New Caledonia, but protected from the ocean waves by the outer reef. At midnight his body was lowered into the unmarked grave. The *Espérance's* chaplain gave the eulogy. All around her, Girardin heard the men weeping. The moon was absent and the night was as black as a charred and empty pot.

Girardin could not comprehend the loss of him. He had put his affairs in order and gracefully, acceptingly, died. With her eyes squeezed closed, she pictured his broad smile and could not believe that she would never see it again. She had never met a man so filled with love of life.

Her mistake had been to imagine that love was possible, that there would be a way out for her, a way to be with her son. God had no forgiveness for her. Instead it seemed she was doomed to have everything taken from her over and over until there was nothing left to give.

The boats ferried the silent mourners back to the ship. She felt unworthy for thinking of herself, of her own loss. A man was dead. A good man was dead. A man of wit and humour, of kindness and intelligence. A man whose sister loved him and did not yet know that he was dead. I am not the only one who has suffered, she told herself, and I do not deserve pity. She opened her eyes. The General was kneeling by the grave, smoothing the sand with the palms of his hands.

D'Auribeau took command of the *Espérance* later that morning. Girardin watched him board the yawl with all his possessions already packed. She hated to see him claim the *Espérance* as his. Just for a moment she thought she saw a look of foreboding in his features, before his stony countenance returned. Perhaps he too wondered how he would replace their beloved captain.

It was three more days before the General ordered their departure. Girardin understood his reluctance. They would be leaving Kermadec behind. It was not right or fair. She could not even leave a token upon his grave.

They left New Caledonia before dawn. In the grey light it was difficult to make out the low island where Huon de Kermadec lay buried. Girardin felt cheated of this last chance to say goodbye. She stood on the deck, hiding the tears on her cheeks as the *Recherche* found a passage through the reefs and out into the open sea.

The General kept to his cabin in a wretched melancholy. In the evenings she sat with him in silence. She knew he blamed himself.

'My ambitions have blinded me,' he confided as he drained his brandy glass. 'God forgive me.'

She could not find the words to reassure him.

'How is it possible to complete these surveys and search for La Pérouse? I am torn. Kermadec would have me dedicate all to the search for him, but if we are to fail, if we can find no trace of La Pérouse and his ships, dare we return to France with no other accomplishments?'

Girardin could not counsel him. He spoke more freely with her than any other aboard the ship, especially as he had long ago stopped using Ventenat as his confessor. All she wanted was to return to France, an option that would not ease the General's conscience. The sacrifice of his friend had to be for some purpose.

Girardin moved numbly through the routine of her days. For the next three weeks, the expedition limped towards the Solomon Archipelago, still desperately short of fresh food and water. All the fruit they had taken on at Tongatabou was long since spoiled by the heat. Rain lashed the ships daily.

At the Santa Cruz Islands, Girardin saw a small flotilla of canoes launch, waving to entice the French ashore. Uncertain of their intentions, the General would not allow it, and neither would the natives be induced to come aboard.

'They remember Mendaña,' Ventenat said to her. 'The Spaniard who tried to settle here in search of Solomon's gold.'

'That was two hundred years ago!' Lieutenant Rossel scoffed, holding up a bolt of red cloth. The men in the canoe warbled in high-pitched glee.

'The Spaniards hunted them down as a show of strength,' continued Ventenat. 'And let their dogs feast on their remains.'

While exploring these waters, the General made few visits to the deck and rarely came to interview the islanders when their canoes drew alongside the ship. Trading was conducted by tossing items into their canoes. Often the price of goods increased after the bargains had been made, and sometimes they refused to pay at all.

Later, sitting with Girardin in his cabin, the General confessed to her that he could not bear to look on their scowling countenances. 'To be among these men fills me with great despair.' He pressed the heels of his hands to his eyes and rested his forehead against his palms. Late at night he walked the deck alone.

Still grieving herself, Girardin was incapable of rousing the General from his lethargy. She knew he felt as she did. Cold. Numb. She went about her duties in a dull haze.

'I have found something,' Labillardière said to her one evening, holding out a plank of wood.

Earlier that day she had seen him interviewing the islanders who approached the ship while Piron sketched each of their ornate canoes.

'It is varnished!' he said. 'It must be from a European ship. The islanders would not say where they had come upon it.'

She felt a spark of interest pierce her numbness.

'I thought you would want to know,' he said with a slight shrug. It was a kindness to her and she was grateful, even if she could not show it.

'And I saw a wooden chisel of French manufacture,' said Saint-Aignan eagerly.

She took the news to the General.

'Could it not be from Carteret's expedition here?' he replied, distracted. Tonight, he seemed distant, muddled. She had noticed he could not finish his train of thought and his voice died away mid-sentence.

'But didn't Carteret find the natives unwilling to trade with him?' she countered.

'Perhaps,' he said. 'I cannot recall.'

'This might be our last chance to search for La Pérouse. It is what Kermadec would want us to do.' Her voice was becoming more sure and steady. They owed this to Kermadec, they owed it to his memory. 'We should investigate.'

'Go ask Lieutenant Rossel. Whatever he thinks is best.' The General stood up from his table and passed through to his sleeping quarters, leaving her sitting alone in his cabin.

Rossel was convinced they must make for Waygiou as quickly as possible for the sake of the General's health. There, he assured her, they would find a safe landfall and fresh food. She knew the General ate little or nothing, surviving only on putrid water and a small roll of plain bread. Coffee gave him spasms. He could not stomach the walnuts soaked in spiced vinegar that Joannet prescribed. The act of dressing exhausted him. She had watched his grief turn to anxiety and delirium. He imagined himself a young boy again and Girardin his sister. Reluctantly, she agreed with Rossel to abandon the search.

Girardin felt guilty. She had failed Kermadec, unable to carry out his last wishes. But they all knew the search for La Pérouse was over.

His officers called for the General to split the expedition ships.

'Go on ahead, sir. For pity's sake, you must preserve your health!' said Rossel.

'I will not leave Captain Kermadec!'

The officers looked to their shoes.

Girardin felt her heart break apart.

Relenting at last, he allowed Rossel to give the order for the *Recherche* to sail ahead. But that morning, as if reprimanded by a vengeful God, the General was seized by a sudden vicious pain in his gut. She watched in horror as he writhed in his chair, face twisted in excruciating pain before he crumpled to the floor in agony. She ran for Renard.

Renard brought Labillardière.

They called for Joannet.

A bilious colic, they all agreed.

She watched in tortured silence as they lowered the General into a bath of water for treatment. Immediately his body shook with violent convulsions and he fell unconscious. By evening, the General was dead.

Chapter 54

Solomon Sea, 21 July 1793

It was dark when Rossel stepped out on the quarterdeck to deliver the news to the crew. Around Girardin there was a deep, profound silence. Disbelief.

D'Auribeau took command of the expedition. He stepped forwards. 'We have lost the best of chiefs, the most tender father.' His voice trailed away.

Girardin could hear the sobs around her, but her cheeks were dry. It was too soon for tears. It was not real. He could not be gone. How could a being, with all its complexity of thought and mind, that presence, be so instantly taken? No! She clenched her fists. She could not have lost the two men who had loved and protected her. She began to shake. She felt undone, unravelled, as though the ties that bound her to home had finally been severed, leaving her adrift. Looking around she thought she saw the same fear on other faces. A sense of irreparable loss, and of being lost. We are orphaned children, she thought.

Girardin locked herself in her room. She threw herself into her hammock and cried until her face was hot and her ribs ached. She wept for Kermadec in a way she had never been able to before. The loss of the General gave her permission. She no longer cared what others might think. She howled her grief. For Kermadec and the lost promise of their love. For Bruni d'Entrecasteaux, the father she'd never had.

At midday of the following day, the cannon shots ripped through her grief and she curled into a ball, cradling her head in her arms. She flinched at each of the thirteen shots as Admiral Antoine-Raymond-Joseph Bruni d'Entrecasteaux was farewelled with full military honours. She heard the weighted splash of his body.

For three days she remained in her cabin. She did not answer her door. She did not take food, nor care to ensure it was provided for others. The scurvy sickness had returned. She scratched at the black rash spreading on her arms and legs. No matter how much she rubbed, she could no longer see the burn mark on her arm. The black pustules had obliterated it. She attacked the rash, digging her nails into her skin. Even that reminder of her son was lost.

She keened when she realised she had missed the anniversary of Rémi's birth. It had passed, lost in the weeks of misery and self-pity. She loathed herself. Her son was now two years old.

Girardin cradled Passepartout in her arms. The lizard was thin—she had forgotten to feed her in these last days of grief—and her skin was dull brown and paper-dry.

'I have made you wear the drab colours of this ship,' she whispered. 'What right did I have to take you from your home?'

On the third day of her confinement, when her ablutions pail was full, when her cabin smelled of piss and shit, when she had no tears left, she heard a knock at her door.

'You can't stay in there forever.'

She recognised the voice at her door. Mérite.

He knocked again. 'Let me in!'

What did he want?

Cautiously, she unlocked the door. Mérite was alone. She stepped back and let him enter.

'Good God, this place reeks.' He winced, covering his nose with his arm. 'It's not healthy. We have to get you out of here.'

She closed the door behind him.

He lit a reed from the lantern he carried and let the flame smoke while he walked around her cabin. When he passed the flame to the wick of her hanging lantern, the golden light swayed. Passepartout watched with a wary eye from her cage.

'What do you want?' Girardin asked, her voice exhausted.

'Crème anglaise and fresh strawberries fed to me on a grass lawn. Dancing and fireworks.'

She stared at him with hollow eyes. 'What are you talking about?'

'We all miss him,' he said. 'But we have to carry on.'

Girardin looked to the floor, expecting her eyes to well up with tears. But by now they were empty.

'We must endure,' he said.

What did this boy know about endurance? What could he know about bearing impossible pain? She sank down in her hammock. She should be angry with him, but the feeling leached away from her. She simply didn't have the energy.

'You need to eat.'

'I'm not hungry.'

'Besnard needs you.'

She grunted. No surprise.

'The savants miss you.'

She raised her eyebrow at him.

'Well, Félix is worried about you.'

She sighed. 'What are you doing here, Mérite? Why do you care?'

'Haven't I always been there? In Van Diemen's Land, New Caledonia? Why would I willingly endure the company of Labillardière?' He smiled. 'The General asked me to keep an eye on you. He would not want to see you like this.'

She narrowed her eyes, wondering how much the General had told him about her. 'I didn't ask for his protection.'

'He loved you like a father. He watched over you. He couldn't help it.'

'Well, the General's gone,' she said, dropping her head. 'Your duty is discharged.'

'I ask you then as a friend. Come, get some fresh air.' He held out his hand.

It galled her that he was right. She couldn't stay in here forever. She could not repeat the same mistakes she had made when Etienne had died. Her grief had cost her everything.

'It's not raining,' Mérite said hopefully.

She let him pull her up. His hand was strong. 'Thank you,' she murmured.

As they left her cabin, she picked up her pail of slops.

On deck, she gulped at the soggy air. She smelled the salt sea, the tar, the scent of recent rain. The deck had been sluiced and the boards steamed.

She followed Mérite as he took a turn about the deck, leading her through the knots of men. She saw fat fingers holding grubby cards. Unshaven faces and yellow teeth, chewing on dry biscuit.

She passed the fishermen smelling of raw bait. They stared at her as she went by. She met their eyes. She held the pail in front of her like a weapon. Let any man come near me and he will wear it, she swore to herself.

'Look there.' Mérite pointed to the horizon. The skies above her head were obstinately grey, but along the horizon was the barest crack of glowing pink. He smiled at her. 'Hope.'

Part Four

Retrouver:
to find something lost

Chapter 55

Boni Harbour, Waygiou Island, 20 August 1793

'Is this not the most beautiful blue you have ever seen?' Mérite asked, coming alongside her at the rail.

A turtle swam through the azure water, the sunlight shifting across its patterned shell. The sun brightened the bay like a translucent jewel. These colours did not exist in France, she was sure of it—except, perhaps, in church windows. She remembered kneeling in the cathedral of Saint-Louis, staring up at the sunlight shining through the blue glass of Mary's robe, Jesus held tight against her. But even then there had been something tainted about the colour. Here the colours were crisp and fresh, newborn.

'Have you ever seen so much fruit? Such variety of produce?' Mérite stared in amazement at the mounds of pumpkin, yam, pawpaw and sweet potato on the deck.

The trading at Waygiou had been cautious, but friendly and surprisingly abundant. The harbour was a disappointing mangrove swamp with rickety huts standing on stilts above the marsh. But, miraculously, food had appeared. Every day the islanders brought more produce to the ship. She drank lemonade and ate oranges. Besnard made a turtle meat soup. The native turkey was delicious. There was laughter, singing and dancing. Saint-Aignan had picked up his violin with renewed appetite.

'I could live here,' Mérite said. 'I could live out my days in an island paradise like this. Remember Tongatabou? Have you ever before seen such lushness, such promise?'

Mérite offered her a piece of pineapple, but she shook her head, thinking instantly of Kermadec. He too had been an optimist. Someone who thought the best of life, despite evidence to the contrary.

'I have a feeling that in this part of the world,' Mérite said softly, 'no one would be left to starve.'

She gave him a sidelong glance. What had this youth seen of starvation? Mérite de Saint-Méry with his well-muscled chest and shoulders that spoke of fine food and safe shelter. He had most likely been fed by the King's navy all his life, and no doubt his father and grandfather before that. What did he know of suffering?

'Have you forgotten the cannibals of New Caledonia?' She reminded him of the men that had pointed at his thighs and smacked their lips with desire.

'But they welcomed us. They fed us, even though they were starving.'

She fell silent. At the bow, Saint-Aignan began to play a merry tune. He hoped to bring the canoes out to trade. She watched him move with the notes, so transported by the music that he did not notice the approaching canoes veer away to the *Espérance* instead.

Mérite kicked off his shoes and leaped up onto the taffrail, balancing with his arms outspread.

'What are you doing?'

'Come in with me!'

'I cannot swim.'

'I will teach you.'

She waved him off. Foolish boy. Mérite jumped, tucking his knees up to his chest, hitting the water with a massive splash that drenched her and caught Félix and Labillardière as they approached.

'Idiot!' Labillardière called, wiping his face.

'Watch out for the snakes here,' said Félix, as he shook the water from his hair. 'They swim.'

Mérite kicked out on his back and grinned.

'It is good to see you revived,' Félix said to her.

She smiled at him, the movement stiff and unfamiliar. 'We are on our way home.'

'Yes, home! At last. My hands itch for soil.' He rubbed them together. 'They have had their fill of salt.'

'A life of discovery is not for you?' she asked.

'I belong in a garden. I would rather watch God's creations grow than squash them flat in dry tomes.' His voice was tart as he turned his head towards Labillardière.

'What will you do when we return to France?' she asked Félix.

'I will take back my breadfruit plants to the Jardin du Roi and become a famous man. One day I shall be director of the King's gardens.'

She heard Labillardière snort.

Félix ignored him. 'And you, Monsieur Girardin?'

What would she do now? All her thoughts and dreams had involved Kermadec. She would need a living to support her son. 'Perhaps I would like to be a gardener too,' she said quietly.

Félix smiled at her with pure delight.

An unusual sensation flushed through her. All it took was dressing like them to prove her worth. She touched her chest. In a strange way these bindings have set me free, she thought. If I can be a man here, I can be a man anywhere. I can be a father to my son. She felt her spirits lift. To Java and then home, she thought.

Shouts rang out from nearby canoes.

'*Boayo, boayo!*'

The natives were urging the sailors out of the water. She saw Mérite floating on his back, arms circling like angel wings, oblivious.

'What are they saying?' she asked Labillardière.

He flicked through his notebook of the Malay language. 'They appear to be warning us about a type of Aloe plant.'

'Not *boaya*,' said one of the crew, a Malay slave they had taken aboard at Amboyna. He shook his head at Labillardière. 'They say *boayo*.' He gnashed his teeth. 'Alligators.'

She gasped. 'Mérite! Get out of the water!'

The cry of 'Alligators!' rang out as the crew called to the bathing men.

Mérite splashed his arms and feet in the clear blue water. 'I am not afraid of alligators,' he boasted.

'Only because he doesn't know what they are,' said Félix.

'Speaking of man-eating beasts,' Labillardière said, pointing to a boat leaving the *Espérance*. It was filled with crates and boxes. She shivered as if a cloud had crossed the sun. The new commander of the expedition, Captain d'Auribeau, was returning to the *Recherche*.

Girardin loosened one of the coils of rope along the side of the ship and threw it out to Mérite. He caught the end of it and let her pull him back to safety.

Girardin watched as Raoul welcomed Captain d'Auribeau aboard, knowing that she had never been more at risk on this ship than at this moment. The royalist sympathiser had a new leader now. If Raoul had spied on her at Versailles, if he knew what she had done for Hébert, then he would tell d'Auribeau. She saw it as clear as these waters, as plain as the scallop shells on the ocean floor. The royalist captain would seek retribution. No one would protect her now.

Captain d'Auribeau's belongings were transferred to the General's cabin and he ordered the flag of expedition commander raised once again on the *Recherche*. Girardin felt hot fury on seeing him take the General's cabin for his own. No one had set foot in the room since he had died. How dare d'Auribeau think to replace the General?

Raoul climbed the quarterdeck carrying a bucket of sea water.

Labillardière cried out, already running, 'Keep away from my breadfruit plants!'

The captain's face boiled red. 'The General tolerated your disrespect, but I shall not!' He flicked his hand to Raoul.

Raoul upended the bucket of sea water over the plants.

'No!' Labillardière dragged him away. 'Imbecile! You are poisoning them.'

'Things will change!' d'Auribeau thundered. 'The new order will not be so lenient. Get those boxes off my quarterdeck.'

Félix groaned and rushed below deck to protect his own plants. She knew he saw his future withering.

Raoul sauntered towards her, confident in his position as overseer of this new order.

Girardin stood her ground. She met his gaze, determined not to flinch. He smirked as he stopped before her. 'The whore,' he said into her ear. She pulled back, eyes wide, searching his face. Raoul leaned forwards and with his warm breath stroking her neck, whispered, 'Who might be next to take their pleasure with you now that the General is dead?'

Her nostrils flared.

'The General gone—' he snapped his fingers '—your Captain Kermadec, too.' He shook his head in mock sadness. 'No one for you to run to. Only me.'

'Never,' she growled.

'I offered you my protection once and I will do so again, for a price. I am a reasonable man.'

If he knew the truth of what she had done for Hébert, for the revolution, Raoul would already have told Captain d'Auribeau. Unless, she reasoned, he thinks only of his profit. Perhaps he thinks his secret knowledge could be turned to his advantage.

'I'm curious,' Raoul said in a low voice. 'Why did Hébert send you here? What does he hope to gain from your charade?'

Ha! He still thinks I am Hébert's cuckoo. He thinks I am in disguise on this ship to serve Hébert.

'Keep away from me,' she hissed. 'Or I will split you from breast to pubis and throw your innards to the fish.'

She saw his surprise as he looked down at the sharpened blade. She pressed the tip of her knife above his groin. It was the tarnished knife with the stag-horn handle she had traded for in Tongatabou. She had spent hours with the whetstone, sharpening the blade.

A hand on her shoulder dragged her back.

'Get about your work, Raoul,' Mérite said.

Raoul looked him up and down dismissively. He mock saluted the younger man and whistled as he sauntered away.

Both Mérite and Girardin were silent, breathing heavily. They shared a look of perfect understanding.

'I can protect you,' he said softly.

She shook her head. 'I can protect myself.'

'The people are starving,' Hébert had said to her. 'Louis has had enough chances, someone must act!'

At last, she thought. At last. Her days whispering in the corridors of Versailles would mean something. This was her moment. Olympe would be proud.

Hébert had Marie-Louise walk along the garden walls every evening. 'Pick an ugly one,' Hébert told her. 'Pick a guard whose head will be turned by a plain girl.' She had not even been incensed by his insult.

The King had sided with the nobles once again. Successive ministers—Turgot, Necker, even Calonne—had all told him he must tax the aristocracy or France would be bankrupt. Each time he tried to change the law the nobles resisted him. She did not trust the nobles; they cared for nothing except defending their privileges.

Something big was planned—Marie-Louise could sense Hébert's excitement.

'He has made a mistake, we have him now!' Hébert meant the banquet for the new troops, brought in to support the King's bodyguard. The banquet was lavish. The soldiers drunk. They danced upon the tricolour cockade. Hébert wrote of the gluttonous orgy while the nobility stockpiled grain to starve the outspoken poor.

When the market women of Paris rallied at the palace gates, Marie-Louise pressed herself to the palace windows along with all the other servants. The women at the gates were a ragged crowd, brandishing their knives and stolen weapons and dragging a cannon among them. They had marched thirteen miles from Paris in the pouring rain, ransacking armouries and gathering thousands in their mob. Whispers went through the galleries. 'They strung up the Abbé Lefèvre because he would not open the stores!'

Marie-Louise was exhilarated. She felt their anger, heard them rattle their pikes against the gilded gates, calling for the bitch, the Austrian whore. The gates held out against the mob and the rain continued to pound the cobblestones. The royal guards spread out along the fenceline, facing down the screaming women.

Her elbow was tapped and a note pressed into her hand. It was from Hébert and simply said: *Tomorrow, at dawn.*

That night, Marie-Louise could not sleep. She was excited, nervous and horrified in turns. What if she failed? This was the moment the revolution had been waiting for, she could feel it. The women, the mothers of France, were going to change their world for the better.

The gate she had chosen was near the southern wing of the château. All was quiet here, away from the main palace gates. On the other side of this wall was the shack she had grown up in. She knew the streets of the town, remembered running through them on a night as dark as this to find the midwife.

She led the guard away from the lamplight and into the shadows, heart pounding. It was real, it was now, it was happening. He said nothing, but grunted while fumbling with his ornate uniform. He lifted her skirts and pressed her back against the stone wall.

It was more painful than she remembered. She squeezed her eyes shut at the sharp stabbing of his penis. *What am I doing? What have I become?*

His thrusting became more urgent, slamming her spine against the wall. She recovered her wits. 'Please, remember to withdraw,' she whispered in his ear, 'My position, I will lose my place here, please withdraw!' She felt him slide from her and press himself against her thigh, and a hot rush of fluid run down her leg. He collapsed against her, breathing heavily.

Hébert had the women waiting and they roared as they charged the gate. The guard pulled himself off her. She sensed his panic as he looked around for his superiors, the realisation dawning that he had left the gate, that he had failed in his duty. The shadows beckoned. She saw him hesitate, but the distant whistle of his fellow guardsmen seemed to steel his resolve and he launched himself into the fray, weaponless.

Marie-Louise pushed herself from the palace wall, her whole body trembling. Her hands were white against her dress. Still the people came through the broken gate, an endless stream of fury. Many thousands trampled the carefully tended grass of the orangerie. The exotic citrus plants were overturned. The pots cracked open. Not just the women of Paris now, but some of the National Guardsmen too, still in uniform. She saw poor townsfolk and farmers together, charging towards the palace, scaling the stone staircase with their pikes lowered. Well-dressed young men, brandishing bottles of liquor, were whipping the crowd on. The women were wild-eyed, hair loose, clothing ragged. Some had torn their bodices and bared their breasts to show the strength of their despair. She heard glass smashing and knew they had entered the palace.

She stumbled after the mob. She saw the body of the guard lying in the dirt, his neck twisted fully around, his eyes staring at her. She doubled over, retching. *I have done this.* His semen was still wet on her leg.

By the time she reached the courtyard the royal family had been dragged out to the balcony. The heads of the Queen's bodyguards were raised on pikes. Beside Marie-Louise, a mother hugged the clothing of her dead baby. Another was hysterical, chanting, 'Kill the bitch! Kill the bitch! Kill the bitch!' These were her people; this was her revolution.

'Come to Paris, Louis, and see what we endure! Be the people's king!'

'She has blinded you!'

'Kill the whore!'

The crowd demanded the Queen. Marie-Louise stood transfixed, watching the Queen reach for the hand of the Dauphin.

'Not with your child,' jeered the crowd.

Marie-Antoinette stepped forwards alone, her face serene. The crowd grew quiet. Muskets were raised and levelled at her breast.

Oh God. Marie-Louise crossed herself. She remembered the face of the guard, twisted around in the dirt. *I have already sacrificed the life of one man today; must I have the death of a queen on my soul?*

Perhaps the crowd had begun to think the same. There was hesitation. The Queen stood alone.

A voice rang out from the mob. *'Vive la Reine!'* Long live the Queen!

Chapter 56

Sourabaya, Java, 27 October 1793

THE PASSAGE DOWN THE TREACHEROUS STRAIT TO SOURABAYA was slow and careful. But as the town drew closer, Girardin's heart beat stronger, each beat bringing her closer to her son.

'We shall soon be home,' Félix muttered to himself. 'Another voyage of eight months at most. I will take my box of seeds and my breadfruit back to André Thouin at the Jardin du Roi. I will be a success.'

She wondered if he knew he spoke this mantra aloud.

She sat with the naturalists as she did each afternoon. Labillardière nursed his three remaining breadfruit plants back to health, keeping them close in a pail beside him. He scowled at Raoul whenever he came near.

Raoul strutted about the deck. He had taken to wearing a tricorn hat and a blue frockcoat, unbuttoned, over his rough sailor's clothes. He styled himself a leader among the crew, someone d'Auribeau could rely upon to keep the men in line.

As the ship made its final tack towards Sourabaya, she stood and went to the bow, feeling the breeze cool her clammy face. The town was split in half by a river. On one side were jumbled Chinese- and Malay-style homes and mosques. On the other were orderly streets, stone mansions and the Calvinist chapels of the Dutch East India Company. She felt uplifted by the sight of the port. It was exactly like Amboyna. All the provisions for a long sea journey would be found here. They could buy salted meat and flour. They had not baked bread in months. Even the hated ship's biscuit would be a joy to behold. They would have brandy, coffee and wine. The holds would be full again for the journey home.

When they at last laid anchor in the soft mud of the bay, she was surprised to see a boat laden with armed Dutch guards approach the ship.

Ventenat came to stand with her. 'What is this about?' he murmured.

The guards filed onto the ship and spread out, their weapons held ready.

Captain d'Auribeau left the helm and addressed the guards. Girardin watched as a letter was presented to the captain.

D'Auribeau read, his lips moving with barely a whisper. She watched his face lose colour and begin to spasm. His voice was soft when he spoke.

'France is at war with the Dutch.'

At war! What did that mean? What did it mean for them?

She saw the same incomprehension on other faces.

'We are prisoners.'

Prisoners. The word reverberated in her head.

'That is outrageous! We are on a mission of science, not warmongery!' Labillardière cried. 'The Dutch have signed a passage of safe conduct.'

'The problem is that our agreements of safe conduct were made with Louis as our king,' d'Auribeau snarled, recovering himself. 'Your revolution has declared France a republic, not a monarchy, and our agreements are no longer valid!'

Shocked voices rose in a clamour. D'Auribeau silenced them with a gesture.

He continued to read. 'In France, an immense disorder reigns.' Tears rolled down his cheeks. 'The King has been executed.'

Pandemonium broke out. Girardin staggered back in shock. Shouts were hurled around her. Instantly the men separated into revolutionary and royalist factions. With those final words, the fragile bonds of kinship, of shared endeavour, hardships and sacrifice, were stretched and torn apart.

Ventenat leaped up to the quarterdeck, suddenly infused with energy. 'The King is dead! The tyrant is dead!'

D'Auribeau's voice cracked like a whip. 'Get that traitor down!'

Raoul tackled Ventenat, pushing him down the stairs and pressing the chaplain's face into the tarred grooves of the deck. The royalist sailors jumped on him. She screamed out as they began to kick his ribs. Labillardière and Félix fought their way through and helped to pull the chaplain to his feet.

Stunned, Girardin listened as more of the letter was read out. France was at war with all the major countries of Europe: England, Prussia, Austria and Spain. There was civil war; the western provinces supported the nobility. Foreign armies threatened Paris.

What has happened in these past two years? Fear escalated around her as the men thought of their families, their wives and children.

Helpless, she watched as the Dutch towed the ships into port and bound them against the dock.

Chapter 57

Girardin felt sweaty and feverish, rolling over in her hammock, unable to sleep. She longed for news of home. When she'd left France she had thought the revolution was over: the National Assembly was in power, they had won. Louis XVI was a king in name only. Her friends had wanted a constitutional monarchy; they'd never wanted to kill the King.

Images of Louis as a boy would not leave her. She saw him standing on the golden statue of Apollo riding his chariot out of the water, running through the labyrinth. She saw the letters he scratched into the gravel for her, the words he taught her. This lonely boy, avoiding his minders and his tutors, had been murdered by his own people. The King was dead. Beheaded.

'Forgive me,' she whispered aloud to the boy who had taught her to write her own name.

After the mob had stormed Versailles, the royal family were taken to Paris and imprisoned at the Tuileries Palace. Marie-Louise was proud. She had done that. She had given them to the National Assembly. To the people.

When Hébert had told her to follow the King to Paris, she obeyed without hesitation. By then, they had been lovers for many months. She no longer kept in touch with Olympe de Gouges and Sophie de Condorcet or any of the Girondists from Sophie's salon. All was Hébert. No one knew what she had done that night at Versailles.

Hébert paid off a chambermaid and Marie-Louise took her place, a nondescript face in maid's clothes, lining up to enter the palace. Her father believed her to be lodged in the Parisian abode of some noble family.

Under house arrest, Louis had no power. No courtiers quarrelled for the honour of removing his chamber-pot. It was Marie-Louise who threw the King's excrement onto the streets of Paris.

'We need someone to keep a close eye on him,' Hébert had told her. 'Make sure he does not plan an escape.'

But Hébert had not told her the truth . . .

There was a knock at her cabin door. Her heart flipped. She reached for her knife.

'It's me,' Félix hissed. 'I have news.'

She unlocked her door and he passed her a roll of papers. 'They were smuggled on board,' he whispered.

She closed the door. Her hands were shaking as she unrolled the bundle. Sickened, she recognised the caricature of Père Duchesne. The old man stood in his long coat and liberty cap in front of his furnace, smoking his pipe. One hand clutched a cone of tobacco, the other his crotch. The caption beneath read: *'I am the true fucking Père Duchesne!'*

Hébert the hypocrite.

'Yes, fuck it, I am again going to declare war on all aristocrats.'

'I am painting a picture in a language they understand,' Hébert had told her. 'I am not preaching to them and telling them how they should think and act.'

'But you are deceiving them!' She propped herself up on one elbow and poked his bare chest playfully. They lay in bed, her naked legs entwined with his. 'There is no Père Duchesne.'

'These people do not want to be told the truth,' Hébert rose suddenly and walked to the window. 'They want to feel it.' He clenched his fists beside his naked thighs. 'When Père Duchesne slaps the face of the whingeing aristocrat and wrings the balls of the whoring bishop, they wish it were them doing it. They want to be Père Duchesne! The more outrage they feel, the more they feel alive.'

He turned to the fire, grasped a poker and prodded the smouldering logs, sending a shower of sparks onto the hearth. 'Did I invent the injustice?' he raged. 'Are there not royalist pamphleteers doing exactly the same as I?'

'Of course there are!' Marie-Louise rushed to wrap her arms around him and laid her cheek on his back. He shrugged her off.

She had believed Hébert. There would be no power among the people if they were not roused by their passions. He saw himself as a conductor. Without him the instruments were nothing more than discordant sounds; with his direction they were transcendent. Hébert gave them focus. He gave them an enemy. He gave them Marie-Antoinette.

'What news do you have for me?' he said, reaching for a robe to wrap around himself.

'Nothing,' she stammered, feeling the coldness of the room on her goose-pimpled skin now that Hébert blocked the fire.

'Nothing?'

'The King signs whatever the National Assembly ask him to. The Queen plays with her children. All is quiet.'

'The Austrian whore is close to her children? Is that natural?'

'Of course it is natural for a mother to love her son and daughter.'

Hébert had smiled at her. 'So tender-hearted.' He had opened the robe he wore and wrapped her in his warmth.

Now, in his persecution of Marie-Antoinette, Hébert excelled himself.

Girardin read on as Hébert accused the Queen of incest with her seven-year-old son. Girardin felt sick. She tried not to think of the things she had told him. The things he had twisted into perversities. How much of this was her fault?

She flicked through the papers and found a cartoon of Olympe de Gouges. She cried aloud in shock. Hébert now attacked her friends. Olympe's trademark white headdress was held aloft by a mob and she stood as bald as a baby.

In black and white he ranted: *The contamination of the old regime lives on, if courtesans and mistresses are allowed to manipulate free men. Fuck, go home! Cease littering our streets with your pamphlets on the rights of bastard children, slaves and other lost causes!*

Olympe spoke out for mercy for the King; the Girondists wanted him disempowered, not made into a martyr. But the Jacobins were in power now. Hébert ridiculed her. *Those fucking meddling women*, he wrote. *Those toothless, lascivious hags*. Père Duchesne brayed for the King's head.

She read of the invention of the guillotine, a beheading machine. How many heads did they need to remove? She was breathless. If they were ever to return to France, what in God's name would they find?

There were royalist papers in among the copies of *Le Père Duchesne*. She read of massacres where the mobs of Paris stormed the prisons with axes, pikes and sabres. With grim purpose, they hacked to death priests, aristocrats and prostitutes. Women were raped before being torn to pieces. She searched for the date . . . September 1792, more than a year ago now. Could it be true? This was horrific.

Girardin rifled through the papers to see what Père Duchesne would say of the massacres. Madame de Lamballe, the Queen's close friend, had been imprisoned because Hébert had accused her of lesbian orgies with the Queen. Hébert had drawn her dead body in caricature, paraded outside the prison where the royal family were held so that the Queen might see her friend with her head hacked off, her guts worn as a belt and her genitals exhibited as a trophy.

Girardin felt nauseated. She had told Hébert that Madame de Lamballe was a confidante of Marie-Antoinette.

Hébert had chosen well. He did not want an enlightened woman; he wanted someone who would do as she was told. Someone who would not ask too many questions. She had been a fool. At the time, she had seen what he was about but had not wanted to believe it. She had seen the Duc d'Orléans step out of Hébert's carriage while she waited in the shadows of the street. He rode about with a member of the royal family and she had never questioned him about it. Now she read these papers and could see the truth. Père Duchesne called Philippe, Duc d'Orléans a true patriot. It was obvious to her now. Hébert was in the pay of the duke. He had orchestrated the downfall of the King not to bring democracy for the people, but so he could install another tyrant in his place.

Marie-Louise had wanted to be like Olympe. She'd wanted to be brave and fearless. She had wanted to *act*. But instead she had let herself be used by Hébert, had danced like a puppet on a string. He cared only for himself. Men like Hébert were opportunists, revelling in the disorder. They saw an opportunity for power and influence and took it. Olympe would never have fallen for his flattery.

She was disgusted by her own weakness. The failings of her character were laid bare. In her need to please him, she had lost all trace of herself.

Girardin was haunted by the look on Louis's face as he gazed up at a painting of two ships in full sail. The windows of the King's chamber were covered, and his face was lit by candlelight. Imprisoned in his chambers at the Tuileries, he had just signed the decree for the mission to rescue La Pérouse. Marie-Louise had watched the minister and his naval officers leave the palace.

'I once thought I could sail around the world,' he said, his voice full of longing. 'Do you remember?'

Marie-Louise had not expected the King to recognise her. They had been children, only seven years old, when they played together in the gardens of Versailles. She paused, motionless.

'But I never made it to the sea.'

Chapter 58

CAPTAIN D'AURIBEAU LEFT THE SHIP TO NEGOTIATE WITH THE Dutch for their release. Mérite was optimistic that the captain would prevail, that the Dutch would honour the agreements of safe conduct and let them sail. He wanted her to have hope and she had tried to appear persuaded, for his sake. But she was filled with dread. Sourabaya. The town drew its name from a mythical battle between a giant white crocodile and a great white shark.

Days passed and the captain did not return. He sent for his belongings. She learned the officers were to be housed with Dutch families ashore. Raoul, too, was given permission to leave the ship. The crew grumbled. Why was he allowed to visit the brothels of town when they were not? Girardin watched him go, dressed in his blue frockcoat and loose white shirt, half officer, half seaman. He tipped his tricorn hat to her with a hot, wet grin.

The port throbbed with the ebb and flow of trading ships. Here, everything was in continual motion. Ships came in from Amboyna, bringing spices from the islands, and from Japan with silk and porcelain. She watched the crates being loaded and unloaded, taken to and fro. The ships from Amsterdam came into dock filled with cloth and silver from Europe and returned loaded up with crates of pepper, mace, nutmeg and cloves. She watched it all. Fishing junks flitted in between the Dutch ships. The pulse of life went on at frenetic pace while the French ships remained trussed and bound with their rudders taken.

Sides of butchered beef and crates of vegetables were carried on board for her to feed the crew, but she saw none of the provisions needed for a long sea voyage. By now, Girardin was convinced that d'Auribeau had failed. She missed the General more than ever. He would have charmed the Dutch. He would've made the Dutch see they were no threat.

The monsoon rains came early. The rain drilled into the deck, chasing everyone below. The crew were falling sick with dysentery. The stretchers came each day to carry more men down the gangplanks, wrapped tight in their bedding, to be taken to the hospital or the cemetery. Only the sick and the dead were allowed to leave the ship.

'Why haven't they released us?' she asked Mérite when he sat with her in the great cabin. Each night she cooked for the officer of the watch. 'We cannot stay trapped here forever. This war might last for years!'

She looked up to the ceiling where a row of black swans hung with their feet crossed and bound, their necks looped over a rail. Along the windowsills, Félix's breadfruit plants climbed towards an open window.

'D'Auribeau does his best,' he said evasively.

'They have sent us no supplies for the journey home!'

Mérite looked away. 'What is there for us back home? The King is dead, disorder reigns, we will return to war and famine. We are better off here.'

She stared at him. 'You can't mean that.'

He shrugged.

'Don't you have a family to go back to?' she asked.

He crossed the room and poured himself another glass of brandy. 'No,' he said.

The silence stretched between them. 'Sorry,' she murmured, regretting her rudeness. She had let her anxiety overcome her. 'Forgive me.'

'I never knew my mother or my father,' he continued. 'I was a foundling.'

Her breath caught in her chest.

'You have heard of the *nourrices*?' he asked. His back was to her. He gazed out the small square windows.

She could not speak.

'My mother was a wet nurse.'

Tears welled in her eyes. This was too cruel. She did not want to listen.

'We lived in squalor. The babies were kept in a darkened room with mattresses on the floor. Every week they would come in from the church and every week we would send more caskets back. I mostly remember hunger.'

Girardin felt sick. She had assumed him to be the pampered son of nobility, grown strong on plenty, and now the truth seemed more horrific for her mistake.

'But I was one of the lucky ones.' He swallowed his brandy. 'I survived.'

'Do you blame her?' she choked.

'The wet nurse?' He half turned to face her.

'No—your mother, your real mother. Do you blame her for abandoning you?'

Above her head, the monsoon rain lashed the glass panes. The noise was sudden and thunderous as she waited, not wanting to hear his answer. Water pooled in the cased window panes and she had the sensation of being pushed underwater. Of drowning.

'I did at first. When I was a child.' He paused. 'But by age eleven I had seen enough of the world to understand.'

Girardin let silent tears seep down her cheeks and drip onto her shirt.

'I forgave her.'

She breathed in deeply, her chest shuddering.

Mérite kept his back to her and she was grateful for it. The pain in her throat was like a swallowed pebble.

'I ran away to sea,' he said amiably. 'And I was lucky. The General found me.'

Girardin wiped her face and pressed the backs of her hands against her eyes.

'The tide washes the beach clean every day. That's what he told me.'

She heard Mérite moving behind her. 'A man can reinvent himself at sea.' He rested his hands lightly on her shoulders. 'Or a woman.'

He bent and kissed the pulse in her neck. Shivers raced down the whole of her left side. She froze. He kissed her again. His breath was soft on her neck.

'Please don't,' she whispered and caught his hand. 'I am old enough to be your mother.'

'What does that matter?' He turned her chair to face him. 'I can protect you. We can stay here, start again. I will get a position with the Dutch. What is there for us in France? Nothing we know remains.'

'I have a son,' she said, her voice cracking. 'And I made a promise to return.'

Chapter 59

When Captain d'Auribeau finally reboarded the ship, he was flanked by a consort of Dutch soldiers. Girardin frowned as he called everyone to the deck. A low, questioning murmur rumbled around her. The crewmen shifted uneasily, casting nervous glances at the heavily armed guards. The crowd parted for d'Auribeau to ascend the quarterdeck. Girardin looked for Mérite and found him among the Dutch guards circling the ship's company. She had not seen him for more than a week, and she wondered if her rejection had angered him. He would not meet her gaze.

A flag was flapping loosely in the uncertain breeze. It was the white Bourbon flag of Louis XVI, now flying at half-mast. She turned her face away from it.

D'Auribeau looked tired and aged far beyond his thirty years, and his hands trembled with palsy. When he began to speak, his voice did not travel well and they all had to shuffle forwards to hear.

'I have negotiated the provisions for our return to France. We can sail!'

Cheering erupted all around her. Could it be true?

'Have we been released?' She turned to Félix. He was dancing a jig on the spot. The sailors threw their arms around each other. Few noticed that d'Auribeau had continued to speak. Girardin looked for Mérite and found him thin-lipped and sweating, eyes darting towards the Dutch soldiers.

'There are conditions,' said d'Auribeau, straining to be heard above the revelry.

Rossel ordered the tocsin rung and its clanging stilled the voices.

'There have been rumours of a republican spy aboard, a man sent to bring down the King's expedition.'

Girardin dared not move, dared not make a sound.

'These rebels make the Dutch nervous. They think we will run to Isle de France and join the republican forces. They think we will betray them.'

She heard a growl of low, questioning voices around her. What did this mean?

'We must flush out the traitors. All personal journals will be requisitioned. The ships will be searched. Those who do not hand over their papers will be punished!'

Girardin gasped and thought of her own secret journal. Was it safe? Had she hidden it well enough? All her letters to her son, to Olympe, all her fears laid bare.

'Furthermore,' snapped d'Auribeau, 'if I read your name, step forwards.'

'What is this?' said a voice from the crowd. It was Ventenat. He was wearing his black cassock and his face looked deathly white.

D'Auribeau read out the list of names. 'Ventenat, Riche, Labillardière, Lahaie, Piron.' Beside her, Labillardière raised his chin defiantly. What did this mean?

'These men are traitors. They are to be arrested immediately.'

'No!' she cried. This was madness, she could not believe it. The chaplain was quickly surrounded by armed men and yanked towards the gangway.

Mérite gripped Félix by his arms. 'Let him go!' Girardin cried. Armand spat on Mérite's shoe and the old sailor was dragged away by a Dutch soldier. His monkey bared its teeth and shrieked.

'What of my collections?' Labillardière said, shouldering Saint-Aignan aside.

'The collections belong to the expedition,' snapped d'Auribeau. 'As such, they will be safe.'

'The breadfruit!' said Félix, as he jerked his arm from Mérite's grasp. 'I must take my plants.'

'Very well.' Captain d'Auribeau waved them away as he retreated inside his cabin to cries of 'Shame!'

She followed Félix to the great cabin with Mérite trailing behind. Félix tore his breadfruit plants from the soil, piling them into a canvas bag. He tucked his chest of stored seeds beneath his arm, the collection more precious to him than a box of jewels.

'How can you do this?' Girardin rounded on Mérite. 'You know they are not traitors.'

'I am following orders.'

'You are saving your skin. You sicken me!'

He took a step back, wounded.

'How could you betray us?' she hissed.

'Girardin,' Félix called.

She went to him. 'This is insanity! She clasped the gardener's arms, disbelieving. This friend who had carried her through all the trials of this journey. 'What will happen to you?'

He bent forwards, his lips lightly brushing the side of her mouth. 'It has been an honour,' he whispered in her ear.

'Enough,' Mérite said, tugging Félix's arm.

The savants were marched from the ship by the Dutch guards. Girardin sank to her knees. The last glimpse she had of them was Labillardière's tall hat moving through the crowded dock and Félix's hand raised in farewell.

Chapter 60

Two soldiers ransacked the ship under the watchful eyes of d'Auribeau and Raoul. They tore apart each of the naturalist's cabins, removing loose boards and slicing open pillows. The great cabin was next. Girardin stood by as they opened the plant presses and tossed the dried plants onto the floor. A row of black swans swung from the ceiling above her head, twisting like hanged men. All the while, Raoul leaned against the wall and leered at her.

D'Auribeau ordered her to unlock her cabin. She clenched her jaw as the soldiers tipped over her chest, scattering her few belongings across the floor. Her string of shells tumbled out, the one she had traded a kerchief for with the boy of Van Diemen's Land, the one she was going to give to her son. She snatched it up and clasped it around her neck.

D'Auribeau thumbed through the book of mathematics and raised an eyebrow at her, but made no comment. She had already torn out the first page with Kermadec's inscription on it and kept it close to her skin. *To MLG, with admiration and love.*

With each stab of the rapier into the bins of tea and grain, her shoulders jerked. Her journal was not found.

As soon as the soldiers were gone, she crumpled to her knees. D'Auribeau had arrested half the crew and let the other half leave the ship. She alone was made to stay on board with a watch posted to guard the ship. He had isolated her completely.

All her friends. Taken.

Many times in her life, Girardin had grieved. Many times she had been brought low. And now those moments of despair engulfed her. She felt the loss of her first child all over again, the ache of losing Etienne, and the raw pain of Kermadec's death. Everyone she dared to love had been taken from her. Her friends peeled away. Even Mérite had turned against her. He was no different from men like Raoul and Hébert, men who chose the side of greatest power.

Abandoned. She recognised this dreadful loneliness. This was not the first time she had been stripped bare, left with nowhere else to turn.

Hébert did not take the news of her pregnancy well. He had risen from the bed, his member shrivelling.

'How do you know it's mine?'

'Don't be ridiculous, my love, how could it be any other?'

'You should have been more careful.' He paced in front of the curtained window.

Marie-Louise bit her lip, feeling panic rising within her. 'I—I thought you might be pleased,' she stammered.

'You meant to trap me, is that it? Contrive a marriage for yourself? The plain daughter of a pompous merchant!'

'But I love you,' she whispered.

'You stupid, stupid bitch. You have ruined everything! Do you think the palace will have a place for an unmarried whore and her bastard? Go back to your papa—I have no use for you now.'

'You should not have slept with your loyal pet then,' she snapped in sudden anger, kneeling up on the bedsheets, one hand resting on the slight mound of her stomach.

Hébert punched her in the mouth. She toppled backwards, sprawling awkwardly on the floorboards. Blood streamed from her lip, and she could feel it throb and swell. With trembling fingers she touched her teeth, checking to see if they remained.

Hébert rushed to her, whispered into her hair, rocking her in his embrace. He promised her he would take care of it. Bring her a tonic. He knew of a woman who dealt with such inconveniences.

Marie-Louise had blamed herself. *I should have been more careful*, she scolded herself. *Why do I always ruin everything?*

Now Girardin was angry.

Hébert had cut her loose. She waited in all the usual places, but he no longer came to collect her in his carriage. On her free afternoon each week she went to the rooms he had rented. He was never there. She had no knowledge of where he printed his broadsheets; he had kept that secret as close as an ingrown hair. Eventually, her increasing girth became too difficult to hide and her pregnancy was discovered. She was dismissed from the Tuileries.

Marie-Louise found a boarding house in Paris with a landlord who did not ask too many questions. She didn't know what to do. She had no way to contact Hébert. At the Club des Jacobins they would not admit her, would not tell her where he lived. She had lurked in the dark street outside their premises in Rue Saint-Honoré and watched for him to arrive. He never did. He had made her promise not to tell anyone that she spied for him, not even Olympe. She had ignored her Girondist friends during her infatuation with Hébert and was too ashamed to seek help from them now. She looked for work, but there was no mistaking the condition she was in. She saw disbelief, disgust, righteous indignation and, only once, pity. Doors closed in her face.

Each day she walked past the turnstile in the church wall: the *tour d'abandon*. How was she to raise a child? With the price of bread and soap escalating, her savings dwindled quickly until all that remained was the price of a coach ticket to Versailles. She had no choice. For the second time in her life she would beg for her father's mercy.

There was a thump at the cabin door. Girardin started. She saw the door handle rattle.

'Open up!'

It was d'Auribeau. He had come back for her. Her chair fell as she stood.

'Now!'

She obeyed.

Captain d'Auribeau entered and closed the door behind him. He looked about, plucking at the fingers of his gloves. She recognised the gesture. He had the same mannerisms as her father. She touched the knife in her pocket and raised her chin.

'Tell me, did you wonder why you were not arrested with your republican friends?'

Girardin felt the bandages around her breasts tighten. So Raoul had finally spoken out of her betrayal of the King and d'Auribeau had come for retribution. Now the moment she had dreaded had come, she felt surprisingly calm. It was almost a relief. She said nothing, awaiting her fate.

'No? Well, I made a promise to a dying man.' He circled around her, speaking softly. 'A promise not to harm a hair of your pretty shaven head.' She felt his breath on the back of her neck.

She closed her eyes.

'I promised the General I would see you safely home. You do want to go home, don't you?'

She clenched her teeth.

'To your child.'

Her breath caught in her throat. He knew about her son. Her heart sounded against her ribs: *All is lost, all is lost.*

'I have seen you playing at being the savant with those traitors to the King.' He stopped and faced her, slapping his gloves against his thigh. 'While that charlatan of a priest plotted to kill the General!'

She gasped. 'That is not true!' This was nonsense. Ventenat would not harm the General.

'Ventenat is a republican spy. A tool of the revolution. He has blood on his hands.'

'You have no proof!' She was confused. Why did he accuse Ventenat of being the republican spy? Had Raoul kept her secret? If so, then what did d'Auribeau want with her?

'Proof is what I expect you to provide for me.' He inclined his head with a snide smile. 'Tell me where the naturalists have hidden their journals, and I will let you sail.' He spread his hands wide as though offering her a perfectly reasonable choice.

Betray her friends and sail home. He was giving her the chance to find her son. Speak out and she could go home. It would be so easy. All this suffering could be over. She stared at him, mute.

The tic in the side of his face jerked. One eye spasmed closed and she saw the effort it took to force it open. 'I could still have you arrested,' he said, 'have you languish here in jail with your friends.' His face screwed in disgust. 'I am sending them into the jungle, far away from any ships that might take them home.'

'What if I do not know?'

His laugh was cold. 'Ah, Marie-Louise. So many men have been curious about you. So many men would want to come and test this aberration of nature.' He flicked his gloves against her bound breasts.

She thought of Raoul and the soiled rope he had thumped against her chest. She wanted to spit.

'Let me give you some time to think on the matter,' the captain said. 'If you do not remember by tomorrow, I will be forced to let the men loose on this ship. Let them satisfy their curiosity. The choice, Mademoiselle, is yours.'

Chapter 61

THE SAFE COCOON OF HER CABIN HAD BEEN SPLINTERED BY d'Auribeau's words, as if he had taken an axe to its door. She could not stay here like a piece of bait laid in a trap. If they came for her, she had no means of escape. Instead, she barricaded herself inside the great cabin, pushing the table and chairs against the door. Behind her, a small window on the portside of the ship was open, showing her the lights of Sourabaya and the black jungle beyond.

Passepartout watched from her cage, large eyes following Girardin backwards and forwards as she paced in front of the window.

'Stop looking at me!' she yelled.

If she betrayed her friends, she could sail home. It was for her son. She had to return. They would understand, wouldn't they? It was only words she would give him. If d'Auribeau found their journals he might even release them. The naturalists were no threat; he would see that if he had their journals. For pity's sake, they collected flowers! But her excuses tasted like bitter greens.

If she said nothing, she would be raped and left to rot in some jungle prison. She looked to Passepartout's cage. Her tail curled around its bamboo bars.

Or she could run.

Outside the window, darkness was falling fast. Through the open panes she could see the stars begin to glow, blinking and waking with the night. She took a deep breath. Creatures called from the jungle with sounds she could not name, creatures she could not even imagine. If she ran now, there would be no returning home.

On the wharf, a spark flared and a flame was passed from pipe to pipe. A row of Dutch soldiers guarded the ship. She slid down against the wall, listening to the steps of the nightwatchmen thud on the deck above her head. D'Auribeau had her trapped. She felt his fingers pinch-grip her throat.

The black swans dangled from the ceiling. She reached for one, slicing open the stitches of its belly with her knife. Taking her journal from the cavity, she tore out each page, ripping it to shreds, obliterating its contents; the letters to Olympe, the messages for her son. He would not have those, at least. She gathered the pieces of confetti and tossed them through the window into the sea. The pieces of her past life floated away on the rippling waves as though she had never existed. She dumped the body of the lifeless swan after it.

The other swans hung from the roof, the stitches in their stomachs hidden beneath their black feathers. It had been Félix's idea. She had watched him sew their journals inside the birds when d'Auribeau first returned to the ship.

She hung Passepartout's cage in the window, then she twisted the latch and opened the door wide. 'Go on,' she urged her. 'Climb out.' But the lizard stared dumbly back. 'Be free!' she shouted. She shook the cage. 'You can leave! Why don't you leave?' She imagined her in the jungle trees, turning a brilliant green and climbing towards the sky.

The bars of the cage reminded her of the bars on her father's windows.

She could have chosen security and safety. Countless other women did so. They accepted their lot in life without question. Why was she not content?

'I could've kept my son,' she sobbed to Passepartout. 'I didn't need to run away.'

Did all freedom come with such trauma? She had carried this guilt across the oceans with her. It had crippled her. It had tricked her into thinking she did not deserve happiness. That she was worthless. Now she crumpled to the floor with the weight of it. She was tired. This guilt had caught her like a bird in a snare, and convinced her that if she struggled too hard to be free she might break her own wings. She had blamed herself for too long. She had to let it go.

The bars were the first thing she had noticed on returning to her father's house. They spoke of wealth, of having something valuable to protect. Inside his house, the rooms were more lavishly appointed, with more rugs and tapestries, more paintings and more furniture than she remembered. All this opulence had narrowed the rooms, she thought as she was led through to her father.

'Girl, what are you wearing?' her stepmother had cried in horror. 'Did anyone see you on our step?'

Marie-Louise looked down at her drab grey apron. Her hair was loose and unwashed. She ignored her stepmother.

Her father had grown in width since she had last seen him. He stood in front of the fire like a squat beetle with an iridescent shell in his brocade vest. He swirled brandy in his glass. His cane rested against the fireplace. Instinctively, she covered her belly with her hands, thinking of her mother.

'I am with child,' she blurted.

'Oh my Lord!' Her stepmother fell about like a wounded moth. She collapsed on the chaise longue, then sprang to her feet. 'Your father is a respected citizen. A burghur. Think of the scandal!'

Her father drew a deep, noisy breath through his nostrils, his lips made rigid with disgust. 'Your lover has discarded you.'

She dropped her head.

Her stepmother strode across the room and slapped her hard across the face. 'You will ruin us all.'

Marie-Louise took it without uttering a sound.

'You think to ask for shelter?' her father growled. 'You have disgraced me! You have fallen from God's grace. He has only contempt for you now.'

She pictured herself plummeting into hell for the life that grew in her belly.

'You know what future awaits you if I were to turn you from this house?'

She nodded, eyes downcast.

'Misery, starvation and death,' he intoned.

'You cannot stay here, if that's what you are thinking,' her stepmother said. 'No respectable family would risk the disease of immorality taking root. If you were our servant we would have no choice but to throw you out!'

'Enough, woman!' her father roared at his wife. 'I decide who can or cannot belong to this family!'

Her stepmother flinched.

'It might be nice,' he continued softly, 'to hear the sound of children in this house.' The glance he sent his wife was cold. She had given him no children.

'I will pray for your sins,' she hissed at Marie-Louise before sweeping from the room. The candle flames stuttered in her wake.

The walls of the salon closed around Marie-Louise. Her father picked up his cane and crossed the short space between them. The point of his cane pressed on the bones of her foot, pinning her to the floor.

'A second time,' he said, putting a hand to her neck. 'You are a slut.'

She felt his grip tighten.

'You should have obeyed my wishes and married as I had first intended, not spread your legs for that piemaker.'

She saw her lovely, gentle Etienne sprawled on the roadside, his skull smashed.

'You may stay in this house, but you must not be seen. For the period of your confinement, you will not go out. You will not go near the windows. We will sew the curtains of your room shut if we must. I will arrange a marriage for you. After the birth of your child we will contrive the "arrival" of you and your husband with your infant to live in this house. We shall be a happy family.'

She remembered Louis, trussed up in the lavish rooms of the Tuileries with the windows covered and gazing longingly at his paintings of wild, tempestuous seas, the white sails of the ships illuminated with promise.

'I just want to look after you and your baby.' Her father's voice like a silk noose. 'A father knows what is best for his child.'

He waited till she nodded before he dropped his hand from her throat.

She fell at his feet to kiss his hand. To obey. But as she knelt, she glimpsed two handsome silver candlesticks on the mantelpiece and calculated the price they would fetch. She could not endure this life her father had planned for her. She would return to Paris. She would find Olympe de Gouges and beg for her help. She would not let herself become her father's prisoner.

Chapter 62

'Let me in!' She recognised Mérite's voice as he knocked at the cabin door.

'Why should I trust you?' she called out, pushing herself to her feet and holding her knife out. 'You chose your side.'

'I had no choice! If I had not signed the order to arrest them, my name would be among them.'

'An honourable man would not betray his friends.' She swallowed, thinking of the choice d'Auribeau had given her.

'An honourable man would not abandon you.'

She paused, her breathing rapid, staring at the door.

'I would not hurt you,' he said.

She closed her eyes, hearing the tenderness in his voice.

'I can help you escape.'

Her heart set up a drumming beat, building faster and harder, like the distant booming of island drums. 'How?'

'There is a spice ship returning to Amsterdam. They are in need of a steward.'

'A spice ship?' She reeled backwards. A Dutch ship, returning to Europe. Was it possible? 'But the guards . . .'

'I have a plan to get you off the ship.'

She hesitated. He was offering her a chance. He was offering hope.

'The surgeon Renard has agreed to it. He will write you a death certificate. We will bring a stretcher to collect your body. Don't you see?'

She would cease to exist. She could begin again. Her wages were already sewn into the hem of her tunic. All her cherished things were carried with her. Her body could be wrapped in bedding and smuggled from the ship. It was possible. She touched the string of shells around her neck.

'Let me in, please. I wouldn't lie to you. Haven't I always been there to protect you?'

Girardin turned back to look at Passepartout, but her cage was empty. She felt a shiver of shock. Passepartout had gone.

Slowly, Girardin dragged the furniture away and unlocked the door.

Mérite stood before her, his face unmasked of bravado. 'The *Vliegende Swaan* leaves tomorrow at dawn. This is your only chance if you want to return for your son.' He reached for her hand. 'You can trust me.'

Suddenly, a dark shape loomed from behind with mallet raised and brought it down on Mérite's head. She cried out as he sank first to his knees, then toppled forwards.

'Touching.' Raoul stepped through the door and kicked Mérite's ankle. The boy did not stir.

Girardin dropped beside Mérite and rolled him back, feeling the dead weight of him beneath her arms. She bent her cheek close to his lips. She could not see his chest rise.

'You bastard!' she screamed at Raoul. He stood with legs spread, tossing the mallet casually from hand to hand.

She bent her face again to Mérite's mouth, and this time she thought she felt his breath whisper across her skin.

'You have killed him,' she accused.

Raoul shrugged and stepped over his body.

Girardin bolted towards the door. She ran for the stairs and up onto the quarterdeck, calling for the night watch. Lanterns swung in the breeze. No one answered her call. The deck was empty.

'Paid them off,' Raoul said as he followed her up to the quarterdeck. 'Settled a few gambling debts.'

The Dutch soldiers stood stationed on the wharf. She backed away to the starboard rail. The water of the harbour glistened, black and slick. Could she swim to shore? Could she swim if her life depended on it?

She faced Raoul with the taffrail pressed against her spine. 'What do you want?' she asked.

'I thought we could have some fun before d'Auribeau lets every man come aboard and poke his stick in you.'

She began to tremble. No, she told herself. I must not let him see my fear. She steadied herself against the rail.

'It amuses me to think I might have Hébert's bitch for myself. It pleases me to imagine his face when I tell him what I did to you.'

He means to terrorise. He enjoys it; do not give him satisfaction. 'How do you know Hébert?' she called out, inching along the side of the ship.

'Hébert, the famous Père Duchesne. I never liked him. Strutting about the Club des Jacobins, boasting of the girl he had wrapped so tightly around his cock that she would do anything for him.

Imagine my surprise when I found Hébert's bitch in disguise aboard this ship!'

The Club des Jacobins? Raoul was at the Jacobin house?

He saw her shock. 'Do you not remember me?' He pressed both his hands across his chest in mock pain. She saw that he no longer had the mallet. 'I was with Fleurieu at the Tuileries when he obtained the King's signature for this mission. I saw you there in your modest cap and apron, Hébert's little cuckoo in the nest. Did you think you were the only republican spy at the palace?'

Her eyes widened. Raoul was among the naval officers with Fleurieu. 'You? You are a republican spy? Not a royalist?' Suddenly it made sense. He could not tell d'Auribeau of her role in the revolution because he would risk revealing his own. 'D'Auribeau accuses Ventenat, but it is you!'

'The idiot priest is a fantasist! Do you really think the National Assembly would place their trust in such a fool?'

'Then what did the National Assembly want with you?' she asked, desperate to keep him talking as she edged away. The buckets and coils of rope threatened to snag her ankles and send her sprawling.

He followed her. 'To keep a ledger, a list of names of men still loyal to the King, those likely to cause trouble. An insurance policy, if you will.' But he was tiring of the game. He feinted, then laughed as she scrambled backwards along the rail. She held her small knife pointing at Raoul's heart. He laughed again and lunged.

She snatched the empty pail at her feet and lobbed it through the air. The bucket clanged as it struck his head. He grunted in surprise. She heard him stumble and swear before she flung herself over the taffrail. Clinging to a ledge she felt her feet dip into the water. Raoul threw the bucket across the deck with a roar of anger.

Her arms burned as she struggled to find footholds on the slippery hull. When she looked up, he was leaning over the side, searching. 'Don't think you can get away from me, bitch.'

She pressed herself flat against the hull.

If she could reach the wharf she would be free. She could sink into the water, feel her way along the hull, and push herself from post to post beneath the wharf. The distance was not far. If she was quiet, she might evade the guards. She could find that Dutch spice ship and be free.

A voice called her name. It was Mérite! He sounded groggy, but he was alive. When she looked up again, the dark shape of Raoul's head had disappeared.

The water lapping at her ankles was warm, like a soothing bath, urging her into the water.

'Marie-Louise,' Raoul sang out. 'I have the boy.'

Her heart thumped against the belly of the ship.

'Come out and play,' he called.

Girardin felt a sudden sense of calm. Her limbs no longer shook. She had made her decision. The toe of her boot caught the lip of a ledge. She may never return for her son, but she could still save this boy. She pulled herself up the side of the ship to stand on the rail.

Raoul held a knife to Mérite's neck.

'Let him go,' she growled.

'Run!' choked Mérite. The knife cut into his throat and a trickle of blood oozed onto his white collar.

She roared as she lunged forwards and threw her entire weight at Mérite. Raoul lashed out. Missed. She pounced on Mérite, wrenching him free of Raoul's grasp as they fell to the deck and rolled away.

Behind her, Raoul screamed in pain. She turned to see a shaft of metal protruding from his stomach. Blood gurgled around the wound. He stared down at the sword and then at her, questioning. She looked back at him in shock, her own blade still in her hand.

The sword in his gut was pulled free, spraying her with blood. Raoul clasped his belly and sank to his knees. Behind him stood a small man, wiping the blood from his rapier with a handkerchief.

D'Auribeau.

D'Auribeau sneered as he stepped aside from the pooling blood. 'Traitor.' He spat on Raoul. 'Fortunately his brother is the better pilot.'

Girardin scrambled to her feet.

Raoul whimpered, pressing his hands to the wound. In the moonlight his blood shone like glossy tar.

Watching d'Auribeau clean his sword, she thought of the great white shark following their boat along the south coast of New Holland. As if it knew that all it needed to do was wait.

'Have you considered my offer?' d'Auribeau asked her.

'You heard Raoul,' she said. 'He was the traitor, not Ventenat.'

'I still do not trust those savants.' The captain scowled. 'They will discredit me. Give me the location of their journals and you can be free. You can sail home.'

'Don't trust him!' Mérite cried. 'He means to sell the ships!'

Girardin glanced at the young man beside her and then to the row of Dutch guards d'Auribeau had stationed along the wharf. In her hand, the stag-horn knife seemed tiny, ineffectual.

D'Auribeau stalked towards her and she stepped back. The deck was rough beneath her feet where the stag's hooves had worn away the wood. She pictured the creature charging down the deck and remembered that effortless leap. She saw his antlers held high above the water, his nostrils flared, swimming for freedom while the doe had quivered, immobile.

D'Auribeau flicked his sword and the lamplight glinting on the blade reminded her of the butcher's knives. She turned her face to the sea, smelling the promise in the salt air.

Girardin reached out her hand to Mérite. He clasped it. Together they ran for the side of the ship and leaped.

Epilogue

France, June 1794

THE *VLIEGENDE SWAAN* ANCHORED IN A COVE SOMEWHERE ALONG the north coast of France. She could not be sure of their exact location, but she knew the ship had steered well away from the naval base at Brest before dipping back towards the coast. In the dark hour before dawn, she climbed into a longboat beside bales of cinnamon, nutmeg and mace. She shivered in the cool morning mist, but felt no fear. A smuggler's lantern winked through the fog and the rowers turned the boat towards it.

Mérite had stayed behind in Java. They had made their way, dripping wet, to the captain of the *Swaan*, a man disinclined to ask questions. The crew of the spice ship was as exotic as its cargo. There were sailors of all colours and creeds—Dutch, Portuguese, Chinese and slaves from the islands—so the arrival of a waif-like Frenchman raised no eyebrows. She said farewell to Mérite with a torn heart. It had felt wrong to leave him behind. But he had gained a position with the Dutch East India Company and could not be convinced to sail home with her. She had made this final journey alone.

A fortune in spices lay in the bales at her back. Corruption was as rife in the Dutch East India Company as syphilis in the navy. She had split the hem of her tunic and bribed the officer in charge of the smuggled shipment. Now his greed was about to deliver her home. She kept her eye on the blinking light. When the rowers leaped out to heave the boat through the mud, she slipped over the side without a backward glance.

Each step through the chilling mud was treacherous. It dragged at her. She heard the wet suck of the tidal mud each time she lifted a foot. She knew there was quicksand along this coast but, strangely, she was not afraid. No alligators lurked in this marsh mud. With each step, the mud became firmer. Each step brought her closer to land.

The grunts of the men grew fainter as she veered away from them. In the grainy light of dawn, she saw the twisted forms of dark trees showing her the way to shore. She tripped as the tidal mud clutched her ankles and fell face first into the slime. It stank like bilge water. She crawled on her hands and knees. She did not stop. The silt turned coarse in her hands. The sharp edges of broken shells pricked her palms. When she stood, cockles crunched beneath her feet. The wet sand was firm as she tottered forwards onto the beach. Land. After so many years at sea. After all she had seen and done. All those she had lost. Home.

Tears ran down her face as she collapsed to her knees.

She felt the release like the crash of a wave upon her back. She crumpled over, letting the relief swirl around her, feeling its foaming embrace. As the wave receded, she wiped her face. She smeared the mud from her skin and breathed deep. She still had a long way to go.

The thought of the journey ahead did not scare her. She was calm as she listened to the birds waking from the darkness. The cove with its low hills of tussock, white rock and trees bent by the wind seemed unusually still. She got to her feet. She would follow the shoreline until she reached a river; it was what the naturalists would do. On her back she carried a knapsack with pies and bread she had baked, just as Etienne had taught her. In her pocket, she carried the telescope that Kermadec had given her. Both men travelled with her.

Her gait was rolling when she set off, her legs unused to solid land after seven months at sea. Her trousers and tunic were caked with wet mud. But it felt good to stretch her legs. Soon she was striding along the beach, confident she would find water. The thought of Labillardière and Félix setting off into unknown forests cheered her. Their courage buoyed her spirits. She hoped that, by now, they had escaped their jungle prison.

At the river mouth she knew she had found her signpost, her marker of the way home. This tranquil seam of water would lead her to a village, and then a town, and then a coach. And she would take the coach to Paris. She pulled back her sleeve. The round welt was vivid red against her pale skin. Not long now, she promised her son.

She followed the river until she was beyond the reach of the tide, and plunged into the water. She scrubbed at herself vigorously, washing the salt and silt from her clothes and ducking her head beneath the water to scratch the dirt from her hair. She scooped up mouthfuls of the fresh water. It was cold and free of salt taint. Even the smell of it was delicious. Climbing out onto the bank, she felt renewed.

Already a breeze was blowing down the valley, pushing the sea mist away. She turned her face to it and held up her arms, waiting for the sun to warm her and the wind to blow the moisture from her. On a distant hill, she saw a line of clothes dancing on a washing line. A dress flapped in the freshening breeze, waving like a signal flag. As she picked her way along the riverbank, she kept her eye on the dress. It strained against its pegs. She imagined the wind might whip it free, let it float on the eddies of air.

The farmhouse was nestled beneath the crest of the hill. She lay down in the long grass, her heart thumping a steady beat against the earth, watching. A girl came out to milk a cow, pulling the teats with practised ease. The girl's head was pressed against the belly of the cow. The yard was empty.

When she took the dress from the line, she left a pile of coins behind.

It was almost evening when she found a barn. No one saw her slip inside and climb up into the rafters. The last shafts of sunlight pierced through knotholes and cracks in the wood. The hay was dusty and made her sneeze, but it was warm.

Stripping off her sailor's clothes, she stared down at her wasted body. It bore the scars of her voyage. The scurvy rash, the protruding ribs, the bruises. She touched the ragged scar across her arm, her rite of passage. She peeled the bindings from her breasts to free her inflamed skin. The flesh beneath the bandages was as soft and translucent as raw fish, and her nipples pressed inwards. She shook her shoulders and felt the air against her skin, the slight sway of her breasts as blood filled them. She flapped her arms like the wings of a bird. Pumping her muscles, thumping her elbows against her ribs, squeezing life into her chest.

The pile of stained clothes lay at her feet. She had shed Louis Girardin as easily as a lizard steps out of its skin. Now she pulled the dress over her head. It was too big for her, but she didn't care. She smiled, stroking the coarse linen, running her fingers along the handstitched seams, admiring the tough and sturdy fabric. It was the colour of a trusted sail. Twirling, she felt air fill her skirt. She laughed with the delight of it, not caring who might hear. A startled mouse sprinted from the hay.

She hardly recognised herself. She was a new person. Free of shame. She believed in herself, she believed she would find her son. And it suddenly occurred to her that she need not wear her father's name. She wondered why she hadn't thought of this before. A rush of effervescence burst through her. She felt lighter. She would take a new name for her family. She was smiling as she pictured them together, mother and son. A warmth spread from her belly as she realised the name had been with her all along. The name her mother gave her. Her middle name.

Victoire.

Author's note

THE MYSTERY OF THE WHEREABOUTS OF LA PÉROUSE AND HIS crew was not solved until 1827, when the wrecks of the ships *Astrolabe* and *Boussole* were discovered at Vanikoro Island in the Santa Cruz Islands between the Vanuatu and Solomon Island groups. This island was sighted by the Bruni d'Entrecasteaux expedition twice, but not explored. Ironically, they named the island after the General's ship—Recherche, the French word for search. It is thought that survivors would have been present at the time of the rescue mission.

Acknowledgements

MARIE-LOUISE LEFT NO WRITTEN RECORD OF HER OWN, HER PRESence was barely mentioned in published records of the voyage, and we learn of her through the impressions of others in private journals. Throughout the writing process I felt a strong sense of doing her story justice. I offer a possible version of her life and I hope this goes some way to bringing her back into the world.

To give her a voice, I chose to tell her story exclusively from her point of view. And in writing from the perspective of the French explorers, I am aware that the voices of the indigenous inhabitants of the countries they visited are missing. I want to acknowledge the limitations of representing contact between cultures from this one-sided viewpoint, and hope that others more qualified than I will share the stories of those cultures.

The characters in this novel are based on real people and I thank them for their stories. I have enjoyed reading the translated journals of the expeditioners and seeing personality revealed by their written words, but in transforming their accounts into story, inevitably they have become my fictional characters. I have relied heavily on the published journal of Jacques-Julien Labillardière, *Voyage in Search of La Pérouse*, as translated by John Stockdale in 1800, and the spelling of names of plants, animals, people and places of the era have come from that source.

This novel would not be possible without the non-fiction works of historians and translators, in particular: Frank Horner, *Looking for La Pérouse: D'Entrecasteaux in Australia and the South Pacific 1792–1793*; Edward Duyker and Maryse Duyker, *Bruny d'Entrecasteaux: Voyage to Australia and the Pacific 1791–1793*; and Lucy Moore, *Liberty: The Lives and Times of Six Women in Revolutionary France*.

There are many people who have supported me on this journey who I want to thank. Firstly, my agent, Gaby Naher, who took me on and gave me the boost I needed to believe in myself. Her skilful advice and advocacy were invaluable. Then the insightful and enthusiastic team at Allen & Unwin: my publisher, Annette Barlow, and editors Christa Munns, Ali Lavau and Genevieve Buzo. It has been a joy to have them care about these characters as much as I do. And thanks to Nada Backovic for creating a beautiful cover.

I am immensely grateful to the readers who gave me encouragement and feedback on early drafts: Lynette Willshire, Shirley Patton, Michael Fletcher, Wendy Newton, Phoebe Reszke, Nelli Parkyn and Barbara Johnson. Writing friends have inspired me: Lillian Hankel, Briony Kidd, Rachel Edwards, Gina Mercer, and I am particularly grateful for the support of the Launceston Nano crew and Gunnabees. Feedback on earlier work helped make me a better writer—thank you John and Shardell Quinn, Sue Clearwater, Jo Ward, Janice Meadows and Rosie Dub. I thank the Tasmanian Writers' Centre for the opportunities to learn from several magnificent authors through their workshops.

In researching this novel I have had some amazing experiences. In Hobart, I had the opportunity to sail on the *Lady Nelson*, where the crew generously gave me a copy of their ship's manual, and to tour visiting ships: the replica *Endeavour* and the *Bark Europa,* where the female crew members were kind enough to speak to me about their experiences. Thank you Chloe Rudkin and Stu Gibson for your warmth and hospitality on my trips back to Hobart. I thank my French language teacher, Peta Frost, at Alliance Française Launceston for being so enthusiastic about this book, Lee and Louise Kingma for being excellent hosts in New Caledonia, and La Muse Artists and Writers Retreat for gathering creative people together, sharing tales and being an inspirational place to spend time revising in a twelfth-century manor in a tiny French village.

Friends and extended family have always been enthusiastic and supportive throughout the many years that it took to write this novel. Please know that I remember your words of kindness and encouragement. I grew up in a family of avid readers where books were the things my sister, Joanna, and I saved up to buy. My parents, Nelli and Vincent Parkyn, created the best sort of start a hopeful writer could have.

To my husband, Paul Johnson, thank you for giving me the space to learn to write and for lifting me up during the inevitable lows. You have been just the sort of pedantic reader, trusted advisor and beloved hand holder I needed. Thank you for sharing my joy.